Gilgamesh The King

Robert Silverberg was born in New York, studied at
Columbia University, and now lives near San Francisco.
He is the author of countless short stories, many novels,
and a substantial amount of non-fiction on archaeological
and historical themes. He has been President of the
Science Fiction Writers of America, was guest of honour
at the World Science Fiction Convention in Heidelberg
in 1970, and at the Bristol Science Fiction Convention in
Manchester in 1976. He has won two Hugo Awards and
three Nebulas. He enjoys gardening, with a particular
interest in fuchsias and cacti, travelling, contemporary
literature and music, and medieval geography.

His most recent books include *Shadrach in the Furnace*,
Lord of Darkness, *The Stochastic Man*, *Capricorn Games*,
Downward to the Earth, *The Second Trip* and the Majipoor
Trilogy, *Lord Valentine's Castle*, *The Majipoor Chronicles*
and *Valentine Pontifex* which are also available in Pan.

Also available by Robert Silverberg in Pan Books

Lord Valentine's Castle
The Majipoor Chronicles
Valentine Pontifex

ROBERT SILVERBERG

Gilgamesh the King

Pan Books London and Sydney

First published 1984 by Arbor House Publishing Company, New York
First published in Great Britain 1985 by Victor Gollancz Ltd
This edition published 1986 by Pan Books Ltd
Cavaye Place, London SW10 9PG
9 8 7 6 5 4 3 2 1
© Agberg Ltd 1984
ISBN 0 330 29223 4
Photoset by Parker Typesetting Service, Leicester
Printed and bound in Great Britain by
Cox & Wyman Ltd, Reading

This is Diana's book

1

There is in Uruk the city a great platform of kiln-baked brick that was the playing field of the gods, long before the Flood, in that time when mankind had not yet been created and they alone inhabited the Earth. Every seventh year for the past ten thousand years we have painted the bricks of that platform white with a plaster of fine gypsum, so that it flashes like a vast mirror under the eye of the sun.

The White Platform is the domain of the goddess Inanna, to whom our city is consecrated. Many of the kings of Uruk have erected temples upon the platform for her use; and of all these shrines of the goddess none was more grand than the one that was built by my royal grandfather the hero Enmerkar. A thousand artisans labored for twenty years to construct it, and the ceremony of its dedication lasted eleven days and eleven nights without cease, and during that time the moon was wrapped each evening in a deep mantle of blue light as a token of Inanna's pleasure. 'We are Inanna's children,' the people sang, 'and Enmerkar is her brother, and he shall reign forever and ever.'

Nothing remains of that temple now, for I tore it down after I came to the throne, and put up a far more splendid one on its site. But in its time it was a wonder of the world. It is a place that will always hold special meaning for me: within its precincts, one day in my childhood, the beginnings of wisdom descended on me, and the shape of my life was shaped, and I was set upon a course from which there has been no turning.

That was the day on which the palace servants fetched me from my games to watch my father the king, divine Lugalbanda, embark upon the last of his journeys. 'Lugalbanda goes forth now to the bosom of the gods,' they told me, 'and he shall live for all time among them in joy, and drink their wine and eat their bread.'

7

I think and hope that they were right; but it may very well be the case that my father's final journey has brought him instead to the Land of No Returning, to the House of Dust and Darkness, where his ghost shuffles about sadly like a bird with crippled wings, feeding on dry clay. I do not know.

I am he whom you call Gilgamesh. I am the pilgrim who has seen everything within the confines of the Land, and far beyond it; I am the man to whom all things were made known, the secret things, the truths of life and death, most especially those of death. I have coupled with Inanna in the bed of the Sacred Marriage; I have slain demons and spoken with gods; I am two parts god myself, and only one part mortal. Here in Uruk I am king, and when I walk through the streets I walk alone, for there is no one who dares approach me too closely. I would not have it that way, but it is too late to alter matters now: I am a man apart, a man alone, and so I will be to the end of my days. Once I had a friend who was the heart of my heart, the self of my self, but the gods took him from me and he will not come again.

My father Lugalbanda must have known a loneliness much like mine, for he was a king and a god also, and a great hero in his day. Surely those things set him apart from ordinary men, as I have been set apart.

The imprint of my father is still clear in my mind after all these years: a great-shouldered deep-chested man, who went bare above the waist in all seasons, wearing only his long flounced woollen robe from hips to ankles. His skin was smooth and dark from the sun, like polished leather, and he had a thick curling black beard, in the manner of the desert people, though unlike them he shaved his scalp. I remember his eyes best of all, dark and bright and enormous, seeming to fill his whole forehead: when he scooped me up and held me before his face, I sometimes thought I would float forward into the vast pool of those eyes and be lost within my father's soul forever.

I saw him rarely. There were too many wars to fight. Year after year he led the chariots forth to quell some uprising in our unruly vassal state of Aratta, far to the east, or to drive away the wild marauding tribes of the wastelands that crept up on Uruk to steal our grain and cattle, or to display our might before one of our great rival cities, Kish or Ur. When he was not away at the wars, there were the pilgrimages he must make to the holy shrines, in spring to Nippur, in the autumn to Eridu. Even when he was home he had little time for me, preoccupied as he was by the necessary festivals and rituals of the year, or the meetings of the city assembly, or the proceedings of the court of justice, or the supervision of the unending work that must be done to maintain our canals and dikes. But he promised me that a time would come when he would teach me the things of manhood and we would hunt lions together in the marshlands.

That time never arrived. The malevolent demons that hover always above our lives, awaiting some moment of weakness in us, are unwearying; and when I was six years old one of those creatures succeeded in penetrating the high walls of the palace, and seized upon the soul of Lugalbanda the king, and swept him from the world.

I had no idea that any of that was happening. In those days life was only play for me. The palace, that formidable place of fortified towered entrances and intricately niched facades and lofty columns, was my gaming house. All day long I ran about with an energy that never failed, shouting and laughing and tumbling on my hands. Even then I was half again as tall as any boy of my own age, and strong accordingly; and so I chose older boys as my playfellows, always the rough ones, the sons of grooms and cupbearers, for of brothers I had none.

So I played at chariots and warriors, or wrestled, or fought with cudgels. And meanwhile one day a sudden horde of priests and exorcists and sorcerers began to come and go within the palace, and a clay image of the demon Namtaru was fashioned and placed close by the stricken king's head, and a brazier was filled with ashes and a dagger put within it, and on the third day at nightfall the dagger was brought forth and thrust into the image of Namtaru and the image was buried in the corner of the wall, and libations of beer were poured and a young pig was slaughtered and its heart was set forth to appease the demon, and water was sprinkled, and constant prayers were chanted; and each day Lugalbanda struggled for his life and lost some further small part of the struggle. Not a word of this was said to me. My playfellows grew somber and seemed abashed to be running about and shouting and whacking at cudgels with me. I did not know why. They did not tell me that my father was dying, though I think they certainly knew it and knew also what the consequences of his death would be.

Then one morning a steward of the palace came to me and called out, 'Put up your cudgel, boy! No more games! There is man's business to do today!' He bade me bathe and dress myself in my finest brocaded robe, and place about my forehead my headband of golden foil and lapis lazuli, and go to the apartment of my mother the queen Ninsun. For I must accompany her shortly to the temple of Enmerkar, he said.

I went to her, not understanding why, since it was no holy day known to me. I found my mother clad most magnificently in a coat of bright crimson wool, a headdress gleaming with carnelian and topaz and chalcedony, and golden breastplates from which hung ivory amulets in the form of fish and gazelles. Her eyes were darkened with kohl and her cheeks were painted deep green, so that she looked like a creature that had risen from the sea. She said nothing to me, but fastened about my neck a figurine in red stone of the wind-demon Pazuzu, as if she feared for me. She touched her hand lightly to my cheek. Her touch was cool.

Then we went out into the long hall of the fountains, where many people were waiting for us. And from there we went in procession, the grandest procession I had ever seen, to the Enmerkar temple.

A dozen priests led the way, naked as priests must be when they come before a god, and a dozen priestesses as well, naked also. After them strode two dozen tall warriors who had fought in the campaigns of Lugalbanda. These were encumbered by their full armor, copper helmets and all, and carried their axes and shields. I was sorry for them, inasmuch as this was in the month Abu, when the scourge of summer lies heaviest on the Land, and no rain falls and the heat is a burden beyond bearing.

Following the warriors came the people of the household of Lugalbanda: butlers, maids, cupbearers, jesters and acrobats, grooms, charioteers, gardeners, musicians, dancing-girls, barbers, drawers of the bath, and all the rest. Every one of them was dressed in a fine robe, finer than anything I had ever seen them wear before, and they carried the implements of their professions as though they were on their way to wait on Lugalbanda. I knew most of these people. They had served in the palace since before I was born. Their sons were my playmates and sometimes I had taken meals in their dwellings. But when I smiled and waved to them they looked away, keeping their faces solemn.

The last person in this group was one who was particularly dear to me. I went skipping up from my place in the rear of the procession to walk beside him. This was old Ur-kununna, the court harper: a long-shanked white-bearded man, very grave of bearing but with gentle twinkling eyes, who had lived in every city of the Land and knew every hymn and every legend. Each afternoon he sang in the Ninhursag courtyard of the palace, and I would sit at his feet for hour upon hour while he touched his harp and chanted the tale of the marriage of Inanna and Dumuzi, or the descent of Inanna to the nether world, or the tale of Enlil and Ninlil, or of the journey of the moon-god Nanna to the city of Nippur, or of the hero Ziusudra, who built the great vessel by which mankind survived the Flood, and who was rewarded by the gods with eternal life in the paradise on Earth that is known as Dilmun. He sang us also ballads of my grandfather Enmerkar's wars with Aratta, and the famous one of the adventures of Lugalbanda before he was king, when in his wanderings he entered a place where the air was poisonous, and nearly lost his life, but was saved by the goddess. Ur-kununna had taught some of these songs to me, and he had showed me how to play his harp. His manner was always warm and tender toward me, with never any show of impatience. But now, when I ran up alongside him, he was strangely remote and aloof: like everyone else, he said nothing, and when I indicated that I would like to carry his harp he shook his head almost brusquely. Then my mother hissed at me and called me back to the place that she and five of her serving-maids occupied at the end of the procession.

Down the endless rows of palace steps we marched, and into the Street of the Gods, and along it to the Path of the Gods that leads to the Eanna precinct where the temples are, and up the multitude of steps to the White Platform, and across it, dazzled by the reflection of the brilliant sunlight, to the Enmerkar temple. All along the path the streets were lined with silent citizens, thousands of them: the whole population of Uruk must have been there.

On the steps of the temple Inanna waited to receive us. I trembled when I saw her. The goddess has since earliest time owned Uruk and all that is within it, and I dreaded her power over me. She who stood there was of course the priestess Inanna of human flesh, and not the goddess. But at that time I did not know the difference between them, and I thought I was in the presence of the Queen of Heaven herself, the Daughter of the Moon. Which in a way was so, since the goddess is incarnate in the woman, though I could not have grasped such subtleties so young.

The Inanna who admitted us to the temple that day was the old Inanna, with a face like a hawk's and terrifying eyes, rather than the more beautiful but no less ferocious one in whom the goddess came to dwell afterward. She was clad in a bright cape of scarlet leather, arranged on a wooden framework so that it flared out mightily beyond her shoulders and rose high above her. Her breasts were bare and painted at the tips. On her arms were copper ornaments in the form of serpents, for the serpent is the sacred creature of Inanna; and about her throat was coiled not a copper serpent but a living one, of a thickness of two or three fingers, but sluggish in the terrible heat, barely troubling to let its forked black tongue flicker forth. As we went past her, Inanna sprinkled us with perfumed water from a gilded ewer, and spoke to us in low chanted murmurs. She did not use the language of the Land, but the secret mystery-language of the goddess-worshippers, those who follow the Old Way that was in the Land before my people came down into it from the mountains. All this was frightening to me, only because it was so solemn and out of the ordinary.

Within the great hall of the temple was Lugalbanda.

He lay upon a broad slab of polished alabaster, and he seemed to be asleep. Never had he looked so kingly to me: instead of his usual half-length flounced skirt he wore a mantle of white wool and a dark blue robe richly woven with threads of silver and gold, and gold-dust was sprinkled into his beard so that it sparkled like the sun's fire. Beside his head rested, in place of the crown he had worn during his life, the horned crown of a king who is also a god.

By his left hand lay his scepter, decorated with rings of lapis lazuli and mosaics of brightly colored seashells, and by his right was a wondrous dagger with a blade of gold, a hilt of lapis lazuli and gold studs, and a sheath fashioned of gold strands woven in openwork like plaited leaves of grass. Heaped up before him on the floor was an immense mound of treasure: earrings and finger-rings in gold and silver, drinking-cups of beaten silver, dice-boards, cosmetics-boxes, alabaster jars of rare scent, golden harps and bull-headed lyres, a model in silver of his chariot and one of his six-oared skiff, chalices of obsidian, cylinder-seals, vases of onyx and chalcedony, golden bowls, and so much more that I could not believe the profusion of it. Standing arrayed about my father's bier on all four sides were the great lords of the city, perhaps twenty of them.

We took up our places before the king, my mother and I in the center of the group. The palace servants clustered about us, and the warriors in armor flanked us on both sides. From the temple courtyard came the great hollow booming of the lilissu, which is the kettledrum that otherwise is beaten only at the time of an eclipse of the moon. Then I heard the lighter sound of the little balag-drums and the shrill skirling of clay whistles as Inanna entered the temple preceded by her naked priests and priestesses. She went to the high place at the rear of the hall, where in a temple of An or Enlil there would be an effigy of the god; but in the temple of Inanna at Uruk there is no need for effigies, because the goddess herself dwells amongst us.

Now began a ceremony of singing and chanting, much of it in the language of the Old Way, which I did not know then and scarcely comprehend today, since the Old Way is woman-religion, goddess-religion, and they keep it to themselves. There were libations of wine and oil, and a bull and a ram were brought forth and sacrificed and their blood sprinkled over my father, and seven golden trays of water were emptied as gifts to the seven planets, and there were more such sacred acts. The snake of Inanna awoke and moved between her breasts, and flicked its tongue, and fixed its eyes upon me, and I was afraid. I felt goddess-presence all about me, intense, stifling.

I edged close to the kindly Ur-kununna and whispered, 'Is my father dead?'

'We must not speak, boy.'

'Please. Is he dead? Tell me.'

Ur-kununna looked down at me from his great height and I saw the white light of his wisdom glowing in his eyes, and his tenderness, and his love for me, and I thought, how like his eyes are to Lugalbanda's, how large and dark, how they filled his forehead! He said gently, 'Yes, your father is dead.'

'And what does that mean, being dead?'

'We must not speak during the ceremony.'

'Was Inanna dead when she descended into the nether world?'

'For three days, yes.'

'And was it like being asleep?'

He smiled and said nothing.

'But then she awoke and came back, and now she stands before us. Will my father awaken? Will he come back to govern Uruk again, Ur-kununna?'

Ur-kununna shook his head. 'He will awaken, but he will not come back to govern Uruk.' Then he put his finger to his lips, and would not speak again, leaving me to consider the meaning of my father's death as the ceremony went on and on about me. Lugalbanda did not move; he did not breathe; his eyes were closed. It was like sleep. But it must have been more than sleep. It was death. When Inanna went to the nether world and was slain, it was the occasion of great dismay in heaven and Father Enki caused her to be brought forth into life. Would Father Enki cause Lugalbanda to be brought forth into life? No, I did not think so. Where then was Lugalbanda now, where would he journey next?

I listened to the chanting, and heard the answer: Lugalbanda was on his way to the palace of the gods, where he would dwell forever in the company of Sky-father An and Father Enlil and Father Enki the wise and compassionate, and all the rest. He would feast in the feasting-hall of the gods, and drink sweet wine and black beer with them. And I thought that would not be so harsh a fate, if indeed that was where he was going. But how could we be so sure that that was where he was going? How could we be so sure? I turned again to Ur-kununna, but he stood with eyes closed, chanting and swaying. So I was left alone with my

14

thoughts of death and my struggle to understand what was happening to my father.

Then the chanting ended, and Inanna made a gesture, and a dozen of the lords of the city knelt and lifted to their shoulders the massive alabaster slab on which my father lay, and carried it from the temple through the side entrance. The rest of us followed, my mother and I leading the procession, and the priestess Inanna in the rear. Across the White Platform we went, down its far side, and toward the west a few hundred paces, until we stood in the sharp-edged shadow of the temple of An. I saw that a great pit had been excavated in the dry sandy earth between the White Platform and the temple of An, with a sloping ramp leading down into it. We arranged ourselves into a group at the ramp's mouth, and all the townsfolk by their thousands formed a great ring around the whole precinct.

Then an unexpected thing: the serving-maids of my mother the queen surrounded her and began to take her rich and costly garments from her, one by one until she stood naked in the bright sunlight in the full view of all the city. I thought of the tale of Inanna's descent, how as she went deeper and deeper into the nether world she gave up her garments and at last was naked, and I wondered whether my mother too was making ready for a descent into the pit. But that was not the case. The lady-in-waiting Alitum, who looked so much like my mother Ninsun that they seemed to be sisters, stepped forward now and put off her own robes, so that she also was altogether bare; and the serving-maids began to put the crimson coat of my mother on Alitum and her headdress and breastplates, and Alitum's simpler robes on my mother. When they were done, it was hard to tell which was Ninsun and which Alitum, for Alitum's face had been daubed with green paint just as had my mother's

Then I saw a playmate of mine, Enkihegal the son of the gardener Girnishag, walking slowly toward me between two priests. I called out as he approached. But he made no answer. His eyes were glassy and strange. He seemed not to know me at all, though only yesterday I had raced with him from one side of the grand Ninhursag courtyard to the other, eight times without stopping.

The priests now began to pluck at my brocade robe and stripped it from me and put my robe on Enkihegal, and gave me his ordinary one. They took my golden headband away, and put that on his head. I was as tall as he was, though he was three years older, and my shoulders were of the same breadth as his. When we were done exchanging clothes they left Enkihegal standing by my side, as Alitum stood by my mother's side.

Now a sledge-chariot came forth, drawn by two asses. It was decorated with blue, red, and white mosaic along the edges of the framework, and had golden heads of lions on its side panels with manes of lapis lazuli and shell; and great mounds of treasure were heaped upon it. Then the charioteer Ludingirra, who had ridden many times to the wars with my father, stepped forward. He took a deep drink from a huge wine-bowl that the priests had fetched, and made a sharp sound and shook his head as though the wine were bitter, and mounted the chariot and drove it slowly downward into the deep pit. Two grooms walked alongside to steady and calm the asses. Afterward a second and a third chariot followed, and each of the drivers and each of the grooms drank of the wine. Into the pit went vessels of copper and silver and obsidian and alabaster and marble, gaming-boards and tumblers, chalices, a set of chisels and a saw made of gold, and a great deal more, all of it magnificent. Then the warriors in armor went down into the pit; and then some of the palace servants, the barbers and gardeners and a few of the fine ladies-in-waiting, with their hair done up in golden braid, and headdresses of carnelian and lapis lazuli and shell. Each of them drank of the wine. All this in silence, except for the steady beat of the lilissu-drum.

Following this, a certain great lord of the city who had been among those carrying the bier of my father from the temple went to his side. He picked up the horned crown that lay beside him, and held it high and showed it to all, as it glinted in the sun. I am forbidden to write the name by which that lord was then known, for afterward he became king of Urul, and one may not write or utter the birthname of one who becomes king; but the king-name he took was Dumuzi. And he who was to become Dumuzi held the horned crown out to the south and the east and the north and the west, and then he put it on my father's head, and a great outcry went up from the people of Uruk.

Only a god wears a horned crown. I turned to Ur-kununna and said, 'Is my father now a god?'

'Yes,' the old harper said softly. 'Lugalbanda has become a god.'

Then I am a god also, I thought. A giddy sensation of high excitement ran through me. Or at least—so I told myself—I am in some part a god. Part of me must be mortal still, I supposed, since I was born of mortal flesh. Nevertheless the child of a god must be a god to some degree, is that not so? It was a bold thing for me to think. But indeed I have come to know that it is the case, that I am in part a god, though not entirely.

'And if he is a god, then will he come back from death as other gods who have died came back?' I asked.

Ur-kununna smiled and said, 'These things are never certain, boy. He is a god, but I think he will not come back. Look you now, bid him farewell.'

I saw three husky grooms of the bedchamber and three charioteers lift the alabaster bier and begin the descent into the pit with it. Before they lifted it they had sipped of the bitter wine. They did not come forth from the pit; no one who had gone down into it had come forth. To Ur-kununna I said, 'What is that wine they all drink?'

'It gives a peaceful sleep,' he replied.

'And they are all sleeping there in the ground?'

'In the ground, yes. Alongside your father.'

'Will I drink it? Will you?'

'You will drink it, yes, but not for many years, I think. But I will drink of it in a few minutes.'

'So you will sleep in the ground near my father?'

He nodded.

'Until tomorrow morning?'

'Forever,' he said.

I considered that. 'Ah. It will be much like dying, then.'

'Very like dying, boy.'

'And all the others who have gone underground, they are dying too?'

'Yes,' said Ur-kununna.

I considered that also. 'But that is a terrible thing to die! And they drink without a murmur, and they walk into the darkness with a steady stride!'

'It is terrible to go to the House of Dust and Darkness,' he said, 'and live scuttling in the shadows and feed on dry clay. But those of us who go with your father go to the home of the gods, where we will serve him forever.' And he went on to tell me what a privilege it was to die in company with a king. I saw the white light of wisdom shining from his eyes again, and a look of sublime joy. But then I asked him if he could be sure that he would go to the home of the gods with Lugalbanda, rather than to the House of Dust and Darkness, and the light of his eyes went out, and he smiled sadly and replied that nothing is ever sure, and most particularly that. And touched my hand, and turned away, and played a little melody on his harp, and walked forward and drank from the wine and went down into the pit, singing as he went.

Others went into the pit too, sixty or seventy people all told. The last two to go were the woman Alitum wearing my mother's coat and jewelry, and the boy Enkihegal wearing mine; and I understood that they were dying in our place. That put a fear in me, to think that if the custom were only a little different, I might have been drinking the wine and going down into the pit. But the fear was only a small one then, because at that time I did not yet have a true understanding of death, but thought of it only as a kind of sleep.

Then the drums were stilled, and laborers began to shovel earth down the ramp and into the pit, where it must have covered everything over, the chariots and the asses and the treasure and the grooms and the ladies-in-waiting and the palace servants and the body of my father, and the harper Ur-kununna. After that, craftsmen fell to work sealing the ramp with bricks of unbaked mud, so that within a few hours there would be no trace of what lay beneath.

Those of us who remained, of the ones who had marched in the original procession, returned to the temple of Inanna.

We were a much smaller group now: my mother and I and the great lords of the city and other important people, but none of the palace servants or warriors, for they were in the pit with my father.

We gathered ourselves before the alter and I sensed the goddess-presence again, close by and almost choking me. A welter of complexities pressed in on my spirit. I had never felt so alone, so forlorn. The world held only mysteries for me. It seemed that I was in a waking dream. I looked about, seeking Ur-kununna. But of course he was not there, and the questions I meant to ask him would not be answered. Which gave me one understanding of the meaning of death, which was, that those who are dead are beyond our speech, and will not answer when we address them. And I felt as if I had been handed a skewer of grilled meat, and then the meat had been snatched away as I was about to eat, leaving me to bite only air.

There was more drumming and chanting and I thought a thousand different things about death. I thought that my father was gone forever; but that was not really so bad, since he had become a god and thus had made me in part a god, and anyway he had never had much time for me because of his absences at the wars, though he had promised to teach me the things of manhood some day. I would learn those from someone else. But Ur-kununna was gone too. I would never hear his singing again. And the boy Enkihegal my playmate, and his father Girnishag the gardener, and all those others who had been part of my everyday life—gone, gone, gone. Leaving me to bite on air.

And I? Would I die too?

I will not let this thing happen to me, I vowed. Not to me. I am in part a god. And although gods sometimes die, as Inanna once had died when she went to the nether world, they do not die for long. Nor would I. I swore never to let death have me.

For there is too much in the world for me to see, I told myself, and there are a multitude of great deeds that must be done. I will challenge death: so I resolved. I will defeat death. I have only scorn for death, and I will not yield to it. Death, you are no match for me! Death, I will conquer you!

And then I thought that if I do somehow die, well, I am in part a god and I am destined to be a king, and at my death I will be translated up into the heavens like Lugalbanda. I will not have to go down into the vile House of Dust and Darkness as ordinary mortals must.

And then I thought, no, there is no certainty of that. Even Inanna went down into that place, though she was brought forth; but if I go there, will I be brought forth? And I felt great dread. No matter who you are, I thought, no matter how many servants and warriors are put to sleep in the funeral-pit to serve you in the afterlife, you may still be sent into that dark loathsome place. The disdain for death that I had felt a moment before gave way to fear, an all-possessing fear that swept across my soul like the great chill of winter. A strangeness entered my mind, the kind of strangeness that comes when one dreams, and I did not know whether at that moment I dreamed or was awake. There was a pressure in my head, almost to bursting. It was a sensation I had never felt before, though I was to feel it many times later in life, and with far more power than in this first light touch. A god was attempting to enter me. Of that I was certain, though I did not know which god.

But I knew even then it was a god and not a demon, and that he bore a message for me, which was, *You will be king, and a great king, and then you will die, and you may not avoid that destiny, try as you may.*

I would not accept the god and his message. There was no room in my soul to admit such things yet. I was only a child.

In my chaos I saw the figure of death before me, all slashing talons and beating wings, and I cried out defiantly, 'I will escape you!' And felt a great bravery in me for an instant, which gave up its place an instant later to dread, and dread, and dread. They are all sleeping now in the pit beside Lugalbanda, I thought. And where will I sleep? Where will I sleep?

Dizziness overwhelmed me. The god battered my mind, demanding admission. But I could neither yield nor resist, for I was paralyzed by the dread of death, a thing that had never afflicted me before. I swayed and reached out for Ur-Kununna, but he was not there, and I fell to the floor of the temple and lay there I know not how long.

Hands lifted me. Arms enveloped me.

'It is his grief that has overcome him,' someone said.

No, I thought. I feel no grief. Lugalbanda's journey is Lugalbanda's task. It is my own task that concerns me, not his, for his task is dying and mine is to live. So it was not grief that cast me to the ground, but the god, trying to enter my soul as I stood there wrapped in dread. But I did not tell them that.

2

In the month of Kisilimu, when the heavy rains of winter sweep like scythes over the Land, the gods bestowed a new king upon Uruk. This occurred at the first hour of the month, that is, at the moment when the moon's new crescent appeared for the first time. There came the beating of drums and the cry of trumpets, and by torchlight we made our way to the precinct of Eanna, to the White Platform, to the temple built by my grandfather Enmerkar.

'A king is come!' shouted the people in the streets. 'A king! A king!'

A city cannot go without a king very long. The gods must be served, which is to say, the proper offerings to heaven must be made at the proper time, for we are their creatures and their servants: so there must be grain, there must be meat. And thus the wells must be freshened and the canals dredged and extended, the fields must be kept green in the dry times, the beasts must be fattened. To achieve those things order must be maintained, and it is the king who bears that burden. He is the shepherd of the people. Without a king all things would fall to ruin, and the needs of the gods, for which they created us, would go unmet.

Three thrones had been erected in the great hall of the temple. The left-hand one bore the sign of Enlil, and the right-hand one had the sign of An. But the throne in the center was flanked on each side by the towering bundle of reeds, looped at the upper end, which is the sign of the goddess; for Inanna holds the power in Uruk.

On the throne of Enlil rested the scepter of the city, and on the throne of An was the golden crown that my father had worn when

21

he was king. But on the throne in the center sat the priestess Inanna so resplendent that it pained my eyes to look upon her.

She wore no clothing that night. Yet she was far from bare, for her body was covered in every place by ornaments, beads of lapis cascading down over her breasts, a plate of gold in a triangle over her loins, golden braid in her hair, a circlet of gold about her hips, a jewel in her naval, jewels at her hips and nose and eyes, two sets of earrings in the shape of the new moon, one of gold and one of bronze. Beneath this her skin was oiled; by the light of the torches she gleamed like a being lit with an inner radiance.

Behind and to the sides of the thrones stood those officials of the court who had not gone down into the pit with Lugalbanda: the high constable, the throne-bearer, the war-chamberlain and the water-chamberlain, the secretary of state, the supervisor of fisheries, the gatherer of taxes, the overseer of stewards, the master of the boundaries, and many more. The only one I did not see among them was the great lord who had placed the horned crown of divinity on my dead father's brow. He was missing for good reason, for he was the man upon whom Inanna had chosen to bestow the kingship this day, and the king at that time was not permitted to enter the temple of the goddess until he was summoned by her to do so. In later years I saw to it that the custom was altered.

The summoning of the new king into the temple was many hours in coming, or so it seems to me in recollection. First came prayer and libations, the invocation of each god in turn, commencing with the lesser ones, Igalimma who is the doorkeeper of the gods and Dunshagana their steward, and Enlulim the divine goatherd and Ensignun the god of charioteers, and so many others that I could hardly keep tally of them, until Enki and Enlil and An finally were reached. The hour was late and my eyelids were heavy, and to remain awake was a struggle.

And I grew terribly restless. No one seemed to remember that I was there, or to care. The chanting droned and droned and at one point I wandered away into the darkness beyond the torchlight, finding an entrance somehow into a passageway that led to a maze of lesser chapels. It seemed to me that I heard the fluttering of invisible wings there, and scratchy laughter far away. I grew fearful and wished I were back in the great hall. But I was unable to find the way. Desperately I called upon Lugalbanda to guide me.

But instead of Lugalbanda, one of Inanna's handmaidens came for me, a tall sparkling-eyed girl of ten or eleven years. All she wore were seven strings of blue beads about her waist and five amulets of pink shell tied to the ends of her hair, and her body was painted down front and sides with serpent motifs. She laughed and said, 'Where are you going, son of Lugalbanda? Are you trying to find the gate of the nether world?'

I despised the mockery in her voice. I drew myself tall, though she remained taller still, and said, 'Let me be, girl. I am a man.'

'Ah, a man! A man, are you! Yes, so you are, son of Lugalbanda! You are a very great man!'

Now I could not tell whether I was being mocked or not. I began to shake from anger at her, and from an inner rage at myself, for not understanding the game she was playing with me. I was too young then. Taking me by the hand, she drew me against her, as though I were a doll, and she put my cheek against the buds of her breasts. I smelled the sharp perfume of her. 'Little godling,' she murmured, and again her tone was somewhere on the borderland between irony and true deference. She stroked me and called me by my name, very familiarly, and told me hers. When I struggled and tried to pull away, she took both my hands in hers and tugged me about so that my eyes looked into her eyes. She held me and whispered fiercely, 'When you are king, I will lie in your arms!'

In that moment her tone held no mockery at all.

I stared at her in amazement. Once again I felt that strange pressure in my brow that was the god brushing against the edges of my soul, merely for a moment. My lip trembled, and I thought I would cry, but I did not permit it of myself.

'Come,' she said. 'You must not miss the coronation ceremony, little godling. One day you will need to know how these things are done.'

She took me back to the great hall just as a great flourish of music was sounded, flutes and double flutes, the long trumpets, the cymbals and tambourines. The new king had made his entrance at last. He was bare to the waist, wearing a flounced skirt below. His long hair was plaited and wound round his head and gathered behind. He lit a globe of incense and set down gifts before each of the thrones, a golden bowl filled with some fragrant oil, and a mana of silver, and a richly embroidered robe. Then he touched his forehead to the ground before Inanna, and kissed the ground also, and gave her a woven basket filled to overflowing with grain and fruits. Now the goddess rose from the throne and stood glittering like a beacon in the torchlight. 'I am Ninpa the Lady of the Scepter,' she said in a voice so deep I could not believe it was a woman's; and she took the royal scepter from the throne of Enlil and gave it to the king. 'I am Ninmenna the Lady of the Crown,' she said, and took the golden crown from the throne of An and placed it upon the head of the king. Then she called him by his birth-name, which from that moment onward could never be uttered again; and then she called him by his king-name, saying, 'You are Dumuzi, the great man of Uruk. So the gods decree.'

There was no mistaking the sounds of surprise in the hall: gasps, murmurs, coughs. What I did not learn until long afterward was the reason for the surprise, which was that the new king had chosen to call himself by the name of a god, and not a minor god at that. No one in memory had done that before.

I knew of Dumuzi the god, of course. Any child would know his tale—the divine shepherd who wooed the goddess Inanna and won her for his wife, and reigned as king in Uruk for thirty-six thousand years, until Inanna, so that she might rescue herself from the demons of the nether world who held her captive, sold him to them to take her place below the ground. To pick that name by which to reign was strange indeed. For the tale of Dumuzi is the tale of the defeat of the king by the goddess. Was that the destiny that Uruk's new ruler sought for himself? Perhaps he had considered only the grandeur of the first Dumuzi, and not his betrayal and downfall at the hand of Inanna; or perhaps he had not considered anything at all. Dumuzi he was, and king he was.

When the rite was done the new king led the traditional procession to the palace for the final phase of his ceremony of investiture, followed by all the high dignitaries of the city. I also returned to the palace, but only to go to my own bedchamber. While I slept, the lords of the realm presented gifts to Dumuzi and laid down their badges and other insignia of office before him, so that he would have the right to select his own officials. But the custom long has been that such changes are never made on the day of the coronation, and so Dumuzi declared, as kings had always declared before him, 'Let everyone resume his office.'

All the same, changes soon were forthcoming. The one most important to me was that my mother and I left the royal palace that had been my home all my life, and took up residence in a splendid but far less imposing dwelling in the Kullab district, westward of the temple of An. It was to An's service that my mother dedicated the rest of her life, as his chief priestess. She is now a goddess in her own right, by my decree, so that she might be reunited with Lugalbanda. For if he is in heaven, then it is fitting that she be at his side. And though I have said that I do not believe he is in heaven, nevertheless it may be that he is, and in that case it would have been remiss of me not to have sent Ninsun to join him there.

It was hard for me to understand why I had been forced to leave the palace. 'Dumuzi is king now,' my mother explained. 'The assembly has chosen him, the goddess has recognized him. The palace belongs to him.' But her words were like the blowing of the dry wind over the plain. Dumuzi could be king, for all I cared; but the palace was my home. 'Will we return to it after Inanna sends Dumuzi to the nether world?' I asked, and she looked stern and told me never to speak such words again. But then in a softer voice she said, 'Yes, I think you will live in the palace again one day.'

This Dumuzi was young and strong and vigorous, and came of one of the greatest families of Uruk, a clan that long had held the sheshgal-priesthood in the temple of Inanna, and the supervisorship of the fisheries, and many another high office. He was handsome and of kingly bearing, with thick hair and a heavy beard.

Yet there seemed something soft and disagreeable about him within, and I did not understand why he had been chosen to be king. His eyes were small and had no shine, and his lips were fleshy, and the skin of him was like a woman's. I imagined he had it rubbed with oils every morning. I despised him from the first moment of his reign. Perhaps I hated him simply because he had become king in my father's place; but I think it was not only for

25

that. At any rate, I harbor no hatred for him now. For foolish Dumuzi I have only pity: even more than the rest of us, he was the toy of the gods.

3

Now my life became very different. My days of play were over, my days of schooling began.

Because I was a prince of the line of Enmerkar and Lugalbanda, I did not have to attend the common tablet-house, where the sons of merchants and foremen and temple administrators are taught to become scribes. Instead I went each day to a small low-roofed room in an ancient little temple at the eastern side of the White Platform, where a priest with a shaven scalp and face conducted a private class for eight or nine high-born boys. My classmates were the sons of governors, ambassadors, generals, and high priests, and they had great regard for themselves. But I was the son of a king.

That created difficulties for me. I was accustomed to privilege and precedence, and I demanded my usual rights. But in the classroom I had no rights. I was big and I was strong, but I was neither the biggest nor the strongest, for some of the boys were four or five years older. The first lessons I learned were painful ones.

I had two chief tormentors. One was Bir-hurturre, the son of Ludingirra, who had been my father's master of the chariots and who had gone down into the death-pit to sleep beside him. The other was Zabardi-bunugga, the son of Gungunum the high priest of An. I think Bir-hurturre bore a grudge against me because his father had had to die when mine had died. What quarrel Zabardi-bunugga had with me, I never fully understood, though possibly it grew from some old jealousy his father had felt toward Lugalbanda. But these two were determined, whatever the reason, to make me see that my high rank and privilege had ended when the crown had passed to the king Dumuzi.

In the classroom I took the front chair. It was my right, to go before the others. Bir-hurturre said, 'That chair is mine, son of Lugalbanda.'

The way he said *son of Lugalbanda*, he made it sound like *son of Dung-fly, son of Trash-picker*.

'The chair is mine,' I told him calmly. That seemed self-evident to me, in no need of defense or explanation.

'Ah. Then the chair must be yours, son of Lugalbanda,' he answered, and smiled.

When I returned from midday recess I found that someone had gone down to the river and captured a yellow toad, and had skewered it into the middle of my seat. It was not yet dead. To one side of it someone had drawn the face of the evil spirit Rabisu, the croucher-in-doorways, and on the other side was drawn the storm-bird Imdugud with her tongue thrust out.

I pulled the toad free and turned to Bir-hurturre with it. 'You seem to have left your midday meal on my seat,' I said. 'Here. This is for you to eat, not for me.'

I seized him by the hair and thrust the toad toward his mouth.

Bir-hurturre was ten years old. Though he was no taller than I was, he was very broad through the shoulders and extremely strong. Catching me by the wrist, he pulled my hand free of his hair and wrenched it down to my side. No one had ever handled me like that before. I felt rage rising in me like a winter torrent rushing down upon the Land.

'Doesn't he want to share his seat with his brother?' asked Zabardi-bunugga, who was looking on with amusement.

I broke loose of Bir-hurturre's grasp and hurled the toad into Zabardi-bunugga's face. '*My* brother?' I cried. 'Yours! Your twin!' Indeed Zabardi-bunugga was amazingly ugly, with a nose flat as a button, and strange coarse hair that grew in widely spaced bunches on his head.

They both came at me at once. They held me with my arms behind my back and jeered at me and slapped me. I had never been held so impiously in the palace, not even in the roughest of play: no one would have dared. 'You may not touch me!' I

27

shouted. 'Cowards! Pigs! Do you know who I am?'

'You are Bugal-lugal, son of Lugal-bugal,' said Bir-hurturre, and they laughed as though he had said something enormously clever.

'I will be king one day!'

'Bugal-lugal! Lugal-bugal!'

'I'll break you! I'll feed you to the river!'

'Lugal-bugal-lugal! Bugal-lugal-lugal!'

I thought my soul would burst from my breast. For a moment I could neither breathe nor see nor think. I strained and struggled and kicked, and heard a grunt, and kicked again, and heard a whimper. One of them released me and I pulled myself free of the other, and went running from the classroom, not out of fear of them but out of fear that I would kill them while the madness was upon me.

The school-father and his assistant were returning just then from their midday meal. In the blindness of my wrath I ran right into them, and they caught me and held me until I was calm. I pointed into the classroom, where Bir-hurturre and Zabardi-bunugga were staring at me and making faces with their tongues, and demanded that they be put to death at once. But the school-father replied only that I had risen from my place without permission, I had spoken to him without permission; and he gave me over to the whipping-slave to cane me for my unruliness. It was not the last time those two tormented me, and occasionally some of the others joined in, the bigger ones, at least. I found I could do nothing against any of this persecution. School-father and his assistant always took their side, and told me I must hold my tongue, I must master my temper. I wrote down the names of my enemies, both my schoolfellows and my tutors, so that I could have them all flayed alive when I was king. But when I came to understand things a little better, soon afterward, I threw those lists away.

Writing and reading were the first things I learned. It is important for a prince to understand such matters. Imagine trusting everything to the honesty of one's scribes and ministers when messages are going back and forth on the battlefields, or when one is engaged in correspondence with the king of another land! If the master cannot read, any kind of deceit may be practised on him, and a great man could be betrayed into the grasp of his enemies.

I wish I were able to claim with any honesty that my reason for turning to those arts was anything so astute and far-sighted. But no such princely notions were in my mind. What attracted me to writing was my notion that it was magical. To be able to work magic, that magic or any other, was tremendously attractive.

It seemed miraculous that words could be captured like hawks in flight, and imprisoned in a piece of red clay, and set loose again by anyone who knew the art of it. In the beginning I did not even think such a thing was credible. 'You invent the words as you go along,' I told the school-father. 'You pretend that there are meanings, but you simply make everything up!' Coolly he handed the tablet to the assistant, who read from it everything that the school-father had read, word for word. Then he called in one of the older boys from another room, and he did the same; and then I was whipped on the knuckles for my doubting. I doubted no longer. These people—ordinary mortals, not even gods—had some way of bringing the words alive out of the clay. So I paid close heed as the school-father's assistant showed me how to prepare the soft clay tablets, how to cut a reed stylus to a wedge-shaped end, how to make the marks that are writing, by pressing the stylus into the tablet. And I struggled to comprehend the marks.

Understanding them was enormously troublesome at first. The marks were like the scratchings of a hen in the sand. I learned to tell the differences out of which their meanings sprang. Some of the marks stood for sounds, *na* and *ba* and *ma* and the like, and some stood for ideas, like *god* or *king* or *plough*, and some showed how a word was meant to stand in relation to the words around it. Then I caught the knack of this wonderful witchcraft. I found that almost without effort I could make the marks yield their meanings to my eye, so that I could look down a tablet and read from it a list of things, 'gold, silver, bronze, copper', or 'Nippur, Eridu, Kish, Uruk', or 'arrow, javelin, spear, sword'. Of course I could never read as a scribe reads, swiftly scanning the columns of a tablet and bringing from it its full wealth of meaning and nuance: that is the task of a lifetime's devotion, and I have had other tasks. But I learned my writing-signs well, and know them still, and can never be deceived by some treacherous underling who means to play me false.

We were taught also concerning the gods, and the making of the world, and the founding of the Land. School-father told us how the heaven and the earth had come forth from the sea, and the sky had been put between them, and the moon and the sun and the planets were fashioned. He spoke of the bright and shining Sky-father An who decrees what must be done, and of Ninhursag the great mother, and of Enlil the lord of the storm, and of the wise Enki and the radiant sun Utu, the fount of justice, and cool silvery Nanna, the ruler of the night; and of course he spoke much of Inanna the mistress of Uruk. But when he told how mankind was created it saddened and angered me: not that we were brought into being to be serfs to the gods, for who am I to question that, but the work was done in such a cruel and slipshod way.

For look, look you, how the job was managed, and how we suffer for our makers' foolishness!

It was at a time when the gods lived like mortals on the earth, tilling the soil and caring for their flocks. But because they were gods they would not deign to work at their tasks, and so the grain withered and the cattle died, and the gods grew hungry. Therefore the sea-mother Nammu came to her son Enki, who dwelled lazily then in the happy land of Dilmun where the lion did not kill and the wolf did not snatch the lamb, and she told him of the sorrow and distress of his fellow gods. 'Rise from your couch,' she said, 'and use your wisdom to bring forth servants, who will assume our tasks and minister to our needs.'

'O my mother,' he replied, 'it can be done.' He told her to reach into the abyss and scoop up a handful of clay from the depths of the sea; and then Enki and his wife the earth-mother Ninhursag and the eight goddesses of birth took the clay and fashioned it, and shaped the body and the limbs of the first mortal being, and said, 'Our servants will look like that.'

Enki and Ninhursag, out of joy at what they had achieved, gave a great feast for all the other gods, and showed them how the creation of mankind would ease their lives. 'See,' he said, 'each of you will have your own estate on the earth, and these beings will assume your tasks and minister to your needs. These will be the serfs who toil, and over them we will place bailiffs and sheriffs and inspectors and commissioners, and above them kings and queens, who will live in palaces just as we do, with butlers and chamberlains and coachmen and ladies-in-waiting. And all of these creatures will toil all day and night to provide for us.' The gods applauded, and drained many a mug of wine and beer; and they all grew gloriously drunk.

In their drunkenness, Enki and Ninhursag continued to bring forth beings out of the clay. They brought one forth that had neither male organs nor female, and they said it would be a eunuch to guard the royal harem; and they laughed greatly at that. And then they brought forth beings with this disease and that, of the body or of the spirit, and set them loose into the world as well. And lastly they made one whose name was 'I Was Born Long Ago', whose eyes were dim and whose hands trembled, and who could neither sit nor stand nor bend his knees. In this way did old age come into the world, and disease and madness and everything that is evil—as the drunken joke of the god Enki and the earth-mother his wife, the goddess Ninhursag. When the mother of Enki, the sea-mother Nammu, saw what he had done, she exiled him in her anger to the deep abyss, where he dwells to this day. But the injury was done; the drunken gods had had their joke; and we suffer under that and always will. I will not quarrel with their having made us to be their creatures and their things, but why did they make us so imperfect?

I asked the school-father that question, and he had me whipped on my knuckles for the asking.

I learned other things that confused and frightened me. These were the tales and legends of the gods, the same ones that the harper Ur-kununna had sung in the palace courtyard. But somehow when the stories fell from the lips of that sweet and gentle old man they had lit a warm light of pleasure in my soul, and when I heard them in the dry precise voice of the pinch-faced school-father they seemed transformed into dark and disturbing things. Ur-kununna had made the gods seem playful and benevolent and wise; but in the school-father's telling the gods seemed foolish and ruthless and cruel. And yet they were the same gods;

and yet they were the same stories; and yet even the words were the same. What had changed? Ur-kununna had sung the gods loving and feasting and bringing forth life. School-father gave us quarrelsome bickering untrustworthy gods who cast darkness upon the world without warning and without mercy. Ur-kununna lived in joy, and walked to his death uncomplaining, knowing he was beloved of the gods. School-father taught me that mortals must live their lives in endless fear, for the gods are not kind. And yet they were the same gods: wise Enki, lordly Enlil, beautiful Inanna. But the wise Enki had created old age for us, and the weakness of the flesh. The lordly Enlil had in his unquenchable lust raped the young girl-goddess Ninlil, though she cried out in pain, and he had fathered the moon upon her. The beautiful Inanna, to free herself from the nether world, had sold her husband Dumuzi to the demons. The gods, then, are no better than we are: just as petty, just as selfish, just as thoughtless. How had I failed to see these things, when I listened to the harper Ur-kununna? Was it merely that I was too young to understand? Or was it that in the warmth of his singing the doings of the divine ones took on a different semblance?

The world that school-father revealed to me was a world that was bleak and chancy. And there was but one escape from that world, to an afterlife that was even more harsh and terrifying. What hope, then? What hope for any of us, king or beggar? That was what the gods had made for us; and the gods themselves are just as vulnerable and frightened: there is Inanna, stripped bare in her descent into hell, standing naked before the queen of the nether world. Monstrous! Monstrous! There is no hope, I thought, not here or anywhere after.

Heavy thoughts, for so young a child, even a child that is the son of a king, and is two parts god and only one part mortal. I was filled with despair. Alone I went one day to the side of the city by the river, and peered over the wall and saw the dead bodies floating in the water, the corpses of those who could not afford a burial. And I thought, it is all the same, beggar or king, king or beggar, and there is no meaning anywhere. Dark thoughts! But after a time I put them from my mind. I was young. I could not brood for ever on such things.

Later I saw the truth within the truth: that even though the gods are as ruthless and as capricious as ourselves, it is also the case that we can make ourselves as exalted as gods. But that lesson was one that I was a long time in learning.

4

Because there is divine blood within me, I grew swiftly to extraordinary size and strength. When I was nine I was bigger than any of the boys in the little temple-school, and I had no more trouble with the likes of Bir-hurturre and Zabardi-bunugga. Indeed they looked to me as their leader, and played the games I called for playing, and gave me the first seat in everything. The only difference between us was that they had hair on their bodies and their cheeks, and I did not.

I went to a sage in the Kullab district and bought from him, for ninety se of silver and half a sila of good wine, a potion made of powdered juniper root, cassia juice, antimony, lime, and some other things, which was meant to hasten the onset of manhood. I rubbed this stuff under my arms and around my loins, and it burned like a thousand devils. But soon hair was sprouting on me as thickly as on any warrior.

Dumuzi launched military campaigns against Aratta, against the city of Kish, and against the wild Martu tribesmen of the desert. I was too young to take part in these wars. But already I was training every day in the skills of the javelin, the sword, the mace, and the axe. On account of my size the other boys were afraid to stand forth on the training-grounds against me, and I had to practice with the young men. When duelling with axes one day with a warrior named Abbasagga, I split his shield in half at a single blow, and he threw down his weapon and ran from the field. After that it was hard for me to find opponents, even among the men. For a time I went off by myself and studied the art of the bow and arrow, although that is a weapon used only by hunters, not by warriors. The first bow that was made for me was too weak, and I snapped it as I tried to draw it; then I bought a costly bow of several woods cunningly laminated together, cedar and mulberry and fir and willow, which better served my purpose. I still have it.

Another thing I learned was the art of building. I studied the mixing of mastics and mortars out of bitumen and other kinds of pitch, the making of bricks, the plastering and painting of walls, and many another humble thing, and in the full heat of the day I labored sweating among the artisans, deepening my skills. One reason I did this is that it is our custom to educate princes in such things, so that they can play their proper roles in the construction and dedication of new buildings and walls. In other lands, I know, princes and kings do nothing but ride and hunt and have sport with women, but things are not like that here. Above and beyond the matter of the responsibilities I expected one day to have to assume, though, I found keen pleasure in mastering those crafts. To make bricks and set them in courses to form a wall gave me a powerful sense of accomplishment, as strong as any that I have had from more heroic endeavors: in some ways stronger, perhaps. And there was something altogether voluptuous about the making of bricks, the mixing of the clay and straw, the pressing of the wet clay into the mould, the scooping away of the excess with the side of my hand.

Of course, there are other and more obvious sources of pleasure, and other sensations more immediately voluptuous. I began my education in those things early also.

My first teacher was a little squint-eyed goat-herder I met in the Street of the Scorpion on a day in late winter. I was ten or eleven and she, I suppose, must have been a bit older than that, since she had breasts, and hair down below. She begged for the bit of golden braid I had wound in my hair, and I said, 'Come with me.'

In a dark cellar atop a pile of old damp straw she earned the price of the braid, though what we did was more like wrestling than coupling. I am not even certain that I entered her that day, so much of a novice was I. But we met two or three more times, and I know that what we did on those occasions was the true deed. I never asked her name or told her mine. She reeked of goat's milk and goat's urine, and her face was coarse and her dark skin was blemished, and she wriggled and writhed in my arms like some slippery creature of the river. But when I embraced her she seemed as beautiful as Inanna, and the pleasure she gave me struck straight through me like the lightning of Enlil. So was I initiated into the great mystery, a little earlier than such things are supposed to happen, and in a highly irregular way.

There were many more after her. The city was full of smudge-faced little girls willing to go with a sturdy young prince for an hour, and I must have sampled half of them.

Then I discovered that the same delights, minus the rank odors and the other little drawbacks, could be had from girls of a higher class. Few refused me, and those who did, I think, said no only out of fear of discovery and punishment. For my part I could never have enough: I felt that when my body quivered with that ecstacy I was entering into direct communion with the gods. It was like being hurled straightaway into the sacred domain. And is that not the truth? The act of engendering is the way of entry into all that is holy. Until you have done it, you dwell outside the bounds of civilization; you are little more than a beast. The joining of flesh and spirit in that act is the thing that brings us close to the gods. I found myself thinking every time, in that wild instant just before the pouring forth of my seed, that this was no ordinary girl of Uruk beneath me, but fiery Inanna herself—the goddess, not the priestess. It is a sacred business.

Apart from all such lofty considerations, I should add that I noticed, very early, that coupling had a wondrous way of calming my spirit. For I boiled then, and for many years thereafter, with turbulent inner frenzies that I scarcely understood and against which I had no defense. I think that hot lust of mine sprang not only from the ordinary passions of the flesh but from something deeper and darker, which was the painful loneliness that assailed me like a wolf in the darkness. Often I felt myself to be the only living being in a world of chilly phantoms. Having no father, no brother, no real friend—set apart from all the others by the godlike strangeness that any simpleton could see lay upon me—I found myself engulfed in a bewildering emptiness of the soul. It stung me and burned me like mountain ice against my skin. So I reached toward women and girls for the only comfort I could find. The fulfillment of passion did at least give me a few hours of respite from that agitation of the spirit.

When I was a month short of twelve one of my uncles, observing in the baths that my body had become that of a man, told me, 'We will go to the temple cloister this afternoon. I think the time is overdue for you.'

I knew what he meant. And I did not have the heart to tell him that I had not waited for a proper initiation.

So when the midday heat had eased a little, we put on kilts of fine white linen, and he drew a narrow red stripe across my shoulders and sliced a lock of my hair, and we went together to the temple of Inanna. We passed through the rear courtyard and crossed a maze of lesser rooms—workshops and toolbins and the library where the holy tablets were stacked—and at last we came to the cloister where the temple priestesses wait to serve worshippers. 'Now you will give yourself to the goddess,' my uncle told me.

For one horrified moment I wondered if he had arranged for me to yield my supposed virginity to Inanna herself. Perhaps the son of a king might in fact warrant such a lofty initiator. By now I had become something of a swaggerer, at least in the inwardness of my thoughts, and I imagine I could have found the valor to couple with a goddess: but to embrace the high priestess was another thing entirely. Her hawk-featured face frightened me; that and the thought of her thickening flesh. She was older than my mother, after all. No doubt she had been the most superb of women once, but now she was aging and said to be unwell, and I had seen when she appeared at the last harvest festival, oiled and bejeweled and practically naked, that her magnificence was going from her. But my fears were absurd. Inanna, whether she be young or old, is reserved only for the king. The priestess whom my uncle had provided for me was a juicy girl of about sixteen, with golden paint on her cheeks and a glittering red jewel mounted in her left nostril.

'I am Abisimti,' she said, touching her hand to breasts and thighs in the holy sign of Inanna. Then she led me into her little chamber, while my uncle went off to make his observances with a priestess of his own.

Abisimti's room contained a couch, a basin, an image of the

goddess. She lit the candles and performed the libations and took me to the long narrow couch. We knelt by it and said the prayers together, her very solemnly, and in a copper brazier she burned the lock of my hair that my uncle had cut off. Then she drew my garment from me and bathed me with a cool cloth. At the sight of my nakedness she frowned.

'How old are you?' she asked.

'In a month, twelve.'

'Twelve? Only twelve?' She laughed prettily and clapped her hands. 'Then the gods have favored you greatly!'

I said nothing, merely stared intently through her light linen robe to the high round breasts half visible beneath.

'How eager you are!' she cried. 'Your first taste of the great mystery, and you can hardly bear to wait a moment longer!'

I dared not lie to a priestess, but I did not want to tell the truth. So I looked away, feigning embarrassment.

Abisimti let her robe drop. But before I could possess her she had to tell me at length of the esoteric meaning of the rite we were about to perform, which I had already comprehended on my own, and then to instruct me in the method and art of coupling. That was also superfluous but I endured it patiently enough. Then we went to it. I pretended to a clumsiness I had long ago outgrown. Even so, Abisimti's eyes were shining when we were done. Was that right, I wondered, for her to take such pleasure in it, she being a priestess? But later I came to see that it is not only right but blessed for the priestess of Inanna to enjoy the devotions of the temple cloister. A common whore may hate her work and detest her customers, perhaps, but a priestess is engaged in the most sacred act of all, which is to bridge the great gulf between mortal and god. That is true of a common whore as well, but the whore does not understand such matters.

In such ways I glided toward manhood. I thought I saw the shape of my life unrolling before me. I would eat well and drink well and enjoy many women, and I would be a warrior and a priest and a prince; and one day Dumuzi would die and I would be called to the kingship of Uruk. I did not question any of that. Plainly it was my destiny. Though I was already well aware that the gods are capricious, I did not think them stupid: and who better to rule over the city, once he was of age, than the son of Lugalbanda? It struck me as inevitable that the assembly of the city would choose me when Dumuzi's time was done.

But meanwhile Dumuzi was king. And Dumuzi, though hardly young—he was at least four-and-twenty then—was far from old. He might easily live another twenty years, if he was lucky on the battlefield. That was a long time for me to wait for the throne. A great restlessness surged in me. I struggled to contain it.

5

One day in this time a slave wearing the badge of Inanna came to me while I was practicing the throwing of the javelin and said, 'You will come now to the temple of the goddess.'

He led me through winding passageways I had never seen before, in the depths of my grandfather's temple, or perhaps even beneath it, in tunnels that descended into the White Platform. By the flickering light of our oil-lamps I saw that the halls here were high-vaulted and richly ornamented with mosaic decorations in red and yellow, which was strange in this place of perpetual night. There was the smell of incense in the air, and a dampness, as if the walls themselves were sweating. This plainly was some holy sanctum, perhaps that of Inanna herself. I was made uneasy by that, as I always was by anything pertaining too closely to Inanna.

I heard the scrambling of small creatures in the darkness, and the sound of harsh congested breathing. Now and then a passage intersected ours, and I saw lamps glowing far away. Twice we came upon wizards or exorcists at work in the hallway by candleglow, crouching against the tiled floors and scattering barley-flour and pungent-smelling tamarisk branches about as they cast their spells. They paid no attention to us. A little while afterward, as I looked down a cross-passage, I had a quick glimpse of three squat brown two-legged creatures with heavy shaggy chests and the hooves of goats, trudging away from us. I am sure I saw them. I have no doubt they were demons. I knew I was in a place of perils, where one world borders close on another, and things that are meant to be invisible cross boundaries that should not be crossed.

We remained on our path, sloping ever downward. At last I arrived at a great door plated with bronze which pivoted on a large round black stone sunk beneath the pavement.

'Go in,' the slave said.

I entered a long narrow room, deep and dark. Its rough brick walls were ornamented with black shale and red limestone set in bitumen, and lamps mounted in four high sconces provided a glimmering light. On the floor two overlapping triangles of white metal were inlaid to form the outline of a six-pointed star.

At the center of that star stood a woman, perfectly motionless.

I was expecting to find myself before Inanna herself, but this was some lesser priestess, taller, younger, and more slender. I felt certain I had seen her before, in the goddess-ceremonies, close at the right hand of Inanna, robing and disrobing her as the rite required: a handmaiden of the goddess, of the inner circle of the temple. For a long silent moment I stared at her, and she at me. Her beauty was extraordinary. It grasped me like a great hand which I could not elude. I felt the power of it seizing and shaking my soul like the hot winds of summer. She was elaborately bedecked: her cheeks were colored with a face-bloom of yellow ochre, her upper eyelids were darkened with kohl, her lower ones were made green with malachite, and her thick lustrous hair had been reddened with henna. She wore rich robes, with the reed-bundle emblem of Inanna embroidered across her breast. A ball of myrrh was burning in a censer that rested on a silver tripod. Her eyes, dark and piercing, traveled across me from shoulder to shoulder, from head to toe: she seemed to be taking my measure.

At length she greeted me by my name, my birth-name. I had no name for her and so I could make no answer. I merely stood there gaping foolishly at her.

Then she said, almost fiercely, 'Well? Do you remember me?'

'I have seen you serving Inanna at the rites.'

Her eyes flashed. 'Of course you have. Everyone has. But you and I have met. We have spoken.'

'Have we?'

'Long ago. You were very young. It must have gone from your mind.'

'Tell me your name, and I will know if we have met.'

'Ah, you *have* forgotten me!'

'I forget very little. Tell me your name,' I said.

She smiled mischievously, and spoke her name, which is one that I may not set down here, for, like my own birth-name, it has been replaced by a holier one and must be abandoned forever. The sound of her name lifted the latch of my memory, and from the storehouse of my mind came a rush of recollection: strings of blue beads, amulets of pink shell, a bare sinuous girlish body painted with serpent designs, budding breasts, a sharp perfume. Was this woman one and the same with that sly child? Yes. Yes. Her breasts were more than buds, now, and her face had grown broader from cheek to cheek, and the wicked sparkle of her eyes was obscured by the womanly cosmetics with which she had painted them. But I was certain that I saw the girl hidden within the woman.

'Yes, I remember now,' I said. 'The day of the naming of the new king, when I was lost in the maze of the temple, and you came after me, and comforted me, and led me back to the ceremony. But you are greatly changed.'

'Not so much, I think. I was already beginning to be a woman, then. I had bled goddess-blood three times. I think I look not so very different now. But you are altogether changed. You were only a child, then.'

'It was six years ago, or a little more than that.'

'Was it? What a sweet child you were!' She shot me a flagrant glance. 'But a child no longer. Abisimti tells me you are truly a man.'

Abashed, appalled, I cried, 'I thought the doings of priestesses were sacred secrets!'

'Abisimti tells me everything. We are like sisters.'

I shifted my weight restlessly. As before, long ago, I felt anger and uncertainty, because I was unable to tell whether I was being mocked. I was strangely helpless before her guile. I had grown older, yes, but so had she; and if I was not much past twelve, she was at least sixteen, and still far ahead of me. There was a sharp edge on her, that cut me wherever I tried to take hold of her.

I said, a little too brusquely, 'Why am I here?'

'I thought it was time we met again. First I saw you one day during the festival, when you were at the temple bearing offerings. My eye fell upon you and I wondered about you, and I asked someone, Who is that man? And she said, that is no man, that is only a boy, the son of Lugalbanda. It surprised me, that you had grown so swiftly, for I thought you were still very young. Then a few days later Abisimti said that a prince had come to her in the cloister and she had conveyed him into manhood, and I asked her which prince that was, and she told me that he was the son of Lugalbanda. I thought I would speak with you again, after hearing Abisimti. The words of Abisimti made me curious about you.'

It infuriated me that I was still too simple to read the meanings between her meanings. Was she saying that she wished to go to the cloister with me herself? So it seemed, or why else had she summoned me, and why else would her eyes be so wanton with me? Well, gladly would I have gone with her—more than gladly! Her beauty drove me wild, even then. But I was not sure that that was what she wanted, and I dared not put it to the test, out of fear of being refused. One may not have the priestess of Inanna for the mere asking, only the ones who wait in the cloister, who have dedicated themselves as holy whores. It is shameful to approach the others, who are set apart as brides of the god, or of the king in whom the god is embodied. I did not know which class she belonged to. And perhaps this was simply a game for her, and I only her plaything, a man-doll now instead of the child-doll I once had been. I felt her spinning webs all about me, and I was lost in them.

She said, 'How has it been for you? What do you do? I never leave the temple; I have no news of the city, except the gossip that the serving-maids bring me.'

'My mother is priestess of An. I do some service at his temple. I study the things a young man studies. I wait to enter into the fullness of my manhood.'

'And then?'

41

'I will do as the gods require of me.'

'Has any god chosen you yet to be his own?'

'No,' I said. 'Not yet.'

'Do you wish it?'

I shrugged. 'It will happen when it happens.'

'Inanna chose me when I was seven.'

'It will happen when it happens,' I said.

'When you know, will you come to me and tell me which god it is?'

She was staring at me very hard. She seemed to be laying some sort of claim to me, and I did not understand why. Nor did I like it. But her power was intense. I heard myself saying meekly, 'Yes, I will tell you. If that is what you want.'

'That is what I want,' she said.

Something became softer about her now: that mischievous edge went from her, and the look that I interpreted as wantonness. From a pouch at her waist she took an amulet and pressed it into my hands, a statuette of Inanna, with great breasts and swollen thighs, carved from some smooth green stone that I had never seen before. It seemed to shine with an inner flame. 'Keep this by you always,' she said.

It troubled me to take it from her. I felt as though the price of that statuette was my soul.

I said, 'How can I accept anything so precious?'

'You may not refuse. That would be a sin, to turn back the gifts of a goddess.'

'The gifts of a priestess, rather.'

'The goddess speaks through her priestess. This is yours, and while you have it, you are under the protection of the goddess-power.'

Maybe so. But it made me uneasy. In Uruk we are all under the protection of the goddess-power; but nevertheless Inanna is a dangerous goddess, who deals in mysterious ways with her subjects, and it is unwise to get too close to her. My father had done his service to Inanna, as a king of Uruk must, but whenever he had gone in private to a temple it had been to Sky-father An. And I myself felt more comfortable with Enlil of the storms than I did with the goddess. But I had no choice but to take the amulet. It may be perilous to worship Inanna but it is far worse to anger her.

When I left her that day I felt strange, as though I had been forced to surrender something of great value. But I had no idea what it was.

I was summoned several more times in the next few months to the audience-chamber at the end of that passageway of demons and wizards deep below the Enmerkar temple. It was the same each time: an inconclusive conversation, a puzzling display of threatening flirtatiousness that led nowhere, a sense at the end that she had outplayed me in a game with rules I did not understand. Often she had some little gift for me, but when I brought her one she would not take it. She wanted to know many things—news of the court, of the assembly, of the king. What had I heard? What were they saying in the palace? She was insatiable. I grew cautious with her, saying little, answering her questions as briefly and vaguely as I could. I did not know what she wanted from me. And I feared the power of her beauty, which I knew was strong enough to sweep me to destruction. With anyone else I would have said, young as I was, 'Come with me, lie with me,' but how could I say such words to *her*? Shielded as she was by the aura of the goddess, she was unattainable, until she gave consent. At a word from her, at the crooking of a single finger, I would have knelt to her. But she did not speak the word. She did not crook the finger. I prayed that the gods would deliver her into my arms, one of these times when she sent for me. But though the warmth of her smile said one thing, the cool icy sparkle of her eyes said another, and held me back from her as though I were a eunuch. She seemed altogether beyond my reach. Yet I had not forgotten the astonishing thing she had said to me in my childhood, on the day of Dumuzi's coronation: *When you are king, I will lie in your arms.*

6

Then it was the month of Tashritu, the season of the new year, when the king enters into the Sacred Marriage with Inanna and all things are reborn. That is the time when the god strides across the threshold of the temple like a rumbling storm and casts his seed into the goddess, and the rains come again after the long dry harsh death-in-life that is the summer.

It is the greatest and most holy festival of Uruk, on which all else depends. The preparations occupy everyone in the city for weeks as the summer wanes. That which has been defiled during the year must be purified by sacrifices and fumigations. Those who are ritually unclean by birth, members of the impure castes, must take themselves outside the walls and build a temporary village for themselves there. Weak and deformed animals must be slain. All houses and public buildings in need of repair are put in order, and the festive decorations are brought forth. Then at last come the parades, led by harpers and tympanists. The whores don brightly colored scarves and the cloak of the goddess. Men adorn their left sides with women's clothing. Priests and priestesses carry through the streets the bloody swords, the double-edged axes, with which the sacrifices have been performed. Dancers leap through hoops and jump over ropes. In her temple Inanna bathes herself and anoints herself and dons the holy ornaments, the great ring of carnelian and the beads of lapis and the shining loin-plate of gold, and the jewels for her navel and for her hips and for her nose and for her eyes, and the earrings of gold and bronze, and the breast-ornaments of ivory. And the god Dumuzi, the bringer of fertility, enters into the king, who goes by boat to the temple district and through the gateway of the Eanna sanctuary, leading a sheep and holding a kid. They stand together on the porch of the temple, priestess and king, goddess and god, while all the city hails them in joy; and then they go within, to the bedchamber that has been prepared, and he caresses her and goes into her and ploughs her and pours his fruitfulness into her womb. So it has been since the beginning, when the gods alone existed and kingship had not yet descended from heaven.

On the day of the new moon that marked the beginning of the new year I went with all the others to the White Platform, to wait outside the Enmerkar temple for the showing-forth of Inanna and Dumuzi. A light wind, moist and fragrant, blew from the south. It was the wind we call the Cheat, which promises springtime, but in fact heralds the winter.

The king appeared, with his sheep, with his kid, at the western end of the platform. The crowd parted to make way for him as he walked slowly up the steps and toward the temple. He looked splendid. The god-light was upon him, and his body gleamed from within.

There is something about performing the Sacred Marriage that exalts any man, I suppose. This was the sixth time Dumuzi had performed the rite since he became king, and each year, watching him cross the platform, I had been astonished by the awe he inspired in me, this man who at all other times seemed to me so ordinary, so flabby of soul. But when the god is in the king, the king is a god. I would never forget how my father had looked on the night of this rite, powerful and grand and immense, glancing neither to one side nor the other as he went past the place where my mother and I stood watching, and entered the temple, and returned with Inanna by his side, and stretched forth his hands to the people of the city, and went inside once again to lead the goddess to her bedchamber. But Lugalbanda had looked majestic at all times. I would not have expected Dumuzi to be able to rival his magnificence; yet on this night each year he did.

Tonight, though, something unusual seemed to be happening. The king and the priestess customarily emerge to show themselves together at the instant when the crescent of the new moon appears above the temple. But this night the moment came and went and the temple door remained closed. I do not know how long we waited. It seemed like hours. We looked toward one another with questioning eyes, but no one dared speak.

Then at last the great brazen door swung open and the holy couple appeared. At the sight of them, the silence grew more intense: it was like a chasm of stillness that engulfed all the sound in the world. But only for an instant. A moment later a low murmuring and hissing could be heard, as those toward the front of the crowd began to mutter and murmur in surprise.

From where I stood, far in the back, I was unable at first to tell what was amiss. There was Dumuzi in shining crown and royal robe of rich deep blue; there was Inanna close by his side. Then I realised that the woman wearing the sacred ornaments of ivory and gold and carnelian and lapis was not Inanna, or at least not the Inanna who had stood forth on this night all the previous years of my life. That woman had been short and sturdy of body, and this one appeared to have been drawn out to a finer consistency, slender, almost frail, and tall, her shoulder virtually of a height with Dumuzi's. And, when a moment later I came to perceive who she must be, I understood that I was about to lose that which had been mine, and I was helpless to prevent it.

I had to see her face. I pushed my way forward, shouldering people aside as though they were dry sticks.

At a distance of twenty paces I looked straight into her eyes, and beheld the dark mischief that sparkled there. Yes, of course, it was she, plucked suddenly from her underground chamber to the height of sacred power in Uruk: no longer handmaiden to the goddess, but suddenly, astoundingly, made into Inanna herself. I could not move. A heaviness invaded my legs and rooted them to the pavement. There was a thickness in my throat, like a lump of sand that could not be swallowed or expelled.

She stared at me but did not seem to see me, though I was more than a head taller than the tallest person around me. The ceremony consumed her entirely. I watched her hand Dumuzi the sacred white flask of honey, and receive from him the sacred vessel of barley. I heard them exchanging the words of the rite: 'My holy jewel, my wondrous Inanna,' he said, and she to him, 'O my husband Dumuzi, you are truly my love.'

Thick-voiced I said to some lord who stood beside me, 'What has happened? Where is Inanna?'

'There is Inanna.'

'But that girl isn't the high priestess!'

'From this evening onward she is,' he replied. And another, on the far side of me, said, 'They say the old one was ill, and worsened

46

all day, and then she died at the sunset hour. But they had another all ready to be consecrated. They brought her forth in a hurry to be bathed and dressed, and she will marry Dumuzi tonight. Which is why there was such a delay.'

I heard the words go echoing through the caverns of my mind, *she will marry Dumuzi tonight,* and I thought I would topple to the pavement.

The king sipped from the flask of honey, and returned it to her so that she could sip of it also. They joined their hands and emptied the vessel of barley on the ground, and poured the golden honey over the seed. The temple musicians strummed their instruments and sang the hymn of the showing-forth of the god and goddess. It was almost done, now. In a few moments they would go within. In the divine bedchamber the handmaidens would take from her the rings and beads and breastplates and the shining three-cornered sheet of gold that covered her loins, and then he would caress her, and speak the words of the Sacred Marriage to her, and then—and then—

I could not stay to watch them any longer.

I turned and rushed from the platform like a maddened bull, knocking down anyone who did not get out of my way quickly enough. From behind me came the music of cymbals and flutes. I could not bear the sound of it. They are in the bedchamber now, I thought, he touches her, he strokes her secret places, his mouth is against her mouth, he will cover her with his body, he will enter her—

I ran blindly this way and that into the darkness, not knowing or caring where I was going. A pain that I had known all too often was once more upon me. I felt alone, outcast, a stranger in my own city. I had neither father nor brother nor wife, nor even anyone I could truly call a friend. My solitude was like a wall of fire around me. I yearned to reach toward someone—anyone—but there was no one. All I could do was run; and I ran on and on until I thought my breast would burst. At last I found myself stumbling through the deserted streets of the district known as the Lion, where the military barracks are. It was not by any accident that my feet had taken me there: when that kind of blindness comes over us, we are guided by the gods. There was then at the center of the Lion district a shrine sacred to the godhood of Lugalbanda, erected there by Dumuzi early in his reign—nothing very grand, only an image of my father a little larger than life size, lit from below by three small oil lamps that burned all night and all day, a small enough tribute to a great king who has become a god. I flung myself down before it and held tightly to the bricks of its base. And I suddenly felt a familiar strangeness enter my mind.

It was the strangeness that first had assailed me on that day of my father's funeral rite, and had touched me in a lighter way two or three times in the years since: a sense of pressure against my brow, the feeling of great invisible wings beating against my soul. But this time it was far more powerful than ever before. There was no withstanding its force. I felt a tingling in my skin, a numbness everywhere. I heard a faint buzzing sound, such as one hears when a distant swarm of locusts rises in the afternoon sky and comes across the plain. And then the buzzing grew louder, as though the locusts now were close at hand and thick black clouds of them were darkening the face of the sun. I smelled the pungent smell of burning candles, though there were no candles anywhere about. Out of the streets and buildings near me rose a cold blue fire that swept over me in flat surging sheets, enveloping me without burning me.

I rose, or, rather, I floated to my feet. I saw before me a tunnel, perfectly round, with smooth shining walls from which a bright blue glow radiated. It drew me toward it. I yielded to its pull. I heard the slow, steady throbbing of a drum, growing louder and louder with each beat. I was without will, utterly in the thrall of the god-power, and that frightened me as deeply as I have ever been frightened in my life. For I felt myself lost, I felt myself drawn down into a place of destruction where all identities are merged in the blue fire that consumes everything.

A quiet voice that arose behind my right ear said, 'Fear nothing. Lugalbanda is with you. There is a covenant between us for all time to come.'

With those words all dread and sorrow and pain lifted from me, and I knew boundless joy, an unending rapture, a sensation of deep ecstasy.

There was no danger. A god was with me, and I was safe. I

resisted nothing now. A god was with me. With every breath I took I breathed in divinity. I made the great surrender. At last I allowed the god to flow through the walls of my soul and enter me and possess me to the fullest.

Fear nothing. Lugalbanda is with you.

I danced a wild dance, roaring and stamping my feet against the ground. Lugalbanda placed in my hands a drum, and I beat upon it and sang a canticle in his praise. Power ran through me, and a great heat. Fearless, I ran forward into the blue tunnel, following a swirling, bobbing globe of brilliant purple light that blazed like a little sun just ahead of me. All night I ran without tiring, through every district of the city, across the Lion and the Reed and the Hive, through Kullab and Eanna, past the royal palace, up the steps of the White Platform and down them again, in and out of this temple and that, past the breweries, the taverns, the whore-houses, the spice market, the river quays, the cattle pens, the slaughterhouses and tanneries, the street of the scribes and the street of the diviners. I looked down into the heart of the earth and saw demons and ghosts toiling in fiery caverns. I perched myself on the right arm of Lugalbanda and flew through the heavens, and beheld the great gods far away in their spheres of crystal, and gave them my salute. I came down to the world again and journeyed from land to land, and sojourned in Dilmun the blessed, and Meluhha and Makan, and the devil-guarded Cedar Mountains, and many another distant place, full of wonders and miracles that I would not have believed, had I been in my ordinary mind.

What happened after that I do not recall. But then it was morning and I found myself lying sprawled on my back in the street in front of the shrine of Lugalbanda.

I felt as stiff and sore as though monsters had been bending each of my limbs the wrong way. I had no idea how I had come to be where I was, nor what had taken place the evening before. But clearly I had spent the night sleeping in the open, and I knew I must have been doing strange things. My jaw ached miserably and my tongue seemed swollen and painful—perhaps I had bitten it once or twice—and there was dried spittle on my chin and robe. Two puzzled-looking young soldiers were bending over me.

'He is alive, I think,' one of them said.

'Is he? His eyes are like glass. Hey, are you alive? You!'

'Speak more gently. He is the son of Lugalbanda.'

'Makes no difference, if he's dead.'

'But he is alive. See, he is breathing. His eyes move.'

'So they do.' And to me: 'Are you indeed the son of Lugalbanda? Ah, I think you are. You wear a prince's ring. Here, then. Here, let us help you.'

I shook away his hand. 'I can manage,' I said in a voice like rusted copper. 'Stand back, stand back!'

Somehow I got myself upright, not without much awkward lurching and staggering. The soldiers stood ready to catch me, looking a little apprehensive, I suppose, on account of my size. But I held my footing. One of them winked and said, 'Been celebrating the Marriage a little too hard, is that it, your lordship? Well, it's no sin. Joy to you, lordship! Joy of the new year!'

The Marriage. The Marriage! Recollection came flooding back, and with it pain. Inanna, Dumuzi, Dumuzi, Inanna.

I turned away, wincing, remembering everything now. And that terrible sense of solitude, of knowing that I stood alone under the uncaring stars, returned to me. Through me once again ran a torment of the spirit that made the aches and bruises of my weary body seem like nothing.

They frowned. 'Will you be all right? Is there anything we can do for you?'

'Just let me be,' I said bleakly.

'As you wish, lordship.' They shrugged and began to move along down the street. 'The sweetness of Inanna be upon you, lordship!' one of them called back to me. And the other laughed and said to him, 'What a very sweet sweetness it must be, this year. Did you see her? The new young one?'

'Ah, did I! What joy the king must have had of her!'

'Enough!' I growled.

And back from them, out of the distance: 'The goddess is dead! Long live the goddess!'

Then they were gone, and I was alone with my pain and my sorrow and my aching and my bewilderment. But I was not altogether alone. I still felt the divine presence, warm and glowing, far back in that place behind my right ear, saying: *Fear nothing. Fear nothing.* For now Lugalbanda was with me, within me, and always would be.

7

Early in the new year, when the festival of the Sacred Marriage was over at last and the funeral rites for the former high priestess had taken place, I was summoned into the presence of She-Who-Is-Now-Inanna. It was a summons that I could hardly reject. Yet I was reluctant to see her, now that the shadow of Dumuzi had fallen between us like a sword.

Three little temple slaves, looking upon me with rounded eyes as though I were some sort of giant demon, led me to the chamber of the goddess in the most holy sector of the Eanna district. No longer would she and I have to meet in obscure chapels along the haunted tunnels beneath the temple. The room in which she received me was a majestic hall of whitewashed brick, with pierced walls through which came fiery spears of sunlight. Along the line where the walls met the ceiling ran a curious row of strange decorations, swelling scarlet globes that looked very much like breasts. Perhaps they were intended to be. The goddess in one of her attributes is the great harlot, the queen of desire.

I waited there a long while, pacing, before she arrived. She swept grandly into the room accompanied by four pages who carried the huge loop-topped bundles of reeds, half again as high as a man, that go wherever Inanna goes. With a quick gesture she sent the pages from us and we were alone.

She held herself tall before me. She looked splendid and triumphant and terrifying. I could see that there was still some girlishness about her, but not very much. Since I last had spoken with her she had been transformed into something beyond my reach and beyond my comprehension.

I thought of her lying naked in the embrace of the king who is the god, on the night of the Sacred Marriage, which was the first night of her high priestesshood, and the taste of bile came to my lips.

She was clad in a simple tufted white robe that covered her from head to foot, with only her right shoulder bare. Her dark hair was parted in the middle and braided into a thick rope that was wound around her head. Her cheeks were lightly tinted with yellow ochre and her eyelids were darkened with kohl, but otherwise she wore no cosmetic. The only tangible sign of her new rank was a delicate coronet of gold chain, woven in the serpent-motif of the goddess, that encircled her forehead. But there were other, subtler signs. The aura of power was upon her. The radiance of heaven's might glowed beneath her skin.

I stared at her, but my eyes could not meet her eyes. I could think only of her body moving beneath Dumuzi's, her lips to his lips, his hand between her thighs, and I burned with chagrin and shame.

Then I reminded myself that the woman who stood before me was not merely someone I had once desired. She was the embodiment of the highest power of the world; she was the goddess herself. The gulf between us was immense. Beside her, I and all my petty desires were nothing.

'Well?' she said after a long while.

I made the goddess-sign to her. 'Queen of Heaven and Earth,' I mumbled. 'Divine Mother. First Daughter of the Moon.'

'Look at me.'

I lifted my eyes. They did not quite reach hers.

'Look at me! Into my eyes, into my eyes! Why this terror? Am I that much altered?'

'Yes,' I whispered. 'Very much altered.'

'And you fear me?'

'Yes. I fear you. You are Inanna.'

'Ah. Queen of Heaven and Earth! Divine Mother! First Daughter of the Moon!'

She put her hand to her mouth and smothered a giggle, and then the giggle escaped as shrill laughter.

Astounded, trembling, I made the goddess-sign again and again.

'Yes, fear me!' she cried, unable to hold back her wild mirth. She pointed imperiously. 'Down and grovel! Fool! Oh, what a child you are! Queen of Heaven and Earth! First Daughter of the Moon!'

I could not comprehend her laughter, ringing in uncontrollable peals. It terrified me. I made the goddess-sign at her once more. She had never been anything other than bewildering to me, even when she was only a naked sparkle-eyed girl with budding breasts, laughing and hugging me fiercely in the corridor and prophesying great things. And the wily young priestess, playing mischievous flirting-games with me to my befuddlement: I had not understood her either. But this was too much, this mockery of the goddess, now that *she* was the goddess. I was frightened. I shivered with fear. Silently I called upon Lugalbanda to guard me.

After a moment she grew more calm, and I felt a little less uneasy. Quietly she said, 'Yes, I am different now. I am Inanna. But I always was: do you understand that? Do you think the goddess did not know from the beginning of time that she would choose my body when she was done with that other one? And now my turn has come. Were you there, the night of the Marriage?'

'I was there, yes. I stood in the front row. You looked straight at me, but you never saw me.'

'The fire of the goddess blinded my eyes that night.'

'Or the fire of the god,' I said rashly.

She stared at me in astonishment and sudden fury. Her cheeks reddened beneath the yellow ochre, and her eyes blazed. But her anger seemed to go as swiftly as it had come. She smiled and said, 'Ah, is that it, Gilgamesh? Is that what gnaws at you?'

I could not speak. My cheeks flamed. I stared at my feet.

She came to me and took my hand in hers. Softly she said, 'I tell you, think nothing of him. Nothing! It was a rite, which I dutifully performed, and that was all it was. It was the goddess who embraced him, and not the priestess. It changes nothing between you and me. Do you understand?'

When you are king, I will lie in your arms.

I looked up, and our eyes met squarely for the first time that day. 'I think I do.'

'So be it, then.'

I was silent. She was still too powerful for me. The force of her was overwhelming.

Then I said, after a time, 'What was that name you called me a moment ago?'

'Gilgamesh.'

'But that is not my name.'

'It will be,' she replied. 'Gilgamesh: He-Who-Is-Chosen. You will reign by that name. It is the name of the old ones, the goddess-people, who held the Land long ago. The knowledge of it came to me as I dreamed, when the goddess first walked with me. Say it: *Gilgamesh. Gilgamesh.*'

'Gilgamesh.'

'Gilgamesh the king.'

'That would be impious to say. Dumuzi is king.'

'Gilgamesh the king! Say it! Say it!'

Once more I shivered. 'Let me be, Inanna, I pray you. If the gods mean to make me king, it will come in proper time. But Dumuzi has the high seat now. I will not name myself king before you, not now, not here in the house of the goddess.'

The anger returned to her eyes. She did not like to be resisted.

Then she shrugged and seemed to put all that we had been saying out of her mind between one instant and the next. In a different voice, flat, businesslike, she said, 'Why are you concealing things from me?'

I was startled by that. 'Concealing?'

'You know what you are concealing.'

I felt a pressure behind my right ear, a warning. Then I knew what she wanted me to tell her, and I feared letting her know it. I said nothing. Speaking with her was like crossing a stream where the footing is tricky: at any moment I might slip and be swept away.

'Why do you hide things from me, Gilgamesh?'

'You must not call me by that name.'

'I suppose not, not yet. But you will not evade me so easily.'

'Why do you think I am hiding something from you?'

'I know you are.'

'Can you see into my mind?'

She smiled enigmatically. 'Perhaps I can.'

I forced myself to stubborn resistance. 'Then I have no secrets from you. You know everything already,' I said.

'I mean to hear it from your lips. I thought you would have come to me days ago to tell me; and when you did not come, I had you summoned. You have changed. There is something new within you.'

'No,' I said. '*You* are the one who has changed.'

'You also,' said Inanna. 'Did I not ask you, when a god has chosen you, to come to me and tell me which god it is?'

I stared at her, amazed. 'You know that?'

'It is easy to tell.'

'How? Can you see it in my face?'

'I could feel it halfway across the city. You have a god within you now. Can you deny it?'

I shook my head. 'No, I will not deny that.'

'You promised to tell me when you were chosen. It was a promise.'

Looking away from her I said in a downcast way, 'It is a very private thing, being chosen.'

'It was a promise,' she said.

'I thought you were too busy to see me—the Marriage festival, the funeral of the old Inanna—'

'It was a promise,' she said.

The whole of the side of my head was throbbing now. I was helpless before her. *Lugalbanda*, I prayed, *guide me, guide me!* But all I felt was the throbbing.

She said, 'Tell me the name of the god who protects you now.'

'You know all things,' I ventured. 'Why must I tell you what you already know?'

That amused her, but it angered her as well. She turned from me and strode up and down the room, and grasped her great reed-bundles and squeezed them tightly, and would not look at me. There was a silence that bound me like bands of bronze. I was choking under its force. It is no small thing to reveal one's personal god: it means surrendering a portion of the strength which that god provides. I was not yet secure enough in my own strength to be able to afford that surrender. But likewise I was not yet secure enough to withhold from Inanna the knowledge she demanded. It was a priestess to whom I had promised, but it was the goddess who laid claim to that promise.

I said very quietly, 'The god who has entered me is my father, the hero Lugalbanda.'

'Ah,' she said. 'Ah!'

She said nothing else, and the frightful silence descended again.

I said, 'You must tell no one.'

'I am Inanna!' she cried, infuriated. 'No one commands me!'

'I ask you only not to tell. Is that a great deal to ask?'

'You may not ask anything of me.'

'Simply promise—'

'I make no promises. I am Inanna.'

The goddess-force flooded the room. The true divine presence creates a chill deeper than the deepest cold of winter, for it draws all the warmth of life toward itself; and in that moment I felt Inanna taking mine, pumping it from me, leaving me a mere frozen husk. I could not move. I could not speak. I felt young and foolish and innocent. I saw rising before me the true goddess incarnate, with yellow eyes glowing like those of a beast in the night.

8

A few days afterward, when I returned to my home after a day at play on the javelin-fields, I found a sealed tablet lying on my couch. This was, I remember, on the nineteenth day of the month: always the unluckiest of days. Hastily I broke open the envelope of brown clay and read the message it contained, and read it again, and read it once more. Those few words inscribed on the tablet struck hard at me. Those words swept me in a single moment away from the comfort of my native city and into a strange life of exile, as though they were not words, but the stormy breath of Enlil the high god.

What the tablet said was: *Flee Uruk at once. Dumuzi means to have your life.*

It was signed with the seal of Inanna.

My instant response was one of blind hot defiance. My heart thundered; my hands rolled up into fists. Who was Dumuzi, that he could threaten the son of Lugalbanda? What did I have to fear from a mere torpid slug such as he? And also I thought: the power of the goddess is greater than the power of the king, so there is no need for me to flee the city. Inanna will protect me.

As I paced up and down in the heat of my anger, one of my servants entered the room. He saw my rage and began to back out, but I called to him to stay. 'What is it?' I demanded.

'Two men, O lord—two men were here—'

'Who were they?'

For a moment his mouth had trouble making words. Then he got it out: 'Slaves of Dumuzi, I think. They wore his red band around their arms.' His eyes were bright with fear. 'They carried knives, my lord. They were hidden in their robes, but I saw the glint of them. My lord—my lord—'

'Did they tell you what they wanted?'

'To speak with you, they said.' He was stammering. Fright had made him pale and sickly-faced. 'I s-s-said you were with the g-goddess, and they answered that they would return—they w-w-w-would return this evening—'

'Ah,' I said softly. 'So it is true, then.' I caught him by the corner of his robe and pulled him close and whispered, 'Keep watch! If you see them nearby, come to me at once!'

'I will, O lord!'

'And say nothing to anyone about where I might be!'

'Not a word, O lord!'

I dismissed him and he scurried out. Once more I began to pace the room. I found myself dry-throated and shaking, not so much with fear, but with rage and dismay. What else could I do except flee? I saw the folly of what I had been thinking a little while before, when I had been so bold. I could go on being bold, yes; but I would surely die for it. How cocky I had been! Asking, who was Dumuzi, that he could threaten the son of Lugalbanda? Why, Dumuzi was the king, and my life was forfeit to him if so he

57

decreed. And if Inanna had any way to protect me, why would she have sent word to me to take flight? I stared into a terrible emptiness. I could not tarry a moment, I knew, not even to seek explanations. In the twinkling of an eye Uruk was lost to me. I must go and go swiftly, without even pausing to bid farewell to my mother, or to kneel at Lugalbanda's shrine. At this moment the two assassins Dumuzi had chosen might be on their way back there to find me. I could not hesitate.

I did not mean to be gone for long. I would take sanctuary in some other city for a few days, or if necessary a couple of weeks, until I could learn what I had done to make myself the enemy of the king, and how the breach could be repaired. I did not then realize that I was setting forth into four years of exile. But so it proved to be.

Numbly, with shaking hands, I gathered together a few possessions. I took as much clothing as would fit in a pack on my back, and my bow and a sword, and the Pazuzu amulet that my mother had given me long ago, and the little goddess-statuette of green stone that I had had from Inanna when she was still just an ordinary priestess. I had acquired a tablet on which some magical phrases were inscribed, things for use in case of injury or illness, and I took that along, as well as a leather pouch of the drug that one burns to drive away ghosts in the desert. Lastly I took a small knife of antique style with a jeweled hilt, not very keen but beloved by me because it had been brought to me by Lugalbanda returning from one of his wars.

At the first watch of the night, star-rise time, I slipped from my house and made my way warily through the narrow tangles of streets, heading toward the North Gate. A light rain was falling. Plumes of white smoke from the lamps of ten thousand houses rose toward the darkening sky. My heart ached miserably. I had never left Uruk before. I had no idea what lay beyond the city walls. I was in the hands of the gods.

The city of Kish was where I chose to go. Eridu or Nippur were much closer and more easily reached; but Kish seemed a safer choice. Dumuzi had great influence in Eridu or Nippur, but Kish was hostile to him. I did not care to arrive at a place where I would immediately be packed up and shipped back to Uruk as a kindness to Uruk's king. King Agga of Kish was not likely to feel any need to do favors for Dumuzi; and Lugalbanda had often spoken of him, I recalled, as a sturdy warrior, a worthy opponent, a man of honor. To Kish, then: to offer myself to Agga's mercy.

Kish lay a great distance away to the north, a march of many days. I could not go by water. There was no ready way for a small boat or a raft to travel upstream on the fast-flowing Buranunu, and it was too risky for me to try to slip aboard one of the great royal sailing vessels that ply the river between cities. But I knew that there was a caravan track that flanked the eastern bank of the river. If I followed it northward and put one foot forward and then the next, sooner or later I was sure to get to Kish.

I walked briskly, and sometimes I ran a light trot, and soon Uruk was falling away behind me in the darkness. I did not halt until the middle hour of the night. By then I had a sense of being far from home, of embarking on a great journey that would take me to the far corners of the world, a journey that would never end. Nor has that journey ended, to this day.

That night I slept in a freshly ploughed field, with my cloak around me and the rain falling in my face. But I slept, and I slept soundly. At dawn I rose, and bathed in some farmer's muddy canal, and helped myself to a breakfast of figs and cucumbers. Then I took myself toward the north once more. I felt tireless, full of inexhaustible energy, and it did not trouble me to walk all the hours of the day. It was the god within me, driving me on, as ever, to more than mortal deeds.

The Land was more beautiful than I had ever imagined. The sky was vast and luminous: it trembled with god-presence. On the rich broad river-plain the first tender grass of autumn was beginning to sprout in the soft meadows after the harsh summer drought. Along the canals the mimosa trees, the willows and poplars, the reeds and rushes, all were stirring with new green growth. The dark-hued river Buranunu ran to my left, rising high above the plain on its bed of its own silt. Somewhere far off to the east, I knew, was the second great river, the swift and wild Idigna, that forms the other boundary of the Land: for when we speak of the Land, we mean the territory between the two

59

rivers. All that lies outside is foreign to us; that which lies within is the dominion allotted to us by the gods.

From the rivers come hardship and danger—terrible torrents, killing floods—but also from them comes fertility, and I saw signs of that great gift on all sides. This we owe to Father Enki. They tell the tale of the wise god taking on the form of a wild bull, who thrust his great phallus into the dry beds of the two rivers and cast forth his seed in mighty spurts to fill them with the sweet sparkling water of life. So it is always: the water of the father gives fecundity to the Land, which is our mother. It was Enki too who, once the rivers were filled with his fertile flow, devised the canals that convey the water of the river to the fields, and brought forth the fish and the reeds of the marshlands, and the green grass of the hills, and the grains and vegetables of the cultivated lands, and the cattle of the pastures, and gave each of these into the hands of its special god.

These things I had heard from the harper Ur-kununna, and from school-father in the classroom; but it had all seemed only words to me. Now it became real. I saw the richly laden fields of wheat and barley. I saw the date palms heavy with unripe fruit. I saw the mulberry and cypress trees, the vines bearing dark glistening grapes, the almonds and walnuts, the herds of oxen and goats and sheep. The Land was thick with life. In the lagoons along the canals I saw wallowing buffaloes, great flocks of birds with brilliant plumage, and an abundance of turtles and snakes. Once I saw a lion with a black mane; but he did not see me. I longed to see an elephant, of which I had heard wondrous tales, but the elephants were elsewhere that season. Of other creatures, though—boars and hyenas, jackals and wolves, eagles and vultures, antelopes and gazelles—there was a multitude.

When I was in the wild places, I hunted hares and geese for my dinners, and found berries and nuts to eat as well. In the villages the farmers took me in and shared with me their beans and peas and lentils, their beer, their golden melons. I told no one my name, nor where I was from; but my bearing was that of a young prince, and perhaps that was why they were so hospitable toward me. In any case it is an offense to the gods to turn away a peaceful stranger. The girls of these farms willingly kept me warm by night, and more than once I regretted having to move along, or debated with myself whether to take some of these tender companions with me. But move along I did, and always I departed from the villages alone; and alone I was when I came at last to the great city of Kish.

My father used to speak generously of Kish. 'If there is any city than can with justice claim to be the equal of Uruk,' he would say, 'it is Kish.' I think that is true.

Like Uruk, Kish lies close by the Buranunu, so that it prospers from the river trade between city and city and from the sea trade that comes up the river from the ocean lands. Like Uruk, it is walled and secure. It has a great many people, though not quite so many as Uruk, which is probably the largest city of the world: my tax-collectors, in the fifth year of my reign, tallied ninety thousands of people, including the slaves. I think Kish has but two thirds as many, which is still a mighty number.

Long before Uruk became great, Kish had already attained the highest power of the Land. This was when kingship had descended from heaven a second time, after the Flood had destroyed the earlier cities. Kish then became the seat of kingship, when Uruk was only a village. I remember the harper Ur-kununna singing us the tale of Etana king of Kish, he who stabilized all the Land and was hailed everywhere as overlord. Etana was the one who soared into the heavens with the aid of an eagle when, because he was childless, he sought the plant of birth, which grows only in heaven.

The wondrous journey of Etana of Kish brought him the heir he desired; but all the same Etana dwells today in the House of Dust and Darkness, and Kish no longer has mastery over all the Land. By the time Enmebaraggesi was king in Kish, greatness had begun to grow in Uruk. Meskiaggasher, son of the sun, became our king, when Uruk was still not Uruk, but only the two villages of Eanna and Kullab. Meskiaggasher made Enmebaraggesi take note of him. After him came my grandfather the hero Enmerkar, who created Uruk out of the two villages; and after him, Lugalbanda. And under those two heroes we won our freedom from Kish and came into our full greatness, of which I have been the steward these many years.

At this time of my boyhood Enmebaraggesi was long dead and

61

his son Agga was king in Kish. On a day of bright winter sunlight I had my first glimpse of his city, rising high on the flat Bur-anunu plain behind a wall of many towers painted a dazzling white, from which long banners in crimson and emerald were streaming. Kish was a two-humped place, I saw, with twin centers to the west and east and a low district between them. The temples of Kish rose on platforms far higher than the White Platform of Uruk, with steps going up and up and up until they seemed to march into the sky. That seemed a grand thing to me, to put the houses of the gods so close to heaven, and when I rebuilt the temples of Uruk I kept the high platforms of Kish in mind. But that was many years afterward.

I was unprepared for the awesomeness of Kish. Everything about it seemed to cry out, 'I am great, I am all-powerful, I am the invincible city.' And I still merely a boy, going out from home for the first time. But there was no room in my heart for fear.

I presented myself before the walls of Kish and a sullen long-bearded gatekeeper came out, idly swinging his bronze mace of office. He looked me over as though I were nothing at all, merely some meat walking on legs. I returned his insolence glare for glare. And with my hand resting lightly on the pommel of my sword I said to him, 'Tell your master that the son of Lugalbanda has come from Uruk to give him greetings.'

9

That night I dined on golden plates in the palace of Agga the king, and so began my four-year sojourn in Kish.

Agga received me warmly: whether out of respect for my father, or out of some crafty intent to use me against Dumuzi, I had no way of telling. Very likely some of each, for he was a man of honor, as I had been told, but also Agga was in every fiber of his body a monarch, who meant to turn everything that came his way to the advantage of his city.

He was a robust pink-skinned man, fleshy and big-bellied, who loved his beer and meat. His head was entirely without hair. He had it shaved every morning in the throne-room of his palace, before an audience of courtiers and officials. The blades that his barbers used were made of a white metal that I had never seen before, and were very keen. Agga said it was iron, which puzzled me, for I thought of iron as a darker stuff and not of much real use: it is soft and will not take a sharp edge. But later I asked a chamberlain, who told me that it was a special kind of iron that had fallen from the sky in the land of Dilmun, and was mixed with another metal without a name which gave it its color and its special hardness. Many times since then I have wished to have a supply of such metal for my weapons, and the secret of working it, but I have been unable to obtain either one.

Be that as it may, I have never seen a man closer shaved than Agga was. His high officials went hairless too, except for those who traced their ancestry to the desert people, whose thick curling hair is too great a chore to shave. I can understand that, for my hair is similar, as was Lugalbanda's. I think I must have some desert blood in me: my height and the texture of my hair and beard argue for that, although my nose is not as sharp and hooked as theirs tend to be. Though every city of the Land has many of these sons of desert-folk living in it, there were more of them in Kish than in any other place I have seen. They must have accounted for full half the population, and I heard their language, so different from ours, almost as often as I heard our own.

Agga knew that I had fled from Dumuzi. He seemed to know a great deal of what went on in Uruk; far more, indeed, than I. But it was no surprise to me that a king as powerful as Agga maintained a network of spies in the city that was his greatest rival. What did surprise me was the source from which his information came. But I did not learn that until much later.

'What have you done,' Agga asked, 'to have caused the king to turn against you this way?'

I had wondered that myself. It was strange that Dumuzi would suddenly choose to look upon me as an enemy, after paying so little heed to me in the six or seven years since the death of my father. During that time I had certainly offered no challenge to his power. Though I was strong and tall beyond my years, I was far from ready for any sort of role in the government of the city. Surely Dumuzi and everyone else realized that. If I had sometimes boasted in my boyhood of becoming king some day, why, that was only a boy's loud talk, while the kingship of my father Lugalbanda had still been bright in my memory. Whatever dreams of royal power I had had since then—and I could not deny that I had had such dreams—I had kept entirely to myself.

But as I sat at Agga's table considering these things, I remembered that there was someone else in Uruk who was much given to the pastime of predicting my destiny, and who seemed to have no doubt I would be king. Had she not whispered of the pleasures we would share when that day came? Had she not gone so far as to devise the name under which I should reign?

And she was one who was close to the ear of Dumuzi.

'What would Dumuzi be likely to think,' I asked Agga, 'if he were to suspect that my soul had been entered by divine Lugalbanda, and his godlike spirit now resided within me?'

'Ah, is that the case?' Agga asked quickly, his eyes gleaming.

I picked up my bowl of beer and sipped at it and offered no reply.

He said after a moment, watching me carefully, 'If that should be the case, or if Dumuzi should merely think it is the case—why, then I believe you would seem very dangerous to him. He knows that he is not worth five hairs of your father's beard. He fears the very name of Lugalbanda. Yet Lugalbanda dead is no menace to the throne of Dumuzi.'

'Yes, that is surely so.'

'Ah,' said Agga, smiling, 'but if it should become known in Uruk that the spirit of the great and valorous Lugalbanda now has come to reside within the sturdy body of Lugalbanda's noble son—and if that son is growing toward an age when he might be expected to begin playing some part in the governing of the city—why, yes, you would seem a great peril to Dumuzi, a very serious peril indeed—'

'Serious enough to have me slain?'

Agga turned up his hands, palms outward. 'What does the proverb say? "The coward sees lions where brave men see only cats"? *I* would have no fear of the ghost of Lugalbanda, if I were Dumuzi. But I am not Dumuzi, and he perceives things in a different way.' He gave me more beer, waving away the slave and pouring from the ewer himself. Then he said, 'If indeed Lugalbanda is the god who has chosen you—and I would not be amazed if that was the case—then you know it was far from wise of you to let Dumuzi have any hint of that.'

'I understand that. But whatever Dumuzi has learned, he has not learned from me.'

'He has learned it from someone, though, and that someone must have learned it from you. Is that not so?'

I nodded.

'Then you have spoken carelessly to a friend who is not a friend, and you have been betrayed, eh? Is that not so?'

Through tight lips I said, 'I asked her not to speak a word of it to anyone! But she would not promise me that. She grew angry, in fact, when I asked the promise of her.'

'Ah. Ah. *She?*'

My face turned red. 'I am telling you more than I should be revealing.'

He laid his hand atop mine. 'Boy, boy, you tell me nothing I don't already know! But you are safe from Dumuzi here. You are under my protection, and no treachery can reach you in my city. Here. Here, take more beer. What good sweet stuff this is! The barley from which they make it is reserved for the use of the king. Here, drink, boy, drink, drink! Drink!'

And I drank, and drank some more. But my mind remained clear, for it was burning with an anger that burned away any drunkenness Agga's beer might have brought me. No doubt of it, she had gone running to Dumuzi with the tale the moment she had had it from me, without once thinking that she might be betraying me into danger. Or was that what she intended? To betray me? Why? I could see no reason for it. Perhaps it had been mere thoughtlessness, her telling Dumuzi the one thing that I had begged her not to tell anyone. And yet again she might have been following some design too subtle for me to comprehend. I understood none of it, only that she was certainly the one who had engineered my exile by giving away my secret to the man most likely to be threatened by it. At that moment such rage rushed through me that had she been within my reach just then I would have struck her down, priestess that she was.

The fury went from me after a while. We sat together late into the night, Agga and I, and he told me tales of his wars with Lugalbanda, and of a day when they had engaged in single combat outside the walls of Kish, axes battering on shields for hour after hour until darkness came, neither man able to inflict a wound on the other. He had always held my father in the highest regard, he said, even when they were sworn to be enemies to the death. Then he ordered another flagon of beer to be opened—I was astounded at how he drank; no wonder there was so much flesh on his bones—and as he grew hazier with liquor so too did his stories, and I could scarcely follow them. He began telling of the campaigns of his own father Enmebaraggesi and of those of my grandfather Enmerkar, stories of wars fought when he had been just a boy, and afterward he drifted off into a jumble of legends of ancient Kish, involving kings who were only names to me, and strange names at that, Zukakip, Buanum, Mashda, Arurim, and the like. As he grew drunker and sleepier I grew more wide awake. But I sensed that he was less hazy than he seemed, and was watching me always with keen vigilance: for I did not forget that this old man before me was king of Kish, the great ruler of a great city, the survivor of a hundred bloody battles, the shrewdest man, perhaps, in all the Land.

He gave me a suite of rooms within the royal palace, very splendid ones, and sent concubines to me in any quantity I desired; and after a while he gave me a wife. Her name was Ama-sukkul. She was a daughter of Agga's own loins, by one of his handmaidens, thirteen years old and a virgin. When he offered her, I did not know what to say, for I was uncertain about the propriety of marrying a woman of a strange city; and I thought I should at least obtain the consent of my mother Ninsun. But Agga felt strongly that a visiting prince of Uruk should not go wifeless in Kish. It was not hard to see that I would offend him deeply if I spurned his hospitality by showing disdain for his daughter. A marriage in Kish, I reckoned, would not be binding upon me in my native city, if ever it seemed desirable to free myself from it. So I took the first of my wives. Ama-sukkul was a cheerful girl, round-breasted and sweet-smiling, though she had little to say: I think she never once spoke except when spoken to, throughout the time of our marriage. I wish we had been closer. But the gods have not given me the good fortune of opening my heart to a woman in marriage. I have had wives, yes: a king must. But they all have been like strangers to me.

I know why that is so. I will dare to say it here, though you will see it for yourself as the tale of my years unfolds. It is because all my life I have been tied in a strange unfathomable way to that dark-souled woman the priestess Inanna, who could never be my wife in the usual way of marriage but who has left no room in my heart for ordinary women. I have loved her and I have loathed her, often at one and the same time; and I have been locked in such struggle of the soul with that woman that I have not tasted the common sort of domestic love with any other. It is the truth. Who is it that believes the lives of kings and heroes are easy?

Agga bound me to him in another way, by placing upon me an oath of allegiance that was meant to carry force throughout my life, even if I became king in Uruk. 'I have sworn to protect you,' he explained, 'and you must swear your loyalty to me in return.'

I wondered about that, whether I was not shamefully selling Uruk to him by making myself his vassal. But when I knelt privately and asked Lugalbanda for guidance, I heard nothing within my soul telling me it was an error to swear the oath. One point that I considered was that in a certain sense everyone in the Land still owed allegiance to Kish, since it was to Kish that the kingship had descended after the Flood, and it had never formally been withdrawn by the gods in all the years since. So by swearing, I was merely confirming a fealty that already had a kind of shadowy existence. It also crossed my mind that it would make little difference to me that I had recognized Agga as my overlord, once I was king in Uruk, so long as I was not required to pay tribute to him or to submit to his commands; and there was nothing in the oath about either of those things. So I swore. By the net of Enlil I swore my loyalty to the king of Kish.

There was no question of my returning to Uruk in a matter of days or weeks, as I had originally imagined I might do. Not long after my arrival in Kish, emissaries from Dumuzi arrived and tactfully but firmly asked Agga to turn me over to them. 'The son of Lugalbanda is sorely missed in Uruk,' they said, most piously. 'Our king craves his counsel, and seeks his strong arm for the battlefield.'

'Ah,' replied Agga, rolling his eyes and looking stricken with great sorrow, 'but the son of Lugalbanda has become my son as well, and I would not be parted from him for all the Land. Tell Dumuzi that I would die of grief, if the son of Lugalbanda were to leave Kish so soon.'

And privately Agga said to me that his spies reported Dumuzi beside himself with fear that I was organizing an army in Kish to overthrow him. In Uruk I had been proclaimed an enemy of the city, he said, and I would surely be slain if ever I came into Dumuzi's grasp. So I remained in Kish. But I managed to send word to my mother that I was healthy and prosperous and was only biding my time until the proper moment for my homefaring.

I found Kish a city not much unlike Uruk in most respects. In Uruk we ate meat and bread, and drank beer and date-wine, and the same in Kish. In Uruk and in Kish the clothing was of wool or of linen, according to the time of the year, and the fashion of wearing it was similar in each place. The streets of Uruk were narrow and winding, except for the grand boulevards, and so were the streets of Kish. The houses were flat-roofed in Uruk, one story or sometimes two, baked brick below, mud brick covered in white plaster above, and so they were also in Kish. The languages that were spoken in Uruk were the same as those spoken in Kish; in Kish they wrote on clay tablets as they did in Uruk, and the characters that they inscribed were the same. The only difference, and it was a great one for me, was in the gods. The chief temples in Uruk, of course, are those dedicated to Inanna and Sky-father An. In Kish no one would deny the greatness of An or the power of Inanna; but the temples in Kish are dedicated to Father Enlil, the lord of storms, and to the great mother Ninhursag. That was strange for me, to find myself constantly in the presence of those gods, and not those of Uruk. I feel more fear than love for Inanna the goddess, but there is love too, and it is hard to live in a place where Inanna is not present. Though everything may be the same externally, it is different underneath: in Kish even the air has a different color, and its taste is different too, because one does not breathe in Inanna with every breath.

It was in Kish that at last I gained full knowledge of the arts of war, which I was somewhat overdue in learning: for I had become a man in years now, and more than a man in size and strength, but I had never had a taste of battle. Agga gave me that first taste, and more—indeed, a rich banquet of it, haunch and flagon.

His wars were conducted in the east, in the rough and hilly kingdom of Elam. This nation is rich in many things that we of the Land lack entirely: timber, the ores of copper and tin, and such stones as alabaster, obsidian, carnelian, onyx. And we have things of value to them: the produce of our overflowing fields, our barley and wheat and apricots and lemons, and also our wool and our linen. So there is good reason for trade between Elam and the cities of the Land, but the gods will not have it so: for every year of peace that we have with the Elamites, there are three years of war. They come down into the lowlands to raid us, and we must send our armies to drive them back, and then to take from them the goods we need.

The father of Agga, royal Enmebaraggesi, had won great victories in Elam and for a while made it subject to Kish. But in Agga's time the Elamites had grown unruly again. Now there was war all along the frontier. So in my second year of exile I went forth with the army of Kish into that broad wind-swept plain behind which lies Susa, the capital of Elam.

I had dreamed battle-dreams for many years, from the time in childhood when my father, home in brief respite from his wars, told me tales of chariots and javelins. I had played at battle on the fields of Uruk, drawing plans of formation and leading my playmates on wild charges against invisible enemies. But there is a song of battle that only a warrior's ears can hear, a high, keening sound that comes through the sluggish air like a blade, and until you have heard that song, you are no warrior, you are no man. I did not know about that song until I heard it, for the first time, beside the waters of a river called the Karkhah in the Land of Elam.

All night long, under a brilliant moon, we made ready for the attack, oiling that which was made of wood or leather, scouring everything of bronze until it gleamed. The sky was so clear that we could see the gods walking about in it, great horned figures, blue against the blackness, striding from cloud to cloud. The giant visage of An, calm, all-seeing, seemed to fill the sky. Great Enlil loomed on his throne, conjuring storms in distant lands. The power of these gods was hot and hard in the air, like the fever-wind. We lit fires to them and sacrificed bullocks, and they came down low to us, so that we could feel the pressure of their divine weight against our hearts. And at dawn, not having had an hour's sleep, I donned my shining helmet, and clad myself in a short skirt of sheepskin with a leather loin-guard beneath, and clambered into my chariot as though this were my twentieth year on the fields of war.

The trumpets sounded. The battle-cry roared from two hundred throats: 'For Agga and Enlil! For Agga and Enlil!'

I heard my own voice, deep and hoarse, crying those same words, words I had never imagined I would find myself uttering:

'For Agga and Enlil!'

And we went forward into the plain.

My charioteer's name was Namhani. He was a broad-shouldered thick-chested man of the city of Lagash who had been sold to Kish when a boy, and he had known no other trade but war: scars covered him like ribbons of honor, some an angry red, some long since faded into the darkness of his skin. He turned to me and grinned just before he charged. He had no teeth, only four or five wicked yellow snags.

Agga had given me a splendid chariot—four-wheeled, not a two-wheeler as is usually provided for novices. The son of Lugalbanda, he told me, could ride in nothing less. To draw it, the king had provided four sturdy asses, swift and strong. I had helped Namhani myself to harness them, fastening the girth-straps about their chests, fitting them to the yoke and collar, attaching the reins to the rings in their upper lips. They were good animals, patient, shrewd. Sometimes I wonder what it would be like to go into battle with a chariot drawn by powerful long-legged horses, rather than our placid asses: but to dream of harnessing horses, those wild and mysterious beasts of the mountainous northeast, is like dreaming of harnessing the whirlwind. They say that in the lands beyond Elam the people have found a way of taming horses and riding them, but I think that is a lie. Now and again in distant lands I have caught sight of black horses sailing like ghosts across storm-swept basins. I see no way such creatures, if they could be captured at all, could ever be broken to our use.

Namhani seized the reins and leaned forward against the leopard-hide that covered the chariot's frame. I heard the groaning of the axle-rod, the creaking of the wooden wheels. Then the asses had the rhythm of it and hit a steady stride, and we went jouncing over the soft spongy ground toward the dark line of Elamites that waited along the horizon.

'For Agga! For Enlil!'

And I, shouting along with all the others, added war-cries of my own: 'Lugalbanda! Sky-father! Inanna! Inanna! Inanna!'

Mine was the fifth chariot: a great honor, for the four in front of mine belonged to the general and to three of the sons of Agga. Eight or ten more came after me. Behind the clattering chariots marched the columns of foot-soldiers, first the heavy infantry protected by helmets and thick cloaks of black felt, with axes in their hands, and then the light skirmishers, all but naked, wielding their spears or short swords. My own weapon was the javelin. I had a dozen of them, long and slender, most beautifully made, in my quiver. I carried also a double-headed axe with which to defend myself when my javelins were gone, and a little sword, a handy little skewer if all else failed me.

As we rumbled toward the enemy, I heard a music upon the wind like no music I had ever heard before: a single note, piercing and fierce, that began amazingly faintly but grew and grew until it filled all the air. It was something like the keening sounds the women make when they mourn the death of the god Dumuzi at the harvest-festival; but this was no mourning-song. It was bright and fiery and jubilant, and heat and light came from it. I did not need to be told what music this music was: it was the battle song, bursting from all our souls at once. For we had fused into a single creature with a single mind, now, those of us who charged the Elamites, and out of the heat of that fusion came the silent song that only warriors may hear.

At the same time I felt the aura of the god upon me, the buzzing droning sound within, the golden glow, the sense of great strangeness, that told me that Lugalbanda was stirring within me. I held myself steady and it seemed to me that I was a rock submerged in a swiftly moving dark river, but I was not afraid. Perhaps my consciousness went from me for an instant. But then I was fully awake again, as awake as I had ever been in my life. At full gallop we came rushing into the Elamite line.

The Elamites have no chariots. What they have is great numbers, and thick shields, and a thickness of soul that some might call stupidity, but which I think is true bravery. They stood piled up before us, heavy-bearded men with eyes dark as a month without moonlight, clad in gray leather jerkins and holding ugly broad-tanged spears. They had no faces: only eyes and hair. Namhani uttered a great roaring shout and guided my chariot right into their midst.

'Enlil!' we cried. 'Agga!' And I: '*Inanna! Inanna!*'

The warrior-goddess preceded us, bowling over the Elamites like gaming-posts. They fell shrieking before the hooves of the four asses, and the chariot rose and fell like a vessel laboring in heavy waters as the wheels passed over their fallen bodies. Namhani swung a great long-handled axe with sharp-angled socket, chopping away with it at any Elamite spearsman who approached us. I gripped the shaft of a javelin in each hand and took my aim. Lugalbanda had told me many times that the task of the vanguard is to destroy the spirit of the enemy, so that the other battle-chariots and the infantrymen behind them can advance more freely. And the best way to achieve that, he said, is to pick out the greatest men of the other side, the officers and the heroes, and slay them first.

I looked about me. I saw mere chaos, a tumult of jostling forms and waving spears. Then I found my man. When my eyes lit upon him, the battle-song grew louder and hotter in my ears, and the glow of Lugalbanda's spirit flared up like the blue flame that comes when date-wine is flung upon a bonfire. *That one. There. Kill him and all else will be easy.*

He saw me, too. He was a mountain chieftain with hair like

black fur, and a shield that bore a demon's face, yellow with blazing red eyes. He, too, understood the importance of killing the heroes first, and I think he had singled me out as a hero, though I was then hardly deserving of any such acclaim. His eyes gleamed brightly; he lifted his spear.

My right arm rose and I cast my javelin without hesitating. The goddess sharpened my aim: the point entered him at the throat, in the small place below his beard and above the rim of his shield. Blood spouted from his lips and his eyes rolled wildly. He dropped his spear and went over backward, furiously kicking his legs.

A great cry, like the sighing of some huge beast, came from the men about him. Several stooped to drag him to safety. That opened a place in the Elamite rank through which Namhani immediately took the chariot. I cast a second javelin with my left hand just as ably as I had the first, and another tall warrior went down. Then we were into the heart of the enemy force, with four or five other chariots flanking us. I saw the men of Kish staring at me and pointing, and though I could not hear what they were saying, they were making god-signs at me, as if they saw a divine mantle in the air above me.

I used all my javelins and did not miss once. Under the force of the charging chariots the Elamites were thrown into confusion, and although they fought bravely their cause was hopeless from the first minutes. One did manage to come up to my chariot and slash at the lefthand-most ass, wounding it badly. Namhani cut the man down with one blow of his axe. Then, leaping out over the poles, the brave charioteer slit the traces with his short-sword, freeing the injured animal so it would not slow us. An Elamite reared up with a spear aimed at Namhani's back, but I took him down with a swing of my own axe, and turned just in time to ram my axe-handle into the gut of one who had hopped upon the chariot from the rear. Those were the only moments of peril. The chariots went on and through, and turned to fall upon the enemy from the rear, and by then our foot soldiers were at work, marching in a frightful phalanx eleven men broad. So went the day for Kish. By nightfall the river ran red with blood and we had ourselves a joyful feast, while the harpers sang of our valor and the wine flowed freely. The next day it took us almost until twilight to divide the booty, there was so much of it.

I fought in nine battles and six small skirmishes on that campaign. After the first battle, my chariot was awarded the second position, behind the general's but ahead of the sons of the king. None of the sons of the king showed anger toward me for that. I took some small wounds now and then, but they were nothing, and whenever I cast my javelin it cost some enemy his life. I was not then fifteen years old; but I am of the blood of gods, and that makes a difference. Even my own men seemed frightened of me. When we had won our third battle the general called me aside and said, 'You fight like no one I have ever seen. But there is one thing I wish you would not do when you go among the enemy.'

'And what is that?'

'You cast your javelins with either hand. I wish you would throw them with one hand or the other, but not with both.'

'But I can cast equally well with right and left,' I said. 'And I think it puts terror into the enemy, when they see me do it.'

The general smiled faintly. 'Yes, that it does. But my own soldiers see it as well. They are beginning to think that you are more than mortal. They think you must be a god, for no ordinary man can fight the way you do. Which may create problems for me, do you understand? It is a good thing to have a hero among us, when we go into battle, yes; but it can be very discouraging, perhaps, to have a god in our midst. Each man of the army hopes to do miracles of valor each day, and that hope strengthens his arm on the field. But when he knows that he can never be the hero of the day, because he is in competition with a god, it saps his spirit and puts a heaviness upon his heart. So cast your javelins with your right hand, son of Lugalbanda, or with your left, but with either one or the other, not both. Do you understand?'

'I understand,' I said. And thereafter I tried to use only my right hand in casting the javelin, for the sake of the other men. In the press of battle, though, it is not always easy to remember that one has promised to use only a certain hand when fighting. Sometimes when I reached for a javelin it was with my left hand,

and it would have been folly to give it to my right one before casting it. So after a time I ceased to worry about such matters. We won every battle. The general did not speak of it to me again.

10

I thought often of Uruk at first, and then less often, and then hardly at all. I had become a man of Kish. In the beginning, hearing reports in Kish of what the army of Uruk had accomplished against the desert tribes or some city of the eastern mountains, I felt a certain pride at what 'we' had achieved, but then I noticed that I was thinking of the army of Uruk not as *we* but as *they*, and the doings of that army ceased to matter at all to me.

And yet I knew, whenever I troubled to think of it, that my life in Kish was leading me nowhere. I lived at Agga's court as a prince, yes, and when it was the season to make war I was accorded high precedence in the camp, almost as though I were a son of the king. But I was *not* a son of the king, and I was aware that I had already risen as high in Kish as I was ever likely to go: a prince, a warrior, perhaps one day a general, nothing more. In Uruk I could have been king.

Furthermore I was troubled as ever by the greatness of that chilly gulf that separated me from other men. I had comrades, yes, fellow warriors with whom I could go drinking or wenching or brawling. But their souls were closed to mine. What was it that cut me off from them? Was it my great size, or my regal bearing, or the god-presence that hovers always about me? I did not know. I knew only that, here as in Uruk, I bore the curse of solitude and had no spell by which I might lift it.

Also thoughts of my mother often crossed my mind. It saddened me that she was fated now to grow old without a son by her side. I sent her little tokens by secret messengers sometimes, and received

75

messages in return from the priests who went as couriers between the cities. She never asked me when I was returning, and yet I knew that that must be uppermost in her mind. Then too I yearned to kneel before the shrine of my father and make the necessary observances to his memory. For though I knew his spirit rode in my soul, and beheld everything that I beheld, nevertheless that did not excuse me from the rites that were due his ghost. I could not perform those rites in Kish. That failure haunted me.

Nor could I banish altogether from my mind the memory of the priestess Inanna, her sparkling eyes, her slender supple body. Each year when autumn came, and it was the time of the Sacred Marriage in Uruk, I imagined I stood in the jostling crowd on the White Platform, seeing king and priestess, god and goddess, showing themselves forth to the people; and bitter anguish rose within me, to think that she would share her bed with Dumuzi that night. I told myself that she had been treacherous to me, or at best faithless; and yet she glowed in my mind and I felt a yearning toward her. The priestess, like the goddess she served and embodied, was a perilous but irresistible figure to me. Her aura was one of death and disaster, yet also one of passion and the joys of the flesh, and something more even than that, the union of two spirits that is the true Sacred Marriage. She was my other half. She knew that and always had known it, from that time I was a boy stumbling around in the dark corridors of the Enmerkar temple. But I was a warrior in Kish, and she was a goddess in Uruk; and I could not go to her, because she had made my life forfeit in the city of my birth through her scheming, or through her thoughtlessness.

In the fourth year of my exile a priest with shaven head, who was newly arrived from Uruk, came to me in Agga's palace and made the goddess-sign before me. He took from his robe a little black goatskin pouch and pressed it into my palm, saying, 'It is a sign to Gilgamesh the king, from the hand of the goddess.'

I had not heard that strange name, Gilgamesh, except once, long ago. And the priest, in using it, made it clear to me who the sender of the pouch must be.

When the priest had departed I opened the pouch in my private chambers. Within it was a small gleaming thing, a seal-cylinder, such as we employ on letters and other important documents. It was cut from a piece of white obsidian so clear that light journeyed through it as easily as through air, and the design carved upon it was intricate and fine, plainly the work of a great master. I called for a scribe and asked him to bring me his best red clay, and carefully I rolled the seal against the clay to see what imprint it made.

There were two scenes depicted on the seal, both drawn from the tale of the descent of Inanna into the land of death. On the one side I saw Dumuzi, dressed in noble garments, sitting proudly on his lofty throne. Before him stands Inanna, clad in sackcloth: she is newly returned from her sojourn in hell. Her eyes are the eyes of death, and her arms are upraised to call down a curse on him; for Dumuzi is the chosen scapegoat whose death will bring about her release from the nether world. The other side of the seal portrayed the sequel to that scene, a cowering Dumuzi surrounded by glowering demons who cut him down with axes, while Inanna looks on in triumph.

I did not think Inanna had sent me that seal merely to awaken in my mind some memory of that great poem. No. I took the seal-cylinder to be a sign, a prophesy, a blunt message. It kindled a fire in my soul: the blood began to flow within me like turbulent riverwater, and my heart soared like a bird newly set free from a trap.

But caution returned, after that first burst of excitement. Even if I had read the message rightly, could I trust it, or her? Inanna the priestess had already led me once into peril; and Inanna the goddess, as everyone knows, is the deadliest of the gods. A message that comes from one, under the auspices of the other, might well be an invitation to doom. I must move carefully. That afternoon I sent word to Uruk, by one of my own slaves, saying simply, 'Hail, Inanna, great lady of heaven! Holy torch, you fill the sky with light!' It is what the newly enthroned king sings, when he makes his first hymn to the goddess: let her see in that what she chose. I signed the tablet with the name she had given me, Gilgamesh, and the royal symbol.

A day or two afterward, Agga called me into the royal throne-chamber, that great echoing alabaster-walled room where he liked to sit in state for hour after hour, and said, 'Word has come to me from Uruk that Dumuzi the king lies gravely ill.'

A joyous surging arose within me like the rising of the waters in the spring. I felt the fulfilling of my destiny now beginning to begin. Beyond doubt, I told myself, this is the confirmation of the message inscribed in pictures on the seal-cylinder. I have read the message rightly: she has already begun to work her deadly spell. And Uruk will be mine.

But to Agga I said only, with a shrug, 'That news causes me very little grief.'

He shook his head, freshly shaven, brows and beard and all, bald as an egg. He tugged at his jowls and leaned forward so that the pink folds of his bare belly piled one atop the other, and he peered down at me with dark displeasure, whether real or feigned I could not tell. At length he said, 'Ah, you invite the anger of the gods, with words like those!'

My cheeks grew hot. 'Dumuzi is my enemy.'

'As he is mine. But he is an anointed king in the Land, who carries the blessing of Enlil upon him. His person is sacred. His illness should grieve us all: and especially you, a child of Uruk, a subject of his. I mean to send an embassy to Uruk to bear my prayers for his welfare. And I intend you to be my ambassador.'

'*Me?*'

'A prince of Uruk, of the line of Lugalbanda, a valiant hero—I could send no one better, not even one of my own sons.'

Amazed, I said, 'Do you mean to send me to my doom, then? For surely it is not safe even now for me to return to Uruk!'

'It will be,' said Agga blandly.

'Can you be certain?'

'Dumuzi suffers with the sickness unto death; you are no threat to him any longer. All Uruk will welcome you, even Dumuzi. There is advantage in this for you, boy: can you not see that?'

'If he is dying, yes. And if he is not?'

'Even if he were not, a safe-conduct is granted to my ambassador. The gods would destroy any city that violated such an oath. Do you think Uruk would dare to lay hands on the herald of Kish?'

'Dumuzi would. If that herald were the son of Lugalbanda.'

'Dumuzi is dying,' said Agga again. 'There will be need soon of a new king in Uruk. By sending you at this time, I put you into the position most useful to you.' He rose slowly from the throne and came down to stand beside me, and laid his arm heavily across my shoulders, as a father might; for in truth he had been virtually a second father to me. Sweat glistened on his scalp. I felt the physical presence of him almost as I might a god's: he was massive, not only in his fleshy bulk but in his deep-seated regal authority. Yet there was the smell of beer on his breath. I did not think Father Enlil would smell of beer, nor An the Sky-father. Quietly Agga said to me, 'It is all quite certain. My information comes to me from the highest power in Uruk.'

'From Dumuzi, you say?'

'Higher.'

I stared at him. 'You are in communication with *her*?'

'We are very useful to one another, your goddess and I.'

In that moment the full truth came to me, and it struck me like the fire of the gods, so that the breath was knocked from me for a moment. I heard the droning buzz of the god-aura within my brain. I saw, enveloping Agga and everything else in the room, a luminous glow, gold with shadows of deep blue within it: the sign of the tempest in my spirit. I trembled. I clenched my fists and struggled to remain upright. What a fool I had been! From the first, Inanna had ruled me. She had engineered the necessity of my flight from Uruk, knowing I would go to Kish and during my exile I would make myself ready to replace Dumuzi upon the throne. She and Agga had conspired that between themselves; and Agga had sent me to his wars and trained me to be a prince and a leader, and now I was ready; and now Dumuzi, no longer needed, was being pushed into the House of Dust and Darkness. I was no hero, but only a puppet, dancing to their tune. I would be king in Uruk, yes: but the priestess would have the power, she and Agga to whom I had sworn the oath. And the son I had engendered upon Ama-sukkul, daughter of the king of Kish, would be king in Uruk after me, if Agga's plan worked its way to its final flowering. So Agga's seed would come to reign in both great cities.

Yet I might still turn all this to my advantage, if I walked warily.

I said, 'When am I to set out for Uruk?'

'Four days hence, on the day of the feast of Utu, which is an auspicious time for the commencement of great ventures.' Agga's hand still tightly grasped my shoulder. 'You will travel in majesty, and they will welcome you with joy. And you will bring with you splendid gifts from me for the treasury of Uruk, in recognition of the friendship that will exist between your city and mine when you are king.'

On the eve of the feast of Utu, the moon, when it appeared, was covered by a veil, which is an omen that is widely understood to mean that the king will attain the greatest power. But the moon did not say which king was meant—Agga the king that was, or Gilgamesh the king that would be. That is the trouble with omens, and with oracles of all sorts: they speak the truth, yes, but one is never sure what the truth may be.

11

My journey toward Uruk was like that of a king already enthroned, and my entry into the city was like that of a triumphant conqueror.

Agga placed at my service three of his finest sailing vessels, of the kind used for the sea trade to Dilmun, with great spreading sails of scarlet and yellow cloth that caught the breeze and sped me downriver swiftly and in the grandest style. I had with me a great richness of gifts from the king of Kish—slaves, stone jars of wine and oil, bales of fine fabrics, precious metals and jewels, effigies of the gods. I was accompanied by three dozen warriors as a guard of honor, and by a good many high officials of Agga's court, among them his astrologer, his personal physician, and his steward of wines, who saw to my comfort at each meal. My wife Ama-sukkul did not come with me, for she was just then about to be delivered of my second son. I would never see her again; but I did not know that then.

At each town along the river the people came out to hail us as we passed by. They did not know who they were hailing, of course—certainly they did not suspect that the kingly bronze-skinned man who returned their homage with a regal wave was one and the same as the fugitive boy who had had their hospitality four years earlier—but they knew that a fleet such as ours must be an important one, and they stood on the banks shouting and waving banners until we were gone from sight. There were at least two dozen such villages, each of a thousand dwellers or more, the northern ones owing allegiance to Kish, the southern ones to Uruk.

By night the astrologer showed me the stars and pointed out the omens in them. I knew only the bright star of the morning and evening, which is holy to Inanna; but he showed me the red star of war, and the white star of truth. All these stars are planets: that is to say, wanderers. Also he showed me the stars of the northern sky that follow Enlil's way, and those of the southern sky that follow Enki's way, and the stars of the celestial equator, which are those that follow the way of An. He taught me to find the Chariot Star, the Bow Star, and the Fire Star. He showed me the Plough, the Twins, the Ram, and the Lion. And he imparted to me much secret knowledge of the mysteries of these stars, and how to know the revelations they offer. He taught me also the art of using the stars to find one's way at night, which was of great value to me in my later journeyings.

Often I would stand by myself in the darkest hours of the night at the prow of my ship and speak with the gods. I asked counsel of Enki the wise, and Enlil the mighty, and Sky-father An, who rises like the arch of heaven above all things. They granted me great favor by entering my spirit, for I know that the high gods have many things to attend to, and the world of mortal men can occupy very little of their time, just as mortal rulers cannot devote themselves greatly to the needs of children or beggars. But those potent princes of heaven inclined themselves toward me. I felt their presence and it was comforting to me. I knew from that that I was indeed Gilgamesh, that is, He-Who-Is-Chosen; for it is not the business of the gods to grant much comfort, yet they granted it to me as I sailed toward the city of Uruk.

On the morning of the ninth day of the month Ululu I came to Uruk under the clear skies and a huge burning sun. Runners had gone ahead, bearing news of my coming, and half the city, so it seemed, was waiting for me when my ships docked at the White Quay. I heard drumming and the sound of trumpets, and then the chanting of my name, my old name, my birth-name, which I was soon to drop from me. There were some ten thousand people, I think, crowded along the rim of the Dike of the ship of An, and flowing from there to the great metal-studded doors of the Royal Gate.

I leaped lightly from my ship, and knelt and kissed the bricks of the ancient dike. When I rose, my mother Ninsun stood before me. She was wondrously beautiful in the brilliant light, almost like a goddess. Her robes were of crimson interwoven with strands of finely drawn silver, and a long curved golden pin fastened her cloak at her shoulder. In her hair she wore the silver crown of the high priestess of An, set with carnelian and lapis, and glinting with highlights of gold. She looked not a day older than when I had last seen her. Her eyes were shining: I saw in them the warmth that emanates not merely from one's own mother but from great Ninhursag, the fountain of repose, the mother of us all.

She studied me a long while, and I knew she was contemplating me both as a priestess and as a mother. I saw her seeing the size and power of my body, and the presence that had come upon me in full manhood. There could have been no stronger confirmation of the godhood of Lugalbanda than the godly body of Lugalbanda's son.

After a time she put out her hands to me and called me by my birth-name, and said, 'Come with me to the temple of the Sky-father, that I may give thanks for your return.'

We walked at the head of a great procession through the Royal Gate and along the Path of the Gods. At each holy place there was a rite to perform. At the small temple known as the Kizalagga a priest wearing a purple sash lit a torch in which spices had been inserted, and sprinkled it with golden oil, and did the rite of the washing of the mouth. At the holy place called Ubshukkinakku another torch was lit, and the pots were broken. Near the Sanctuary of Destinies a bull was sacrificed, and its thigh and its skin were seared and offered up. Then we ascended to the temple of An, where the old high priest Gungunum mixed wine and oil and made a libation at the gate, smearing some of it on the doorsockets and some on the gate itself. When we were within, he sacrificed a bull and a ram, and I filled the golden censers and made the offering to the Sky-father and to all the other deities in their turn.

Throughout all this I asked no questions and spoke no words out of turn. It was like moving through a dream. In the distance I heard the steady beating of the lilissu-drum, that is beaten only in the hour of an eclipse, and at the time of the death of kings; and I knew that Dumuzi the king was dead, and that they were going to offer the kingship to me.

I had not yet felt the goddess-presence. Nor had I laid eyes on the priestess Inanna. Thus far Uruk had withheld the goddess from me, and I had moved only in the presence of the Sky-father, to whom my mother is dedicated. But I knew Inanna would be manifested to me shortly.

'Come,' said Ninsun, and we crossed from the precinct of An to the precinct of Inanna, and up the steps of the White Platform toward the Enmerkar temple.

Inanna waited for me there.

The sight of her drew a gasp of amazement from me. In the four years of my absence, time had burned all the girlishness from her. She had entered into the deepest ripeness of her womanhood and her beauty had become overwhelming. Her dark eyes gleamed with the old wanton sparkle, but also with strange power where there had been mere mischief before. She seemed taller, and more slender, with the blades of her cheekbones sharply outlined; but her breasts were fuller than I remembered. Her deep-hued skin was shining with oil. The only garments she wore were the ornaments of the goddess, the earrings and the beads, the golden triangle at the lions, the hip-jewels and the nose-jewels and the navel-jewels.

I felt the heavy musky aura of goddess-presence and the buzzing aura of god-presence both at once. The slow steady beating of the drum penetrated my soul and invaded it utterly, so that the drum became me, and I became the drum. I felt myself stretched taut in the sunlight as the felt-covered paddles descended again and again. My eyes met Inanna's and I was drawn toward those dark immensities just as long ago I had been drawn toward the eyes of my father Lugalbanda, and I yielded

83

myself for a moment and let myself drift into a pool of darkness.

She smiled, and it was a terrifying smile, the smile of the Inanna-serpent.

In a low husky voice she said, 'The king Dumuzi has become a god. The city is without a king. The goddess requires this service of you.'

'I will serve,' I said, as all my life I had known I was destined one day to say.

Though I knew that it was Agga and Inanna who had conspired to give me this throne, for reasons of their own advantage, that did not matter to me. When I was king, I would be king: no one would own me, no one would use me. So I vowed to myself: I would be king, when I was king. Let them tremble who thought to have it otherwise!

They had everything in readiness. At a signal from Inanna I was taken aside, into a small three-sided building adjoining the temple where the preparations for high services are done. There I was stripped and bathed by half a dozen young priestesses, and then I was anointed in every part of my body with sweet-smelling oils, and my hair was combed and brushed and plaited and gathered behind my head, and they gave me a skirt of flounced wool to cover myself from my hips downward. Finally I gathered into my arms the gifts that a new king must offer to Inanna, and I went slowly forward from the robing-room out into the terrible blast of the summer sunlight, and to the vestibule of the Enmerkar temple. And went within to claim my kingship.

There were the three thrones, the one with the sign of Enlil, the one with the sign of An, and the one flanked by the reed-bundle of Inanna. There was the scepter. There was the crown. And there on the center throne sat Inanna, priestess and goddess, radiant now in all her awful majesty.

Her eyes met mine. She looked close upon me, as if to say: *You are mine, you will belong to me.* But I met her gaze steadily and evenly, as if to answer: *You much misjudge me, lady, if that is what you think.*

Then it began, the great ceremony, the prayers and the libations. About me stood the officers of Dumuzi's reign, the chamberlains and stewards and overseers and tax-gatherers and viceroys and governors, who soon would be dependent upon my mercies. The flutes sounded, the trumpets played. I lit a globe of black incense; I laid down my gifts before each of the thrones; I touched my forehead to the ground before Inanna, and kissed the ground, and gave the proper gifts to her. It seemed to me that I had done this a thousand times. I felt new strength flowing through me as though my blood had doubled in volume, as though my breath was the breath of two men, and both of them giants.

Inanna rose from the throne. I saw the beauty of her long arms and graceful neck; I saw her breasts swaying beneath the blue necklaces of beads. 'I am Ninpa the Lady of the Scepter,' she said to me, and took the scepter from the throne of Enlil and handed it to me. 'I am Ninmenna the Lady of the Crown,' she said, and lifted the crown from the throne of An and let it rest upon my brow. Her eyes met mine; her gaze was burning, burning.

She spoke my birth-name, which would never again be heard in the world of mortals.

Then she said, 'You are Gilgamesh, the great man of Uruk. So do the gods decree.' And I heard the name from a hundred voices at once, like the roaring of the river in the time of flood: 'Gilgamesh! Gilgamesh! Gilgamesh!'

12

That night I slept in the palace of the king, in the great bed of ebony and gold that had been my father's, and Enmerkar's before him. The family of Dumuzi had already departed from the place, all his wives, his plump doughy daughters; the gods had not granted him sons. Before I went to my bed I confirmed in their position all the officers of the kingdom, according to the tradition, though I knew I would remove most of them from office

85

in the months to come. And I feasted most royally with them, until spilled beer ran in foaming torrents along the channels of the feasting-hall floor.

At the evening's end the chamberlain of the royal concubines asked me if I meant to have a woman with me in the night. I said that I did, as many as he could supply; and he supplied them all night, seven, eight, a dozen of them. From the eagerness of them I suppose Dumuzi had been making little use of them. I embraced each one only once, and sent her out and called for the next. For a moment, in their arms, it seemed almost as if I might be able to fill that hollow place within my soul that gave me such torment. Indeed I could—for a moment, for half an hour, and then the pain came rolling back in upon me like a storm cloud. One woman alone might have freed me from this distress, I thought. But that woman, the woman I would have chosen for myself that night had I been free to choose, was of course not for me to have—not then, not until the new year and the rite of the Sacred Marriage. But I allowed myself to imagine that I was with her, as I pressed my body against this concubine and that one.

At dawn I found that I still had vigor in me. I rose and went by foot, disdaining all bearers, to the cloister of the holy priestesses. There I asked for the priestess Abisimti, who had initiated me into manhood. It seemed to me that there was terror in her eyes, as much perhaps for my great height and strength as for the fact that I was now the king. I smiled and took her hand in mine, and said, 'Think of me as that boy of twelve with whom you were so gentle.'

I was not gentle with her that morning, I suspect. Great strength had come upon me, greater even than I had already had, simply from having assumed the kingship. And there was the godhood within me as well. Three times I had her, until she lay back panting fitfully, looking a little dazed and plainly hoping I was sated. Nothing could have sated me that day; but for her sake I spared her further toil. Abisimti was as beautiful as I remembered her, with skin like cool water and breasts round as pomegranates; but her beauty was to Inanna's as the moon is to the sun.

So passed my first day in the kingship. Hour by hour I felt the power and the greatness flowing into me. On my second day I received homage from the assembly of the city.

If a stranger were to ask how the king of Uruk is chosen, why, any citizen of the city would reply that he is chosen by the assembly. And in truth that is the case; but that is not the entire case.

The assembly elects, but the gods direct, and in particular it is Inanna, speaking through her priestess, who makes known the one who is to be king. Nor does the kingship pass automatically, as it does in Kish and as I hear it does in many other cities, to the son of the king. We understand these matters differently. We think that there is a divine inwardness that some men have, a kind of grace, which makes them fit to be king. If that grace happens to pass from father to son, as it had from Enmerkar to Lugalbanda, and from Lugalbanda to me, it is only because a father often passes his traits to his son—his stature, his breadth of shoulders, the turn of his nose, and, perhaps, his kingliness. But it does not necessarily happen that way. Not all our kings have been the sons of kings.

Once the assembly has chosen the king, the assembly may only advise, not command. If there is disagreement between the assembly and the king, the king's wishes will prevail. This is not tyranny; this is the inherent outcome of the correct choice of king. For, mark you well, in time of crisis and doubt it is vital that a city speak with a single voice. And have the gods not indicated which voice that voice should be, by making him the king? The assembly, in its discourse with the king, tunes that voice as a harper tunes his strings; but when the voice speaks, it is the voice of the king, which is to say, it is the voice of the city, it is the voice of heaven. And if the king in his speech does not speak with heaven's voice, everyone will know it, and heaven will cast him from his place.

These matters were much on my mind when the men of the assembly paid their ceremonial call on me in the audience-chamber of the palace. First came the free citizens, what we have always called the house of men: those who speak for the boatmen and fishermen, the farmers and cattlebreeders, the scribes and jewelers and carpenters and masons. They passed through, and put down their gifts before me, and touched their hands to my ankles in the customary way. When that was done, the elders of the assembly came, those who speak for the great estates, the princely families, the priestly clans. Their gifts were more weighty, their scrutiny of me more intense. I met their gaze evenly and with assurance. I was aware that I was the youngest man in the room, younger than any of the elders, younger than any of the house of men. But I was king.

I felt the sacred force that is a king's glory, and I revelled in it. But even then a dark shadow lay upon my joy, for I remembered Lugalbanda laying upon his alabaster bier, and I remembered the day I had stood by the city wall and watched the corpses of the poor go floating down the river. I was mindful always of the bleak jest the gods have played upon us, even on those who are of a greatness approaching theirs: *Never forget that you are mortal, never forget that you have but a brief moment of grandeur and then you are dragged off to the House of Dust and Darkness*. Such matters chilled my warmest moments. Yet I was young; yet I was strong; I pushed the thought of death from me as often as it arose within me, and told myself, as I had when I was a child: *Death, I will defeat you! Death, I will devour you!*

'All during the time of Dumuzi,' said the great landowner Enlil-ennam, 'we waited for your return. For Lugalbanda is within you.'

I looked at him, startled. Was that fact such common knowledge in Uruk? But then I realized that he meant it only as a manner of speaking. It was merely as if he said, *Lugalbanda's blood flows in your veins*. And everyone knew that.

'It has been a dark time for us,' said white-haired Ali-ellati, whose standing of nobility could be traced back ninety thousand years. 'Signs and omens became confused. The gods gave no clear answers. The portents were sinister. We lived in fear and foreboding. It was because of the king. Yes: because of the king.'

'And what manner of king was Dumuzi?' I asked.

'Well, he was not Lugalbanda,' Enlil-ennam said, smirking broadly. 'He was not Enmerkar.'

'He was not even Dumuzi,' said Lu-Meshlam, whose estates were like a little kingdom in themselves. 'Sufficient to be Dumuzi, if one cannot be Enmerkar. But he was not even Dumuzi!' And they all laughed at that.

'What are you telling me?' I asked.

Piece by piece they unfolded a tale of weak and sorry kingship, this one speaking a little while, then another taking up the story. A silly man, swollen with pride—ill-starred projects, abortive military adventures, the raising to power of upstarts and nonentities, foolish quarrels with the great men of the city, neglect of the rituals, public funds consumed on absurdities while necessities went unrepaired—the sad account went on and on. Once the dam was broken, the flow of their accusations was unending. I felt some embarrassment for their sake, listening to it all: for who had put Dumuzi forth to be king, at the time of my father's death, if not they? The old priestess Inanna must have had a reason for proposing him, and they for accepting him, and I think that reason must have been that he was pliant and malleable, very soft metal indeed. But the nine years of his kingship had not, so it seemed, brought them the advantage they had hoped to have out of it. Which was small surprise, if they had knowingly chosen a weak man. So now they were turning, eagerly, gladly, hopefully, to a stronger one, in whose veins the blood of greatness flowed. I could not help feeling some scorn for their folly. But I was swift to pardon them. They saw their error; they were redeeming themselves now from it; and, if they had not comported themselves according to the way of the gods when they chose Dumuzi, so be it. The fault had not been theirs. The fault was the gods'.

'Tell me of the death of Dumuzi,' I said.

They became evasive. 'Heaven withdrew the kingship from him,' said Lu-Meshlam, and the others nodded sagely.

'I understand that,' I said impatiently. 'But how did he die?'

They looked at one another. No one would speak. I had to draw it from them. A lingering, horrible death, they said. A slow wasting-away, in great pain. The gods forsook him and many demons entered him: Ashakku, Namtaru, Utukku, Alu, the fever-maker, the sick-maker, the evil spirit, the diabolical one. No door could shut them from his body. No bolt would turn them back. Through the gateways of Dumuzi they glided like snakes. Through the hinges of his spirit they blew like the wind. The diviners had struggled mightily, but there was no healing him, not even any understanding of the malady that consumed him.

The old priest Arad-Nanna said, when the elders were done with this grim recital, 'His mistake was in the choice of his name. There is a doom upon Dumuzi that was proclaimed at the first day of time. How could he have hoped to escape it, with such a name, in this city of all cities?'

I was preoccupied with other thoughts at that moment and I suppose I did not pay close attention to those words of Arad-Nanna. Only afterward, when I sat alone thinking these matters through, did I see their likely meaning. *In this city of all cities.* The city of Inanna, he meant. Who is the ultimate ruler of Uruk, beyond assembly, beyond king? Why, it is the goddess, and none other! And it is in the nature of the goddess that she is destined to destroy the god Dumuzi, the holy shepherd: we have that tale taught us from childhood. Had the priestess Inanna re-enacted, with the king Dumuzi, the downfall that the goddess Inanna works each year in heaven upon the god Dumuzi? Everything cried out *yes* to that. She had sent me that seal-cylinder, while I was still in Kish, showing the death of Dumuzi, the triumph of Inanna, and I had taken it for word that she was casting some spell which would bring an end to him. But had she settled for mere spells, or had she made use of actual potions? I thought back through what they had told me of the king's sufferings, his fevers, his agonies, his wasting away. And I grew uneasy. If Inanna could slay one king, she might slay another, when she saw fit. And in Uruk every king plays the role of Dumuzi to the goddess, whether his name be Dumuzi in fact, or Lugalbanda, or Enmerkar—or Gilgamesh.

This I pondered, Inanna and Dumuzi, Dumuzi and Inanna. My mind returned, as it often had since my childhood, to that tale of her descent into hell, in that time when she longed for conquest beyond her allotted realm.

Holding sway over heaven and earth was not enough for her. She must also have the nether world, the realm where her older sister, Ereshkigal, rules. So she dons her great scarlet robes of power, her crown, her double strand of lapis beads, her breast-plate, her ring, the lapis measuring-rod and line of her authority; and she goes to that place in Uruk which is the gateway to hell, and makes her way downward. 'If I do not return in three days,' she tells the goddess Ninshubur, her vizier, her right hand, 'get you to Father Enlil, beg him to set me free.'

At the first gate of the nether world the gatekeeper blocks her way and demands to know why she has come. She offers a false answer, but the gatekeeper is not deceived; he has instructions from his queen Ereshkigal to deprive Inanna of her power and bring her to humility. And so at the first gate the gatekeeper takes her crown from the goddess; and at the second gate he demands the lapis beads; and thus it is at each of the seven gates, until the scarlet royal robe itself is taken from her, and she enters the throne-room of Ereshkigal naked, bowing down low. For anyone who comes before the queen of the nether world must do so naked, even if she be the queen of heaven. What a humbling for proud Inanna! Nor is she given the chance to assail her sister's throne: the judges of the lower realm surround her at once, they utter their judgment, and Ereshkigal fastens the eye of death on her. Just like that, Inanna is slain. Her corpse, like a side of rotting meat, is hung from a peg on the wall. And there she remains, for a day and a second day and a third, and in the world it is wintertime, for Inanna is gone from it.

Then Ninshubur takes herself to Father Enlil and begs mercy for the dead Inanna; but Enlil will not lift a hand to save her. Nor will Nanna of the moon, to whom Ninshubur turns next. But the wise and compassionate Enki, who knows the water of life, is willing to come to her aid. Enki sends two messengers into the nether world, and they find Ereshkigal in the pangs of childbirth. 'We can lift this pain from you,' they tell her, but they must have a gift in return, and the gift they ask is the corpse of Inanna. Ereshkigal yields; the envoys ease her pain; and then they take the dead Inanna from the wall and restore her to life. But she must not leave the nether world, Ereshkigal insists, unless she provides someone in her place.

Ah, and who will Inanna send? Why, who else but Dumuzi her husband? He sits upon his splendid throne beneath the great apple tree in Uruk, clad in shining garments and all unmoved by Inanna's torments. Yes, Dumuzi will be the one. Where is Inanna's love? Ah, there is no love! It is her life or Dumuzi's, and she does not hesitate. Dumuzi has shown no grief over Inanna's disappearance; perhaps he feels well rid of his troublesome consort. And so he is doomed. She looks upon him with the eyes of death, and cries out to seven demons, 'Seize him! Take him away!' The demons take him by his thighs; they break the flute that he has been playing; they gash him with axes so that his blood pours forth. He flees. They follow. He appeals to the gods to spare him, and they aid him in his flight, but Inanna is implacable, and at last he is seized and slain and carried down into hell. It is the time when the great death of summer settles over the Land, that time when Dumuzi is taken away. In summer he must die, though he returns in the autumn, with the rains, with the new year, to celebrate the Sacred Marriage with Inanna and bring about the new birth of all things. Where is the mercy of Inanna, in this tale? There is no mercy. Inanna is a force that will not be gainsaid. Dumuzi must die, he who is the king, he who is the god.

To all this I gave most careful thought. Inanna had made me king, that much was certain: she and Agga both, working in some sly alliance. She had made me, but she could unmake me also. I would be on my guard, I resolved, against any further playing out in Uruk of the tale of the goddess and god.

On the third day of my kingship, Inanna summoned me. When the goddess beckons, even the king must hasten.

We met in a small room of the temple, not at all majestic, with pink-washed walls and a few lopsided rickety chairs that a poor scribe would have deemed too shabby for his house. She wore a plain robe and her face was unpainted. Two days earlier she had been goddess and priestess both, terrible in her majesty and over-whelming in her beauty. The woman I saw now had not troubled this day to assume the goddess. Her beauty was with her at any time, but the grandeur of it did not shine forth. It was just as well; I had had little sleep in my two nights of kingship, and confronting Inanna in her majesty is an exhausting business for anyone, even one who is in part a god.

I wanted to have the truth from her concerning Dumuzi's death. But how could I ask it outright? 'Did he die at your hands? Did you drop poison in his bowl, priestess?' No. No. Should I say, 'I am grateful for your slaying my predecessor, so I might have his throne'? No. Or, perhaps, 'I am young and new in these matters of state. Tell me, is it the custom for the goddess to murder a worthless king, when the city can no longer tolerate his worthlessness?' No. Nor did I choose to bring up the old matter of my having been forced into exile: 'Did Dumuzi grow so suddenly frightened of me, perhaps, because you happened to tell him that the spirit of Lugalbanda had entered into me?'

No, I said none of these things. Nor did she, who had looked upon me with such fierce hunger in years gone by, favor me with the flashing eyes now, the savage grin of triumph, the fiery embrace toward which her scheming had been directed so long. She took care to convey to me nothing but what was fitting between priestess and king on the first ceremonial visit of his reign: cool formality, a strict observance of the rites. Inanna and the king are not meant to embrace in passion, except on the night of the Sacred Marriage, and that is but once a year.

So in the appropriate phrases she congratulated me upon my ascension, and offered me her blessing; and I, just as formally, pledged myself to serve the goddess in kingly manner. We shared sweet wine from a single bowl, and ate of the charred meat of an ox that had been sacrificed at dawn. When all that was done, we talked, like two old friends who had not seen one another for a long while, of the past, of our first meeting in the Enmerkar temple, events of my boyhood, how tall and strong I had grown in the four years of my exile, and so on and so on, but everything offhand and distant. She spoke of the death of certain princes and great men while I had been away. That led her eventually to the subject of the death of Dumuzi: she looked sad, she sighed, she cast down her eyes, as though the king's passing had been a great sorrow to her. I searched her face but saw no clues. 'With my own hands I ministered to him,' said Inanna. 'I put cool cloths on his forehead. I mixed the medications myself, the quunabu and the kushumma, the duashbur seeds, the root of nigmi and arina. But nothing availed. From day to day he withered and shrank.' I felt a chill, as she talked of mixing medicines for Dumuzi, and wondered what devilish things she had mixed into those powders to hasten him onward to the next world. But I did not ask. I think I know what truths lay beneath my unspoken questions. But I did not ask.

13

Now the full weight of kingship fell upon me, and it was far heavier a burden than I had ever imagined. Nevertheless I think I bore it well.

There were the rituals to perform, the offerings and sacrifices. I expected that. But so many, so many! The Feast of the Eating of Barley, the Feast of the Eating of Gazelles, the Feast of the Blood of Lions, this feast and that one, a calendar of ceremonies that was unsparing of the king's time and strength. The gods are insatiable. They must be fed constantly. I had not been king for ten days when I found myself wholeheartedly sick of the reek of roasting flesh and the thick sweet smell of freshly poured blood. You must understand that I was still hardly more than a boy: I knew it was my duty, all this ritual, but I would rather by far have been cracking heads together in the wrestling-house, or hurling javelins on the field of war, than spending my days and nights at spilling the blood of beasts in these high ceremonies. Yet I moved past that early revulsion, and performed my tasks as I knew I must. The king is not only the leader in warfare and spokesman of the gods in matters of statecraft; he is the highest of the high priests, which is a formidable job.

So on the proper evening I would come forth on the roof of the temple of An in the first night watch, when the star of An had appeared, and preside at the golden table where a feast for the Sky-father had been laid out, with food also for the wife of An and for the seven wandering stars. To these great ones I offered the flesh of cattle, sheep, and birds, beer of the best quality, and the wine of dates, poured from a golden ewer. I made an offering of every kind of fruit, and spread honey and aromatic spices on the seven golden incense burners. I went around to each of the four horns of the altar and kissed it to renew its holiness.

I drank wine and beer and milk and honey, and even oil, until my stomach was bloated from it. In some rites I had to sip from ewers of blood, which I never have come gladly to do. I wore heavy robes for certain rituals and in others I was altogether naked. There was never a night without some observance, and often there were some by day, as well. The gods must be fed. I began to feel like a cook and a serving-boy.

And like a butcher also, sometimes. For one rite they brought me a sacrificial ox too fat to stand: it looked like a great tub of fat. It peered at me with great brown sad eyes as if it knew I was its death approaching, but it was too placid to protest. They held its head up and put the blade in my hand. 'The gods created you for this moment,' I told it. 'Now I return you to them.' I cut its throat with a single stroke. The ox, panting, sighing, sank on its fore-limbs, but was a long time dying; I thought I heard it weep. I let its warm blood gush over my naked skin until I was slippery with it from head to toe. This is what it is to be a king in Uruk.

There were restrictions and constraints upon me. On this day of the month I could not eat beef, and on that one I might not have pork, and on another I was forbidden any cooked meat at all. On a certain day it was perilous for me to eat garlic; on another day, for the sake of the security of the commonwealth, I was required to abstain from intercourse with women; on a day of setting-out of boundary-stones in the fields I must not go within sight of the river; and so forth. Many of these things seemed absurd to me, but I observed them all. Some of them I still perform. But some I have discarded with the years, and I have never seen any hardship come to me or to Uruk for my having done that.

These obligations and burdens of kingship grew less oppressive as I became accustomed to them. Now and again I found myself yearning for the freer and more vigorous life I had led as a warrior of Kish; but such feelings passed quickly by, like the birds of winter that flash silver in the blue sky. I did what was required of me, and did it ungrudgingly. A king who grudges his own tasks is no king, but a mere imposter.

There was one rite I would have performed not merely ungrudg-ingly, but altogether eagerly. But I had begun my reign at the height of summer; that one had to wait until the new year. I speak of the Sacred Marriage, when Inanna would at last lie in my arms.

At last the heat abated and that soft sweet wind, the Cheat, swept out of the south. The scent of the warm sea travels on that wind; I stood a long time on the terrace of the palace by myself, breathing deep, drawing it into my lungs. It is the harbinger, I thought. The season now changes; the rains return; the time arrives for tilling and sowing. And before the fields may be sown, the goddess must be. I trembled with anticipation.

That morning the chamberlain in charge of such things told me I must cease lying with the palace concubines now, for the festival-time was nigh. The days of purification had arrived, when the seed of the king must be dedicated entirely to Inanna. I laughed and said that I would gladly make that sacrifice, though within a day or two I had other thoughts about that. I have always felt the surge of desire as the shore feels the surge of the sea, that is, something that comes steadily, insistently, unceasingly. Nothing can check the sea-surge; and when I sought to check that other surge within myself, I found it almost as difficult as it would have been to halt the waves from crashing against the beach. I had not gone without a woman's embrace for as much as half a day since coming into manhood, I think. Now I decreed for myself a great drought of the passions, that parched my blood most amazingly. It was a very hard time for me. I withstood it, but only because I knew that my reward would be Inanna, coming to me as the cool winter rains do after the hellish summer.

All ordinary business of the city halted. The festival prepara-tions began, the repair and cleansing of buildings, the sacrifices, the fumigations, the parades. Exorcists were busy in every part of Uruk, driving the demons beyonds the walls. Priests marched out into the dry fields and sprinkled them with holy water from golden ewers. Those who belonged to the unclean castes went to their temporary villages outside the city, and anyone who was a stranger to Uruk also was asked to leave.

I remained secluded in the palace, fasting, bathing, eating no meat, touching no woman. All day long I breathed the fumes of sacred royal incense, burning in long-legged braziers. I slept hardly at all, but spent my nights in prayer and chanting. Gods came and went in my bedchamber, great shadowy figures who stood by my side a little while. One night I felt the presence of Enlil; on another, I woke from a light doze to see the hooded figure of Enki before me, with eyes blazing like red embers. The visits of these gods and others left me cold with dread. No one, not even a king, can go easy in such presences. If there had been some good friend by my side then whom I loved, it would have been less difficult for me to face those spirits. But in that time I was alone. They walked about my room and passed through me as though I were not there, and each time they did I felt a bleak gray wind blowing into me out of the nether world. At this season of the year, when the dry death that is summer still grips the Land, the nether world is very close: its mouth lies just below the gateway that opens into Uruk.

Gungunum, the high priest of An, came to me on the third morning. My servants dressed me in the fullest of my royal regalia, and I went with him to the chapel of the palace. There I knelt before the Sky-father. Then Gungunum stripped me of all my ornaments of rank, and slapped my face, and pulled my ears, and otherwise humbled me before the god, and made me swear that I had nothing that was evil in the sight of the gods; and when that was finished, he lifted me and dressed me with his own hands, and gave me back my kingship.

Afterward he handed me a bowl that contained tender slivers of the heart of the palm, the young bud of the date tree. We hold this tree to be holy, for it has as many uses as there are days in the year, and gives us food and drink, and fibres for ropes and nets, and wood for our furniture, and everything else: it is a godly tree. So I took the bowl from the priest and ate the slivers of the heart of the palm, and Dumuzi immediately entered into me.

I mean the god Dumuzi, of course, not that silly shallow king who had taken that name upon himself. The heart of the palm is the power of the tree to produce new fruit, and when I ate it, that power, which is Dumuzi the god, passed into me. All fertility now was embodied in me. I was the rainfall; I was the rising sap; I was the flower; I was the seed. I was the force that could engender dates and barley, wheat and figs. From me would come the rivers. From me would flow wine and beer, milk and cream. The god throbbed within me, and I was bursting with the new life of the new year. When I looked down at my naked body I saw the rigid scepter of my maleness standing out far in front of me like a third arm, and there was a pulsing within it.

But Dumuzi without Inanna is useless. It was time now for me to release the power of the god into her receptive loins.

So, then—at last, at last—the night of the Sacred Marriage was at hand. The moon had vanished into the place of its slumber. That morning I had bathed in pure water from the font of the temple of An, and then handmaidens oiled my body, omitting no part of it, using the golden oil pressed from the richest of dates. I put on my crown and my robe, leaving the upper half of my body bare. They took me to the dark windowless Dumuzi-house at the edge of the city, where I spent half the day in silence, emptying my mind of everything but the god. I tell you that I was like a man in a dream, void of all self, possessed entirely by Dumuzi. And at nightfall I went by boat—the journey must be done by water, so that the king glides into the city as seed does into the womb—to the quay nearest the Eanna precinct, and from there on foot to the White Platform and the temple where the goddess awaited me.

I mounted the Platform at its western end, looking neither to the left nor to the right. I led a black-fleeced sheep by a leather leash, and held a tiny kid resting on my arm, as offerings to Inanna. I suppose the air was warm or cool that night, and the stars were bright or perhaps veiled by mist, and possibly there was a breeze on which the perfume of young blossoms drifted, or possibly not. I could not tell you. I saw and felt nothing, except the gleaming temple before me, and the smooth brick of the Platform beneath my bare feet.

I entered the temple and gave the kid to a priestess and the sheep to a priest, and went to the long chamber. Inanna stood there. If I live twelve thousand years I will never see a sight more glorious.

She was as bright as a polished shield. She glistened in her splendor. They had bathed her, they had anointed her, they had draped her nakedness with ivory and gold and lapis lazuli and silver. Sheaths of alabaster surrounded her thighs and a triangle of gold lay over her loins. Clear blocks of lapis rested upon her breasts. Strands of gold braid were woven through her hair. But those were mere ornaments. I had seen them all before, worn by her on the night of her first Sacred Marriage to Dumuzi, and worn by her predecessor in the time of Lugalbanda. What awed me was not the magnificence of her jewelry but the magnificence of the goddess that shined through from beneath. Just as I had become the embodiment of the virile power—there was that insistent throbbing between my legs to remind me of that—so too was she the blazing essence of the female, now. From that golden triangle at the base of her belly came wave upon wave of intense power, like the brightness of the sun.

Smiling, she extended her hands toward me, fingertips outstretched. Her eyes met mine. I leaped back across the chasm of years to that moment, in this very temple, when the girl Inanna had found me wandering, and stroked me and spoke my name, and looked into my eyes and told me that I would be king, and that she would lie in my arms one day: my cheek against the little buds of her breasts, her perfume pungent in my nostrils. Now indeed everything that she had prophesied had befallen, and we stood face to face in the temple on the night of the Sacred Marriage, and her dark eyes, gleaming like onyx by torchlight, were ablaze with goddess-fire.

'Hail, Inanna!' I whispered.

'Hail, royal husband, fountain of life.'

'My holy jewel.'

'My husband. My true destined love.'

Then she laughed a very human laugh. 'See? It has all come to pass. Has it not? Has it not?'

I heard the music of the showing-forth. My fingers touched hers—just the tips, but it was fire! fire!—and together we walked down the corridor and out upon the porch of the temple. The door swung open before us. The bright crescent of the new moon rose above the temple. A thousand pairs of eyes stared back at me out of the night.

We spoke the words of the rites. We sipped from the flask of honey, and poured the vessel of barley out on the ground. We stood with joined hands during the singing of the hymn of the showing-forth. Three naked priests pronounced blessings. The blood of the kid, my gift, was daubed on my forearm and on her cheek. The seared meat of my other gift, the sheep, was offered to us on plates of gold, and we took one mouthful each. It took me twelve hundred years to swallow that little morsel of meat.

Once again we entered the temple, preceded and surrounded by priestesses and priests, musicians, dancers, all leaping and chanting about us as we made our way to the bedchamber of the goddess. It was a small high-vaulted room, strewn with soft green rushes made sweet-smelling with the oil of cedar. The bed that was at its center was of the blackest ebony, inlaid with ivory and gold. A sheet of the finest linen covered it, bearing the emblem of Inanna. All about the bed lay heaps of freshly harvested dates, still clustered as they had come from the tree: the true treasure of the Land, more precious than any gem. She broke one date from a cluster and put it tenderly in my mouth, and then I made the same offering to her.

You may think that at this point I was maddened with desire and impatience. But no, no, the god was in me and I had a god's divine calmness. How many years in the making had this Marriage been? What did a few minutes more matter, now? I remained tranquil while the priestesses of Inanna removed the jewels from her, the beads, the alabaster sheaths, the rings, the ornaments of her ears, her eyes, her hips, her navel. They took from her the beads that covered her bosom, and laid bare her breasts, which were high and round and stood forth like those of a girl, although she was past twenty. They lifted the latch of her golden loin-covering and revealed to me the inner zone of her womanhood, dark and deeply thatched and richly perfumed. And then the same women undid my robe and uncovered my body; and when we were both naked they went from the room and left us with each other.

I went close to her. I stood before her. I watched the rising and falling of her breasts. She drew her tongue across her lips, slowly, making them gleam. Her eyes traveled shamelessly over my body; and mine made the journey over hers, lingering at fullness of breast, breadth of thigh, the dense rich nether beard that concealed the well of womanhood. I took her lightly by the hand and led her toward the couch.

For a moment, as my body hovered above hers, my god-self flickered and went from me and my mortal self returned. And I thought of all the intricacies of my dealings with this woman, how she had baffled and bewildered me. I thought of her wantonness, her dark playfulness, her mystery, her power. I thought also of that other Dumuzi, the mortal one, whom she had embraced year after year in this same rite, and then, when he was of no further use

100

to her, had casually slain. Then the god reasserted himself in me and all these thoughts went from me, and I said, as the god must say to the goddess in this moment, 'I am the shepherd, I am the ploughman, I am the king: I am the bridegroom. Let the goddess rejoice!'

I will not tell you what further words passed between us on that night. The things that the goddess must say to the god, and the god to the goddess, you already know, for those words are the same every year; and the things that the priestess said to the king, and the king to the priestess, can easily be guessed, and are of no interest. Besides god and goddess and king and priestess, there were also a man and a woman in that room; and as to the words that were said by the woman to the man and by the man to the woman, why, I think they are the secrets of that woman and that man, and I will not tell them, though I have told so much else. Let those words remain our mystery. The greater mystery that we performed that night, you can imagine. You know what rites of lips and nipples, of buttocks and hands, of mouths and loins, must be acted out by the sacred couple. Her skin was hot, burning like the ice of the northern mountains. Her nipples were hard as alabaster in my hands. We did all that must be done, before the final thing, and when it was the moment for that, we knew it without saying it. To enter her was to glide in honey. As we joined, she laughed, and I knew it to be as much the laughter of the girl of the corridor as the goddess on high. I also laughed, to be having the fulfillment of my desire after so long a waiting; and then our laughter was lost in a deeper, heavier sound. When we moved together, she spoke in babbling phrases that I did not know; the woman-language, the goddess-language of the Old Way. Her eyes rolled upward so that I saw only the whites. Then my own eyes closed, and I gripped her tightly with both my arms. The god-power, flowing from me like liquid fire, brought the goddess-power within her to its fruition. In the outpouring of my seed the new year was born. A cry of rejoicing burst from my lips and from hers, and we heard the answering melodies of the musicians who waited outside the bedchamber. It was then that we spoke with each other, first with our eyes and our smiles, then with words. In a little while we began the rite anew, and then again, and again and

101

again, until the dawn brought the new year's blessing to us, and we went quietly from the temple to stand naked in the gentle rain that our coupling had summoned into the Land.

14

So, then, passed the night of the Sacred Marriage, when Inanna and I were united at last. But it was the goddess and the god who had been married, not the priestess and the king; and once the festival was over, we went on in our separate lives, she in the isolation of her temple, I amidst my concubines in the palace. I did not so much as set eyes on her for some weeks. When I did, at the rite of casting wheat-seed, she treated me in a cool and formal way. That was right and proper: but I hated it. The taste of her was still on my tongue. Yet I knew I would not embrace her a second time until the season of the new year had come round again, twelve months hence. I ached from that knowledge.

Ties of ritual and responsibility kept us in constant communication, all the same. In Uruk the king is the right arm of the goddess, and her sword; and she is the holy staff on which he leans. Without the goddess, there would be no king; without the king, the goddess could not touch the souls of the people. So they are forever joined, twin centers of the city, one revolving about the other and all else revolving about both of them.

The gentle rain of Tashritu gave way, early in the month Arahsamna, to rains that were not gentle at all: torrential downpours that came sweeping out of the north nearly every day. The dry soil drank greedily at first, but soon its thirst was slaked, and still the storms roared across the Land. In this time I began to give close thought to the condition of the canals. They had not been kept in proper repair during the last year of the reign of Dumuzi. If the rains continued with such force and the silt were not cleared from the canals we might very well suffer from flooding by early spring.

I was deep in the midst of these matters, conferring with my water-chamberlain and my overseer of canals and three or four other high officials, when my viceroy of the palace entered the royal chamber. A priest of the temple of Enmerkar, he said, had come with a message from Inanna. She had urgent need of me. A demon, it seemed, had taken up residence in her huluppu-tree, and I must drive it away.

My mind was full of the needs of the canals, and I made no attempt, I suppose, to veil my impatience. I looked at the viceroy in amazement and said bluntly, 'Can she find no other exorcist?'

There was some muttering from the officials who sat at the table with me. I heard their disapproving tone, and thought at first that they were as annoyed as I was by this interruption of our work; but no, what troubled them was my surly refusal, not Inanna's ill-timed request. They peered at me uneasily. For a moment no one would speak.

Then the overseer of canals murmured, not looking directly at me, 'It lies in the province of the king to do such tasks, my lord, when they are asked of him.' Sudden perspiration put a sheen on his face.

I spread my hands wide before him. 'We have important work—'

'The summons of Inanna may not be ignored, O majesty,' said my viceroy softly, touching his forehead with the greatest tact.

'The canals—' I said.

'The goddess,' said the water-chamberlain.

'Do all of you feel this way?' I asked, glancing about me at them all.

This time no one spoke. But there was no mistaking their insistence. I yielded, and I yielded smiling. I know no other way to yield, but with a smile. What could I do? There was no help for it: busy as I was, I must go at once to the temple, and rid Inanna's tree of its demon.

This huluppu-tree was, and for that matter still is, a great towering thing of graceful weeping boughs, which was planted by the goddess in the garden of her temple five thousand years ago.

The ground where it grows is so holy that a pinch of the black soil from its roots is enough to cure many ailments of the spirit; in springtime barren women come to it and embrace its trunk, and many are made fertile by the dripping of its sap; and a green tea is brewed from its leaves that is sometimes used in divining the future. It is a noble and sacred tree, and I would not have had it come to any harm. But it seemed to me that Inanna might well have looked after her own tree just then, and left me free to look after the canals.

In the second watch of the morning—the rain had stopped for a time; the sky was bright and clear, the air had the newly washed scent of early winter—I went to the temple garden in the company of a band of the younger men of the palace. The huluppu-tree, vast and spreading, stood in the northeast corner of the enclosure, looming above everything else. Half a dozen wailing priestesses stood close beside it, and a dozen old women of the city shuffled slowly in a wide circle about it, chanting a tuneless dirge.

One did not need to be an expert gardener to know that something was amiss with the tree. The rain had swept nearly all of its long narrow leaves from it, and they lay piled in huge mounds. Those that had not yet fallen were withered and yellowing, and the branches themselves looked limp and lax. I went to it and put my hands against its thick wrinkled bark, as though trying to feel the demon that had taken up residence within it. But all I felt was thick wrinkled bark.

I had brought with me a certain Lugal-amarku, a little hunch-backed man with black eyebrows that met above his nose, who knew spells and exorcisms. He put his hands to the tree too, and pulled them back as though they had been burned.

'Well?' I said. 'What do you discover?'

'Not one demon, my lord. Three!'

'Ah,' I said. 'Three, is it?' That was tiresome. I thought of the silt clogging the canals, and the rain that surely would return in a few days. Three demons, then? Three?

From behind me came a whispering of the priestesses and the old women. I looked about, and saw Inanna striding toward me, heedless of the muddy ground that flecked her white robe at every step. It was only the second time I had seen her since the dawn following the Sacred Marriage. Instantly there flashed into my mind the vision of that night, Inanna before me, her face hot and flushed, her breasts heaving. But the vision passed. Brusquely she made toward me the sign that the high priestess makes when she greets the king, and I made the goddess-sign to her.

'You must save the tree,' she said immediately.

'It houses three demons, I am told.'

'Ah, you see that also?'

I nodded toward Lugal-amarku. 'Not I. He sees it.'

The hunchback said, turning his palms outward modestly, 'It is apparent, my lady.'

'So it is,' she said, and went to the tree. She glanced toward me. 'Here: look. The snake who knows no charm has made his dwelling here. And in the crown of the tree the Imdugud-bird has built her nest, and rears her young. And here, in the trunk: the vampire Lilitu now resides, the maid of desolation, the eater of souls.'

I stared. Inanna's words fell upon me like the tolling of leaden bells. Was this what it was, to be king in Uruk? Must I carry out some impossible task every morning, and three to do on special days? The snake who knows no charm? The Imdugud-bird? The vampire Lilitu? There was indeed a hole in the ground at the base of the tree, opening between two of the huge tangled roots. I peered in, but I saw nothing. Nor could I see a nest in the crown, nor any demon-house in the middle of the trunk. I glanced from Inanna to Lugal-amarku, and back toward Inanna again. Three demons, and my task to drive them out! If only I could shrug, and walk away, and return to my palace to grapple with problems that could be seen and felt! But I could not. I must do Inanna's bidding in this thing, or all Uruk would know within the hour that Gilgamesh had shirked his tasks and that he feared the invisible world. I felt such despair as I cannot tell you, as I stood there thinking, *ah, my canals, my canals, my canals!*

Then I said, 'We will deal with these things, and quickly.'

I gave orders to Lugal-amarku to concoct a potion so foul, so stinking, that no creature could resist it, not even the snake who knows no charm. Bring it here within the hour, I told him. I sent one of the men of my band—he was the warrior Bir-hurturre, my

105

old schoolmate and boyhood tormentor, now taken into my closest counsel—back to the palace to fetch my great axe. And I bade the priestesses to get me a length of thick and sturdy rope from the Enmerkar temple. We would deal with these demons then and there. Even so early in my reign I had come to my basic idea of governing, which is that everything may be achieved through decisiveness and the show of clear determination.

The hunchback returned, not in an hour but in half that time, carrying a deep brazen beaker filled with some bubbling yellow stuff, flecked with bits of green and red, a substance so noxious and pestilent that I was surprised it did not eat holes in the bronze. He looked proud of himself. I clapped him lustily on his hump, rubbing it hard for luck, and cried, 'This will do it, Enlil! There's nothing better for the job!'

Gagging and half puking from the stench, I took the beaker from him and emptied it into the hole at the base of the tree. The earth hissed as that stuff touched it. I will offer an oath that the edges of the hole drew back as if in loathing. We waited. The snake who knows no charm obeys neither An nor Enlil nor even Inanna, the mistress of all serpents. But in moments there was a stirring in the earth, and angry yellow eyes flared within the hole, and a forked black tongue came flickering forth.

'Give me my axe,' I said quietly to Bir-hurturre.

Slowly, slowly, the snake glided from its hole. Its skin was dark as night, with bands of yellow upon it, and its supple body was nearly of the thickness of my arm. Behind me, the priestesses chanted holy names over and over and over, and even my own men were whispering incantations of defense. Yet I felt no fear of it, perhaps because it looked so forlorn, so sickened and bemired by Lugal-amarku's dreadful fluid. Ordinarily I am not one to slay an enemy whom I have at such a disadvantage; but there was no time for such tender niceties now. I raised my axe and in a single swift blow split that serpent in two. The sundered halves coiled and uncoiled and leaped wildly, and from the mouth of the snake came a wild roaring, and I think it meant to spit its venom upon me, but I was not harmed. I heard sobbing and prayer behind me.

After a few moments the snake lay still.

'One,' I said.

Now I took the thick rope from the temple, and wound it about the trunk of the tree, and tied it behind my back in such a way that when I put my feet against the tree and held the rope I could pull myself upward, and walk, more or less, up the side of the tree. This I did, higher and higher, climbing with ease. The bark was rough and ridged, and from it, as I bruised it with my feet, came the fragrance of almond blossoms, or of heavy wine.

Soon I reached the middle of the trunk, where they had told me the demoness Lilitu was making her home, that dark maid who dwells in ruined places and brings sorrow on wayfarers. I suppose that if I had allowed myself pause to think, I would have felt sore afraid. But there are times when it is perilous to pause to think. I held both ends of the rope in one hand and slapped the other lustily against the trunk. 'Lilitu? Lilitu? Do you hear me? I am Gilgamesh king of Uruk.' I laughed, to show I had no dread of her. 'Hear me, Lilitu! I forbid you this tree, which is Inanna's! I forbid you! I forbid you! Begone, begone, begone!' Would she obey? I believed she would. Inanna's name has great power among such creatures. I slapped the trunk twice more, but did not wait for an answer, and went climbing higher.

'Two,' I said.

In the crown of the tree, so Inanna had said, the Imdugud-bird nested her young. I peered through the close-packed branches and did not see her, but it seemed to me that I felt her presence. I pulled myself upward, no longer clambering up the trunk now but going hand over hand from branch to branch.

'Imdugud?' I said softly. 'Imdugud, it is I, Gilgamesh son of Lugalbanda.'

She is the most fearsome of birds, the storm bird, bearer of thunder and rain, whose body is that of an eagle and whose head is that of a lioness. She is the bird of destiny, who decrees the fates and utters the word which none may transgress; and she is bound to no city, to no god, but goes wherever she will, alone, independent. Yet I had no reason to fear her. My father had spoken of her often, and warmly. When he was young, in Enmerkar's time, he had gone at Enmerkar's behest as emissary to many distant realms, and his wanderings brought him at last to the land of Zabu at the end of the world. When he sought to go home to Uruk, he found that he could not, for that is a journey from which none return. Yet he was undaunted. He discovered in that land the nest of the Imdugud-bird, and when the Imdugud was away, Lugalbanda entered her nest, and offered honey and bread and sheep-fat to her young, and painted their faces with the colors of honor, and put crowns upon their heads. The Imdugud, when she returned, took great pleasure in what Lugalbanda had done, and bestowed her favor and friendship upon him, offering him whatever reward he would have of her. 'Decree a safe journey homeward for me, then,' he said, and so she did, and in time he made his way unharmed to his native city.

Gently I said, peering into the branches of the crown, 'I am the son of Lugalbanda, O Imdugud. But this tree is Inanna's; and I ask you in Lugalbanda's name to make your home elsewhere. Will you do that, Imdugud? For Lugalbanda's sake, who loved you well, will you do that?'

I heard no reply; and there was no movement in the almost leafless branches. I clung in silence, scarcely breathing. I did not feel the presence of the storm bird any longer. It seemed to me then that the Imdugud, if she truly nested there, had listened to me, and had obeyed, and had risen from the tree with her nestlings and now was soaring high above the Land. At any rate I gave her my thanks.

'Three!' I called to those who waited below.

Before I left the tree I climbed about in the crown, putting my feet in turn on each of the great branches. The sixth or seventh one that I came to had, I thought, something of death about it. It was stiff and unyielding, and felt dry and strange to the touch. Such a branch must be removed, or it would spread its deadly magic to the rest of the tree. So I called out to the onlookers to stand back, and raised my axe and hacked at the branch until I had severed it entirely. It was of immense size, as big in girth as some trees are altogether, and it was no small labor to cut it loose, but finally it fell. I hurled it outward so it would clear the branches below it and land in an open place of the garden. Then I swung myself downward, leaping the last of the way and landing on my feet with a joyous shout. Inanna, pale and silent, looked at me in a way I had never seen from her before: there was awe in her eyes.

'The demons are gone from your tree, lady,' I said.

I felt the warmth of work well done. Whether I had driven off Lilitu and the Imdugud, or even if they had truly been there, who can say? But about the snake there could be no doubt; and a little later in the winter the huluppu-tree of Inanna began to sprout new leaves, so that by spring it looked as healthy as it had before. Perhaps the fiery breath of the snake at its roots had been doing it injury, or perhaps the other two demons had indeed been haunting it as well. I could not say. I say only that the tree recovered, after I had done my work in it.

From the dead limb that I had cut off, Inanna had a throne and a couch made for herself. Out of the remaining wood she caused a gift to be fashioned for me, a drum and a drumstick, most elegantly carved by the craftsman Ur-nangar, whose hand must be guided by Enki himself. The drumstick was so perfectly balanced that it seemed almost to fly into my hand when I but reached for it, and it needed only the smallest movement of the wrist to make the most intricate of drummings. The drum itself was polished smooth until its surface felt like the skin of a maiden's buttocks; and for the drumhead Ur-nangar used the hide of an unborn gazelle, stretched taut and held in place by sinews made of its mother's gut. There has never been such a drum, nor such a drumstick, in all the world, to equal the one that Ur-nangar made for me at Inanna's behest. It is lost to me now, and I think not a day goes by but that I wished I had it again.

During the years that it was with me, I used the drum of Ur-nangar in two particular ways. One, that was best known to the citizens of Uruk, was as a summons of war: when it was time for the troops to gather, I went forth into the plaza outside the palace and beat a brisk tattoo, and everyone knew what I meant by it. 'Listen,' they would cry, 'Gilgamesh drums us to war!' And at its sound all the city began to stir, knowing that soon there would be new heroes made, and also new widows.

The other use for the drum was far more private. It was the doorway into the world of the gods, for me. Maybe there was goddess-power in the drum, coming as it had out of Inanna's holy huluppu-tree, or maybe some remnant of the Imdugud-bird's magic clung to it. I do not know.

This was its gift: when I retired to my innermost room and began quietly to beat on it in a certain way, it carried me up and out of myself and into that realm where Lugalbanda dwells. With it I could bring on at will all those things that arose in me when the god-aura was upon me. I would feel the droning and the buzzing, I would see a luminous glow in tones of gold or vermilion or deepest blue, I would find an entrance into another place, whether it was a ladder going up into the sky or a column of black water into which I sank or a tunnel, curving downward and away from me, inviting me to run along its shining cylindrical walls. And that place was the god-place. When I was there, I changed my shape, I soared, I flew. I shrieked like an eagle, I roared like a lion. I jouneyed into the underworld and into the lands of monsters. I supped with gods and demigods. I danced with spirits. I spoke the languages of dreams. I became the mate of the Thunderbird; I saw all things, all wisdom was open to me. I think Etana of Kish must have had such a drum, and made use of it in order to leap into the sky, instead of going aloft on the wings of an eagle as the old tale would have us believe.

I did not use the drum often that way. It was too strange and frightening, and too deep a drain on my energies, which I needed for the daily tasks of kingship. When I came back from such a flight, my jaws ached and sometimes my tongue was swollen as if I had bitten it in my ecstasies, and I felt dazed and weary for hours or even days afterward. So it was a secret thing, which I did only when the need was great upon me, whether for reasons of my own soul's hunger or because the city was faced with a peril that I alone could master. When I sat alone tapping on that drum I was close to being a god.

15

The rains returned, more intense than ever, and the problem of the canals became urgent.

In the days before my nation came into the Land, when the people of the Old Way were here, those who used sickles made of clay and lived in mud huts, there were no canals. Each spring, when the snows melted on the mountains of the north, the Two Rivers would rise and burst from their banks and the waters would pour out over the fields, drowning the crops and the villages. Some years the flooding was great, and the work of years was destroyed. In other years the waters retreated quickly under the hot sun of the dry season, and there was no moisture left to keep the crops alive. Even in the flood years, when water covered the valleys all summer long, much of the Land remained desert, too dry for any use, and there was no way of conveying the water from the drowned places to the parched places. It was a dreadful way to live.

When we conquered the goddess-people and took the Land from them, we found another way. It was Enlil's son who showed us, Ninurta, the warrior god, god of the stormy south wind.

It happened that Ninurta fell into a quarrel with the demon Asag, who dwelled in the nether world; and Ninurta went down into the nether world and slew this demon after a terrible battle. But the slaying of Asag loosed a great calamity upon the Land: for it was Asag who held in check the dragon Kur, which is the river that flows through the nether world. When Asag died, the Kur broke free and rose up out of the earth to the surface, and the vile waters of the subterranean river poured forth into the lands of daylight and everything was flooded.

Great were the lamentations of the gods who had charge of the fields and gardens, and those who carried the pickaxe and basket. The Kur covered the Land and famine was severe. Nothing grew except the weeds that will grow in all circumstances. But at this dark time Ninurta found a way. He gathered a heap of stones in the mountains and sent them floating like drifting rain clouds to the Land. These he piled up, then, over the place where the Kur had burst out of the nether world, and damned it so that its waters could no longer escape. Once this was achieved he built dikes to contain the flood-water, and canals to guide it into the beds of the Two Rivers and from the rivers to the fields. So the dragon was contained and its depredations halted. And now the fields brought forth abundant grain, the vineyards and orchards yielded their fruit, and the harvest was heaped up in great hills in the granaries.

Since then it has fallen to us to maintain and extend the canals: it is our chief work, the great duty that underlies all others, for on the canals all our prosperity depends. At times of high level on the rivers they allow us to lead the dangerous waters aside into storage channels. When the rivers begin to fall, we close the sluices, and retain the water to use in the dry months. Other canals carry water from these reservoirs into the cultivated fields, and even into lands that once were desert. Thus the rivers, once our great enemies, now are our servants. By controlling the level and the flow, we spare our fields from the menaces of flood and of drought. Quays and wharves now rise along the shores of our cities, where once we had only muddy swamps. All across the land spreads the network of water-channels, linking field to field, village to village, city to city.

But the soil of the land is deep and soft, and easily breaks away under the force of the current in spring, so that the canals are filled and silt blocks their mouths. We cannot afford that. If the canals become too shallow, water will not flow down from one to the next, and soon nothing will flow at all, and then when the rivers are in spate disaster will fall upon us as if the dragon Kur has returned. So we must toil constantly at maintaining the canals. It is each farmer's responsibility to look after his little canal, and it is the responsibility of the overseer of each village to see that the greater feeders are in order, and it is the responsibility of the officials of the government to survey the main channels. But the final responsibility falls to the king: he must understand the grand design, and know where it is weakening, and give the orders to send forth the armies of repair. Dumuzi had let that responsibility slip. For that alone, he can never be forgiven; and for that alone, he merited being sent to the House of Dust and Darkness.

There was little that I could do during the worst of the rainy season but look through the surveyors' reports, and decide where it was most essential to begin the repairs. Soon the tablets were piled high all about me, basket upon basket of them, bearing the close-packed inscriptions that told of Uruk's peril. Scribes stood at my right shoulder and at my left to read them to me, but I called upon them rarely: it seemed better to me to do my own reading, so long as I had the skill. It gave me a stronger grasp of what needed to be done.

In midwinter the rains relented, and we began our task. The rivers and canals were high from the constant downpours, but not seriously so: the real danger would not arrive until the snows of the north began to thaw. But there was little time to spare.

I chose as the place to begin the canal known as the Mouth of Ninmah, which lies just north of Uruk and conveys our drinking-water to us. It was in bad need of dredging and scouring, but that was no serious matter, for it called for nothing more than sweat and the straining of muscles. But also the embankments and regulating sluices were in need of rebuilding, particularly the main dam, which my engineers told me might very well be swept away by the first brunt of the spring flood.

It is an old custom, in starting any great work of construction, that the king must make and put into place the first brick. Whether this custom has been honored by each and every king, I cannot say; but I took gladly to it, since it has always been one of my great pleasures to toil as an artisan does. My star-watchers chose a propitious day for the ceremony. On the night before, I tied back my hair and went in a simple robe to the small temple of Enlil, where I bathed myself and spent the night alone, sleeping on the floor of black stone. In the morning the sun shone splendidly. I went to the temple of An and made an offering of cattle and goats without blemish. Then, at the shrine of Lugalbanda, I performed the ritual gesture of hand to the face, and felt the god my father stirring within me. And when the midday hour came I went to the place where bricks are made, wearing a head-pad and carrying builders' tools on my head.

Priests of the several craftsman-gods stood about me beating their drums as I began my task, working half-naked like any laborer in the sun. First I made a libation, pouring the water of good luck into the frame of the mold. Then I lit a fire of aromatic wood, to drive off impurities and any evil spirits that might be lurking about. I smeared the mold with honey and butter and fine oil of the best quality. Now I took the clay and wet it until it puddled, and mixed the straw with it, and trod upon it; I took the holy hod and scooped up the mixture, and pressed it into the mold; I smoothed the face of the bricks with my hands, and put them out in the drying-place to dry. There was no rain that night; I think I would have flayed my star-watchers alive if there had been. On the morrow, we had the ceremony of the breaking of the mold, when I kindled more aromatic wood, and seized the mold by its handles and drew it away, and lifted out the first brick. I raised it to the sky like a crown.

'Enlil is satisfied,' I cried.

Indeed he should have been. The brick was perfect. The gods had accepted my service, which was a sign that the period of trial was past and Uruk would be sustained.

Throughout those days I worked alongside the others in the making of bricks, and the transporting of them to the canal, and the stacking of them in great rows. Then, when the star-watchers once again announced a propitious day, we carried out the task of closing the flow into the canal. It was not easy; two men lost their lives at it. But we achieved it. In those days I knew no moderation, neither for myself nor for those about me, when there was the work of the city to be done. I stood for an hour in mid-winter, in the deepest part, holding my arms outstretched while they wove the fabric of the barrage about me. It was necessary for me to do it, not so much because I was king, but because I was the tallest and the strongest of the men. When we had accomplished the closing, we opened the farther sluices and drained the canal, and set about the job of repairing its lining. I placed the first brick, which was the brick I had made with my own hands on that other ceremonial day. We labored until darkness, and at dawn we returned, and so it was day after day: I would not let them rest, for the time was short and the task urgent. I never tired. When the others grew weary, I went among them, clapping my arm to their shoulders and saying, 'Come, fellow, rise up, the gods require our service!' And, weary as they were, they rose up and worked again. I drove them hard

114

—I drove them unsparingly—but I drove myself even harder. Great pyres of aromatic wood purified the place of our toil, and Enlil was pleased, and the work went swiftly and well. All was well with Uruk that winter. When the high waters came in spring, the canals received and stored the flow, and there was no flooding. I rejoiced in my kingship.

16

Then on the first day of summer messengers from Agga of Kish appeared, and demanded that I pay tribute to him.

There were three of them, officers of the court, men known to me from my stay in Kish. I did not realize, when they arrived, that they had come as enemies. I received them warmly and offered a great feast in their honor, and we sat far into the night, talking of times gone by, the feasts in the palace of Agga, wars against the Elamites, the turns of fate that had enmeshed this one and that one whom I had known in Kish. I opened the wine of the cask of Enki for them, and slaughtered three of the oxen of the fields of Enlil. 'Tell me,' I said, 'how goes it with the lordly Agga, my father, my benefactor?' And they told me that Agga was well, that his love for me was great, that when he spoke with his gods he never failed to ask them to provide for my continued welfare. I gave each of the envoys a choice concubine and sent them into the finest of the chambers of state for the night. The next day they told me they carried a message from Agga the king, and they put before me a tablet of large size, sealed in a jacket of costly white clay that bore the royal seal of Kish. Their eyes, when they put this tablet before me, were flickering swiftly; I should have taken that for a sign.

'We ask leave to withdraw,' they said, and I dismissed them.

When they were gone, I broke open the jacket of white clay and drew the tablet forth, and began to read it. And my eyes grew wider and wider with every line I read.

It began in a routine way, the usual formulas, *Agga son of Enmebarragesi, king of Kish, king of kings, lord of the Land by merit of Enlil and An, to his beloved son Gilgamesh son of Lugalbanda, lord of Kullab, lord of Eanna, king of Uruk by merit of Inanna,* and so on and so forth, followed by pious expressions of wishes for my continued good health and prosperity, and so on and so forth, followed by expressions of regret that Agga had heard no word lately from his beloved son Gilgamesh, no tidings of the kingdom which Agga had placed into the hands of his beloved son. That was my first hint of impending trouble, this reminder that Agga had helped to make me king of Uruk; it was true, yes, but perhaps it was a little tactless of him to call attention to the point. It was not as though he had raised me up out of utter obscurity to give me my crown: I was the son of a king, and the chosen of the goddess.

But swiftly I saw what he was after. It was implied right in his formula of greetings: 'king of kings, lord of the Land'. That was the ancient title of the king of Kish, which no one ever had formally bothered to challenge. But Agga's use of it now seemed plainly to say that he regarded me as a vassal. And, indeed, I *had* sworn an oath of fealty to him when I came as a young fugitive to his city. I read on, feeling a growing uneasiness.

Now began the demands for tribute.

He did not quite call it tribute. He spoke of it as the 'gift', the 'offering', the 'donation of my love'. But it was tribute, all the same. So many sheep, so many goats, so many barrels of oil, so many jars of honey; this many gur of date-wine, this many mana of silver, this many gu of wool, this many gin of fine linen; so many male slaves, so many female ones, of such-and-such ages. The request was couched in the most bland and pleasant terms, with no hint of ultimatum. He seemed to be saying that it was unnecessary for him to use threatening language, since these gifts and donations were self-evidently owing to him from me, from the loyal son to the benign father, from the vassal to the serene overlord.

I was thrown into confusion. This letter of Agga's stole not only my kingship but my manhood from me. Yet I had sworn fealty to him, had I not? By the net of Enlil I had sworn it. And now I was caught in that net. My cheeks blazed; tears of anger came to my eyes. I read his message four times over, and each time the words

116

were the same, and they were damning words. I should have foreseen this, but I had not. Agga had taken me in when I was homeless; Agga had given me rank and privilege in his city; Agga had conspired with Inanna to make me a king. And now he was presenting his bill. But how could I pay his price, and still hold my head up among the kings of the Land, and among the people of Uruk?

By darkness I went alone to the shrine of Lugalbanda and knelt and whispered, 'Father, what shall I do?'

The aura of the god came upon me and I heard Lugalbanda within me saying calmly, 'You owe Agga love and respect, and nothing more than that.'

'But my oath, father! My oath!'

'It said nothing of tribute. If you pay him these things, you sell yourself and your city to him forever. He is testing you. He wants to know whether he owns you. Does he own you?'

'No one owns me but the gods.'

'Then you know what you must do,' said Lugalbanda within me.

I passed the night in prayer, before this god and that, wandering restlessly about the city from temple to temple. The only one I did not consult was Inanna, though she was the goddess of the city. For to do that I would have to confess myself to the priestess Inanna, and I did not want her to know my shame in this matter.

In the morning, while the envoys of Agga were being diverted with women and singing, I sent out messengers to all the elders of the assembly, telling them to come at once to the palace. In rage and anxiety I strode back and forth before them, corded veins standing out on my neck, sweat on my forehead, until I could bring myself finally to speak.

Then I said, 'We are asked to submit to the house of Kish. We are called upon to pay tribute.' They began to mutter, those old men. I held up the tablet of Agga and shook it angrily and read the list of demands aloud. When I was done I stared about the room and saw their faces: pale, drawn, fear-ridden. 'How can we submit to this?' I asked. 'Are we vassals? Are we serfs?'

'Kish is very mighty,' said the landowner Enlil-ennam.

'The king of Kish is the overlord of the Land,' said old Ali-ellati, of venerable noble lineage.

'It is not a great amount of tribute,' said the wealthy Lu-Meshlam mildly.

And they all set up a nodding and a bowing and a muttering, and I saw that they were dead set against any defiance of Kish.

'We are a free city!' I cried. 'Are we to surrender?'

'There are wells to dig and canals to dredge,' said Ali-ellati. 'Let us pay what Agga demands, and go about our business in peace. War is very expensive.'

'And Kish is very mighty,' said Enlil-ennam.

'I call for your pledges,' I said. 'I will defy Agga: give me your support.'

'Peace,' they said. 'Tribute,' they said. 'There are wells to dig,' they said.

They would not hear of war. In despair I sent them away, and summoned the younger house of the assembly, the house of men. I read Agga's lists of demands to them, I spoke to them of my anger and indignation, and the house of men gave me the answers I wished to hear. I knew how to speak to them. I fanned the fires of their tempers, and appealed to their courage; for if they also went against me, I was lost. I had the power of overruling the elders if I must, but I could not make war if both the houses of the assembly were against me.

The house of men did not fail me. They gave me no talk of having wells to dig and canals to dredge. They shouted their scorn at the idea of tribute. I cried out for war, and they cried it louder back to me. Do not submit, they said. Let us smite the house of Kish with our weapons, they said. You will shatter Kish, they said—you, Gilgamesh, king and hero, conqueror, prince beloved of An. One after another the men of the house of men rose up and called out such ringing words as those. What was there to fear in the coming of Agga? they asked. His army is small, its rear-guard is feeble, its men are afraid to lift up their eyes.

I put a higher value on the army of Agga than they did, and I had better reason for my opinion. But I rejoiced at their words all the same, and my spirit brightened. For how could I have accepted vassalhood? Whatever Agga thought I might have pledged to him, my strength of kingship was at stake in this, my strength of manhood. I could not reign in Uruk at the sufferance of the king of Kish.

So, then, it was resolved: we would cast our lot for freedom. We would defy Agga. We would spend the summer preparing for war. Let him come, I said to the house of men. We will be ready for him.

I went to the palace and came upon the ambassadors of Agga in their debauch, and said to them, cold as stone, 'I have read the letter of my father Agga your king. And you may tell him this, that I overflow with boundless love for him, and I feel the highest gratitude for the favor he has shown me. I send him my warmest embrace. That is the only gift I send him: my warmest embrace. There is no need for any other gift-giving between father and son, is there? And Agga is my second father. Tell him, then: I embrace him.'

That night the envoys departed for Kish, carrying with them my filial embrace, and nothing more.

Now we began our preparations for war. I will not say that the prospect saddened me. I had not heard that wild hot music in the air since the days when I had fought for Agga in the land of Elam, and that was already several years behind me. A man must make war now and then, especially if he is king, or he will begin to rust from within: it is a matter of keeping one's edge, of maintaining the sharpness of one's spirit, which will go blunt soon enough in any case, but far more swiftly if left unhoned. So it was a time of polishing chariots, of oiling the shafts of javelins and spears, of sharpening blades, of taking the asses from the stables and letting them remember what it is like to run. Although the heavy heat of summer lay upon us, there seemed a crispness in the air of Uruk in those first few days as though it were the finest midwinter day. It was the excitement, the anticipation. The young men were as thirsty for battle as I was. That was why they had shouted down the elders, that was why they had voted for war.

But there was a surprise for us all. No one in the Land makes war in the summer, if it can be avoided. Why, in those months the air itself will go ablaze, if one moves too swiftly through it. So I was sure we had all the summer long to make ourselves ready for

Agga. I was wrong in that. My judgment was altogther confounded. For Agga must have been expecting my defiance, and his armies were ready; surely they must have set forth from Kish on the very day his envoys returned with my message. Trumpets brought me the news as I slept among my women, at dawn on the sultriest morning of the summer. Boats of Kish had come swiftly down the river, months before I expected them. The troops of Agga were at the quay. The waterfront was in their hands; the city was besieged.

It was the first full testing of my kingship. I had never led a city in war. I stepped out on the terrace of the palace and beat the war-drumming upon the drum that was made from Inanna's tree. It was the first time I had sounded that drumming in Uruk, though it would not be the last. My heroes gathered about me with darkened faces. They were uncertain of my leadership. Many had fought in the wars of Dumuzi, some had fought in the armies of Lugalbanda, there were even some who might remember Enmerkar; but not one had fought under me.

'Where is one with heart,' I said, 'who will go to Agga and ask him why he trespasses here?'

That splendid warrior Bir-hurturre stepped forth. His eyes were shining. He had grown tall and strong, and I think there was no man more valiant in all of Uruk. 'I am the one to go,' he replied.

I put troops behind each of the gates of the city wall, the High Gate and the Royal Gate and the North Gate and the Holy Gate, the Ur Gate and the Nippur Gate, and the rest. I sent patrols to move along the perimeter of the wall to guard against the men of Kish, should they try to scale the wall with ladders, or to chop their way through the brick. Then we opened the Water Gate, and Bir-hurturre went out to parley with Agga. But before he had gone ten paces the men of Kish seized him and dragged him away. This was done by the order of Agga son of Enmebaraggesi, he who had told me that heralds were under sacred protection. Perhaps he meant only the heralds of Kish.

Zabardi-bunugga came running to me with the news. 'They are torturing him, my lord! May Enlil eat their livers, they are torturing him!' Zabardi-bunugga was now my third-in-command, a sturdy man, no lovelier of face than he had been in boyhood, but loyal and steadfast. He told me that he had mounted the wall by the lookout post of Lugalbanda's tower and had seen the men of Kish assaulting Bir-hurturre in plain view, striking him, beating him, kicking him as he lay in the dust. 'Enlil will have their livers!' he cried. And he told me that when he had ascended the wall, the men of Kish had called out to him, asking if he were Gilgamesh the king. To which he had shouted back that he was not, that he was nothing in comparison with Gilgamesh the king.

'Will we ride out to them now?' he asked.

'Wait a little longer,' I answered him. 'I'll go up the wall so that I can see what kind of enemy we have.'

I strode quickly through the streets. Faces peered at me from the rooftops: the ordinary people, frightened, chilled. It was many years since an enemy had come to the gates of Uruk; they did not know what to expect, and they dreaded the worst. At the watchtower of Lugalbanda I ran up the wide brick stairs two and three at a time, carrying a yellow-and-blue banner that I had seized from one of the tower guardsmen, and I stepped out onto the wide platform at the top of the wall.

My blood sang in my ears as I looked out at that sea of invaders.

The longboats of Agga crowded our quays. The troops of Kish swaggered along the wharves. I saw the banners of Kish, crimson and emerald. I saw tough tanned faces, men I knew, the warriors with whom I had swept through the forces of Elam as though they were mere fleecy clouds. Under the fierce midsummer sun they wore their coats of thick black felt without show of discomfort; the light gleamed like fire from their shining copper helmets. I saw two of the sons of Agga; I saw six high officers of the Elam campaign; I saw Namhani, my old charioteer, and he saw me and waved and pointed and grinned his snag-toothed grin, and called me by the name by which I had been known in Kish.

'No,' I roared back. 'Gilgamesh! I am Gilgamesh!'

'Gilgamesh,' they answered me. 'Look, it is Gilgamesh, Gilgamesh the king!'

I carried no shield and I stood exposed against the sky, but I felt no fear. They would not dare aim a shaft at the king of Uruk.

I scanned them from south to north, the hundreds of them, perhaps the thousands. They had set up tents; they were here to stay for a lengthy siege.

'Where is Agga?' I called. 'Bring out your king. Or is he afraid to show himself?'

Agga came. If I was unafraid of showing myself upon the wall, he could do no less. From one of the far tents he emerged, moving slowly, fatter than ever, a mountain of flesh, pink-skinned, freshly shaved from scalp to chin. He carried no weapons; he leaned on a staff of black wood carved in curves and angles that troubled my eye. When he stood close below me I made a gracious sign of reverence to him and said in a calm voice, 'I bid you welcome to my city, father Agga. If you had sent word of your visit, I would have been better prepared to entertain you.'

'You look well, Gilgamesh. I thank you for the embrace you sent me.'

'It was only my obligation.'

'I had expected more.'

'Indeed, so you had. Where is my herald Bir-hurturre, father Agga?'

'We are discussing matters with him, in one of our tents.'

'They tell me he was beaten and kicked and thrown down in the dust, and taken off for torture, father Agga. I think I treated your envoys with more kindness.'

'He was unruly. He lacked politeness. We are teaching him courtesy, my son.'

'In Uruk I teach such lessons, and no one else,' I said. 'Return him to me, and then I will invite you within for the feast that is my obligation to so noble a guest as you.'

'Ah,' said Agga, 'I think I will invite myself within. And I will bring your lackey with me, when I am done with him. The lord of the Land decrees it.'

'So be it,' I replied. I turned away, and threw down my banner on the side within the wall. It was the signal: we opened every gate at once, and came riding forth upon the men of Kish.

When an enemy comes to the gate of a walled city, it is often best to wait within, especially if the enemy has been so rash as to arrive in summer. In that dry time there is no food outside the walls,

122

except whatever is stored in the outlying granaries, and when that is gone, there will be nothing left for the besiegers. Within, we had supplies enough to see us through to winter, and fresh water aplenty. They would suffer more keenly than we, and eventually they would withdraw: that is the usual wisdom.

But the usual wisdom usually does not apply. Agga understood these things as well as I; far better, in fact. If he had chosen to lay siege in summer, plainly he did not mean the siege to be a lengthy one. And so I guessed that he intended a direct attack. The walls of Uruk—Enmerkar built them—were not high, then, as the walls of great cities go. No doubt there were ladders aplenty on those boats of Agga's, and in a little while warriors of Kish would be scrambling up our walls in a hundred places at once. Meanwhile their axewielders would be attempting to breach the ramparts from below: I knew those axes of Kish, which could readily cut through the old bricks of our wall. So it was pointless to sit inside the city waiting for them to attack. I had more men at my command than Agga had brought with him; once they were within the walls, tossing torches about, we would be at their mercy, but if I could defeat them on the quay we would be saved. We had to carry the attack to them.

We burst forth in chariots out of five gates at once. I think they had not expected us to emerge so soon, or even for us to emerge at all. They were confident and arrogant, and thought I would bow my knee to Agga without a struggle. But we fell upon them with axes high and spears flashing. Zabardi-bunugga's chariot was in the vanguard, with ten others just behind it, carrying the finest heroes of the city. The men of Kish met that first wave with valor and energy. I knew how well they could fight; I knew them, indeed, better than my own soldiers. But while the first skirmishes were under way I came down from the wall and entered my own chariot, and led the second wave of the assault myself.

I will be very plain about it: when the men of Kish beheld me, it struck them with terror and froze their souls. They had known me in the Elam wars, but though they remembered me they did not remember me as well as they should have, until they saw me riding into their midst, casting my javelin equally well with my right hand and my left. Only then did they remember.

'It is the son of Lugalbanda!' they cried, and they began to panic.

There is no pretending otherwise: I know no finer music than the music that sings through the air of the battlefield. Joy rose in me, and I rode into the enemy like the emissary of death. My charioteer that day was the brave Enkimansi, a narrow-faced man of thirty years who acknowledged no fear whatever. He drove the asses forward, and I stood high behind him, hurling my weapons as though I bore the wrath of Enlil upon Kish. My first cast took the life of a son of Agga; my second and third slew two of his generals; my fourth pierced the throat of one of the envoys who had borne Agga's message to me. 'Lugalbanda!' I cried. 'Sky-father! Inanna! Inanna! Inanna!' It was a cry that these men of Kish had heard before. They knew that a god rode among them that day, or at least a godling, with divine keenness to his sight and divine strength to his arm.

Into the breach made by Zabardi-bunugga and the rest of the front line of chariots I followed, cutting a deep hole in the forces of Kish. Behind me came my footsoldiers, crying out, 'Gilgamesh! Inanna! Gilgamesh! Inanna!'

I give the men of Kish credit for courage. They tried their best to slay me, and only some fast work with my shield and some deft maneuvering by the skillful Enkimansi kept me from harm. But there was no halting me. Terror overcame them despite themselves, and they turned and ran toward the water; but we cut them off from the sides and began to chop them apart.

It was over far more swiftly than I could have hoped. We sent multitudes of them rolling in the dust. We reached their longboats and took them, and cut their prows off and carried the images of Enlil away as trophies. We got Bir-hurturre free, and found him still well, though he had been shamefully bloodied and bruised. As for Agga, we fought our way through to him—he was no fighter himself, not at his age, but he was surrounded by a ring of a hundred picked guardsmen, who perished to the last man—and took him prisoner. Zabardi-bunugga led him to me as I stood leaning against my chariot, drinking a flask of beer of Kish that I had taken from one of the stewards.

Agga was dusty and sweating and flushed, and his eyes were red with weariness and dismay. There was a small wound on his left shoulder, only a scratch, but it shamed me to see that he had been touched. I gestured to one of my field surgeons. 'Clean and bind the wound of the king of kings,' I said. Then I went up to Agga and to his amazement I knelt before him. 'Father,' I said. 'Royal master of the Land.'

'Don't mock me, Gilgamesh,' he muttered.

I shook my head. Rising, I put the flask of beer in his hand, saying, 'Take this. It will ease your thirst, father.'

He regarded me bleakly. Slowly he put his hand to his belly and kneaded the thick rolls of flesh. Rivulets of sweat ran down him, cutting through the dust that lay on his skin. I will not deny it: I savored my triumph, I doted on his discomfiture. It was sweet wine to me.

'What will you do with me?' he asked.

'You will be my guest at the palace this evening, and for two days thereafter. Then we will have the rite of the burying of the dead; and then I will send you back to Kish. For are you not my lord, the king of kings, to whom I have sworn my loyalty?'

He understood me now, and anger flared in his eyes; but then he laughed, and looked sadly about his warriors and his sons heaped in the blood-soaked dust, and his mutilated longboats, and he nodded. 'Ah, is that it?' he said after a time. 'I did not think you were so shrewd.'

'My debt is paid now, is that the case?'

'Ah,' he said, 'that is the case. Your debt is paid, Gilgamesh.'

17

So it was done. I gave a great feast to Agga, and sent him back to Kish with what was left of his army.

But before he left I had sad news from him: my wife Ama-sukkul his daughter was dead, and both the children she had borne for me. These tidings went through me like blades. Death, there is no place to hide from you! I thought of how on my last day at Kish I had embraced her and patted her swelling belly so lovingly. The child in being born had been the death of her, though, and he perished with her; and then our first-born son had languished for lack of his mother and went quickly from the world. Doubtless the gods had not intended for me to plant my seed in Kish. I have had other sons since, many of them, but I wonder often what those two would have been like had they grown to manhood. And the sweet little Ama-sukkul: she was a gentle person and not the least loved of my wives.

In the hour of Agga's departure I insisted on pledging myself once again in fealty to him. This I did of my own free will, as everyone saw. Such a pledge given freely is a sign not of submission but of strength: it is a gift, it is a splendid offering, which loosed me rather than bound me. It was my way of acknowledging what Agga had done for me in the past, when he helped me gain my kingship upon the death of Dumuzi, and it freed me forever from any real sort of vassalage. At last I was king in my own right, through prowess in battle and greatness of soul. It would not be wrong to say that the true beginning of my reign could be dated to the time of the war with Kish.

But if it was the true beginning of my kingship, it was the end of Agga's, though he lived on a little while after. He withdrew within the walls of Kish and was not heard from again outside it. When he died it was the end of the dynasty of Kish after thousands of years, for Mesannepadda king of Ur marched north and seized the city. Soon we had reports that Mesannepadda had put to death the last of Agga's sons and taken the throne for himself; and thereafter he called himself king of Kish instead of king of Ur. I allowed this to happen because I was preoccupied with other matters at that time, as I will duly tell; and later I had my own reckoning to make with the king of Ur and Kish.

The first thing I did, when the excitement of the war had begun to recede a little into memory, was to rebuild the walls of Uruk. In truth I did not so much rebuild them as build them anew, for the old walls of Uruk were as no walls at all, compared with the ones that I constructed for the city. Perhaps they were good enough for

Enmerkar's time; but I had seen the walls of Kish. I knew what city walls should be.

A wall must be high, so that the enemy cannot scale it with his ladders. It must be thick, so it cannot easily be breached. It must have a deep and broadly based foundation, so it cannot be undermined and tunnels cannot be dug beneath it. All that is evident enough; but the walls of Uruk were barely adequate in all those respects. We needed, also, more towers from which we could observe the approaches to the city, and a wide parapet along the top of the wall where defenders could take up positions and aim their fire upon the heads of the invaders. In particular there had to be guard-towers and parapets flanking each of the city gates, since the gates are the weak points in any wall.

All the rest of the summer there was scarcely anything done in Uruk but the making of bricks and the building of the wall that I think will be known until the end of days as the Wall of Gilgamesh. As in the repair of the canals, I worked alongside the common artisans, and I think no one worked as hard as I: I built that wall with my own hands, and that is the truth. Nor was there any artisan more skillful than I in the placing of the bricks as it must be done, on edge, leaning sideways against one another in careful rows, each row leaning in the direction opposite the one below it. That is the only true way to build. We ripped away the old wall of Enmerkar so that the city stood naked, and then, quickly as we could, we put up the new wall, or, rather, the walls, for there are two of them. The seven wise sages themselves could not have designed a better plan. I used only kiln-baked bricks, for what is the use of building with mud, and having to do it all over again five years later? And they were the finest of bricks. The outer wall shines with the brightest of copper, and the inner wall, a gleaming white, is a wall without equal anywhere. The foundation terrace is, I think, the mightiest ever built. The wall of Uruk is famous throughout the world. It will last twelve thousand years, or I am not Lugalbanda's son.

I would not have you believe we finished the entire wall in a single summer. In truth, there has been no year of my reign when we have not continued to work on it, strengthening it, increasing its height, adding new parapets and watchtowers. But in that first summer we built the greater part of it, sufficient to defend us against any enemy we could imagine.

In those early months I was in the fullest flush and most robust joy of my kingship. Scarcely did I even take the time to sleep. I worked all day at the things a king must do, and made my people work as I did. I suppose I made them work too hard; indeed, I drove them to exhaustion, and they began to call me tyrant behind my back. But I did not realize that. My energies were immense, and I did not understand that theirs were not. When their day's toil was done, they wanted nothing but sleep. But I would feast magnificently with my court by evening, and then at night there were the women. Perhaps I was excessive, with the women, though I did not think so then. My appetite for them was like the unceasing hunger of the gods for meat and drink. I had my concubines, I had the priestesses of the holy cloister, I had the casual women of the town, and even they were not sufficient. You must never forget that I am in part a god, by my descent from Lugalbanda, and also from Enmerkar who called himself the son of the sun; and a god's force blazes within me. How could I deny that force? How could I stifle it? The god-presence throbbed in me like the beating of a drum, and I marched to its tune.

Within my joy and vigor, though, I must tell you there was a hidden melancholy. All Uruk waited upon me, yet I never could forget that I was a man alone, a lofty and isolated figure. Perhaps it is that way with everyone: I do not know. But it seems to me that others are bound in close league with wives, sons, friends, companions. I who had never had a brother, who had scarcely known his father, who had been set apart by size and strength from his playfellows, was now as king cut off as though by colossal walls from the normal flow of human intercourse. There was no one around me who did not fear me and envy me and in some way draw back from me. And I saw no way of altering that; but the toil by day and the feasting by evening and the women by night were my consolations for this pain of separation. Especially the women.

My chamberlain of the royal concubines was hard pressed to meet my needs. When the wandering tribesfolk of the desert came to Uruk for the market, he brought their girls to me, tawny long-legged girls with dark shadows about their eyes, and wide thin-lipped mouths. When wedding contracts were drawn in the city, the brides were given first to me before their husbands had them, so that I might bring divine grace upon them. If the wife of one of my noblemen pleased me, that man would convey her to the palace for the night without murmur, should I ask for her. No one spoke out against me. No one would; no one could; I was the king; my strength was like the strength of the host of heaven. I saw nothing wrong in what I did. Was it not my privilege, as king, as god, as shepherd of the people? Could I be left in need, when my hungers raged so powerfully? Ah, the wine, the beer, the music, the singing of those nights! And the women, the women, their sweet lips, their smooth thighs, their swaying breasts! I never rested. I never halted. The beating of the drum was unrelenting. By day I led the men in the building of walls or the playing of the games of war, until they were dull-eyed and drooping with fatigue, and by night I swept my way through their women as a raging fire roars through the dry grass of summer.

I never grew weary. I was making Uruk weary of me, but I did not know that yet.

Now it was the season of the new year, and once again the time of the Sacred Marriage arrived. I had been king of Uruk a year and some months. Tonight the goddess would open to me for the second time. I performed the rituals of purification, I meditated in darkness and silence in the Dumuzi-house, and when evening came they took me in the traditional way, by boat, toward my union with Inanna.

And as I debarked at the very quay where I had shattered the forces of Agga, and strode into the city through a gate in the wall I had built with my own hands, I felt a great surge of pride in what I had achieved. I felt like a god, in truth: not like one who merely has some godly blood in his veins, but in truth a god, a wearer of the horned crown, who walks through the bright heavens in splendor. Was I wrong, to feel such pride? I had come from exile to receive the crown; I had repaired the canals; I had crushed the most powerful of foes; I had built the walls of Uruk, and all this before I had reached my twentieth year. Was that not godlike to have done? Did I not have reason for pride?

And now the goddess awaited me.

In these months I had had little in the way of dealings with her, only the customary sacrifices and rituals that required both our presences. We had scarcely spoken otherwise. There were times when I could have gone to her to seek counsel or blessing, and I had not. There were times when she might have sought me out, and she did not. I think I understood even then why we were keeping such a wary distance from one another. In Uruk we were like rival kings; she had her zone of power, and I had mine. But already I was extending the reach of my zone. This was not with the intent of provoking her enmity, but simply because I knew no way to be king, other than to exercise power to the fullest. When I had made war on Agga, I had not asked her consent: it seemed too risky, when I had already met the opposition of the house of elders to the war. The war had to be fought; and with Inanna against me I would not be able to levy the army I needed; and therefore I did not consult Inanna. I feared the interference her power could create. I was even then concerned with placing myself beyond the range of that power. And, she, seeing the growing strength of my own authority, had drawn back, uncertain of my intentions, unwilling to challenge me before she understood my purposes more completely.

But on the night of the Sacred Marriage all such dreary considerations of state are set aside. I went to her in the long chamber of the temple and found her glittering in her oils and ornaments. I hailed her as my holy jewel, and she greeted me as royal husband, fountain of life; and we performed the rite of the showing-forth; and when that was done we went within, to the chamber of the sweet-smelling green rushes, and the handmaidens of the goddess undid her sheaths of alabaster and plates of gold and left her naked to me.

When we were alone I put my hands to her sleek shoulders, and stared deep into the shining mysteries of her eyes, and she smiled at me as she had smiled that first time when we were children, a smile that was in part warm and loving, in part fierce, intense, challenging. I knew she would devour me if she could. But on this night she was mine. She had grown no less beautiful in the twelve months gone by. Her bosom was deep, her waist narrow, her hips were broad; her fingernails were long as daggers, and painted the color of the moon in eclipse. She beckoned me to the bed with a single small gesture of her hand.

We glided down to it and embraced. Her skin was like the fabrics they weave in heaven. My body rose over hers. Her back was arched beneath me. Her fingers dug into the cords and sinews of my shoulders, and she drew her knees toward her breasts and turned them outward, and her lips parted, her tongue came flickering out, her breathing was a thick heavy hissing. She kept her eyes open all the while, as women rarely do. I saw that. For I kept my eyes open also, throughout every moment of that night.

At dawn I heard the coming of the new year's first rain, a faint muffled drumming against the ancient white brick of the temple platform. I slipped from the bed and looked about me for my robe, so that I could take my leave. She lay facing me; she was watching me the way a serpent watches its prey.

'Stay a while longer,' she said softly. 'The night is not yet done.'

'The drum is beating. I must go.'

'All the city sleeps. Your friends lie sprawled in drunken dreams. What can you do alone at this hour?' She made a purring sound. I mistrust serpents that purr. 'Come back to my bed, Gilgamesh. The night is not yet done, I tell you.'

With a smile I said, '*You* are not yet done, you mean.'

'And are you, then?'

I shrugged. 'We have performed the rite. And performed it amply, I think.'

'So the insatiable one is sated, for the moment? Or are you merely bored with me, and ready to begin the search for your next woman of the day?'

'You speak cruelly, Inanna.'

'But not without truth, Gilgamesh? You never have enough. Not enough women, not enough wine, not enough toil, not enough warfare. You rage through Uruk like a torrent, sweeping everything before you. You are a burden under which all the city groans. The people cry out for mercy from you, so terribly do you oppress them.'

That stung me. My eyes went wide with surprise. 'I, an oppressor? I am a just and wise king, lady!'

'Perhaps you are. No doubt you think you are. But you

overwhelm and crush your own people. You march the young men up and down the drilling-fields, up and down and up and down, until everything gets black before their eyes and they fall down from exhaustion, and still you have no mercy on them. And the women! No one has ever consumed women as you do. You use them as though they are playthings, five, six, ten a night. I hear the stories.'

'Not ten,' I said. 'Not six, not five.'

She smiled. 'That is how they tell it. They say that no one can content you, that you are like a wild bull. They look at me and say, 'Only a goddess can satisfy him.' Well, there is a goddess within me, and you and I have passed this night together. Are you content, for once? Is that why you are so eager now to leave?'

I was eager to leave now because I had no defense against this onslaught of hers. But I would not admit that to her. Stiffly I said, 'I wish to walk by myself in the rain.'

'Walk, then, and then come back.' Her eyes flashed. She had the force within her of a snapping whip. I picked up my robe, hesitated, let it fall again and stood naked before her. There was the musky odor of our night's lovemaking in the chamber. The last of the incense still sputtered in the bowl. Her lips were taut, her nostrils were flaring. In a low harsh voice she said, 'Will you come back? For you there are ten women every night, Gilgamesh. For me there is only you, one night a year.'

Suddenly I feared her less, hearing her trying to wheedle me that way with pity.

'Ah, is that how it is, Inanna? No one else, all the year long?'

'Who else but the god may touch the goddess, do you think?'

I grew more bold. I dared to tease her a little. 'Not even in secret?' I asked playfully. 'Some lusty slave, summoned in the darkest watch of the night—'

Fury flared in her. She pulled her hands toward her breasts. Her fingers tightened, so that they looked like claws. 'You say such a thing, under the temple's own roof? Shame, Gilgamesh! Shame!' Then she softened. Cat-like still, she stretched, she purred again, she raised one knee and let her foot slide down the calf of her other leg. More gently she said, 'There is only you, one night of the year. I swear it, though it makes me feel soiled that you should require me to take oath on it. There is only you. I am not yet ready to let you leave me. Will you stay? Will you stay just a little while longer? It is only the one night I have, this one night.'

'Let me cleanse myself first in the rain,' I said.

I stood some time outside the temple, in the virgin air of the rainswept dawn. Then I went back to her. Cat or serpent, priestess or goddess, I could not refuse her, not if it was the only night of the year that she might know an embrace. And the rain, washing the night's staleness from me, had reawakened my strength and my desires anyway. I would not refuse her. I wanted her. I went to her and we began the night afresh.

18

Early in the new year a strange dream came to me, and I was unable to make any sense of it. Later that night came a second dream just as strange, just as unreadable.

I was troubled that I had so little understanding of these dreams. The gods often speak to kings as they sleep, and perhaps I was being given some knowledge important to the welfare of the city. So I went to the temple of An and took my dreams to my mother the wise priestess Ninsun.

She received me in her chamber, a dark-walled room with heavy pilasters painted crimson. Her cloak was black, bordered below with a broad band of beads of lapis, gold, and carnelian. There was about her, as always, a supreme tranquility and beauty: all might be in turbulence, but she was ever at peace.

She took my hands between her small cool ones and held them a long while, smiling, waiting for me to speak.

'Last night,' I said after a time, 'I dreamed that a feeling of great happiness came upon me, and I walked full of joy among the other young heroes. Night fell, and the stars appeared in the heavens. And as I stood beneath them one of the stars plunged to earth, a star that bore in itself the essence of Sky-father An. I tried to lift it, but it was too heavy for me. I tried to move it, but I could not. All Uruk gathered around to watch. The common people jostled; the noblemen dropped down and kissed the ground before the star. And I was drawn to it as I would be drawn to a woman. I put a carrying-strap on my forehead and braced myself and with the help of the young heroes I lifted it and carried it to you. And you told me, mother, that the star was my brother. That was the dream. Its meaning baffles me.'

Ninsun appeared to stare off into some great empty space. Then she said, still smiling, 'I know the meaning.'

'Tell me, then.'

'This star of heaven, that attracted you as a woman might attract you—it is a strong companion, it is a loyal friend, your rescuer, your comrade who will never forsake you. His strength is like the strength of An, and you will love him as you love yourself.'

I frowned, thinking of that vast loneliness that I believed was the inescapable price of my kingship, and how weary I was of it.

'Friend? What friend do you mean, mother?'

'You will know him when he comes,' she said.

I said, 'Mother, I dreamed a second dream the same night.'

She nodded. She seemed to know.

'An axe of a strange shape was lying in the streets of great-walled Uruk,' I said, 'an axe unlike any of the axes familiar to us. All the people were gathering around it, staring, whispering. As soon as I saw it, I rejoiced. I loved it: again, I was drawn to it as I would be to a woman. I took it and fastened it at my side. That was the second dream.'

'The axe you saw is a man. He is the comrade who is destined for you—'

'The comrade, again!'

'The comrade again, yes. The brave companion who rescues his friend in a time of need. He will come to you.'

'May the gods send him swiftly, then,' I said with great fervor.

And I leaned forward close to her and told her something I had never revealed to anyone before: that I was in terrible need, that a great chilling loneliness assailed me in the midst of all my power and plenty. Those were not easy words to speak. Twice my tongue stuck fast, but I forced it to say the words. My mother Ninsun smiled and nodded. She knew. I think it was she that had induced the gods to fashion a companion for me. When I left her temple that morning I felt a lightness in my soul, as of the lifting of storm-clouds after they have hung heavy in the air for many days.

About the time these dreams were coming to me a great strangeness—so I was afterward told—was befalling a man I did not know, a certain hunter, Ku-ninda by name. This Ku-ninda was a man of one of the outlying villages, who had his livelihood from trapping wild game; but this time when he went out into the wilderness on the far side of the river to inspect the traps he had set, he found them all torn apart. Whatever beasts might have been snared in them had been set free. And when he went to look into the pits he had dug, he discovered that they had all been filled in.

This was a great mystery to Ku-ninda. No civilized person will disturb the traps of a hunter or fill in his pits: it is a discourtesy, and an ignoble act. So Ku-ninda searched for the man who had done these things to him; and soon enough he caught sight of him. But he was like no man Ku-ninda had ever seen. He was of huge size, naked, rough and shaggy all over, covered with dark coarse hair everywhere, more like a beast than a man, a wild creature of the hills. He carried himself like an animal, crouching, grunting, snorting, running swiftly on the balls of his feet. The beasts of the wilderness seemed to have no fear of him, but ran freely at his side: Ku-ninda saw the wild man among the gazelles on the high ridges, grazing with them, fondling them, eating grass as they ate grass. Ku-ninda was troubled by the strangeness of what he saw. He made more traps. The wild man sought them out and destroyed them, every one. One day Ku-ninda encountered the wild man at the watering-hole: they stood face to face. 'You, wild one: why do you disturb my traps?' Ku-ninda demanded. The wild man made no reply, but only sniffed the air. He growled, he snarled, he bared his teeth, he glared with fiery eyes. A spume of spittle came forth and rolled down into his thick beard. Ku-ninda was no coward, but he shrank back: his face was frozen with fear, and terror numbed his limbs. Again the next day they met at the watering-place, and the day after that, and each time, when the wild man saw Ku-ninda, he growled and snarled, and Ku-ninda did not dare go near him. And at last, seeing that the shaggy stranger was making it impossible for him to hunt, Ku-ninda yielded, and went back empty-handed to his village, greatly downcast.

He told this tale to his father, who said, 'Go you to Uruk, and set yourself before Gilgamesh the king. There is no one more mighty than he: he will find a way to help you.'

When next it was my audience-day for the common people, there was this Ku-ninda waiting in the audience-hall, a strong and sturdy man of more than middle height, with a lean hard face and keen penetrating eyes. He was clad in black skins, and he had the smell of sinews and blood about him. He put an offering of meat before me and said, 'There is a wild fellow in the fields who tears up my traps and frees my catch. He is as strong as the host of heaven and I dare not approach him.'

It seemed strange to me that this sturdy Ku-ninda could show fear of anyone or anything. I asked him to tell me more, and he spoke of the growling, the snarling, the baring of teeth; he told me how the wild man ran with the gazelles on the high ridges, and grazed beside them in the grass. Something in that stirred me deeply and held me fascinated. My skin crept a little with wonder and amazement, and the hair prickled on my neck. 'What a marvel,' I said. 'What a mystery!'

'Will you slay this creature for me, O king?'

'Slay him? I think not: it would be a pity to slay him for no other reason than being wild. But we can't let him run loose in the fields, I suppose. We will trap him, I think.'

'Impossible, majesty!' Ku-ninda cried out. 'You have not seen him! His strength is as great as yours! There is no trap that could hold him!'

'There is one, I think,' I said, with a smile.

An idea had come to me as Ku-ninda spoke: a notion out of one of the old tales that the harper Ur-kununna had sung in the courtyard of the palace when I was a boy. I think it was the tale of the goddess Nawirtum and the devil-monster Zababa-shum, or perhaps the goddess was Ninshubur and the monster was Lahamu: I do not remember, and the names are I suppose not important. The point of the tale was the power of womanly beauty over the forces of violence and savagery. I sent to the temple cloister for the holy courtesan Abisimti, she of the round breasts and long shining hair who had initiated me into the rites of fleshly love when I was young, and told her what I would have to do. She hesitated not at all. There was true holiness in Abisimti. She was in all ways a servant of heaven, and her way of giving service was to give it without question, which is the only true way.

So Ku-ninda took Abisimti with him out onto the steppe, out into the hunting-lands, to the watering-hole where Ku-ninda had had his encounters with the wild man, three days' journey from Uruk. There they waited a day and a second day, and the wild man was among them. 'That's the one,' said Ku-ninda. 'Go to him now, use your arts upon him.'

All unafraid and unashamed, Abisimti went to him and stood before him. He growled, he grunted, he frowned, not knowing what sort of creature she might be; but he did not snarl, he did not bare his teeth. She unfastened her robe and disclosed her breasts to him. I think he must have never seen a woman before, but the power of the goddess is great, and the goddess made the beauty of the holy whore Abisimti manifest to his understanding. She uncovered herself and showed him her soft ripe nakedness, and let him fill his nostrils with the rich perfume of her, and lay down with him and caressed him, and drew him down atop her so that he might possess her.

It was his initiation. He had been like a beast; by embracing her he became like a man. Or it would be just as true to say that by embracing her he became a god. For that is the way that the divine essence enters into us, through the rite of the true life-giving act.

Six days and seven nights they lay together coupling. I will testify myself to Abisimti's skills: I could have sent no one to him who was wiser in the ways of the flesh. When she lay with Enkidu—for that was the wild man's name, Enkidu—she surely must have made use of all her wisdom with him, and after that he could never be the same. In those hot days and nights the wilderness was burned from him in the forge of Abisimti's passion. He softened, he grew more gentle, he gave up his savage grunting and growling. The power of speech came into him; he became like a man.

But he did not know yet what had befallen him. When he had

taken his fill with her, he rose to return to his beasts. But the gazelles ran off in fright as he approached. The smell of mankind was on him now, the smell of civilization. The wild creatures of the steppe no longer knew him, and they drew away from him. As they fled he would have followed them, but his body was held back as though bound with a cord, his knees would not serve him, all his swiftness was gone. Slowly, bewilderedly, he made his way back to Abisimti, who smiled tenderly and drew him down beside her. 'You are no longer wild,' she said, with gestures more than with words, for he was not yet good with words. 'Why do you still want to roam with the beasts of the steppe?'

Now she told him of the gods, and of the Land, and of the cities of men, and of great-walled Uruk, and of Gilgamesh its king. 'Rise up,' she said. 'Come with me to Uruk, where every day is a festive day, where the people are resplendent in wondrous robes. Come to the temple of the goddess, that she may make you welcome in the world of men, and to the temple of the Sky-father, where you will receive heaven's blessing. And I will show you Gilgamesh, the joyful king, the hero radiant in manhood, strongest of men, who lords it over one and all.' And at those last words his eyes grew bright and his face became hot, and he said, in his thick-tongued way that was still freighted with the sounds of the beasts, that he would indeed go with her to Uruk, and to the temple of Inanna and the temple of An. But chiefly he wished to be shown this Gilgamesh, this king, this so-called strong man. 'I mean to challenge him,' Enkidu cried. 'I will show him which one of us is stronger. I will let him feel the might of the man of the steppes. I will change things in Uruk, I will reshape destinies, I who am the strongest of all!' Or such, at any rate, were the words that Abisimti reported to me afterward.

Thus was it carried out, the snaring of the wild man Enkidu. In accordance with the strategy I had devised, he was caught in the softest and sweetest of traps, and brought away from the fields of beasts into the world of settled folk.

Abisimti divided her garments, clothing him with one half and herself with the other, and took him by the hand; and like a mother she led him to the place of the sheepfolds close by the city. The shepherds gathered around him: they had never seen anyone like him. When they offered him bread, he did not know what to do with it, and held it in his hand staring at it, confused, embarrassed. He was accustomed to eating only the wild grasses and berries of the fields, and to sucking the milk of wild creatures. They gave him wine, and it bewildered him, and when he tasted it it made him gag and choke, and he spat it out.

Abisimti said, 'This is bread, Enkidu: it is the staff of life. This is wine. Eat the bread, drink the wine: it is the custom of the Land.'

Cautiously he nibbled, cautiously he sipped. His fear went from him; he smiled, he ate more gladly, he gobbled bread until he was full, he drank down seven goblets of strong wine. His face glowed, his heart exulted; he leaped about, he danced a merry dance. Then they took him and they groomed him, they rubbed the tangles out of his matted hair, they trimmed him and clipped him and anointed him with oil, and gave him decent clothing, so that he came to look more like a human being, although one who was of more than usual size and more than usual hairiness.

He lived some while among the shepherds. Not only did he learn to eat the food of men and drink the drink of men and wear the clothes of men; Enkidu learned to work as men must do. The shepherds taught him how to use weapons, and made him the watchman of their flocks. By night, while the herdsmen slept peacefully, he patrolled the fields, driving away the beasts that came to raid the sheepfold. He chased lions, he caught wolves, he was the tireless guardian of the sheep—he who had been as a wild beast himself. No word of any of this was brought to me. I confess that I had forgotten all about the wild man of the steppes, so busy was I with the tasks of kingship and with the pleasures by which I eased my heart's ache.

One day at this time Enkidu and Abisimti were sitting in a tavern that the herdsmen were fond of frequenting, when a wayfarer came in, a man of Uruk, and called for a beaker of beer. The stranger, seeing the courtesan Abisimti, recognized her, and he nodded to her and said, 'Count yourself fortunate that you are not living in Uruk these days.'

'Why, is life so unlucky in the city?' she asked.

'Gilgamesh oppresses us all,' said the stranger. 'The city groans beneath him. There is no containing the force of him, and he exhausts us. And he practices abominations: the king defiles the Land.'

At that, Enkidu looked up and said, 'How so? Tell me what you mean.'

The stranger replied, 'There is a house of assembly in the city that is set aside for the people, where they celebrate their marriages. The king ought not to intrude there; but he enters it, even while the wedding drums are beating, he seizes the bride, he demands to be first with her, before the husband. He says that this right was ordained by the gods at the time of his birth, from the time the cord that bound him to his mother was cut. Are such things right? Are such things proper? The wedding drums roll, but then Gilgamesh appears to claim the bride. And all the city groans.'

Enkidu grew pale on hearing this, and great anger came over him. 'It must not be!' he shouted. And to Abisimti he cried, 'Come, take me to Uruk, show me this Gilgamesh!'

Abisimti and Enkidu set out at once for the city. When they came within the walls he caused a considerable stir, so broad were his shoulders, so powerful his arms. Crowds gathered about him, and when they heard from Abisimti that this was the famous wild man who had been setting trapped animals free on the plains, they pressed close, gawking, whispering. The bravest of them touched him to feel the strength of him. 'He is the equal of Gilgamesh!' someone cried. 'No, he is not as tall,' said another, and a third said, 'Yes, but he is broader in the shoulders, his bones are stronger.' And they said, 'A hero has arrived! He is one that was suckled on the milk of wild beasts! Finally Gilgamesh has met his match! At last! At last!'

This was the man, this Enkidu, whose coming had been foretold in my two dreams. He was the companion whom the gods had provided to lift me from my loneliness, to be the brother I had never had, the comrade with whom I would share all things. To the people of Uruk he was also a godsend for whom they had long prayed, but for a different reason. For it was indeed the case— though I did not know it—that they had been groaning under the burden of my reign, that they feared my surging energies and condemned me for arrogance. So the people of Uruk had asked the

140

gods to create my equal and send him to their city: my double, my second half, matching me stormy heart for stormy heart, in order that we would contend with one another, and leave Uruk in peace. And now that man had come.

19

It was the day of the wedding of the nobleman Lugal-annemundu and the maiden Ishhara. The wedding drums were beating, the bridal bed had been laid out. The maiden was desirable to me, and at nightfall I made my way to the assembly-house of the people to take her to the palace.

But as I was crossing the marketplace known as the Market-of-the-Land, which lies just across the street from the assembly-house of the people, a burly figure rose up out of the shadows and blocked my path. He was a man almost of my own height, no more than a finger's breadth or two shorter: I had never seen anyone else so tall before. His chest was deep and heavy, his shoulders were wide, wider even than mine, his arms were as thick as an ordinary man's thighs. By the flickering light of my servants' torches I stared close into his face. His chin thrust boldly forward, his mouth was broad, his brow was strong and dark; and there was something fierce and smouldering in his eyes. His beard was thick, his hair was shaggy. And how calm he was, how self-assured! Look at him standing in my way! Did he not know I was Gilgamesh the king?

I said quietly, 'Step aside, fellow.'

'That I will not do.'

It amazed me to hear such words. I will not say that I felt fear, but I was put on my guard, for I knew this could be no common citizen. My yeomen stirred uneasily and began to draw their weapons. I beckoned them to hold back. Going closer to the stranger, I said, 'Do you know me?'

'I think you are the king.'

'So I am. It is not wise to bar my way like this.'

'Do you know *me?*' he asked. His voice was rough and deep, his accent uncouth.

I said, 'Not at all.'

'I am Enkidu.'

'Ah, the wild man! I should have guessed as much. So you have come to Uruk, now? Well, what do you want with me, wild man? This is not the hour for presenting petitions to the king.'

Bluntly he said, 'Where are you going, Gilgamesh?'

'Am I answerable to you, then?'

'Tell me where you are going.'

Again my yeomen stirred. I think they would gladly have speared him dead, but I held them back.

In some irritation I answered, waving beyond him to the assembly-house, 'Over there. To attend a wedding. From which you delay me, wild man.'

'You may not go,' he said. 'Do you mean to take the bride for yourself? You may not have her!'

'I may not? I may not? What strange words to offer a king, wild man!' With a shrug I said, 'This ceases to amuse me. Once more I tell you: step aside, fellow.'

I moved forward. But instead of yielding the way, he put out his foot to prevent me, and then he laid hold of me with his hands.

It is death to touch the king in such a fashion. I left no space, however, for my yeomen to strike him down; for as he touched me a sudden terrible rage sprang up in me, and I grabbed him as if I meant to hurl him to the far side of the marketplace. Instantly we were grappling in a tight embrace, and the spearmen could not have struck him without wounding me; so they stepped back and let us go at it, not knowing what else to do.

In the first moments I saw that he was my equal in strength, or nearly so. That was something new to me. In my boyhood, in my days of military training in Kish, in the roistering frolics with the young heroes of my court after I had become king, I had wrestled often, purely for the sport of it, and I had always sensed in the first laying-on of hands that the man with whom I had contended was at my mercy; I could throw him whenever I chose. That was satisfying only when I was a child. When I grew older I lamented it, since it robbed the wrestling of sport, to know that the power of victory was mine for the taking, at any moment, always. This was different. I had no assurance. When I tried to move him, he did not budge. When he tried to move me, it took all my strength to resist. I felt as though I had crossed over into some strange other world where Gilgamesh was no longer Gilgamesh. What I tasted was not fear—I do not think it was fear—but something almost as unfamiliar. Doubt? Uncertainty? Unease?

We fought like maddened bulls, snorting, lurching up and down, never once releasing one another. We shattered doorposts and made the walls of the buildings shake. Neither of us was able to prevail. Because he was of my height, or nearly so, we stared eye to eye as we contended; his eyes were deep-set and reddened with strain, and they gleamed with an astonishing wildness. We grunted; we bellowed; we roared. I shouted out defiance in the language of Uruk and the language of the desert folk and any other language I could think of; and he muttered and stormed at me in the language of the beasts, the harsh growling of the lion of the plains.

I yearned to kill him. I prayed that it be given to me to break his back, to hear the sharp snapping sound of his spine, to toss him like a worn-out cloak into the trash-heap. Such hatred went through me as made me dizzy. You must understand that no one had ever stood up to me in this way before. He was like a mountain that had risen in the night across my highway. How could I have felt, if not enraged: I the king, I the invincible hero? But I could not defeat him, nor he me. I cannot tell you how long we strained and struggled, and my strength and his were in equal measures.

But there is godhood in me, and Enkidu was altogether mortal. In the end it was inevitable that I would prevail. I felt my strength holding, while his was beginning to wane. At last I planted my foot firmly on the ground and bent my knee, and was able to catch him and pull him down, so that his feet flew up beneath him and he lost his balance.

In that moment every vestige of hatred for him went from me. Why should I hate him? He was splendid in his strength. He was close to being my equal. As a river batters down a dam, so did love for him sweep away all my anger. It was a sudden love so deep that it swept upon me like the fullest torrents of springtime and entirely conquered me. I bethought me of my dream—of that piece of starstuff which had fallen from the heavens and which I had been unable to budge. In the dream I had braced myself and with the greatest of efforts I had lifted it and taken it to my mother, who had told me, 'This is your brother, this is your great comrade.' Yes. I had never known a man so much my equal in so many ways, so fitted to me as though joined by a master carpenter. I clove to him in that moment as if we were of one flesh in two bodies, long sundered, now united. That was what I had felt, while my strength was being tested by his. That was what had passed between us as we struggled. I went to Enkidu and raised him from the ground and embraced him a second time, not in strife now, but in love. Great sobs shook me, and him also; for we both knew in the same moment what had passed between us.

'Ah, Gilgamesh!' he cried out. 'There is not another one like you in all the world! Glory to the mother who bore you!'

'There is one other,' I said, 'who is like me. But only one.'

'No: for Enlil has given you the kingship.'

'But you are my brother,' I said.

He looked at me, dazed like one who is roused too soon from sleep. 'I came here meaning to do you injury.'

'And I the same to you. When I saw you would block my way, I imagined myself cracking you in half, and throwing the pieces of you aside like gnawed bones.'

He laughed. 'You could not have done it, Gilgamesh!'

'No. I could not. But I meant to try.'

'And I to cast you down from your high place. I could have done that, if the luck had gone with me.'

'Yes,' I said. 'I think you could. Try it again, if you will. I will be ready for you.'

He shook his head. 'No. If I cast you down, if I do you grave injury, I will lose you. I will be alone again. No, I would rather have you for a friend than an enemy. That is the word I mean. *Friend. Friend.* Is that not the word?'

'A friend, yes. We are too much alike to be enemies.'

'Ah,' said Enkidu, frowning. 'Are we alike? How so? You are

the king, and I am only—I am—' He faltered. 'A shepherd's watchman is all I am.'

'No. You are the king's friend. The king's brother.'

I had never thought I would be able to say those words to anyone. Yet I knew them to be true. 'Is it so?' he asked. 'Shall we not fight again, then?'

With a grin I said, 'Of course we'll fight! But it will be as brothers fight. Eh, Enkidu? Eh?' And I took him by the hand. Forgotten now was the wedding, forgotten was the maiden Ishhara. 'Come with me, Enkidu. To Ninsun my mother, the priestess of An. I would have her meet her other son. Come, Enkidu. Come now!' And we went to the temple of the Sky-father, and knelt in the darkness before Ninsun; and it was very strange and wonderful for us both. I had thought the loneliness would be with me forever; and here it was gone, suddenly, vanished like a thief in the night at the moment of the coming of Enkidu.

That was the beginning of that great friendship, the like of which I had never known before, and will never know again. He was to me my other half; he filled a place in me where there had been an emptiness.

But it has been whispered that we were lovers as men and women are. I would not have you believe that. That was not the case at all. I know that there are certain men in whom the gods have mixed manhood and womanhood so that they have no need or liking for women, but I am not one of them, nor was Enkidu. For me the union of man and woman is the great holy thing, which it is not possible for a man to experience with another man: they say that they do experience it, those men, but I think they deceive themselves. It is not the true union. I have had that union, in the Sacred Marriage with the priestess Inanna, in whom the goddess resides. Inanna too is my other half, though a dark and troubled half. But a man may have several halves, or so it seems to me, and he may love a man in a way that is altogether different from the way in which he finds union with a woman.

That kind of love that exists between man and man existed between Enkidu and me. It sprang to life in the moment of our wrestling, and it never faded thereafter. We did not speak of it with one another. We did not need to speak of it. But we knew its presence. We were one soul in two bodies. We scarcely had to voice our thoughts, because we could hear them unspoken in one another. We were well matched. There is a god within me; there was the earth within him. I come from the heaven downward; he came from the ground upward. Our meeting-place was the place between, which is the world of mortal men.

I gave him rooms in the palace, the grand white-walled suite along the southwestern wall that previously had been reserved for the use of visiting governors and kings of other cities. I provided robes of the finest white linen and wool for him, and gave him maidens to bathe and oil him, and sent him my barbers and my surgeons to trim and polish the last traces of wildness out of him. I awoke in him a love of fine roasted meats, and sweet strong wines and rich foaming beer. I gave him the skins of leopards and lions to bedeck himself and his rooms. I shared all my concubines with him, holding back none for myself alone. I had a bronze shield made for him engraved with portrayals of the campaigns of Lugalbanda, and a sword that gleamed like the eye of the sun, and a richly ornamented red and gold helmet, and spears of the most exquisite balance. I taught him myself the arts of the chariot, and the casting of the javelin.

Though there remained always something rough and earthy at the core of him, nevertheless he quickly came to take on the outer look and manner of a noble of the court, dignified, accomplished, handsome. I tried even to have him taught to read and write, but he drew the line at attempting that. Well, there are many great men of the court who lack that skill also, and few who have mastered it.

If there was jealousy of him at court, I suppose I did not notice it. Perhaps there were some in the inner circle of heroes and warriors who turned away bitterly, saying behind his back and mine, 'There is the king's favorite, the wild man. Why was he chosen, and not me?' But if they did, they hid their scowls and mutterings very well. I prefer to think that no such envious feelings existed. It was not as though Enkidu had displaced some earlier favorite. I had never had a favorite before, not even such old comrades as Bir-hurturre or Zabardi-bunugga; I had never allowed anyone so close. They saw at once that the companionship I enjoyed with Enkidu was one of a different sort from anything I had known with them, just as his strength was of a different sort from theirs. There was no one like him in the world; and there was nothing like our friendship.

I took him completely into my confidence. I made every aspect of myself open to him. I even allowed him to watch me when I went into seclusion to beat the drum made of the huluppu-tree in the special way that put me into a trance. He crouched beside me as I disappeared into that other realm of blue light; and when I came out of it I found myself lying with my head cradled against his knees. He was staring at me as though he had seen the god emanating from me: he touched my cheekbones, he made holy signs with his fingertips. 'Can you show me how to go to that place?' he asked. And I replied, 'I will, Enkidu,' but he could never reach it, try as he would. I think it was that he had not been touched in an inward way by the god as I had been; he had never felt the fluttering of the great wings in his soul, he had not heard the droning and the buzzing, or seen the crackling aura, that are the first signs of being possessed. But often I let him sit beside me as I drummed, and he guarded me when I rolled about on the floor and thrashed and lashed my arms and legs in the ecstatic fit.

When there was work to do—the construction of canals, the strengthening of the wall, whatever labor the gods decreed for me—Enkidu was by my side. At the rituals he stood near me, and handed me the sacred vessels, or lifted the offerings of oxen and sheep to the altar as easily as if they were birds. When it was the season of hunting, we hunted together, and in that he was my superior, since he knew the wild beasts with a brother's knowledge. He stood with his head thrown back and sniffed the air, and said, pointing, 'That way is lion. That way is elephant.' He was never wrong. We went time and again into the marshes or the steppes or the other places where the great beasts dwelled, and there was no beast that did not fall to us. Together we killed three strong male elephants in the great bend of the river, and we carried their hides and teeth to Uruk and hung them up for a show on the facade of the palace. Another time he built a pit covered with branches and we captured an elephant alive, and brought it to the city also, where it stood bellowing and snorting in an enclosure for the whole winter until we offered it to Enlil. We hunted lions of the two kinds, the black-maned ones and those without manes, from our chariot: like me, Enkidu cast his javelins with the right hand or the left, with equal accuracy. I tell you, we were one soul in two bodies.

He was different from me, of course, in many ways. He was louder and far more boisterous, especially when he had had overmuch wine, and he had a low taste in wit, roaring endlessly with laughter over jokes that would make a child's nose wrinkle with distaste. Well, he was a man who had been reared among beasts. He had a dignity, a natural one, but it was not the dignity of one who had grown up in a palace with a king for a father. It was good for me to have Enkidu booming and roistering at my side, for I am too serious a man for my own good, and he lightened my hours, not as a court jester does with his carefully devised jollities, but in an easy and natural way, like a cool crisp breeze on a sultry sweltering day.

He spoke out with complete honesty. When I took him into the Enmerkar temple, thinking he would be overwhelmed by its beauty and majesty, he said at once, 'It is very small and ugly, is it not?' I had not expected that. Afterward I began to see my grandfather's great temple through Enkidu'a eyes, and indeed it did appear small and ugly to me, and old, and in bad need of repair. Instead of repairing it I tore it down and built a splendid new one, five times its size, atop the White Platform: that is the temple that stands there now, which I think will win me fame through the thousands of years to come.

It cost me some little trouble with the priestess Inanna, when I tore the Enmerkar temple down. I told her what I meant to do, and she looked at me as if I had spat upon the altars and replied, 'But it is the greatest of temples!'

'The one that was there before it, that Meskiaggasher built, was also the greatest of temples, in its day. No one remembers it now. It is in the nature of kings to replace temples with greater temples. Enmerkar built well, but I will build better.'

She glared at me sourly. 'And where will the goddess live, while you are building your temple?'

'The goddess inhabits all of Uruk. She'll live in every house and in every street and in the air about us, as she does now.'

Inanna was furious. She summoned the assembly of elders and the house of men to declare her protest; but no one could stop me from building the temple. It is in the province of the king to enhance the grandeur of the goddess by offering temples to her. So we swept the Enmerkar temple away, down to its foundations, although we left intact those demon-haunted ancient underground passageways beneath it: I did not want to meddle with those. I brought in limestone blocks from the limestone country to be the new foundations of my temple, and laid it out on a scale that no one in Uruk had ever imagined before. The citizens gasped in surprise when they came to watch the work and saw the length and breadth of what I intended to build.

In building the new temple I made use of everything I had learned of the craft. I raised the height of the White Platform until it towered halfway to heaven, and put my temple high on its foundations above that, as the temples are in Kish. I made the walls thicker than anyone had ever thought to make walls, and I supported them on immense columns as sturdy as the thighs of the gods. By way of ornament for the walls and columns I devised a new thing so wondrous that I should be remembered for it alone, even if all my other achievements are forgotten. This was, to drive thousands of long pointed cones of baked clay into the mud-plaster that covered the walls and columns, before it had hardened. Only the heads of these cones were allowed to remain visible, and they were painted in red or yellow or black, and placed one next to the other to form dazzling colorful patterns in diagonals and zigzags and lozenges and chevrons and triangles. The result is that wherever the eye looks within my temple, it is delighted by vividness and complexity: it is like seeing a vast tapestry, woven not with colored wools but of an uncountable number of small bright roundels of painted clay.

Enkidu thought also that the small shrine to Lugalbanda that Dumuzi had erected years ago by the military barracks in the Lion district was unworthy of my father. I had to agree: and I tore that down too, and built a far more appropriate one, with arches and pilasters of great size all covered over with my cone-mosaic decorations in brilliant colors. At the center of it I put the old image of

149

Lugalbanda in black stone that Dumuzi had erected, for it was a noble enough representation, and I would not lightly discard anything made of a material so rare as the black stone; but I surrounded it by tripod-mounted lamps against mirrors of bright copper, so that a dazzling light filled the shrine at every hour. We painted the walls with pictures and leopards and bulls, as offerings to Enlil of the storms, whom Lugalbanda loved. At the dedication I poured the blood of lions and elephants over the tiles of the floor. Can anyone say that the hero Lugalbanda merited anything less?

There were no wars in those years. The Elamites were quiet, the Martu desert tribesmen went marauding elsewhere, the collapse of the dynasty of Agga of Kish removed a powerful menace to our north. That the king of Ur had made himself king of Kish did not trouble me; Ur and Kish are far apart, and I saw no way that he could combine the power of the two cities in league against us. So we lived a calm and easy life in Uruk, growing rich in peace, fattening ourselves with trade instead of going forth to seek the booty of warfare.

In those years the merchants and emissaries of Uruk went everywhere at my bidding, to the great enhancement of the city. From the mountains in the east they brought beams of cedar-wood fifty and even sixty cubits in length, and logs of urkarinnu-wood to the length of twenty-five cubits, which we used for the beams of the new temple. From the town of Ursu in the mountain of Ibla they fetched zabalu-wood, great beams of ashukhu-wood, and the timber of plane-trees. From Umanu, a mountain in the land of Menua, and from Basalla, a mountain of the land of Amurru, my envoys returned with great blocks of the rare black stone, out of which the craftsmen fashioned new images of the gods for all the older temples. I imported copper from Kagalad, a mountain of Kimash, and with my own hands I made a great mace-head out of it. Out of Gubin, the mountain of huluppu-trees, I brought huluppu-wood, and from Madga came asphalt to use in the plat-form of the temple, and from the mountain of Barshib I fetched blocks of the sumptuous nalua-stone by boat. I laid plans to send expeditions even farther, to Magan, to Meluhha, to Dilmun. The city thrived. It grew daily in splendor. I took a wife, and she bore me a son; and I took a second wife, as was my right. There was peace. On the night of the new year I went to the temple I had built, and lay with fiery Inanna in the rite of the Sacred Marriage: each year she clung more fiercely to me, and her body moved with greater abandon, as she received in a single night the whole year's fulfillment of her hungers. I had the love of Enkidu to buoy me through my days. The wine flowed freely; the smoke of burning meat rose each day to the gods, and all was well. This was how I thought my reign would be forever and ever. But the gods do not grant such ease forever and ever: it is a miracle when they grant it at all.

20

One day I came upon Enkidu and found him in a bleak and downcast mood, scowling and sighing and well-nigh close to tears. I asked him what troubled him, though I was fairly sure that I knew; and he said, 'You will think me a fool if I tell you.'

'Perhaps I will, and what of it? Come, speak it forth.'

'It is foolishness, Gilgamesh!'

'I think not,' I said. I gave him a close look and said, 'Allow me a guess. You grow restless in our civilized life of ease, is that not it? You've become weary of dallying here in idleness.'

His face reddened and he replied, startled, 'By the gods, how did you know that?'

'It takes no great wisdom to see it, Enkidu.'

'I would not have you think I want to return to my old life and run naked on the steppe.'

'No. I doubt that you do.'

'But I tell you, I'm becoming soft here. The edge of my strength is going from me. My arms are limp, my breath comes short.'

'And the hunting trips we make? And the games we play on the jousting-field? Not enough, are they, Enkidu?'

In a low voice I could barely hear he said, 'I am ashamed to say it. But they are not enough.'

I put my hand to his arm. 'Well, they are not enough for me either.'

He blinked in surprise. 'What is that you say?'

'That I feel the same restlessness you do. My kingship binds and confines me. The tranquility that I've labored to achieve for the city has become my enemy. My soul is troubled even as yours is. I yearn as much as you for adventure, Enkidu, for danger, for mighty deeds that will raise up my name before mankind. I chafe here. I long to take a great journey.'

It was the truth. All was so serene in Uruk that being the king did not seem much different to me from being a shopkeeper. I could not accept a shopkeeper's lot, for the gods had put divinity in me, and the divine part of me was and is unsleeping, forever questing, forever unsatisfied. That is the jest the gods have played on me—that I yearn for peace but am not satisfied when I attain it; but I think I have solved the riddle of that jest now, as I will tell you in its proper time.

'Ah, is it so?' he said. 'You suffer as I do?'

'Exactly as you do.'

He laughed. 'We are like two overgrown boys, casting about for new diversions. But what will we do, then, Gilgamesh? Where can we go?'

I gave him a long steady look. Slowly I said, 'There is a place known as the Land of Cedars. For some time now I have been thinking of undertaking an expedition to that place.' That was not the truth: the idea had leaped into my mind that moment. 'Do you know of it, Enkidu?'

With a frown he said, speaking somewhat darkly and grimly, 'I know of it, yes.'

'Would it cure your restlessness, do you think, to go there with me?'

He moistened his lips. 'Why that place, Gilgamesh?'

'We have need of cedar. It is a splendid wood. There is none of it in the Land.' I was not being devious with him. It was the truth. But also I had chosen the Land of Cedars for its sharp and bracing air, which I thought would bring Enkidu out of his melancholy.

And above and beyond that, there was talk of late that the Elamites were staking claim to all the land around the cedar forest. I could not permit that.

'There are other places where you can obtain cedar.'

'Perhaps. But I mean to go to the Land of Cedars for it. They say it's wondrous country there, high and green and cool, very beautiful.'

'And very dangerous,' said Enkidu.

'Is it?' I shrugged. 'Better and better! You said you were growing restless dallying here in civilized ease—that you are hungry for challenge, for peril—'

He said, looking as abashed as I had ever seen him, 'Possibly you offer more than I bargain for.'

'What? *Too much* peril, is that it? Did those words come from Enkidu's lips? I never thought to hear you speak in a cowardly way.'

His eyes flashed; but with an effort he kept himself in check. 'There is a fine line, brother, between cowardice and common sense.'

'And is it common sense to fear a skirmish with a few Elamites?'

'No, not with Elamites, Gilgamesh.'

'Then what—'

'Are you not aware that the Lord Enlil placed the demon Huwawa at the gateway to the Land of Cedars to guard the holy trees?'

I nearly laughed out loud at that. Indeed I had heard tales of the demon of the forest; every forest has its demon or two, and terrifying tales abound. But generally demons can be propitiated or otherwise turned aside; and I had not expected Enkidu to care a rat's eyelash for beings of that sort in any case.

I said lightly, 'Well, there is some such story. But perhaps the demon will be busy elsewhere when we get there. Or perhaps the demon isn't as ferocious as the tales make him out to be. Or perhaps, Enkidu, there's no demon in the forest at all.'

Quietly Enkidu said, 'I have looked upon Huwawa with my own eyes.'

His words had the force of a blow in the belly, so hushed was his voice, so taut with conviction. Now it was my turn to blink with amazement. 'What?' I blurted. 'You have actually seen him?'

'When I was still ranging through the wilderness with the wild beasts,' he said, 'I wandered once far to the east, and came into the forest where the cedars grow. It extends ten thousand leagues in every direction; and Huwawa is everywhere in it. There is no hiding from him. He rose up before me and roared, and I thought I would die of fright; and I am no coward, Gilgamesh.' He looked at me very closely. 'Am I a coward, do you think? But Huwawa rose up and roared, and when he roars it is like the roaring of the storms that bring the great floods. I thought I would die of fright. His mouth is fire itself, his breath is death.'

I still could not believe it. 'You say that you saw the face of the demon?' I asked.

'I saw it. There is nothing more frightening in this world. This Huwawa is a monster beyond belief. His teeth are like the fangs of a dragon. His face is a lion's face.' Enkidu was trembling. His eyes were gleaming with the recollection of terror. 'When he charges, it is like the onrushing waters of the river. He devours trees and reeds as though they are grass.'

Dully I said yet again, 'You saw the demon!'

'I saw him, Gilgamesh. I was lucky to get away. He turned aside; he forgot me. I would not get away a second time. He will slay us. I tell you this: if we go to the Land of the Cedars, *he will slay us*. He perceives everything that happens in that forest. He can hear the sound of the wild heifers roaming in the woods, even if they are sixty leagues away. There's no escaping him. The contest is unequal.' He shook his head. 'Gilgamesh, Gilgamesh, I am hungry for some great exploit as you are: but are you hungry for death?'

'Do you think that I am?'

'You mean to go to the Land of Cedars.'

'For the sake of adventure, yes. For the sake of making my heart beat faster in my breast. But I have no hunger for death. It is the love of life that draws me to the Land of Cedars, not any craving for dying. You know that.'

'Yet to enter the lair of Huwawa—'

'No, Enkidu. I have seen the corpses floating on the river, and it weighs heavy on my soul, seeing them and knowing that that is

154

our fate too. I abhor death. Death is my enemy.'

'Then why go—'

'Because we must.'

'Ah, why must we? We can go north! We can go south! We can go—'

'No,' I said. The fire was upon me now. It pained me to see Enkidu languishing in such fear. His soul had softened in Uruk; he would die of it if I did not pull him forth. For his sake we must undertake this thing, no matter the risks. 'There is only one place we can go, and that is the Land of Cedars.'

'Where we will most certainly die.'

'I am not so certain of that. But consider this, friend: only the gods live forever under the sun, and even they taste death now and then. As for mortals like us, what we attempt is nothing but empty air, the blowing of the wind. Yet we must attempt it, I think, even so.'

'And die. I have never known you so eager for death, Gilgamesh. No matter what you say, that is how you seem.'

'No! No! I mean to fend off death as long as I can. But I will not live in fear. How can it be, Enkidu, that you are afraid?'

This time my jeering roused no anger in him. He looked away, scowling, bleak-faced.

'I have seen Huwawa,' he said sullenly.

Now I grew angry myself. This was not the Enkidu I knew.

'Well, then,' I cried, 'fear him! But I will not. Stay back where it is safe, then. Come with me to the Land of Cedars, yes. The journey will refresh you; the keen air will awaken your soul. But when we are in the forest, I will let you walk behind me. What if he slays me? If I fall to him, well, at the least of it I will have left behind me a name to last forever. They will say of me, "Gilgamesh has fallen to fierce Huwawa." That is no disgrace, eh? Where can there be any disgrace in falling to a demon so dreadful that he frightens even the hero Enkidu?'

His eyes met mine. He grinned fiercely, and his nostrils flared. 'How sly you are, Gilgamesh!'

'Am I? How so?'

'To tell me you'll let me walk behind you.'

'It will be safer for you there, Enkidu.'

'Do you think so? And have everyone in Uruk say afterward, "That is Enkidu, he walked behind his brother in the forest of the demon"!'

'But if the demon frightens you—'

'You know I will walk at your side when we come into Huwawa's domain.'

'Ah, I would not require that of you—you who have seen the dreadful Huwawa.'

'Spare me your mockery,' said Enkidu wearily. 'I will stand beside you. You know that, Gilgamesh. You have known it from the beginning.'

'If you are unwilling to go—'

'I tell you, *I will stand beside you!*' he bellowed. And we laughed and seized each other in a great hug, and made an end to all this talk: and I let the word go out that I soon would set forth from Uruk to the Land of Cedars.

I cannot tell you how many times, as we made our preparations for the journey, I asked Enkidu to describe the demon for me. Each time he offered the same words. He spoke of the roaring, the mouth like fire, the vast outpouring of storm-force. Well, I could not give him the lie: there was no artifice in Enkidu, he had not the slightest trace of the skills of deception. Plainly he had seen the demon, and plainly the demon was no trifling foe. From time to time we all see demons, for they are everywhere about, lurking behind the doors, in the air, on the rooftops, under bushes; I had seen demons often enough myself; but I had never seen one to match Huwawa. Still, I felt no fear. The very fear Enkidu had voiced only sharpened my resolve to fetch cedars from Huwawa's forest.

I chose fifty men to go with us, among them Bir-hurturre, but not Zabardi-bunugga, for I told him that he must remain to command the army of the city while I was away. I had great adzes cast for felling the trees, of a weight of three talents each, with handles of willow and box-wood; and my artisans made for us swords worthy of heroes, with blades of two talents' weight each, and golden sheaths, and pommels on the hilts that only a big man's hand could grasp. We gathered together our finest axes, our hunting-bows, our spears. Even before the day of departure I heard the war-song humming in my ears, which I had not heard in too long a time, and I felt like a boy again, I felt fresh blood coursing hot in my veins.

Of course the elders were gloomy. They formed a delegation on the quay and marched into town through the Gate of Seven Bolts, chanting prayers in their dour long-faced way. The people gathered around them in the Market-of-the-Land and began to chant and weep too, and I saw there was going to be trouble; so I went to the marketplace and presented myself before the elders. It was not hard to predict what they would say: 'You are still young, Gilgamesh, your courage is greater than your wisdom, your heart leads you into something rash. You take a road you have never traveled, and you will be lost. You are strong, but you will never prevail against Huwawa. He is a being of a monstrous kind; his roaring is like that of the storm-flood, his mouth is fire itself, his breath is the breath of death.' And so on and so forth. Which was exactly what they said. I heard them out; and then I replied, smiling, that I would seek the protection of the gods and that I was confident the gods would protect me, as they always had in the past. 'It is a road I have never traveled, I admit,' I said, 'but I go without fear. I go with joyful heart.'

When they saw there was no changing my mind, they altered their tune. Now they warned me simply not to be too sure of my own strength. Let Enkidu go first, they said. Let him lead the way, let him protect the king. To this advice I listened calmly, smiling still, not entering into any dispute with them. They told me also to place myself under the mercy of Utu of the sun, who is the god who guards those in danger, and I swore to go that very day to the temple of Utu and offer him two kids, a white one without blemish and a brown one. I would beg the aid of Utu, and I would promise him a glorious offering of praise and gifts if he granted me a safe return. And on my journey to the Land of Cedars I would perform this rite and that one, this observance and that, to insure myself against all harm. I promised these things in all sincerity. I was not unaware, after all, of the perils.

When the elders were done plaguing me, it was the turn of the priestess Inanna, who summoned me to the temple I had built for her and said angrily, 'What is this madness, Gilgamesh? Where are you going?'

'Are you my mother, to speak to me this way?'

'Hardly. But you are king of Uruk, and if you die in this venture, who will be king after you?'

Shrugging, I said, 'That is for the goddess to determine, is it not, and not I. But have no fear, Inanna. I will not die on this journey.'

'And if you do?'

'I will not die,' I said again.

'Is it so important to attempt this thing?'

'We must have the cedar.'

'Send your troops, then, and let them fight with the demons.'

'Ah, and would you have me tell them that I am afraid of Huwawa, and send them in my place, while I sit here comfortably at home all the rest of my days? I will go, Inanna. That much is settled.'

She stared at me furiously. I felt, as I always did, the power of her beauty, which was in its fullest ripeness now; and I felt also the force of her love for me, which had raged within her like the fire of the heavens since we were children; and I felt, beyond that, the anger that she had for me because she was unable in any way to fulfill that love as women and men ordinarily do.

I thought also of those times, one night a year, when she and I had come together in the bed of the goddess, when she had lain naked in my arms with her breasts heaving and her thighs parted and her fingers clawing the skin on my back, and I wondered whether I would live to embrace her that way again. For in my way I loved her also, though my love was always mixed with a certain mistrust and more than a little dread of her wiles. We were silent a time. Then she said, 'I will make offerings for your safety. And go, get you to your mother the old queen, and ask her to do the same.'

'I mean to go to her next,' I said.

It was true, Enkidu and I crossed the city to the wise and great Ninsun, and I knelt before her and told her that I was setting out on an uncertain road, with a strange battle to fight. She sighed, and asked why it was that the gods, having given her Gilgamesh for a son, had endowed him with such a restless heart; but she made no attempt to dissuade me from going. Instead she rose and cloaked herself in her holy crimson robe, and donned her breast-plate of gold and her necklaces of lapis and carnelian, and put her tiara on her head, and went to the altar of Utu on the roof of her dwelling. She lit incense to him and spoke to the god for a time; and then she returned to us, and turned to Enkidu, saying, 'You are not the child of my flesh, strong Enkidu, but I adopt you as my son. Before all my priestesses and votaries I adopt you.' She hung an amulet about Enkidu's neck, and embraced him, and said to him, 'I entrust him to you. Guard him. Protect him. Bring him back safely. He is the king, Enkidu. And he is my son.'

The praying and discussion were done with at last; and I led my men forth out of Uruk the city, to the Land of Cedars.

21

Swiftly we went up out of the warm lowlands, leaving behind us the groves of date-palms and the golden breast of the desert, and rose into the cool green high country to the east. We traveled in forced marches from dawn to dusk, crossing seven mountains one after the other without pausing, until at last the forests of cedar stood before us, uncountable legions of trees ranging along the slopes of the rough land ahead. It was strange for us to see so many trees, the Land having scarcely any. They made the jagged hills look almost black. They seemed like a hostile army, waiting calmly for our onslaught.

There was another great strangeness in those fanged ridges and rocky gullies: the fires of the outcast gods and demons that rose out of the stone here and there, and their thick black oily outpourings, which came rolling down toward us like the sluggish snakes of the nether world. For we were entering the land that is known as the Rebel Lands, into which the gods who rose up against Enlil were

159

exiled. Here did the victorious warriors Enlil and Ninurta and Ningirsu cast their banished enemies in that great battle of gods long ago; and here they still sulked, still rumbling and growling and shaking the earth, still giving off their great blasts of smoke and fire and letting their serpents of oil seep from the depths of the ground. With each step we took we penetrated deeper into this dark realm, knowing all the time that sinister deities with angry red eyes snorted and puffed beneath our feet.

Yet we allowed ourselves no fear. We paused at the proper times and made the proper observances to Utu, to An, to Enlil, to Inanna. When we camped at night we dug wells and let the holy waters rise to the surface as offerings. At the last, before sleep, I invoked Lugalbanda and took counsel with him, for he had been in these lands himself, and had suffered greatly from the noxious fumes and blasts of the rebel gods. His presence was a strong comfort within me.

Enkidu knew this country well. Like the wild creature he once had been, he guided us through the unending trackless leagues without fail. He took us around the places that had been burned and blackened by the hot breath of dangerous spirits. He led us past the regions where the land had slipped and broken and heaved upward and was impassable. He brought us past thick deep oily slicks that lay like black lakes upon the breast of the earth. Nearer and nearer did we draw to the inner forest itself, to the domain of the demon Huwawa.

Now we were amidst the first outlying cedar trees. If we had come only for wood, I suppose we could have chopped down twenty or sixty of the trees and returned happily with them to Uruk, claiming triumph. But we had not come only for wood.

Enkidu said, 'There is a great gate here, sealing off the sacred groves within. We are very near it now.'

'And Huwawa?' I asked.

'On the other side of the gate, not far.'

I peered close at him. His voice was strong and steady, but yet I was not entirely sure of him. I had no desire to injure his pride; but after a moment I asked, 'Is all well with you thus far, Enkidu?'

He smiled and said, 'Do I look pale? Do you see me quaking with fear, Gilgamesh?'

'In Uruk I heard you speak with great respect of Huwawa. There is no escaping him, you said. He is a monster beyond belief, you said. When he roared, you thought you would die of the fright of it. You said those things.'

Enkidu shrugged. 'I said those things in Uruk, perhaps. In cities men grow soft. Here I feel my strength returning. There is nothing to fear, my friend. Follow me: I know where Huwawa dwells, and the road he travels.' And he put his hand to my arm and squeezed it, and locked his arm hard around mine.

A day later we came to the wall of the forest, and to the great gate.

I had wondered about that wall since Enkidu first told me of it. The Land of Cedars lies in the unsettled borderland between the Land and the country of the Elamites, and ownership of it has been in dispute at least since the days of Meskiaggasher, the first king of Uruk. Since it is a territory that cannot be farmed, we have never tried to take formal possession of it, but whenever we found need of cedar-wood we have freely entered into it and collected all that we wanted. It was a serious business if someone was building walls through the forest. It is one thing if Enlil chooses to post some dread fire-demon here to guard the trees in his name: I have no say in what Enlil does. But I would not tolerate the setting-up of walls here by any black-bearded Elamitish mountain king who meant to try to claim the whole forest for his dirty ragged tribesfolk.

The moment I saw the wall I knew that Elamites and not Huwawa or any other spirit had built it. It had the mark of men all over it, and not very skillful men at that. Cedar logs, roughly squared and indifferently bound with withies, were piled in a helter-skelter fashion along a crudely slashed track that stretched off in both directions as far as the eye could see: the pink heart-wood of the trees was sadly exposed, as if the timber had been flayed rather than planed. Anger rose in me at the sight of this huge clumsy wall. I looked about at my men and said, 'Well, shall we knock the thing apart and go into the forest?'

'You should see the gate first,' said Enkidu.

The gate lay half a league around to the south. Even before I reached it I gasped in surprise. It rose high above the wall, more a

161

tower than a gate, and it was superb in every aspect. That gate would have been no disgrace to the walls of Uruk. It too was of cedar, trimmed and cut by a master's hand, and framed and joined with high skill. Its pivot and rod were wondrously smooth and its great jamb was superbly fitted.

'A gate of the gods!' Bir-hurturre cried. 'A gate put up by Enlil himself!'

'A gate that no Elamite could have built, at any rate,' I said, going close to inspect it.

Indeed it was perfection. Not only was it flawlessly built, it was magnificently adorned: carved upon the finely seasoned wood of its face were monsters and serpents and gods and goddesses, in Elamitish designs that I remembered having seen on the shields of the warriors I slew in my campaigns for Agga of Kish. Mounted high at the top of the gate were three huge horns set close together, much like the massive horns that the Elamites carve and place on the facades of their temples. And down the sides of the wall were inscriptions in the barbaric Elamitish script, which is awkwardly patterned after our own: pictures of beasts, vases, jugs, stars, mountains, and many other things, tumbling together in some sort of declaration indecipherable to me. The carvings were nicely done, but it seemed a foolish way to write, this silly making of pictures.

Then I saw something that angered me, low down on the left-hand side of the gate. It was an inscription in the wedge-shaped characters of the Land, clear and unmistakable, saying, *Utu-ragaba the great craftsman of Nippur built this gate for Zinuba king of kings, king of Hatamti.*

'Ah, the traitor!' I exclaimed. 'Better that he had stayed in Nippur than to come here and render such excellent service to an Elamite lord.' And I lifted my axe to smash the face of the gate.

But Enkidu caught my arm and stayed me. I looked about at him, frowning.

'What is it?'

His eyes were aglow. 'The gate is very beautiful, Gilgamesh.'

'So it is. But see, here, this writing? A man of my own nation constructed it for our enemies.'

'That may be,' said Enkidu indifferently. 'All the same, beauty is beauty, and ought not to be desecrated. Beauty comes from the gods, does it not?' I think you should not shatter the gate. Step aside, brother, and let me force it instead. What does it matter if a traitor built it, so long as his work was righteously accomplished? The gods clearly guided his hand. Do you not see that?'

It amazed me to hear him reason in this fashion; but I saw the wisdom in his words, which humbled me, and I yielded to him. I wish now that I had not. Enkidu stepped boldly forward and pushed the edge of his axe against the bolt, and thrust at the gate with all his strength, so that cords and sinews stood out all over his body. He grunted mightily under the strain and the gate swung open before him; but in that moment he cried out in a strange choking way and dropped his axe, and slapped his left hand to his right arm, which suddenly was dangling down as limp as a length of rope. He fell to his knees, moaning, desperately rubbing his arm.

I knelt beside him. 'What is it, friend? What has happened to you?'

In a thick voice he muttered, 'There must have been a demon in the gate. Look, I have hurt my arm! All strength is gone from my hand! It is torn within, Gilgamesh. It is ruined, it is useless. Come, see for yourself.' And indeed his hand was fearfully cold to the touch, and swung like a dead thing, and the skin looked strangely blotched and mottled. He was trembling as if some ague had come into him. I heard the chattering of his teeth.

'Wine!' I called. 'Bring wine for Enkidu!'

The wine warmed him, and his shivering ceased; but his hand remained lame, though we heated it and rubbed it for hours. Indeed he did not begin to recover the use of it for many days, nor was it ever fully the same again. That was a sad thing, that such a hero as Enkidu should lose a part of his strength, especially when it had been for the sake of preserving something of beauty. What was worse, the fear of Huwawa returned to him when he injured himself, for he was convinced that the demon had put a curse on the gate; now he drew back, unwilling to pass through the gate that he himself had opened for us.

It grieved me that he felt fear again, and that our comrades should see him in such a state. But he would not go through the gate, and I could hardly leave him behind. So we made camp in that place and stayed there some time, until he ceased to writhe in anguish and said he felt the power of his hand returning. Even then he was reluctant to go forward. He sat in dismal bleak silence, lost in brooding. Fear was upon him like a dreadful bird of night that clung with terrible talons to his shoulder. I went to him and said, 'Come, dear friend, it is time to move on.'

He shook his head. 'Go without me, Gilgamesh!'

Sharply I said, 'It makes me ache to hear you speak like a weakling. Have we traveled so far, and come through so many dangers, only to turn back at the gate?'

Just as sharply he replied, 'When did I ask you to turn back?'

'No, you never did.'

'Then go on without me!'

'That I will not do. Nor am I willing to go back empty-handed to Uruk.'

'If that is so, you leave me no choice. Must I come with you, then? Am I to be swept along by whatever you wish?'

'I would not force you,' I said in no little distress. 'But we are brothers, Enkidu. We should face all perils side by side.'

He gave me a bitter jaundiced look. 'We should, should we? And if I am unwilling?'

I stared. 'This is not like you.'

'No,' he said gloomily, with a sigh. 'This is not like me. But what can I do? What can we do? When I hurt my hand a great terror entered me, Gilgamesh. I am afraid. Do you understand that word? *I am afraid*, Gilgamesh!' There was a look in his eyes, I had never seen there before: terror, shame, self-reproach, anger, fifty somber things gleaming there at once. His face was glossy with sweat. He looked around as if fearing that the others had overheard us. In a low anguished voice he said, 'What can we do?'

I shook my head. 'There is a way. Here: stand close by me, take hold of my robe. My strength will go into you. Your weakness will pass. The trembling will leave your hand. And then let us go down into the forest together. Will you do that?'

He hesitated. Then he said, 'Do you think I am a coward, Gilgamesh?'

'No. You are no coward, Enkidu.'

'You called me a weakling.'

'I said it pained me to hear you speak like a weakling. It is because you are not a weakling that it pained me. Do you understand that, brother?'

'I understand.'

'Come, then. Let me heal you.'

'Can you do that?'

'I think I can.'

'Do it, then.'

He came to me and stood close; he reached for my robe and held it a moment; then I embraced him so tightly that my arms quivered. After a moment he grasped me with equal strength. We did not speak, but I could feel his fear leaving him. I could feel his courage returning. He seemed to be becoming Enkidu again, and I knew that he would journey onward with me into the forest.

'Go,' I said. 'Make yourself ready. Huwawa awaits us. The heat of combat will warm your blood and strengthen your resolve. I think there is no demon that can harm us, if we stand side by side. But if we fall in the struggle, why, we will leave a name that will last forever.'

He listened without replying. After a time he nodded and rose and touched his hand to mine, and trampled out our campfire, and went off to oil his weapons. In the morning we passed through the gate and into the forest of cedars, not in any foolhardy way, but with boldness and determination.

It was an awesome place. It was almost like a temple: I felt the presence of gods all about me, though I did not know which gods they were. The cedars were the loftiest trees I have ever seen, rising like spears into the heavens, with clear open space between them; but so dense were their crowns that the sunlight could scarcely penetrate the cover they made. It was a green and silent world, cool, full of delight. Ahead of us lay a single mountain, beyond doubt an abode of the gods, a fitting throne for the highest of them. But also about us lay the presence of Huwawa: we felt him, and we saw the traces of him, for there were certain zones of the forest where the underground gases and fires had broken through, and that was the mark of the demon.

Yet there was no immediate sign of him. We went deeper, until

165

darkness halted us. As the sun began to descend I dug a well and made the water-offering, and scattered three handfuls of fine meal before the mountain, and asked the gods of the mountain to send me a favorable dream. Then I lay down beside Enkidu and entrusted myself to sleep.

In the middle hour of the night I woke suddenly, and sat bolt upright, utterly awake. By the smouldering light of our fire I saw Enkidu's gleaming eyes.

'What troubles you, brother?'

'Was it you that awakened me?'

'Not I,' he said. 'You must have had a dream.'

'A dream, yes. Yes.'

'Tell me.'

I looked inward and saw the mists lying heavy on my mind, like thick white fleece; but behind them I caught sight of my dream, or of some part of it. We were crossing a deep gorge of the cedar mountain, Enkidu and I, in that dream; against the great bulk of the mountain we seemed no larger than the little black flies that buzz among the swamp-reeds; and then the mountain heaved like a ship tossed on the bosom of the sea and began to fall. That was all I could remember. I told the dream to Enkidu, hoping he would be able to read it for me; but he shrugged and said it was an unfinished vision, and urged me to return to it. I doubted I would sleep again that night, but I was wrong, for as soon as I closed my eyes I was dreaming once more. And it was the same dream: the mountain was toppling upon me. A rumbling rockslide swept my feet from under me, and a terrible light glared and blazed intolerably. But then a man appeared, or a god, I think, of such grace and beauty as is not found in this world. He pulled me out from under the mountain and gave me water to drink, and my heart took comfort; he raised me and set my feet on the ground.

I woke Enkidu and told him my second dream. He said at once, 'It is a favorable dream, it is an excellent dream. The mountain you saw, my friend, is Huwawa. Even if he falls on us, we will defeat him, do you see? The gods stand by you: tomorrow we will seize him. We will kill him. We will cast his body on the plain.'

'You sound very certain of that.'

'I am certain,' he said. 'Now sleep again, brother. Sleep.'

Once more we slept. This time the cedar mountain devised a dream for Enkidu, and not a cheering one: cold rain-showers fell upon him, and he huddled and shivered like the mountain barley in a winter storm. I heard him cry out, and awakened, and he told me his dream. We did not search for its meaning. There are times when it is best not to probe a dream too deeply. One more time in that dream-thronged night I let my chin rest upon my knees and gave myself up to sleep; and yet again I dreamed, and again I woke amazed from it, startled, trembling.

'Another?' Enkidu asked.

'Look how I shake!' I whispered. 'What awakened me? Did some god pass by? Why is my flesh so numb?'

'Tell me, did you dream again?'

'Yes. I dreamed a third dream, more frightful even than the others.'

'Tell it.'

'What did we eat, that gave us such dreams tonight?'

'Until you tell it, it will burden your soul.'

'Yes. Yes,' I said. But still I held back from it, though its horrendous images still blazed in my mind. He was right: one must tell dreams, one must bring them into the light, or they will bore your soul like maggots. After a moment I took a deep breath and said, speaking in a slow halting way, 'That is what it was. The day was calm, the air was still. And then suddenly the heavens shrieked, the earth cried out in booming roars. Daylight failed; darkness came. Lightning flashed, and fires blazed on the horizon. The clouds grew heavy and death came raining down from them. Then the brightness vanished. The fire went out, and everything about us was turned to ashes.'

Enkidu shivered. 'I think we should not sleep again tonight,' he said.

'But the dream? What of the dream?'

'Come, rise, walk with me, brother. Forget the dream.'

'Forget it? How?'

'It is only a dream, Gilgamesh.'

I looked at him, puzzled. Then I smiled. 'When the omens are favorable, you say the dream is excellent. When the omens are grim, you say it is only a dream. Do you not see—'

'I see that the morning is near,' he said. 'Come, walk with me in the forest. We have heavy work to do at dawn.'

Yes, I thought. Perhaps he was right. Perhaps the dream did not bear close inspection. The morning would bring great challenges: we needed all our courage about us.

By first light I roused my men. We donned our breastplates and swords and grasped our axes, and set out down the slope into the valley that lay before the cedar-covered mountain. This was the place, said Enkidu, where he had encountered Huwawa that other time he had been here. The demon had risen up without warning from the ground, he said: he had been lucky to escape.

'Today,' I said, 'it will be Huwawa who is lucky to escape. And when we have done with him, we will see to these Elamites who build walls around a forest, eh, brother?' And I laughed. It felt good to be going to war. No matter that our enemy was a demon. No matter that my last dream and Enkidu's had been full of dark omens. There is a joy in going to war: there is poetry in it, there is music. It is what we were meant to do on this world, those of us who are warriors. You will not understand this, you who sit at home in cities and grow fat. But true warfare is not mere mindless destruction: it is the setting to rights of those things which must be set to rights, and that is a holy task.

As we went forward I felt a rumbling in the earth, distant but unmistakable. It seemed perhaps as though one of the horn-crowned gods might be stirring and walking to and fro down there. That gave me some pause. I will do battle against demons with a glad heart, but what hope is there in contending against the gods? I prayed to Lugalbanda that I was mistaken, that the far-off underground thundering that I felt did not portend the anger of Enlil. Let it merely be Huwawa awakening, I prayed. Let it be just the demon, and not the god.

Behind me I heard my men murmuring uneasily. 'What is this demon like?' asked one, and another said, 'Dragon's fangs, lion's face,' and another said, 'He roars like the whirlwind,' and yet another said, 'Feet with claws, eyes of death.' I looked back at them and laughed out loud and cried, 'Yes, go on, frighten yourselves! Make him really awesome! Three heads, ten arms!' And I cupped my hand to my lips and called into the mist-shrouded forest, 'Huwawa! Come! Come, Huwawa!'

The earth trembled again, more vehemently.

I rushed onward, Enkidu beside me and the others keeping close pace just behind. There was a single great cedar that stood like a mast before us, higher than all the others, and I thought, this is the way to summon Huwawa. So I unslung my axe and set to work at it with all my might, and Enkidu worked on its other side, cutting the lesser notch to guide it in its falling. I felt a great heat entering the air, which was strange, this still being the coolest part of the morning. A third time there were tremors beneath my feet. Something was awakening, no question of it, something vast and fierce, hot and furious. In the distance I saw the treetops swaying. I heard the tearing and crackling of branches. With stroke upon stroke we cut away at that great cedar, until it was on the verge of toppling.

Then to my horror I became aware of the droning and buzzing that told me the god-presence was surging within me. My fit was coming upon me as surely as though I had drummed it into wakefulness. Not now, I begged desperately. Not now! But it would have been easier to hold back the eight winds. The veins of my neck swelled up and beat with a hard pulsation. My eyeballs throbbed as if they meant to leap from their sockets. My hands tingled. Each stroke of the axe against the wood sent fire through my veins.

'Chop, brother, chop!' Enkidu called from the far side of the cedar. He did not understand what was happening to me. 'We have it, now. Another four strokes—three—'

I felt ecstasy and terror both at once. The air about me was blue and sizzling. A river of black water was rising from the earth. A golden aura surrounded everything I could see. The god was seizing my mind.

The earth shook and bucked and heaved wildly. I called out to Lugalbanda three times.

Then I heard Enkidu's voice roaring above all the confusion: 'Huwawa! Huwawa! Huwawa!'

The demon came, but I did not see him just then. The blackness overtook me; the god swallowed me up.

22

When next I perceived anything that made sense to me I found myself lying on the ground with my head in Enkidu's lap. He was rubbing my forehead and shoulders, which was most soothing. I ached everywhere, but most especially in my face and neck. The great cedar was down; indeed, most of the trees around us were toppled or partly toppled, as if half the forest had been thrown over in the earthquake. Dark fissures furrowed the ground in a dozen places. Directly in front of us the earth had split wide open and a horrendous column of smoke, black with fiery streaks in it, was belching forth straight up to the sky, making a noise like that of the bellowing of the Bull of Heaven upon the last day of the world.

'What is that thing?' I said to Enkidu, pointing at the roaring column of smoke.

'It is Huwawa,' he said.

'That? Is Huwawa nothing but smoke and flame?'

'That is the form he has taken today.'

'Did he have another form, that time you were here?'

'He is a demon,' said Enkidu with a shrug. 'Demons take whatever appearance they please. He is afraid to strike, for he feels the god in you. He hovers there, pouring himself forth. This is the moment to slay him.'

'Help me to my feet.'

He lifted me as though I were a child, and set me aright. I felt dizzy, and swayed, but he steadied me, and then the dizziness passed. I planted my feet on the ground. The earth beneath me was thrumming from the force of the outrush of Huwawa from his subterranean lair, but otherwise it was firm again. Whatever had stirred down there before the quake, whether it had been horned Enlil or only his minion Huwawa, was no longer troubling the pillars and foundations that uphold the world.

I stepped forward and looked upon Huwawa.

It was difficult to get close. The air in the vicinity of that smoky column was foul and oily, and lay upon my lungs like something slimy. My head pounded, and not only from the aftermath of my fit. I bethought me of the time of which they tell when Lugalbanda, traveling in these eastern parts, was overcome by a smoke-demon much like this on the slopes of Mount Hurum, and was left for dead by his comrades. 'We must be careful,' I told the others, 'to keep the demon-stuff from entering into our nostrils.' We cut apart the hems of our robes and wrapped them over our faces, and took care to breathe the smallest of breaths while we peered into that noxious smoke.

The crevice that had opened in the earth to release Huwawa was not large: I could span the width of it between my two hands. Out of it, though, the demon came boiling upward with enormous force. I looked, trying to see the face and eyes, but I saw nothing but smoke. I cried out, 'I conjure you, Huwawa, show yourself as you are!' But still I saw nothing but smoke.

Enkidu said, 'How can we slay him, if he is only smoke?'

'By drowning him,' I replied. 'And by smothering him.'

I pointed toward the side, where the earthquake had set free some underground spring. A little rivulet now was running toward the bottom of the valley: the water was warm, from the breath of the god beneath the earth, I suppose, and steam was rising from it. We drew ourselves together and formed a plan. I put thirty of my men to work digging a channel to guide the stream sideways toward the mouth through which Huwawa raged into the air; and I assigned the others the task of trimming the trunk of the great cedar, cutting a length about twice the length of a man from it and giving it the form of a pointed stake. We worked swiftly, lest the demon take on its solid form and attack us; but the god-presence in me still seemed to hold it at bay. To be certain of safety I set three men at work chanting and making signs without pause.

When we were ready I called out, 'Huwawa? Do you hear my voice, demon? It is Gilgamesh king of Uruk who slays you now!' I looked to Enkidu, and for an instant, I tell you in truth, I felt fear and doubt. It is no little thing to slay a demon who is in the service of Enlil. Also I wondered after all whether there was need to slay him—whether it might not be sufficient only to seal his hole and leave him bound in there. I tell you my heart was moved with compassion for the demon. Does that sound strange? But it is what I felt.

Enkidu, who knew my soul as he did his own, saw me waver. He said to me, 'Hurry, now, Gilgamesh! This is no moment for hesitating. The demon must die, brother, if you have any hope of leaving this place. There is no arguing it. Spare him and you will never make it back to your own city and to the mother who bore you. He will block the mountain road against you. He will make the pathways impassable.'

I saw the wisdom of that. I raised my hand and gave the signal.

In that moment my men chopped an opening in the earthen dam that they had built across the rivulet, and let its waters pour forth into the new channel that ran toward Huwawa's blowhole. I watched the cascade of steaming water flow swiftly to its home: and when it reached the crevice and tumbled in, there arose such a wailing and howling from the depths that I could scarcely believe it. A white jet of hot cloud rose up in the heart of the black cloud, and I heard thunder and roaring. The ground trembled as though it would begin to heave and upsurge all over again. But it held fast. The crevice drank the stream, and the stream poured onward, giving it all it could drink. The red sparks dimmed within the black column; the foul smoke wavered and came in choked spurts.

'Now,' I said, and we raised the cedar stake.

I bore the brunt of the weight, though Enkidu with his one good hand offered more force than any other man could have provided whole and healthy, and seven or eight of my other men ran alongside us, giving support. We carried that tremendous stake at a dead trot until we were poised over the smoking hole, as close to it as we could manage, with our eyes running tears and our faces red from holding our breaths; and then we rose up on the tips of our feet and we thrust forward and downward and rammed it into the opening.

We leaped back, thinking the earth might erupt. But no: the demon was weakened or drowned by the water, and he could not force the wooden plug. I saw some coiling strands of smoke break from the earth a little distance away; but then they were gone, and we heard nothing more.

All was deathly still. The blaze and the glory that had been

Huwawa was quenched. There was no smoke, there was no fire, only the afterstench that stained the air and assailed our nostrils, and even that was quickly beginning to dissipate in the cool sweet cedar forest. I think they will say of Enkidu and me, when the tellings and retellings of the story begin to change it as these stories always are changed with time, that we rushed upon Huwawa and cut off his head; for the harpers of the days to come will not understand how we could slay a demon with nothing more than a dammed stream and a sharpened stake. So be it; but that was what we did, whatever they may tell you when I am not here to testify to the truth.

'He is dead,' I said. 'Come, let us purify the site, and get ourselves onward.'

We cut cedar boughs and laid them over the demon's tomb, and made the offerings, and said the words. Afterward we chose fifty fine cedar logs to bring back with us to Uruk, and we stripped them and loaded them; and when we were done with that, we returned to the wall that the Elamites had built and scattered it apart as though it had been made of straws, though for beauty's sake we left intact the splendorous gate that the traitor Utu-ragaba had fashioned for the mountain king.

When we were taking our leave of the place, a hundred Elamitish warriors came upon us, and asked us in the name of their king why we were trespassing here. To which I replied that we were not trespassing at all, but merely coming to gather a little wood for our temple, which had required us to slay the demon of the place. They found this insolent of me. 'Who are you, man?' their leader demanded.

'Who am I?' I asked of Enkidu. 'Tell him.'

'Why, you are Gilgamesh king of Uruk, greatest of heroes, the wild bull who plunders the mountains as he pleases: Gilgamesh the king, Gilgamesh the god. And I am Enkidu your brother.' He clapped his belly and laughed and said to the Elamite, 'Do you know the name of Gilgamesh, fellow?' But the Elamites were already in flight. We followed after them and slew about half, and let the others go, so that they could bring word back to their king that it was unwise to build walls about the forest of cedars. I think he came to see the wisdom of that, for I heard no more of such walls, nor of Huwawa the dreadful, and in years afterward we had all the cedar we required from that forest without hindrance.

23

It was a triumphant time. We marched into Uruk as joyous as though we had conquered six kingdoms. There was a kind of madness in our pride, I think, but I think it was a pardonable pride. One does not kill a demon every day, after all.

So we celebrated our exploits in the Land of Cedars and our safe return with feasting and laughter. But there was a touch of discord at the outset of that night of glorious revelry, and there was another before it ended.

As we approached the city walls in late afternoon with our booty the Royal Gate swung open, and through it rode a welcoming party of many chariots, led by Zabardi-bunugga. Trumpets sounded, banners waved; I heard my name shouted over and over. We halted and waited. Zabardi-bunugga, riding up to me, hailed me with upraised hands and presented me with the bundle of barley-sheaves that is the customary salute to a returning king. He made his thanksgiving offering for my safety, and then together we poured out a libation to the divine ones. Good loyal flat-faced Zabardi-bunugga: what a worthy prince!

When these ceremonies were done we embraced in a less formal way. He nodded graciously also to Enkidu, and smiled his greetings to Bir-hurturre. If there was any envy about Zabardi-bunugga because he had not taken part in our grand adventure, I did not see it. I told him how the journey had gone; but he already knew that, for runners had gone ahead bearing news of our victory. Then I asked how things had fared in Uruk during my absence, and a shadow passed across his eyes, and he looked away as he said, 'The city prospers, O Gilgamesh.'

It was not hard to perceive the uneasiness about him, the

hesitation, the discomfort. I said, 'Does it, in all truth?'

In a restless way he replied, 'May I ride with you into the city?'

I beckoned him into my chariot. He glanced toward Enkidu, who rode beside me; but I shrugged as though to say, whatever you have to say to me, it is fitting that my brother hear it as well. Which Zabardi-bunugga understood without needing to say it. Lightly he stepped up into the chariot, and Enkidu gave the signal for the procession to continue through the city's great gate.

'Well?' I said. 'There is trouble, is there? Tell me.'

In a low voice Zabardi-bunugga said, 'The goddess stirs. I think there is danger, Gilgamesh.'

'How so?'

'She broods. She frets. She feels that you have cast her into eclipse, that you overreach yourself. She says that you ignore her, that you fail to consult her, that you go your own way as though this is not at all the city of Inanna, but has become only the city of Gilgamesh.'

'I am king,' I said. 'I bear the burden.'

'She would remind you, I think, that you are king by grace of the goddess.'

'So I am, and I never forget it. But she must remember that she is not the goddess, but only the goddess' voice.' Then I laughed. 'Do you think I speak blasphemy, Zabardi-bunugga? No. No. It is the truth: we must all remember it. The goddess speaks through her; but she is only a priestess. And I bear the burden of the city each day.' As we came near the gate of the city I said, 'What evidence do you have of this wrath of hers?'

'I have it from my father, who says she visited him in the temple of An to consult ancient tablets, writings from the time of Enmerkar, the annals of your grandfather's reign, the record of his dealings with the priestess of his time. She has been to the archives of the priests of Enlil also. And several times she summoned the assembly of elders to meet with her while you were away.'

Lightly I said, 'Perhaps she is writing a book of history, eh?'

'I think not, Gilgamesh. She seeks ways of bringing you in check: she looks for precedent, she searches for trustworthy strategies.'

'Do you merely suspect this or do you know?'

'It is certain knowledge. She has been speaking out, and many have heard her. Your journey angered her. She said so to your mother, to my father Gungunum, to some of the assembly of elders, even to her acolytes: she made no secret of her fury. She says it was presumptuous of you to undertake the venture without first seeking her blessing.'

'Ah, was it? But we needed the cedar. The Elamites had built a wall in the forest. It was not only a sacred quest, Zabardi-bunugga: it was a war. Decisions concerning warfare lie in the province of the king.'

'She sees it otherwise, I think.'

'I will educate her, then.'

'Be wary. She is a troublesome woman.'

I laid my hand upon his wrist and smiled. 'You tell me nothing new, old friend, when you tell me that. But I will be on my guard. And you have my thanks.'

We rode through the gate. I turned from him and lifted my shield high, so that it caught the last glow of the waning day and sent lances of golden light into the crowd that lined the grand processional highway. Half the city had turned out to welcome me. 'Gilgamesh!' they cried, till their voices were hoarse. 'Gilgamesh! Gilgamesh!' And they used the word that means *divine*, which is not used ordinarily of a king while he still lives. 'Gilgamesh the god! Gilgamesh the god!' I felt abashed; but only a little, for it would have been folly to deny the godhood within me.

Zabardi-bunugga's warnings had darkened my homecoming somewhat. But I had not been greatly surprised to hear them: Inanna had been quiescent too long, and I had for some while been expecting difficulties from her. Well, we would see; but I chose not to brood on these matters just now. It was the night of my homecoming; it was the night of my triumph.

At the palace I oiled and polished my weapons and put them in their storehouse, and said the laying-to-rest prayers over them. Then I went to the palace baths and opened my braid so that my hair streamed down my back, and the handmaidens rinsed the grime of the journey from it. Afterward I chose to leave my hair loose and long. I wrapped a fine fringed cloak about me and fastened a scarlet sash at my middle and even put on my royal tiara, which I did not wear often. When all that was done I called my fifty heroes about me, and Enkidu, and we gathered in the great hall of the palace for a feast of roasted calves and lambs, and cakes of flour mixed with honey, and beer both of the strong and the mild kinds, and royal palm-wine, the thickest and the richest in the Land. We even drank the wine made of grapes, which we bring in from the territories in the north, dark purple stuff that makes the soul soar upward. We sang and told tales of the warriors of old, and we stripped and wrestled by firelight, and we enjoyed the maidens of the palace until we felt sated; and then we bathed and dressed ourselves in our finery again and paraded out into the town, playing on fifes and trumpets and clapping our hands as we strutted about. Ah, it was a fine time, a splendid time! I will never know another like it.

In the silver-gray hours of the dawn slumbering heroes lay sprawled in heaps all about the palace, snoring forth their wine. I felt no need of sleep; and so I went to bathe at the palace fountain. Enkidu was with me. His robes reeked of drink and the juice of meat, and I suppose mine must have been no better. Bits of straw and charred twigs from the fire were in our beards and hair. But the cool fresh water refreshed and cleansed us as though it were a font of the gods. As I emerged I looked about me for a slave to bring us clean robes, and I caught sight of a slender figure at the far side of the courtyard, a woman, wearing an ashen-hued robe of some thin shimmering fabric, and a shawl pulled up around her face so that her features could not be seen. She appeared to be heading in my direction.

'You, there!' I called. 'Come here and do us a service, will you?'

She turned to me and lowered her shawl, and I saw her face. But I did not believe what I saw.

'Gilgamesh?' she said softly.

My breath went from me in astonishment. This could only be some apparition. 'A demon!' I whispered. 'Look, Enkidu, she wears Inanna's face! It must be Lilitu come to haunt us, or is it the ghost Utukku?' Fear and awe struck me like the clangor of a brazen bell, and I shuddered, and groped in my discarded clothes for the little amulet of the goddess that the young priestess Inanna had given me so long ago.

In the same soft voice she said, 'Have no fear, Gilgamesh. I am Inanna.'

'Here? In the palace? The priestess never leaves the temple to see the king: she calls the king to wait on her in her own domain.'

'This night it is I who comes to you,' she said. She was close beside me, now, and it seemed to me she was telling the truth: if this was some demon, it had more skill at mimicry than any demon I knew. And what demon, anyway, would dare to put on the guise of the goddess within the walls of the goddess' own city? Yet I could not understand the presence of Inanna in the palace precinct. It was not right. It was not done. My loins grew cold and there was a chill at the back of my neck, and I picked up my robe and draped it about me, soiled and sweaty though it was. Enkidu was staring at her as though she were some ravening beast of the fields, all fangs and teeth, making ready to spring.

I said hoarsely, 'What do you want with me?'

'Some words. Only some words.'

My throat was dry, my lips were cracking. 'Speak, then!'

'What I have to say, I would rather say in privacy.'

I glanced at Enkidu, who was scowling now. It displeased me to send him away; but I knew Inanna well enough to realize she would not be moved on this point. Sadly I said, 'I ask you to leave us, friend.'

'Must I go?'

'This time you must,' I said, and slowly he went from the courtyard, looking back several times, as if he feared the priestess would pounce on me the moment he was gone.

She said then, 'I saw you from the temple portico, when you paraded through the town this evening with your heroes. You have never looked more beautiful, Gilgamesh. You were as radiant as a god.'

'The joy of my victory put that glow upon me. We slew the demon; we obtained the wood; we cast down the wall the Elamites had raised.'

'So I have heard. It was a wondrous victory. You are a hero beyond compare: they will sing of you in ages yet to come.'

I stared into her eyes. At this hour, by this pale gray dawn-light, they seemed a color I had never seen before, darker even than black. I studied the flawless arches of her eyebrows; I made scrutiny of her fine straight nose and the fullness of her lips. There was heat coming from her, but it was a cold heat. I could not tell whether she stood before me as goddess or as woman; the two seemed mixed in her even more than usual. I thought of the warnings I had had from Zabardi-bunugga, and I knew from what he had said that she was my enemy; but she did not appear to be an enemy at this moment.

'Why are you here, Inanna?'

'I could not help myself. When I saw you in the evening I said, I will go to him when his feast is done, I will come to him before the dawn comes, I will offer myself.'

'Offer yourself? What are you saying?'

Her eyes were shining strangely, like silvery suns rising at midnight. 'Marry me, Gilgamesh. Be my husband.'

I was altogether dumbfounded at that.

In a halting way I said, 'But it is not the proper season, Inanna! The new year festival is still some months away, and—'

'I am not speaking now of the Sacred Marriage,' she said crisply. 'I speak of the marriage between man and wife, who live under the same roof, and bring forth children, and grow old together in the manner of husbands and wives.'

Had she spoken in the language of the people of the moon I could not have been more bewildered.

'But such a thing is impossible,' I said, when I found the use of my tongue again. 'The king—the priestess—never since the founding of the city—never in all the time of the Land—'

'I have spoken with the goddess. She gives consent. It can be done. I know that it is new and strange. But it can be done.' She took a step toward me, and put her hands to my hands. 'Hear me, Gilgamesh. Be my husband, give me the gift of the seed of your body, not one night out of the year but every night. Be my husband and I will be your wife. Listen, I will bring splendid gifts to you: I will harness for you a chariot of lapis and lazuli and gold, with wheels of gold, and brazen horns. You will have storm-demons to draw it for you, in place of mules. Our dwelling will be fragrant of cedars, and when you enter it, the threshold and dais will kiss your feet.'

179

'Inanna—'

There was no halting her. As though chanting in a trance she went on: 'Kings and lords and princes will bow down before you! All the yield of mountains and plains will they bring you as tribute! Your goats will bear triplets, your sheep will drop twins! The ass that carries burdens for you will outrun the swiftest of mules; your chariots will prevail in every race; your oxen will be without rivals, if only you let me bring my blessings upon you, Gilgamesh!'

'The people would not allow it,' I said numbly.

'The people! The people!' Her face became harsh and dark; her eyes turned cold. 'The people could not prevent us!' Her grip on my hand grew tighter: I imagined I could feel my bones moving about. In a low strange tone she said, 'The gods are angered with you, Gilgamesh, for the killing of Huwawa. Do you know that? They mean to take revenge on you.'

'It is not so, Inanna.'

'Ah, do you walk with the gods as I walk with the gods? I tell you, Enlil grieves for the guardian of his forest. They will have a blood-price from you for the death. They will make you grieve as Enlil grieves. But I can shield you from that. I can intercede. Give yourself to me, Gilgamesh! Take me as your wife! I am your only hope of peace.'

Her words fell upon me like an icy torrent that knew no mercy. I wanted to run from her; I wanted to bury my head in some soft dark place and sleep. All this was madness. Marry her? There was no way that could be. I thought for a wild moment of what it would be like to share her bed night after night, to feel the fire of her breath against my cheek, to taste the sweetness of her mouth. Yes, of course, what man would refuse such joys? But marriage? To the priestess, to the goddess? She could not marry; I could not marry her. Even if the city would permit it—and the city would not, the city would rise up instantly against us and give our corpses to the wolves—I could not bear it. To go humbly to the temple with my wedding gifts, kneeling before my own wife because she was also the goddess, the Queen of Heaven—no, no, it would be my ruin. I am the king. The king must not kneel. I shook my head as though to sweep away a gathering fog that grew thick in my spirit. I began to understand the truth. Her scheme became clear to me: a compound of greed and lust and envy. Her aim was to ensnare me in her trap, and bring me down. If she could not break the power of the king any other way, she would break him through marriage. Because she was a goddess she would make me kneel for her as no man, certainly no king, ever kneels to his wife. The people would laugh at me in the streets. The dogs themselves would howl at my heels. But I would not let her make me subservient to her. I would not let her buy me into this slavery with her body. And all her talk of the anger of gods, which she alone could avert from me—no, that must be some silly lie meant to frighten me. I would not let myself be threatened, either.

As these things became clear to me, a hot rage rose in me like fire on a summer mountain. Perhaps it was from having been awake all the night, perhaps it was the wine, perhaps it was some dark floating demon of the dawn air that entered into my spirit; or maybe it was simply that I was full of the overweening pride that came of my victory over Huwawa; but I grew intemperately fierce. I pulled my hand free of hers and loomed high above her and cried, 'You are my only hope, you say? What hope do you offer me, except the hope of pain and humiliation? What could I expect, if I were so foolish as to take you in marriage? You bring only peril and torment.'

The angry words poured from me. I would not and could not halt. 'What are you? A brazier that goes out in the cold. A back door which keeps out neither wind nor rain. A leaky waterskin that wets its bearer. A sandal that trips its wearer?'

She gaped at me, amazed, as I had been amazed when she had come to me with this talk of marriage.

I went on and on. 'What are you? A shoe that pinches its owner's foot. A stone that falls from a parapet. Pitch that defiles the hand, a palace that collapses on its inhabitants, a turban that does not cover the head. Marry you? Marry *you*? Ah, Inanna, Inanna, what folly, what madness!'

'Gilgamesh—'

'Where is there any hope for a man who falls into Inanna's snare? The gardener Ishullanu—I know that story. He came to you with baskets of dates, and you looked at him and smiled your smile, and said, "Ishullanu, come close to me, let me enjoy you, touch me here and touch me there." And he shrank back in terror of you, saying, "What do you want with me? I am only a gardener. You will freeze me as the frosts freeze the young rushes." And when you heard that you changed him into a mole and cast him down to tunnel in the earth.'

She said, astounded, 'Gilgamesh, that is only a tale of the goddess! That was not my doing, but the goddess' long ago!'

'It is all the same. You are the goddess, the goddess is you. Her sins are yours. Her crimes are yours. What has befallen the lovers of Inanna? The shepherd who heaped up meal-cakes for you, and slaughtered the tender kids: he wearied you and you struck him and turned him into a wolf, and now his own herd-boys drive him away, and his own dogs bite his thighs—'

'A fable, Gilgamesh, a story!'

'The lion you loved: seven pits you dug for him, and seven more. The bird of many colors: you broke his wing, and he sits in the grove now, crying, "My wing, my wing!" The stallion so noble in battle: you ordained the whip and the spur and the thong for him, and made him gallop seven leagues, and ordered him to drink from muddied water—'

'Are you mad? What are you saying? These are old tales the harpers tell, tales of the goddess!'

I suppose I was in a kind of madness. But I would not relent. 'Have you ever kept faith with one of your lovers? And will you not treat me as you treated them?' She opened her mouth to speak, but nothing came forth, and into her silence I said, 'What of Dumuzi? Tell me of him! You sent him down into hell.'

'Why do you throw fables in my face? Why do you keep reproaching me with things that have nothing to do with me?'

I ignored her. I was in a madness. 'Not Dumuzi the god,' I said. 'Dumuzi the king, who ruled in this city, and died before his years. Yes, tell me of Dumuzi! Dumuzi the god, Dumuzi the king, Inanna the goddess, Inanna the priestess—it is all the same. Every child knows the tale. She snares him and uses him and has her triumph over him. You will not do that with me.' Then I caught my breath and wiped my brow and in another voice entirely said, very coldly, 'This is the royal palace. You have no business being here. Go. *Go!*'

She reached for words and again no words came, only little wrathful stammering sounds. She gaped and stammered and backed away, her eyes hot, her face flaming. At the door she halted a moment and gave me a long chilling look. Then she said in a quiet calm voice that seemed to rise from the depths of the nether world, 'You will suffer, Gilgamesh. That I promise. You will feel pain beyond any pain you have ever imagined. So the goddess pledges.' And she was gone.

24

That year at the time of the new year festival the heat of the summer did not break, the moist wind called the Cheat did not blow from the south, and there was no sign of rain in the northern sky. These things gave me great fear, but I kept my uneasiness to myself, saying nothing even to Enkidu. After all, there had been other dry autumns in the past, and the rains had always come sooner or later. If this year it was later rather than sooner, nevertheless they would come. Or so I believed: so I hoped. But my fear was great, for I knew that Inanna was my enemy.

On the night of the ceremony of the Sacred Marriage she and I stood face to face for the first time since the visit she had paid to the palace that time at dawn. But when I came to the long chamber of the temple to greet her, her eyes were like polished stones, and she greeted me with the silence of a stone, and when I said, 'Hail, Inanna,' she did not reply, as Inanna must, with the words, 'Hail, royal husband, fountain of life.' I knew then that a doom had come to lie upon Uruk, a doom of her making.

I did not know what to do. We performed the showing-forth on the temple portico, we carried out the rites of the barley and honey, we went to the bedchamber and stood before the bed of ebony inlaid with ivory and gold. All this while she said not a single word to me, but I knew from her eyes that her hatred for me was unabated. The handmaiden-priestesses took her beads and breastplates from her, and lifted the latch of her loin-covering, and left her naked before me, and uncovered my body to her, and went from the room. She was as beautiful as ever, but yet there was no glow of desire upon her: her nipples were soft, her skin did not have the sheen of fleshly fire. This was not the Inanna I had known so long, the woman of unquenchable passion. She stood beside the bed with folded arms and said, 'You may stay here or not, as you wish. But you will not have me tonight.'

'It is the night of the Sacred Marriage. I am the god. You are the goddess.'

'I will not have the king of Uruk enter my body this night. The wrath of Enlil falls upon Uruk and its king. The Bull of Heaven will be loosed.'

'Will you destroy your own people?'

'I will destroy your arrogance,' she said. 'I have gone to my knees before Father Enlil—I, the goddess! Father, I said, turn loose the Bull of Heaven to bring down Gilgamesh for me, for Gilgamesh has scorned me. And I said to Enlil that if he did not do this thing, I would smash the door of the nether world and shatter its bolts, I would throw open the gate of hell and raise up the dead to devour the food of the living, and the hosts of the dead in the world would be greater than the number of the living. He yielded to me: he said he would loose the Bull.'

'Out of anger at me, you bring down years of drought upon Uruk? The people will starve!'

'There is grain in my warehouses, Gilgamesh. The people have paid their tithes to the goddess, and I have stored grain enough to last through seven years of seedless husks. I have fodder set aside for the cattle. When the hunger strikes, Inanna will be ready to give aid to her people. But you will already have fallen, Gilgamesh. They will have cast you from your high place, for bringing the wrath of the gods upon them.' Her voice was very calm. She stood naked before me as if it was nothing at all to reveal her body, as if she were only a statue of herself, or I a eunuch. I looked at her and there was nothing I could say or do. If the goddess did not embrace the god in the Sacred Marriage there would be no rain; but how could I force her? It would have been worse, if I had forced her.

She told me again, 'You may stay or not, as you wish.' But I had no wish to spend the night shivering in the cold gale of her wrath. I gathered my splendid kingly robes and draped them about me and made my way from the temple in sorrow and in fear.

In the palace I found Enkidu with three concubines, celebrating the night of the Sacred Marriage in his own way. Rivers of dark wine ran across the floor and half-eaten joints of roasted meat were on the table. In great surprise he said, 'Why are you back so soon, Gilgamesh?'

'Let me be, brother. This is a sad night for Uruk.'

He did not seem to hear me. 'Are you done with your goddess so soon? Why, then, have a goddess or two of mine!' And he laughed; but his laughter died away in a moment, when he saw the wintry bleakness of my face. He shook himself free of the girls who were twined all over him, and came to me and put his hands on my shoulders, and said, 'What is this, brother? Tell me what has happened!'

I told him; and he said, 'If this Bull of hers is to be set loose in the city, why, we will have to catch it and put it back in its pen, will we not? Is that not so, Gilgamesh? How can we allow a wild bull to run free in Uruk?' And he laughed again, and threw his arms around me in his great bearish embrace. For the first time that evening my heart rose, and I thought, perhaps we will withstand this: perhaps we can contend successfully with her, Enkidu and I.

But there was no rain. Day upon day the sky was a sheet of brilliant blue in which Utu's great eye stared remorselessly down on us. The scorching wind was a knife slicing into the earth, hurling aloft the dry mud of the riverbanks and the sand of the gray and yellow desert beyond. Suffocating dust-clouds fell upon us like shrouds. The barley withered in the fields. The fronds of the palms grew black with dust, and drooped like the wings of crippled birds. Thunder came, and lightening, and dreadful flares of light covered the land like a cloth; but the storms were dry storms, and still there was no rain. Enlil was our enemy. Inanna was our enemy. An ignored us. Utu would not hear us. The people gathered in the streets and cried out,

'Gilgamesh, Gilgamesh, where is the rain?' and what could I tell them, what could I tell them?

Then far to the east the earth shook and the hills roared and there came such a belching of flame and foul gas as to make the outpouring of Huwawa seem like a sweet gentle breeze. I had an army of a thousand men in that territory, searching out the places where the Elamites were descending to our domain, and of those thousand men scarce half returned to Uruk. 'It was the Bull of Heaven breaking loose,' they told me. 'The sky grew dark and black smoke arose, and there was a landslide that roared, and we saw the Bull in the air over our heads. Three times he snorted; and with his first snort he slew a hundred men, and a hundred more with the second, and with the third snort two hundred more. The earth shook, the hills roared, the Bull of Heaven breathed foulness upon us. The smell of it is in our nostrils still. And now the Bull marches upon Uruk.'

What was I to do? Where could I turn?

'It is the Bull,' the people cried. 'The Bull is upon us!'

'The Bull still grazes in the temple pasture,' I said. 'All will be well. These tribulations soon shall end.'

And I looked toward the blazing sky, and said inwardly to Lugalbanda, *Father, father, go to Enlil, ask him for rain.* But there was no rain.

Inanna kept to her temple. She accepted no petitions, she performed no rites. When the people gathered before the White Platform and begged for mercy, she sent her maidens out with word that they had come to the wrong place, that they should go to Gilgamesh for mercy, for it was Gilgamesh who had brought this evil upon the land. Again, they came to me. But what could I tell them? What could I do?

The wind grew more fierce. A story arose in the town that this wind that blew was the wind of the nether world, a demon-wind that carried the seeds of death and decay up to us out of the House of Dust and Darkness. I said it was not. It was whispered in the town that there was a curse upon the wells, and they soon would fill with blood, so that the vineyards and palm groves would run red with it. I told them it would not happen. The rumor spread in the town that an army of locusts was flying toward us out of the

186

north, and soon the sky would darken under their wings. They will not come, I said.

I gave the people grain from my storehouse. I provided fodder for the cattle. But there was not enough, not nearly enough. It is not the province of the king to provide the grain in time of drought and famine; it is the province of Inanna. And Inanna withheld herself from the people, and withheld her grain. Nor did the people hate her for it: she let it be known in the town that Uruk must first be purified, and then she would open her granaries to the needy. They understood. I understood. She meant to bring me down.

And at the last she loosed the Bull within the confines of the city. I mean the bull that grazed in the temple pasture, the one that embodied in himself the might and majesty of the gods. For twenty thousand years, or twice twenty, there have been bulls in the pasture of Inanna's temple, great bulls, mighty bulls, giant bulls without equal in the Land; they grow fat and huge on the grain of the temple offerings, and wear garlands of fresh flowers in every season of the land, and heifers are brought to them daily for their pleasure, and when they die—for they do die, even they, these bulls who play the part of the Bull of Heaven—they are buried in the temple grounds with rites worthy of a god. I cannot tell you how many bulls have been buried there in the years of Uruk, but I think that if that pasture were to be ploughed, the ploughman would turn up a sea of horns.

Never once does the bull leave the pasture of the temple, once he has taken up residence there. Guards are posted night and day to see that that does not happen; and though he snort like Enlil himself, and paw the ground and crash with all his force against the gate, he cannot go free. But on the holy midwinter day, when the drought stood at its worst and the sky was gray with swirling dust and those of us whose senses were most keen could smell the reek of the deadly black outpourings that were rushing into the air from the vents of the Rebel Lands far to the east—on that day when calamity was already rife in Uruk, Inanna turned loose the Bull of Heaven into the streets of the city.

The outcry of grief and terror that arose was like nothing that had ever been heard in Uruk before. I think that cry must have resounded in Kish; I think they must have heard it in Nippur; perhaps even in the Elamite lands they looked up and said, 'What is that awful cry out of the west?'

In my palace I trembled with dismay and woe. It seemed to me now that I must go to Inanna, and kneel to her, and yield to her, and deliver up the city to her; for otherwise the people all would perish, or else I would be cast down from my high place. It had begun to seem to me that I must after all be responsible for this ruin that had come upon Uruk, that it was I and not Inanna who had brought these evils to the city, even as she was saying. Perhaps the gods were indeed taking their vengeance for the death of Huwawa. Perhaps I had erred in refusing to make the priestess my queen. Perhaps—perhaps—perhaps—

I had never known such despair as on that day when Inanna's bull pranced and snorted in the streets of Uruk. It was Enkidu who lifted me from it. He found me grieving in the palace, and drew me up and embraced me and said, 'Come, brother, why do you weep? Deliverance is at hand!'

'Do you know that the Bull of Heaven is loose in the city?' I asked him.

'Yes, Gilgamesh, yes, the bull is loose! And this is our moment. Can we turn back the dry winds? Can we call rain from the heavens? Can we turn sand into water? No, no, no, none of those things can we do: but we can kill a bull, brother. We can surely kill a bull. Now at last Inanna has poured all of her fury into a single vessel. Let us go out there, Gilgamesh: let us break that vessel.' His eyes were glittering with excitement. His body throbbed with strength. I took heart from his vigor. I smiled for the first time in I cannot tell you how many days, and I embraced him until he grunted with the force of my embrace. 'Come, brother,' he said, and we went out into the dry and dusty streets to seek the Bull of Heaven.

It was the noon hour. The streets were empty in that terrible heat. But I did not need to ask the way to the bull. Its presence announced itself in the city like the heat of a heated anvil: I felt the red glow of it hot against my cheeks. As did Enkidu, in whom the wisdom of the wilderness still lived. He held his face to the wind, he flared his nostrils wide, he turned his head so that his ears

188

gathered in all the sounds; and he pointed, and we went forward. In the district known as the Lion we saw the dung of the bull fresh in the streets, with a golden aura about it, and blue-headed flies buzzing above it but not daring to touch it. In the district known as the Reed we found the carts of the merchants overturned, and their merchandise strewn in the path, for the bull had come this way. And in the district known as the Hive, where the streets press close upon one another and there is scarcely room to walk, we saw bricks ripped loose from the buildings where the bull had run between them.

A little while on, we came upon something worse: the cobblestones stained bright with blood, the sounds of bitter sobbing and wailing, and a man and a woman standing like statues, blank-eyed. The man held a child's broken body in his arms. A boy, I think, four or five years old, who must have darted into the bull's path. I prayed that Enlil had granted the child a swift death; but what mercy would the god grant the mother and the father? As we ran past, the woman recognized us. Without saying a word she held her hand out toward me, as though to beg me, *O king, give me back my son.* I could not do that for her. I could give her nothing to ease her sorrow but the blood of the bull, and I did not think that would be enough.

This little death, I thought, must be tallied to Inanna's account. Is that how she serves her people, by killing their innocent children with her furious vengeful beast?

Enkidu and I sped onward, grim-faced, intent. A few moments more and we turned into the great open space known as the Place of Ningal: and there we came upon the bull himself, prancing wildly like a playful calf.

He was white—all the bulls of the temple are white—and he was huge, and his eyes were rimmed with red, and his horns were long and sharp as spears, but they curved in a strange wicked way almost like the frame of a lyre. I saw splashes of the child's blood on the hooves of his forelegs, and on his pastern. When we came upon him he smelled our sweat, and halted and turned and glared at us out of eyes that blazed like coals; and he snorted, he stamped, he lowered his head, he seemed to be making ready to charge. Enkidu looked at me, and I at Enkidu. Together we had slain

189

elephants and we had slain lions and we had slain wolves. We had even slain a demon that came belching out of the ground like a column of fire. But we had never slain a bull, and this was a bull enjoying the first heady measure of freedom after too long in captivity. He was full of his own power, and the power of Father Enlil was in him besides; for I did not doubt that this bull was the Bull of Heaven today, just as at certain times Inanna the priestess is Inanna the goddess, and the king of Uruk is Dumuzi the god of the fields. So we caught our breaths and we made ready to meet his thrust, knowing it would not be an easy combat.

I beckoned him with my hand. 'Come to us,' I said, whispering it, making my voice seductive. 'Come here. Come. Come. Come. I am Gilgamesh: this is Enkidu my brother.'

The bull stamped. The bull snorted. The bull lifted his great head and tossed his horns. And then he charged, running with great grace and majesty. He appeared almost to float as he came across the worn brick pavement of the Place of Ningal.

Enkidu, laughing, cried out to me, 'What sport this will be, brother! Play him! Play him, brother! We have nothing to fear!'

He ran to one side, and I to the other. The bull stopped in midstride and pivoted and whirled and charged again, and halted a second time and pivoted and whirled, kicking up dust. He seemed almost to frown as we darted back and forth around him, laughing, slapping each other on the shoulders. The bull cast his foam in our faces and brushed us with the thick of his tail. But he could not run us down; he could not bring us to earth.

Five times the bull charged, and five times we skipped past him, until he was angry and perplexed. Then he charged once more, feinting with demonic intelligence and feinting again, changing his course as lithely as any dancing-boy of the temple, going now this way, now that. Fiercely he sprang at Enkidu with lowered horns, and I feared that my brother would be gored: but no, as the bull drew near Enkidu reached out and clamped one hand to each of his horns and swung himself up in a single swift leap, twisting in mid-air so that when he landed he was astride the bull's back, still grasping the horns.

Now began such a combat as I think the world had never seen before. Enkidu atop the Bull of Heaven grappled with him by the horns, twisting his head this way and that. The bull in rage reared high on his hind legs to throw him off, but could not do it. I stood before them watching in joy and delight. It seemed to me that my friend must now have fully recovered the strength of his hand, for he held so tight against so great a power; but even if he were not fully recovered, his strength was still sufficient to maintain his grip. The bull could not rid himself of Enkidu. He roared, he stamped, he hurled flecks of spittle about, and still Enkidu held on. Enkidu turned all his enormous strength to the breaking of the bull, forcing him into weariness, making him lower his mighty head. I heard Enkidu's booming laughter, and rejoiced; I saw Enkidu's massive arms bulging with the strain, and took pleasure in the sight. I watched the bull grow sullen and downcast. But then the combat took a different turn. The bull, having rested a moment, summoned new strength, and plunged and leaped and plunged and leaped again, striving with renewed ferocity to hurl Enkidu to the ground. I feared for him; but Enkidu showed no fear at all. He clung, he held, he twisted the great head from side to side; once again he forced the bull's muzzle toward the ground.

'Now, brother!' Enkidu called. 'Strike, strike now! Thrust in your sword!'

It was the moment. I rushed forward and took the hilt of my sword in both my hands, and rose to my greatest height, and drove the sword downward. I thrust it in between the nape and the horns, forcing it deep. The bull made a sound like the sound of the going out of the sea when the tide is dwindling, and a film came over the blazing fury of his eyes. For a moment he stood entirely still, and then his legs turned to water beneath him. As he fell, Enkidu sprang clear, landing beside me, and we laughed and embraced and rested a little time beside the dying bull until he was dead. Then we cut out his heart and made an offering of it on the spot to Utu of the sun.

When that was done I looked about me, and when I looked toward the west, toward the rampart of the city, I saw figures upon the wall. I touched Enkidu's arm and pointed.

'It is your goddess,' he said.

In truth it was. Inanna and her handmaidens were on the wall. She must have watched the battle with the bull; I could feel the heat and the force of her wrath even at this distance. I cupped my hands and called out to her, 'See, priestess! We have slain your bull: the rains soon will come, I think!'

'Woe to you,' she replied in a voice like a voice out of hell. And to her maidens and the other onlookers she cried, 'Woe to Gilgamesh! Woe to him who dares to hold me in contempt! Woe to the slayer of the Bull of Heaven!'

To which Enkidu replied back, 'And woe to you, croaking bird of doom! Here: I make my offering to you!'

Boldly he ripped loose the private parts of the dead bull and flung them with all his might, so that the bloody flesh landed on the rampart almost at her feet. He laughed his rumbling laugh and called to her, 'There, goddess! Does that appease you? If I could get hold of you, I'd drape you in the bull's own guts!' At that blasphemy she cursed us again, both Enkidu and me; and the women beside her on the wall, the priestesses, the handmaidens, the temple courtesans, the votaries of all sorts who had come with her to see us destroyed by the bull that now lay dead at our feet, set up a great wailing and a lamentation.

25

I would not even let her have the carcass of the bull to bury at the temple grounds: I meant to deny her everything. I summoned the butchers and had the meat cut into strips and given freely to the dogs of the town, to show my contempt for Inanna and her bull. But the horns of the bull I took for myself. I turned them over to my craftsmen and my armorers, who were wonderstruck by the length of the horns, and their thickness. I commanded them to plate the horns with lapis lazuli to a thickness of two fingers, for I meant to hang them on the wall of the palace. So great were they that they had a capacity of six measures of oil: I filled them with the finest of ointments, and then I poured the oil out at the shrine of Lugalbanda, in honor of the god my father who had brought me this triumph.

When all this was done we washed our hands in the waters of the river and rode together through the streets of Uruk to the palace. The people crept forth one by one from their houses to see us, and after the first had come out the others took heart, until a great multitude lined our path. Heroes and warriors of Uruk were there, and girls playing lyres, and many more. Boastfulness took hold of me, and I called out to them, 'Who is the most glorious of the heroes? Who is the greatest among men?' They called back, 'Gilgamesh is the most glorious of the heroes! Gilgamesh is the greatest among men!' Why should I not have been boastful? Inanna had set loose the Bull of Heaven; and I had slain it—Enkidu and I. Did we not have the right to boast?

There was feasting and celebration at the palace that night. We sang and drank until we could revel no more, and we went to our beds. In that night the wind called the Cheat began to blow; and the air grew soft and moist. Before morning the first rain that had fallen all that winter began to fall upon Uruk.

That day was the peak of my glory. That day was the height of my triumph. I felt there was nothing I could not achieve. I had increased the wealth of my city and made it preeminent in the land; I had slain Huwawa; I had slain the Bull of Heaven; I had brought rain to Uruk; I had been a good shepherd to my people. Nevertheless after that day I knew little joy and much sadness, which I suppose is the lot that the gods had intended for me even while they permitted me my moments of triumph. That is the way of life: there is grandeur, and there is sorrow, and we learn in time that the darkness follows upon the light whether or not we choose to have it that way.

In the morning Enkidu came to me, looking somber and weary, as though some great darkness of the soul had visited him while he slept. I said, 'Why is it that you carry yourself so mournfully, brother, when the bull lies dead and the rains have come to Uruk?' He sat down by the side of my couch and sighed and said, 'My friend, why are the gods in council?' I did not understand; but then he said, 'I have had a dream that lies heavy on me, brother. Shall I tell you my dream?'

He had dreamed that the gods were sitting in their council–chamber; An was there, and Enlil, and heavenly Utu, and the wise Enki. And Sky-father An said to Enlil, 'They have killed the Bull of Heaven, and they have killed Huwawa also. Therefore one of the two must die: let it be the one who stripped the cedar from the mountains.'

Then Enlil spoke up and said, 'No, Gilgamesh must not die, for he is king. It is Enkidu who must die.' At this Utu raised his voice to declare, 'They sought my protection when they went to slay Huwawa, and I granted it. When they slew the Bull, they made an offering of his heart to me. They have done no wrong. Enkidu is innocent: why should he die?' Which enraged Enlil, and he turned angrily to heavenly Utu, saying, 'You speak of them as though they are your comrades! But sins have been committed; and Enkidu is the one who must die.' And so the argument raged until Enkidu awakened.

I was quiet for a time when he had finished, and I kept my face a mask. Such a dire dream! It filled me with fear. I did not want him to see that. I did not want to face that fear myself. Fear gives dreams power that they might otherwise not have. I resolved to let this dream have no power, to sweep it aside as one would sweep aside a dry reed.

At length I said, 'I think you ought not to take this too close to heart, brother. Often the true meaning of a dream is less obvious than it seems.'

Enkidu stared in a dismal way at the floor. 'A dream portending death is a dream portending death,' he said sulkily. 'All the sages will agree on that. I am a dead man already, Gilgamesh.'

I thought that was nonsense, and I told him so. I said he was not dead so long as he lived, and he looked full of life to me. I said also that it is folly to take any dream so literally that you let it govern your waking life. I will not pretend that I fully believed that, even as I said it: I know as well as anyone that dreams are whispered into our souls at night by the gods, and that they often carry messages worth heeding. But I found nothing in this dream that Enkidu might do well to heed, and much that would be harmful if brooded upon. And so I urged him to put all gloomy thoughts behind him and go about his business as if he had heard nothing but the chattering of birds in his dream, or the murmuring of the winds.

That seemed to hearten him. Gradually his face brightened, and he nodded and said, 'Yes, perhaps I take this thing too seriously.'

'Too seriously by half, Enkidu.'

'Yes. Yes. It is my great fault. But you always bring me back to my right senses, old friend.' He smiled and gripped my arm. Then, rising, he dropped into a wrestler's crouch and beckoned to me. 'Come: what do you say to a little sport to lighten the day?'

'A fine idea!' I answered. I laughed to see him turn less doleful. For an hour we wrestled, and then we bathed; and then it was time for me to attend to the meeting of the assembly. By midday I had put Enkidu's dream behind me, and I think so had he. For a moment it had darkened our lives; but it had passed like a shadow across the ground. Or so I believed.

A few days later, as an act of thanksgiving for the lifting of the Bull of Heaven from the city, I decreed that we would perform the rite of purification known as the Closing of the Gate. That was something which had not been done in Uruk for so long that not even the oldest priests remembered the exact details of it. I set six scholars to work for three days searching through the library of the Temple of An for an account of the rite, and the best they could find was a tablet written in such an antique way that they could hardly make out the picture-writing it bore. 'Never mind,' I said. 'I will ask Lugalbanda for guidance. He will show me what must be done.'

I meant to make certain that the passageway which runs downward from Uruk into the nether world was properly sealed, since Inanna had threatened to open it as part of the loosing of the Bull of Heaven. In her wrath she could actually have done some harm to the gate, so that evil spirits or perhaps the ghosts of the dead might be able to drift up through it into the city. So I must be sure the gate is shut, I thought, and I devised a rite intended to accomplish that. I drew the procedure out of the hazy memories of the oldest priests and the writing on that ancient tablet and my own sense of what would be fitting. It was a proper rite, I think.

Yet if I had to do it over again, I would let the gate of hell stand open for a thousand years, rather than have what happened that day befall me.

The gate is one of the oldest structures in Uruk—some say even older than the White Platform, and that, of course, was built by the gods themselves. The gate lies a hundred twenty paces east of the White Platform. It is nothing more than a ring of weather-beaten kiln-baked bricks of a very old-fashioned shape, surrounding a stout round door of flaked and rusted copper that lies flat on the ground, like a trapdoor. A ring is set in the middle of that door, fashioned of some black metal that no one can identify. Two or three strong men pulling on that ring with all their might can raise the door out of the ground. When the door is lifted it reveals a dark hole that is the mouth of a tunnel, scarcely wider than the shoulders of a sturdy man, which slopes down under the earth. If one goes down into it one comes after a short time to a second gate which is nothing more than some metal bars mounted from floor to ceiling of the tunnel like the bars of a cage. On the far side of that the angle of the tunnel's descent becomes much steeper, and if one were mad enough to follow it one would come eventually to the first of the seven walls of the underworld itself. Each of those walls has its gate; the demon Neti, gatekeeper of the nether world, guards them: and behind the seventh wall is the lair of Ereshkigal, Queen of Hell, sister of Inanna.

Until the ill-starred day when I chose to do the rite of the Closing of the Gate no one had passed through that gate for thousands of years. The last to do it, so far as I knew, was the goddess Inanna long ago, when she made her unhappy descent into hell to challenge the power of Ereshkigal. Since then the dread tunnel surely had gone unentered. Although we pull the door from the ground once every twelve years for the rite known as the Opening of the Gate, in which we cast libations into the tunnel to propitiate Ereshkigal and her demon hordes, no one in his right mind would step as much as half a stride across its threshold.

We commenced the Closing of the Gate at the noon hour sharp, when it is the middle of the night in the nether world and I thought it likely most of the demons would be at rest. The day was warm and bright, though it had rained in the dark hours. Enkidu was at

196

my side, and my mother Ninsun just behind me; arrayed in a circle about me were the chief priests of all the temples of the city and the high members of the royal court. The only great personage of Uruk who did not attend was Inanna. She remained brooding behind the walls of the temple I had built for her. Beyond the circle of dignitaries were lesser priests by the double dozen, and hundreds of musicians ready to make a fierce outcry with drums and fifes and trumpets if spirits should begin coming forth through the gate when we opened it. And behind them were all the common citizens of Uruk.

I nodded to Enkidu. He put his left hand to the ring of the door, and I my right, and we lifted it. Though it was said to be a mighty task to open that door, we pulled it from the ground as easily as if it had been a feather. Out of the pit came the stale, sour odor of old air. My hands were cold. My face was set hard and tight. I felt the chill of death coming from the nether world. I stared downward but I saw nothing but darkness after the first few steps.

I held my spirit tautly in check. There are some places that arouse such fear we dare not think of the peril; we act without giving thought, for to think is to be lost. That was how I acted then. I gave the signal, and we began the ceremony.

The rite that I had devised began with an offering of aromatic barley seed, which I tossed into the opening myself. If any dark beings were lurking just within the tunnel, perhaps they would busy themselves down there quarreling over the barley, and would not emerge even though the gateway was open. Then the priests of An and Enlil and Utu and Enki came forward and made libations of honey, milk, beer, wine, and oil. That insured us the good will of the high gods. A small child, the daughter of a priest, led a white sheep forth, and I sacrificed it with one quick clean stroke of my blade at a sacrificial stand that Enkidu had erected at the edge of the passageway. Blood of a startling brightness spurted as if from a fountain and ran down along the little creature's slender white throat, and it quivered and sighed and looked at me sadly and died. That was intended as a gift to the gatekeeper Neti, so that he would prevent spirits and demons from emerging into our world. I drew a band of the blood across my forehead and another down my left cheek as a protection for myself.

When these things were done, the priests and I knelt at the rim of the tunnel and chanted spells of sealing, to weave a band of magic across the opening as our final line of defense. I knew that neither the lower gate nor the trapdoor would have any real effect on a spirit that was determined to come forth. The gate and the door were useful merely in keeping living folk from straying into the underworld; but it was by incantations alone that the dwellers beneath could be made to stay where they belonged.

I was frightened. What man would not be, however brave a face he offered to the world? The nether world itself stood open before me. I heard the black waters of its hidden rivers lapping at unseen shores. The pungent acrid smoke of its deadly vapors rose and coiled like hungry serpents about me. But yet, fearful though I was, I was excited also, and filled with a high boldness of purpose. For I was Gilgamesh who had said, even as a boy, *Death, I will conquer you! Death, you are no match for me!*

So we wove our spells. 'All you who would do us harm, whoever you may be, you whose heart conceives our misfortune, whose tongue utters mischief against us, whose lips poison us, in whose footsteps death stands: I ban you!' I cried. 'I ban your mouth, I ban your tongue, I ban your glittering eyes, I ban your swift feet, I ban your toiling knees, I ban your laden hands. By these conjurings I bind your hands behind your back. Whether you are a ghost unburied, or a ghost that none cares for, or a ghost with none to make offerings to it, or a ghost that has none to pour libations to it, or a ghost that has no descendants, whatever cause leads you to wander, nevertheless I compel you to remain below. By Ereshkigal and Gugalanna, by Nergal and Namtaru, I conjure you never to pass these gates. By the might of Enlil that is in me—by An and Utu, by Enki and Ninazu, by Allatu, by Irkalla, by Belit-seri, by Apsu, Tiamat, Lahmu, Lahamu—'

That was the chant I chanted. I bound the beings below by every name that they might hold holy, except for one; I did not bind them in the name of Inanna. Though she was the patron goddess of the city, I would not bind them in her name. I knew that such a binding would be of no avail so long as Inanna's priestess was my enemy.

And because I had not bound them by Inanna's name, I was not certain that any of my spells would be of value. So I had with me at the ceremony my sacred drum, which the craftsman Ur-nangar had made for me out of the wood of the huluppu-tree. I meant to beat on it in my special way and put myself into my trance in front of all the people of Uruk, a thing I had never done before; and then I would send my spirit down into the tunnel, I would venture even to the gates of the underworld, for when I was in my trance there was no barrier to my roving. In that way I would be able to see for myself whether our spells had truly sealed the passage against those terrible creatures of black smoke and dank musty vapor.

I said to Enkidu, 'There should be revelry and dancing while I do this. Give the order: have the musicians strike up.'

Almost at once the sound of trumpets and fifes filled the air. I bent low over my drum and began the slow quiet tapping I knew so well. I felt myself in the presence of the great mystery of mysteries, which is the life beyond life that the gods alone can know. All awareness of the solid world about me faded. There was only my drum and my drumstick, and the steady subtle rhythm of my drumming. It took possession of my soul. It seized me, it lifted me. I saw an aura coming out of the tunnel, rising like flame, cool and blue. There was a buzzing in my ears, a droning, a crackling. I felt a stirring within my body, as though some wild thing were moving about inside me. My breath came fast; my vision dimmed. I was overflowing; a sea was rising out of me and engulfing me.

But then just as the full ecstacy was about to come upon me, and I was making ready to launch myself from my body, there came a shriek from behind me that cut through my soul as an axe cuts through wood, and ripped me from my trance; a shrill harsh outcry, piercing and fierce, over and over.

'Utu! Utu! Utu!'

Gods, what a scream! The unearthly sound jolted me and shook me and stunned me. I went numb and pitched forward, all but insensible, as though I had been struck between the shoulders. Enkidu caught me by the shoulders and held me, or I would have toppled down the tunnel; but my drum and my drumstick fell from my frozen hands. I watched with horror as I saw them disappear into the dark mouth of the nether world.

At once almost without thinking I started to scramble down

after them. But Enkidu, still gripping my shoulders, hauled me roughly back and flung me to one side as though I were a sack of barley. 'Not you!' he cried angrily. 'You must not go into that place, Gilgamesh!' And before I could say or do anything he ran down the steps that led into the earth, and vanished entirely from sight in that black pit.

Dazed, I peered after him. I could not speak. There was an overwhelming silence all about me: the musicians were motionless, the dancers were still. Out of that silence rose a single sound, a muffled sobbing or whimpering that came from a girl of eight or ten years who lay writhing on the ground not far away, held down by one of the priests. It was she who had screamed in that terrible way and had broken my trance; I saw that the beating of my drum must have worked on her soul much as it did mine, but even more powerfully. The drumming had driven her not into the trance of ecstasy but into a terrible fit, under the force of which her mind had given way. Her convulsions still continued. They were frightful to behold.

And Enkidu? Where was Enkidu? Trembling, I stared into the tunnel, and saw only blackness. I found my voice and called his name, or croaked it, rather, and heard nothing. I called again, more loudly. Silence. Silence. '*Enkidu!*' I cried, and it was a great wail of pain and loss. I was sure he had been set upon by the minions of Ereshkigal; perhaps they had already carried him off to hell. 'Wait!' I shouted. 'I'm coming after you!'

'You must not,' said my mother sharply, and suddenly three or four men were at my elbows ready to hold me back. If they had tried to restrain me I would have hurled them over the city wall into the river. But there was no need of that, for just then I heard the sound of a choking cough close by in the tunnel, and Enkidu came slowly up out of it. He was holding my drum and my drumstick in his hand.

He looked ghostly. He was like one who had returned from the dead. All color was gone from his skin: his face seemed bleached, so pale was it. His hair and beard were gray with dust, and his white robe was badly soiled. Great tangles of cobwebs were snarled about his body, and even over his mouth; he was trying to brush at them with his shoulders as he emerged into the light. He stood there a moment dazzled and blinking. There was a look in his eyes of such wildness, such strangeness, that I scarcely knew him to be my friend. Those who had been standing near me backed away. I felt almost like backing away from him myself.

'I have brought back your drum and your drumstick, Gilgamesh,' he said in a voice like cinders and ashes. 'They fell a long way: they were beyond the second gate. But I went on my hands and knees until I touched them in the dark.'

I stared at him, appalled. 'It was madness. You should not have gone into that tunnel.'

'But you had dropped your drum,' he said, in that same strange whisper. He shivered and rubbed his shoulder against his face again, and coughed and sneezed from the dust. 'I had to try to bring it back. I know how important it is to you.'

'But the dangers—the evils—'

Enkidu shrugged. 'Here is your drum, Gilgamesh. Here is your drumstick.'

I took them from him. They did not feel right; it was as if they had lost eleven parts out of twelve of their weight. They were so light I thought they might float out of my grasp. Enkidu nodded. 'Yes,' he said. 'They are different now. I think the god-strength must have gone out of them. It is a terrible place, down there.' He shuddered once more. 'I could not see anything. But as I crawled, I felt bones breaking beneath me. Old dry bones. There is a carpet of bones in that tunnel, Gilgamesh. People have gone down into it before me. But I think I may have been the first one to come out.'

Something hung in the air between us like a curtain. The strangeness that had come upon him in that other world now screened his soul from mine. I felt I could not reach him; I felt almost as though I did not know him any longer. A sense of irretrievable loss choked my soul. The Enkidu I had known had vanished. He had been to a place I dared not enter and he had returned with knowledge that I would never be able to comprehend.

'Tell me what you saw there,' I said. 'Were there demons?'

'I told you: it was dark. I saw nothing. But I felt their presence. I felt them all around me.' He gestured toward the gaping tunnel. 'You should close up that pit, brother, and never open it again. Seal the door, and seal it again and seven times over.'

I thought I would burst with rage, to see him so shattered for the sake of my drum. How could I call back the moment? Cling to the drum lest it fall into that hole, cling to Enkidu lest he go rushing off after it? But all that was engraved forever in the book of time. Bitterly I said, 'I will seal it, yes. But it is too late, Enkidu! If only you had not gone down there—'

He smiled a faint wan smile. 'I would do it for you again, if I had to. But I hope I will not have to.' Then he came close to me. I could smell the dry smell of dust and cobwebs that were on him. In a voice like a torch that has gone out he said, 'I saw nothing while I was in the underworld because everything was black there. But there was one thing I saw with my heart and not with my eyes, and it was myself, Gilgamesh, my own body, which the vermin were devouring as though it were an old cloak. Those were my own bones I crawled on in that tunnel. And now I am frightened, old friend. I am very frightened.' He put his arms lightly to my shoulders and gave me a dusty embrace. Gently he said, 'I am sorry that your drum has lost its god-strength. I would have brought it back to you as it was, if I could have done it. You know that: I would have brought it back to you as it was.'

26

I think it was the next day that Enkidu's illness began. He complained that his hand, the one he had injured when forcing the gate in the forest of cedars, felt chilled. An hour or two later he spoke of a stiffness and a soreness in that arm. Then he said he was feverish, and took to his bed.

'It is as it was in my dream,' he said gloomily to me. 'The gods have met in council, and they have decreed that I am the one who must die, because you are king.'

'You will not die,' I said with a loving anger in my voice. 'No one dies of a soreness in the arm! You must have hurt it again while you were crawling about in that foul tunnel. I have sent for the healers: they will set you aright before nightfall.'

He shook his head. 'I tell you I am dying, Gilgamesh.'

It frightened and maddened me to hear him so weary and faint. He was yielding to whatever demon had seized him, and that was not like him. 'I will not have it!' I cried. 'I will not let you die!' I knelt beside his bed. He was flushed and his forehead was shiny with sweat. Urgently I said, 'Brother, I cannot abide losing you. I beg you: speak no more of dying. The healers are on their way, and they will make you well again.'

I watched over him as a lioness watches over her cub. He muttered, he moaned, his eyes were veiled by a film. He said that his head hurt him and his mouth pricked him, his eyes troubled him, his ears were singing. His throat choked him, his neck muscles hurt. His breast, his shoulders, and his loins hurt him; his fingers were cramped; his stomach was inflamed; his bowels were hot. His hands, his feet, and his knees were aching. There was no part of his body that did not trouble him. He lay trembling, gripped by death or the fear of death, and I felt for his sake that fear as well. Seeing him in mortal terror I was reminded of my own mortality, which tormented me like a knife in my flesh. It was the old enemy, and though he was coming to call not on me but on my friend, he could not but awaken my own fear of him. But I was determined: I had already resolved not to yield to death myself, nor would I allow him to have Enkidu.

I did whatever seemed useful. Perhaps it was the presence of the drum in the palace that was afflicting him, I thought, by carrying some taint of the nether world. I did not know, but I would not take the chance. The drum was hateful to me now. I ordered priests to take it outside the city walls and burn it, using such rites as will dispel those spirits. Greatly did I lament its loss, but I would not keep it by me if it made Enkidu ill. So the drum was burned. Yet Enkidu did not recover.

The healers came, the most skilled diviners and exorcists in the city. The first who viewed him was old Namennaduma, the royal baru-priest, the great diviner. His consultation was lengthy; for several hours he studied Enkidu, consulting the omens so that he could make a preliminary diagnosis and prognosis. Then he summoned me to the sickroom and said, 'There is great danger.'

'Drive it away, seer, or you will find yourself in danger even greater,' I said.

Namennaduma must have heard such threats before: my harsh words did not seem to trouble him. Calmly he replied, 'We will treat him. But we must know more. Tonight we will consult the stars, and tomorrow we will do the divination by sheep's-liver. And then the treatment can begin.'

'Why wait so long? Do your divining today!'

'Today is not auspicious,' the baru-priest said. 'It is an unlucky time of the month, and the moon is unfavorable.' I could not argue with that. So off he went to study the stars, and into the room came the azu, the water-knower, the man of medicines. This doctor touched his hand to Enkidu's breast and to his cheek, and nodded and scowled, and took certain powders from his pouch. Then he said to me, as though I were some sort of azu myself, 'We will give him the powder of anadishsha and the ground seeds of duashbur, mixed into beer and water. That will cool the fever. And for his pain, the lees of the dried vine and the oil of the pine tree, made into a poultice. And to help him sleep, the powdered seeds of nigmi, and an extract of the roots and trunk of arina, combined with myrrh and thyme, in beer.'

Hope made my breath come short. 'And will he be healed, then?' I asked.

With some irritation the water-knower replied, 'He will be in less pain, and his fever will relent. Healing must come afterward, if it comes at all.'

That night Enkidu slept only a little, and I none at all.

In the morning Namennaduma returned. His face was grim, but he refused to speak of what he had learned in the stars, and when I commanded him to tell me he simply peered at me as if I were a madman. 'It is not a simple prognosis,' he said, and shrugged. 'We must do the liver-divination now.'

A statue of the healing-god Ninib, son of Enlil, was brought into the room. A small white sheep was tethered in front of it. I stared at that little sad-eyed animal as though it held the power of life and death over Enkidu itself. Namennaduma performed prayers and purifications and libations, and slaughtered the sheep. Then with

204

brisk swift strokes he cut open its belly and drew forth the steaming liver, which he examined with the skill of his sixty years of this art. He studied the position it had held within the belly of the sheep—'the palace of the liver,' he called it—and then he pored over the liver itself, its lobes and veins, its curves and indentations, its little fingerlike projections. At length he looked up at me and said, 'The shanu is double and so is the niru. That is an evil omen, king.'

'Find a better one,' I said.

'See, king, this: there is a lump of flesh at the bottom of the na.'

I felt my anger rising. 'So? What of it?'

Namennaduma grew uneasy. He sensed the stirring and heating of my wrath, and knew what it could mean for him. But if I had hoped to frighten him into finding an answer that would comfort me, I did not succeed. Straightaway he replied, 'It means that a curse lies on the sick one. He will die.'

His voice fell upon my ears like mallets. Now I was enraged. There was thunder in my brain. I came close to striking him. 'We will all die!' I roared. 'But not yet, not so soon! A curse on you, for your foul omens! Look again, baru-priest. Find the true truth!'

'Shall I deceive you with the words you prefer to hear, then?'

He delivered those blunt words in so quiet and unflinching a tone that my fury at once went from me: I realized I was in the presence of a man of strength and majesty, who would not bend the truth of his art even if it were to cost him his life. I brought myself into check and when I could speak in a normal voice again I said, 'The truth is what I want. I have no liking for the truth you offer me: but at the least I admire the way you tell it. You are a man of honor, Namennaduma.'

'I am an old man. If I anger you and you slay me, what is that to me? But I will not lie to please you.'

'Are all the omens bad?' I asked, speaking softly, cajolingly, almost begging him.

'They are not good. But he is a man of immense strength. That may yet save him, if we follow the right procedures. I promise nothing: but there is a chance. It is a very small chance, king.'

'Do what can be done. Save him.'

The baru-priest laid his hand gently on my arm. 'You

205

understand it is forbidden to physicians to treat one whose case is hopeless. That is a defiance of the gods: we may not do it.'

'I'm aware of that. But you have just said there is a chance to save him.'

'A very small one. Another diviner might say the case is hopeless, and refuse to continue. I tell you this, king, because I want you to remember that there are perils in going against the wishes of the gods.'

With an impatient sigh I said, 'So there are. Now call in the exorcist and the water-knower, and set them to the task of healing my brother!'

And so they went to their work.

An army of healers surrounded Enkidu's bed. Some busied themselves with sacrifices and libations, pouring out milk, beer, wine, bread, fruit, enough to feed a legion of gods, and killing any number of lambs and goats and suckling pigs. While that was going on the ashiptu, the exorcist, began his incantations. 'Seven are they, seven are they, in the Ocean Deep seven are they,' he chanted. 'Ashakku unto the man, bringing fever. Namtaru unto the man, bringing disease. The evil spirit Utukka unto the man, against his neck. The evil demon Alu unto the man, against his breast. The evil ghost Ekimmu unto the man, against his belly. The evil devil Gallu unto the man, against his hand. The evil god Ilu unto the man, against his foot. Seven are they; evil are they. These seven together have seized upon him: they devour his body like a consuming fire. Against them I will conjure.'

As he chanted, I paced the room, counting my steps a thousand times from wall to wall. I felt the god closing his fist on Enkidu: it was an agony for me. He lay with clouded eyes and thickened breath, scarcely seeming to understand what was taking place. The rituals proceeded for hours. When the healers left, I remained by the bedside. 'Brother?' I murmured. 'Brother, do you hear me?' He heard nothing. 'The gods have chosen to spare my life, but you are the price I must pay! Is that it? Ah, it is too much, Enkidu!' He said nothing. I began to speak the words of the great lamentation over him, slowly, haltingly, but I got no more than a little way. It was too soon to speak those words for Enkidu: I could not do it. 'Brother, will you go from me?' I asked. 'Will I ever see you again?' He did not hear me; he was lost in a fevered dream.

During the night he awakened and began to speak. His voice was clear and his mind seemed clear, but he showed no sign of knowing that I was there. He spoke of that time he had hurt his hand in the forest of cedars, in order to spare the beautiful gate; and he said aloud that if he had known then that any such affliction as this would come upon him as a result, he would have raised his axe and split that gate like a curtain of reeds. Then he spoke bitterly of the trapper Kuhninda, who had discovered him on the steppe. 'I call curses down on him, for putting me in the hands of the city people!' Enkidu cried, in a hoarse crazed way that frightened me. 'Let him lose all his wealth! Let the beasts he would trap escape from his snares! Let him be denied the joy of his heart!' He was silent a time, calmer, and I thought he had returned to sleep. But suddenly he sat up and raved again, this time speaking of the sacred harlot Abisimti: 'I curse the woman too!' He had been wild and simple, he said, and she had forced him to see things as men see them. He had not felt sorrow, or loneliness, or the fear of death, until she had caused him to understand that such things existed. Even the joy she had brought him was tainted, said Enkidu: for now that he was dying he felt a stabbing pain at the thought of the loss of that joy. But for her he would have remained ignorant and innocent. Bitterly he said, 'Let this be her doom for all time to come: she will wander the streets forever! Let her stand in the shadow of the wall! Let drunken men strike her and use her foully!' He rolled over toward the wall, coughing, growling, muttering. Then once more he subsided.

I waited, fearful that the next he would curse would be Gilgamesh. I dreaded that, even if his mind was in disarray. But he did not curse me. When next he opened his eyes he looked straight at me and said, in his normal voice, 'Why, brother, is it the middle of the night?'

'I think it is.'

'The fever is easing, perhaps. Have I been dreaming?'

'Dreaming, yes, and raving, and talking aloud. But the medicines must be having their effect.'

'Raving? What sort of things have I said?'

I told him that he had spoken of the gate at which he had injured himself, and of the trapper, and of the harlot Abisimti, and that he had cursed them all, for leading him to this pass.

He nodded. His brow darkened. For a troubled moment he did not speak. Then he said, 'And did I curse you too, brother?'

Shaking my head I answered, 'No. Not me.'

His relief was immense. 'Ah. Ah. How afraid I was that I might have done it!'

'You did not.'

'But if I had, it would have been the fever speaking, not Enkidu. You know that.'

'Yes. I know that.'

He smiled. 'I have been too harsh, brother. It was not the gate's fault that I hurt myself. Nor Ku-ninda's, that I was snared. Nor Abisimti's. Is it possible to call back curses, do you think?'

'I think it can be done, brother.'

'Then I call back mine. If it were not for the trapper and the woman, I would not have known you. I'd not have learned to eat bread fit for gods, and drink the wine of kings. I'd not have been clothed with noble garments, and had glorious Gilgamesh for my brother. So let the trapper prosper. Yes, and the woman, why, let no man scorn her. Let kings and princes and nobles love her, and heap up carnelian and lapis and gold for her, and forsake their wives for her. Let her enter into the presence of the gods. There! I call back my curses!' He looked at me strangely and in a different voice said, 'Gilgamesh, am I going to die soon?'

'You will not. The healers are doing their work on you. A little while longer, and you will be your old self again.'

'Ah. Ah. How good it will be to rise from this bed, and run and hunt beside you, brother! A little while longer, you say?'

'Just a little while.' What else could I say? Why not let him have an hour of peace amid his pain? And hope was rising in me for his return to health. 'Sleep now, Enkidu. Rest. Rest.'

He nodded and closed his eyes. I watched him nearly until dawn, when I fell asleep myself. I was awakened by the healers returning, bringing beasts for the morning sacrifices. Quickly I looked toward Enkidu. He had not sustained the night's recovery. He seemed feverish again, and wandering in delirium. But I suppose there will be many relapses, I told myself, before this thing is lifted from him.

That day they did the divination by oil-bubble and water, gathering around in a little circle to observe the patterns the oil made as it floated in the cup. 'Look,' said one, 'the oil sinks and rises again!' And another said, 'It moves in an easterly direction. It disperses and covers the cup.' I did not trouble to ask what these omens meant. I had become certain of Enkidu's restoration.

They performed the incantation of Eridu on him. The priests fashioned a figure of Enkidu out of dough, and sprinkled the water of the incantation on it: water the life-giver, water the all-cleansing. By prayer and ritual they drew a demon from him into a pot of water, which they broke, spilling the demon into the fireplace. They took another demon out in a piece of string, which they tied in knots. They peeled an onion, throwing the peels one by one into the fire, demon after demon. There were many more such spells.

Meanwhile the physician went about his work also, setting out his potions of cassia and myrtle and asafoetida and thyme, his bark of willow and fig and pear, his ground turtle-shell and powdered snake-skin, and the rest. Both salt and saltpeter figured in his healing draughts, and beer and wine, and honey, and milk. I noticed the exorcists looking sourly toward the doctor as he mixed his medicines, and he at them: no doubt there is some rivalry between them, each thinking that he alone is the true worker of the cure. But I know that one is useless without the other. The medicines ease pain and make the swellings go down and soothe the chilled brow, but unless the demons be driven out as well, what good are the potions? It is the demons who bring the sickness in the first place.

Because I knew that the illness of Enkidu came by decree of the gods, to punish us for our pride in killing Huwawa and destroying the Bull of Heaven, I felt I should take the medicines too. Perhaps the same disease lurked in me as in Enkidu, though I had been spared its effects by divine command; and perhaps Enkidu would not be rid of his affliction until I too had been purified. So whatever potion Enkidu drank I swallowed also, and foul-tasting

209

stuff it was, most of it. I gagged and choked and retched over it, but I drank it all down, though often it left me dizzy the better part of an hour afterward. Did I achieve anything by doing that? Who knows? The ways of the gods are beyond our comprehension. The thoughts of a god are like deep waters: who can fathom them?

Some days Enkidu seemed stronger. Some days he seemed weaker. For three days running he lay with his eyes closed, moaning and making no sense. Then he awakened and sent for me. He looked pale and strange. The fever had ravaged his flesh: he was hollow-cheeked and his skin hung loosely on his frame. He stared at me. His eyes were dark glowing stars ablaze in the caverns of his face. Suddenly I saw the unmistakable hand of death resting on his shoulder, and I wanted to weep.

I felt utterly helpless. I the son of divine Lugalbanda, I the king, I the hero, I the god: for all my power, helpless. Helpless.

He said, 'I dreamed again last night, Gilgamesh.'

'Tell me.'

His voice was calm. He spoke as though he were twelve thousand leagues away. 'I heard the heavens moan,' he said, 'and I heard the earth respond. I stood alone and there was an awful being before me. His face was as dark as that of the black bird of the storm, and his talons were the talons of an eagle. He seized me and held me fast in his claws: I was crushed up against him, and I was smothering. Then he changed me, brother, he turned my arms to wings covered with feathers like a bird's. He looked at me, and led me away, down to the House of Darkness, down to the dwelling of Ereshkigal the queen of hell: along the road from which there is no way back, down to the house which no one leaves. He took me into that dark place where the dwellers sit in darkness, and have dust for their bread and clay for their meat.'

I stared at him. I could say nothing.

'I saw the dead ones. They are clad like birds, with wings for garments. They see no light, they dwell in darkness. I went into the House of Dust and I saw the kings of the earth, Gilgamesh, the masters, the high rulers, and they were without their crowns. They were waiting on the demons like servants, bringing them baked meats, pouring cool water from the waterskins. I saw the priests and priestesses, the seers, the chanters, all the holy ones: what

210

good had their holiness done them? They were servants.' His eyes were hard and glittering, like gleaming bits of obsidian. 'Do you know who I saw? I saw Etana of Kish, who flew in heaven: there he was, down below! I saw gods there: they had horns on their crowns, they were preceded by thunder as they walked. And I saw Ereshkigal the queen of hell, and her recorder Belit-seri, who knelt down before her, marking the tally of the dead on a tablet. When she saw me she lifted her head and said, "Who has brought this one here?" Then I awoke, and I felt like a man who wanders alone in a terrible wasteland, or like one who has been arrested and seized and whose heart pounds with fright. O brother, brother, let some god come to your gate, and strike out my name and write his own in its place!'

I was all pain, everywhere in my soul, and I think in my breast also, as I listened to this. I said, 'I will pray to the great gods for you. It is a dire dream.'

'I will die soon, Gilgamesh. You will be alone again.'

What could I say? What could I do? Sorrow froze me. Alone again, yes. I had not forgotten those days of bleakness before the coming of my friend and brother. Alone again, as I had been before. Those words were like a knell to all my joy. I was chilled; I had no strength.

He said, 'How strange it will be for you, brother. You will journey here and you will journey there, and the time will come when you turn to me and say, Enkidu, do you see the elephant in the marsh, Enkidu, shall we scale that city's walls? And I will not answer you. I will not be beside you. You will have to do those things without me.'

There was a hand at my throat. 'It will be very strange, yes.'

He sat up a little way and turned his head toward me. 'Your eyes look different today. Are you crying? I don't think I've ever seen you cry before, brother.' He smiled. 'I feel very little pain now.'

I nodded. I knew why that was. Sorrow bent me like a weight of stone.

Then the smile faded and in a harsh somber voice he said, 'Do you know what I regret most, brother, apart from leaving you to be alone? I regret that because of the curse of the great goddess I must die in this shameful way, in my bed, wasting slowly away. The

211

man who falls in battle dies a happy death: but I must die in shame.'

That did not matter to me as it did to him. The thing that I struggled with then had nothing to do with such delicate matters as shame and pride. I was already bereaved while he still lived; I suffered his loss. It made no difference to me how or where that loss had been inflicted.

'Death is death, however it may come,' I said, shrugging.

'I would have had it come in a different way,' said Enkidu.

I could say nothing. He was in the grip of death and we both knew it, and the words would not alter anything now. The baru-priest Namennaduma had known it from the first, and had tried to tell me, but in my blindness I would not see the truth. Enkidu's death had come to him; and Gilgamesh the king was helpless against it.

27

He lingered eleven days more. His suffering increased each day, until I could barely bring myself to look upon him. But I stayed by his side until the end.

At dawn on the twelfth day I saw his life leave him. At the last moment it seemed to me in the darkness that there was a faint red haze about him; the haze rose and drifted away, and all was dark. That was how I knew he was dead. I sat in silence, feeling the solitude come rolling in upon me. At first I did not weep, though I remember thinking that the wild ass and the gazelle must be weeping, now. All the wild creatures of the steppes were mourning Enkidu, I thought: even the bear, even the hyena, even the panther. The paths in the forests where he used to dwell would weep for him. The rivers, the streams, the hills.

I reached out and touched him. Was he growing cold already? I could not tell. He seemed merely to be sleeping, but I knew this was not sleep. The fevers that had burned through him had left their mark on his features in these twelve days, making him gaunt and shrunken; but now he looked almost like his old self, calm, his face at ease. I put my hand to his heart. I could not feel it beating. I rose and drew the linen bedcloth over him, tenderly, as a husband might veil his bride. But I knew that this was no veil, it was a shroud. And then I wept. The tears came slowly at first, tears being very odd to me: I made a little sniveling sound, I felt a warmth at the corners of my eyes, my lips clamped themselves tight together. After a moment of this it was easier. Some dam within me broke, and my grief came freely. I paced back and forth before the couch like a lioness who has been deprived of her cubs. I tore at my hair. I ripped at my fine robes and flung them down as though they were unclean. I raged, I stormed, I roared. No one dared approach me. I was left alone with my terrible grief. I stayed beside the body all that day, and another, and another after that, until I saw that the servants of Ereshkigal were claiming him. I knew then that I had to give him up for burial.

Therefore I gathered myself together. There was much that I needed to do.

The parting-ritual, first. I went to the cabinet where such things are kept and brought forth a table made from elammaqu-wood, upon which I set a bowl of lapis and a bowl of carnelian. Into one I poured curds, into the other I poured honey; and I carried the table to the terrace of Utu and put it out into the sunlight as an offering. I said the proper words. When I spoke the great lamentation now it was without faltering.

Then I called the elders of Uruk to me. They knew, of course, what had happened, and they wore the colors of mourning on their arms. They looked somber, but it was only on account of my loss, not for any loss of their own: Enkidu had meant nothing to them. That angered me some, that they had not perceived Enkidu's virtues as I had perceived them. But they were only ordinary men: how could they have known, how could they have understood anything. They were ill at ease, seeing how great my grief was. They did not expect that of me, precisely because I was not an ordinary man. They had thought of me as a being beyond mere mortal things like grief: a god dwelling among them, or some such thing. Probably I had done much to foster that belief. But now my eyes were rimmed with red, my face was pale and swollen. They could not comprehend such a show of humanity in me. Gilgamesh the king, Gilgamesh the god—well, yes, but I was also Gilgamesh the man. I had suffered greatly in the splendid isolation of my kingship, though no one about me had realized that I suffered; and then I had found a friend; and now that friend had been stolen from me by the demons. Therefore I wept. What did they expect?

I said, 'I weep for my friend Enkidu. He was the axe at my side, the dagger in my belt, the shield I held before me. He was my brother. The loss is great. The pain cuts deep.'

'All Uruk mourns your brother,' they told me. 'The warriors weep. The people in the streets weep. The ploughmen and the harvesters weep, Gilgamesh.' But their words rang hollow to me. It was the old story: they were telling me what they thought I wanted to hear.

'We will bury him as though he had been a king,' I said, so they would comprehend what Enkidu had been.

They looked startled at that, thinking perhaps that I might have it in mind to send my household staff, or even a few of the elders themselves, into the grave to keep Enkidu company. But I had no such thought. I understood death better now than I had on that day when the household of Lugalbanda had gone one by one under the earth into his tomb; I saw no merit in causing other brothers to weep, and sons and wives, for Enkidu's sake. So I told them only to prepare for a ceremony of great splendor.

I called out the finest of the city's craftsmen, the coppersmiths, the goldsmiths, the lapidaries. I ordered them to make a statue of my friend—the body of gold, the breast of lapis. I had the grave-diggers dig a shaft in the open place beside the White Platform and line its walls with bricks of baked clay. I gathered together Enkidu's weapons and the skins of the animals he had slain, to be buried with him; and also I provided rich treasure to be put beside him, cups and rings and alabaster goblets and jewels and such.

I went to each temple in turn and formally asked the high priest to take part in the burial of Enkidu. The one temple that I did not visit was the one that I had built for the goddess. In truth it was proper and necessary for Inanna to be present at the funeral of any

214

great man of Uruk; but I did not want her there. I held her responsible for Enkidu's death: I was certain she had called his doom down upon him with her curses, in her anger at my over-shadowing her power in the city. I would not have her at the funeral of the friend she had ripped from me; I would not give her the chance to gloat over the great wound she had inflicted on me. Let her stay huddled in her temple, I thought. No one but her handmaidens had seen her since the day of the loosing of the Bull of Heaven. That was how I preferred it to be.

But it was not how she preferred it to be. On the day of the funeral I led the march from the palace to the grave-shaft, weeping all the while, and stood beside the priests and my mother as we made the sacrifices of oxen and goats and poured out the libations of milk and honey. The hunter Ku-ninda was with me; the sacred harlot Abisimti was with me also. They had known Enkidu even longer than I, and they mourned him nearly as deeply. Abisimti's eyes were reddened with weeping, her garments were torn; Ku-ninda, stark and silent, stood with clenched fists and lips clamped tight, holding back fierce sorrow. I had them both aid me in performing the rites. Just as we were coming to the point in the service where the pure cool water is poured as a refreshment for the dead man as he goes to the House of Dust and Darkness, there was a stirring behind me, and I turned and saw Inanna amidst a little group of her priestesses.

She looked more like hell's queen than heaven's. Her face was painted ghostly white, and her eyelids and even her lips were blackened with kohl. She wore a dark stark robe falling straight from her shoulders and her only ornament was a dagger of polished green stone that dangled between her breasts from a lanyard of woven straw about her neck. Her priestesses were clad in the same fashion.

The ceremony came to a halt. There was a hard crackling silence all about me.

She looked toward me in the coldest hatred and said, 'A funeral, Gilgamesh, without asking the consent of the goddess?'

'I do as I please today. He was my friend.'

'Inanna still rules, nevertheless.'

My glance rested unwaveringly on her eyes. I returned hatred

215

for hatred, frost for frost. In clear measured tones I said, 'I will bury my friend without Inanna's help. Go back to your temple.'

'I speak for the goddess in Uruk.'

'And I am king in Uruk. I speak for the gods.' I raised my arm and swept it about broadly. 'See, the priests of An and Enlil are here, and the priests of Enki, and the priests of Utu. The gods have given their blessing to the laying to rest of Enkidu. If the goddess is absent today, well, it does not matter so much, I think.'

She glared at me and for a long moment did not speak, did not even vent breath. She seemed to be swelling up; I thought she would explode. The fury in her face was awesome.

Then she said, 'Beware, Gilgamesh! Your defiance goes beyond the bounds. You have seen already what my curse can do: I would not want to place it on the king of Uruk. But I will if I must, Gilgamesh. I will if I must.'

In a low cold voice I replied, 'You beware also, priestess! Your curse may be dangerous, but so is my sword. I tell you, take yourself away from here this moment, or I will make a libation to Enkidu's shade with your blood. I tell you: before everyone, Inanna, I will split your belly open.'

It was a frightful moment. Had anyone ever spoken to the priestess of the goddess in such a way? I was swept by an excitement that was almost like a high drunkenness. I felt giddy. My breath came in quick hard gusts; my heart hammered at the cage of my ribs.

She stared. 'Are you mad?'

I put my hand to the hilt of my sword. 'I will if I must, Inanna. I will if I must. Go, now.'

I think I would have slain her in front of all Uruk, if she had defied me then. I think she knew that, too. For she gave me one final glare, like the cold fiery glare of that serpent whose eyes breathe poison. But I did not fall; I did not flinch; I returned her glare, fire for fire, chill for chill. And then at last she swung about and went sweeping back with her women toward her temple.

When she was out of sight I let my arms hang limp and my breath come soft, for I was strung tight as a bow. When I was calm again I turned to the priest who still held the beaker of water and said, 'Come, let us continue.'

216

He handed me the water, and I poured it out into the grave, and said the words. Afterward I pulled my headband off, and tore my garments, and broke my bracelets and my necklace. My body ached in twenty places; there was a pressure against my eyes, and a heaviness in my breast, and the hand at my throat had tightened until I could scarcely breathe. This was the end of the rite: now Enkidu's journey into darkness was complete and I had no way to hide from my bereavement. He was gone. I was alone. The pain rose up within me like a fountain and flooded me. I threw myself on the ground and wept for Enkidu for the last time. Then it was done. I grew calm; I lay still; after a while I arose, saying nothing to anyone. With my own hands I sealed the shaft with bricks, and the other priests covered it over with earth.

I returned to the palace alone. I sat in silence all that day in my innermost chamber, seeing no one. I listened to hear Enkidu's laughter tumbling in torrents through the halls. Silence. I listened for the sound of his hands slapping against the door to summon me. Silence. I thought of going out to hunt, and imagined myself turning to him to take a javelin from him: he would not be beside me. I felt a hunger for him that I knew could never be eased. Why, I wondered, had I been singled out for such a loss? Because I was king? Because my life had gone only from triumph to triumph, and the gods themselves were jealous of me? Perhaps I had been given Enkidu only so that he might be taken away; perhaps this was all the design of the gods, to let me taste happiness so that I could learn the true taste of grief afterward.

I was alone. Well, I had been alone before. But it seemed to me, that day of the burial of my friend, that I had never been alone in the way that I was alone now.

28

They say that all wounds heal in time. I suppose they do, in one way or another, though often they leave thick raised scars in their place. One day flowed into another and I waited for the scars to form over the place where Enkidu had been ripped away. I wandered the halls of my palace and did not hear his laughter, and I did not see his great burly form swaggering about the terraces, and I thought that soon I would become accustomed to his absence; but that did not seem to happen. Every day I was reminded by some little thing that he was no longer here.

I could not bear it. I had to take myself away from Uruk. Wherever I looked in Uruk I saw the shadow of Enkidu falling across the streets. I heard the echoes of Enkidu's voice in the jabber of the crowds. There was no place to hide from memory. It was a kind of madness, I think: a pain beyond reason. It invaded every corner of my soul and rendered everything meaningless that once had mattered to me. At first what gnawed at me and ached in my gut was only the loss of Enkidu, but then I came to see that the real source of my pain lay even deeper: it was not so much the death of Enkidu that tormented me, as it was my awareness of the fact of death itself. For I knew that I would, in time, reconcile myself even to the departure of Enkidu: I was not so great a fool as to think that wound would never heal. But how could I reconcile myself to the loss of all the world? How could I reconcile myself to the loss of *myself*? Again and again in my life I had begun to wrestle with that question, and had stepped aside from it; but the death of Enkidu raised it once more, and this time it could not be avoided. Death will come, Gilgamesh, even for you. That is the thing I saw in the air before my face, the black mocking mask of death. And the knowledge of the inevitability of that death robbed my life of all its joy.

As on that day of the funeral of my father Lugalbanda long ago I fell into such sharp terror of dying that I could hardly breathe. I sat upon my high throne, thinking, Enkidu has died and shuffles about now within that place of dust, cloaked like a bird in gloomy feathers, making his evening meal out of cold clay. And soon enough I must go to that dark place too. One day a king in a grand palace, the next a mournful creature flapping his wings in the dust—was that the fate that awaited me? I remembered how as a boy I had vowed to conquer death. *Death, you are no match for me!* So I had boasted. I was too proud to die; death was an affront I could not bear, and I would deny death his sway over me. But could that be? Death had defeated Enkidu; beyond any doubt death would come for Gilgamesh as well, in his proper time. And the certainty of that drained all strength from me. I did not want to be king any longer. I did not want to perform the sacrifices and pour out the libations and repair the canals and lead my troops in war. Why go to such trouble, when our lives are like the lives of the little green flies that buzz about for a few hours at twilight and then perish? What sense is there in striving so hard? We are given friends and then the friends soon are taken away: better not to have had the friend at all, I thought. And, thinking in that fashion, I came to see all human action as without value or purpose. Flies, flies, buzzing flies: we are nothing more than that, I told myself. Death is the gods' great joke upon us. What sense in being a king? King of the flies? I would be king no longer. I would flee this city, and go out into the wilderness.

Thus it was the fear of death that drove me from Uruk. I could not be king any longer: I was an empty man. Under the shadow of the dread of death I went forth alone out of the city.

I told no one where I was going. I did not know that myself. I did not even say that I was leaving at all. I appointed no regent; I left no instructions for what was to be done in my absence. It was a madness that was upon me. Between midnight and dawn I slipped away, taking no more with me than the little I had carried that time I had fled to Kish when I was a boy.

Despair governed me. Woe lay heavy on my every thought. Fear nestled like a venomous serpent behind my breastbone. My hair was unkempt: I had not allowed it to be cut since the first day of Enkidu's illness. My only garments were a lion's rough hide and a peasant's sandals: I renounced my elegant robes and cloaks and all of that. I think no one seeing me depart would have recognized me as Gilgamesh the king, so wild and frightful did I look. I scarcely would have known me myself, I think.

So did I wander dismally off into the steppe, following no plan, seeking no path, hoping only to find some place where I might elude the hounds of death.

I could not tell you now what route I took. I think I began by going east toward Elam, into that green wilderness where Enkidu first was found, as though I believed I might discover another one just like him out there. But soon I turned north to the land they call Uri, and then I may have swung around to the west where the Martu people dwell, and after that I do not know. I paid no heed to the rising of the sun, or to its setting. I was in a madness. I walked by day or by night, and slept wherever I chose, or did not sleep at all; and I walked without knowing where I was nor where I had been. I am sure, at least, that I was at all times outside the boundaries of the Land. Several times I think I came up against the walls of the world, and looked out into the places that are beyond the compass of the earth. Maybe I went into those places; I do not know. I was in a madness.

I felt fear of things I had never feared before. One night in a mountain pass where the air was cold and thin and stung the nostrils, the smell came to me of lions: a bitter smell, sour and keen. If I had been Gilgamesh, and had had Enkidu beside me, we would have run up the rocks even though it was dark and hunted those lions for their skins, and made cloaks out of them before we slept. But Enkidu was dead and I was not Gilgamesh: I was no one, I was mad. Fear came over me and made me tremble. I raised my eyes to the moon, which hung like a great white lamp above the sharp peaks, and cried out to Nanna the god, 'Protect me, I beg you, for I am afraid.' Those words, *I am afraid*, sounded strange to me even as I said them: there was that much of Gilgamesh still alive within me. *I am afraid*. Had I ever spoken those words before? I had been afraid of death, yes, I suppose. But to be afraid of lions?

Nanna took pity on me. He caused me to fall into a deep sleep despite my fear. I dreamed of gardens and orchards; and when the morning light woke me I saw the lions all around me, rejoicing in life. I felt no fear now. I took my axe in my hand; I drew my dirk from my belt; I ran among those lions like an arrow speeding from the bow, and struck at them and scattered them and killed more than one. That was better than cowering and snuffling in fear. But I was a madman still.

In another place where the trees were thick and squat and had leaves like sharp little awls I saw the Imdugud-bird perched on a branch with her heavy red talons deep into the wood. Or rather the Imdugud-bird saw me, and knew me, and called out, 'Where are you going, son of Lugalbanda?'

'Is that you, Imdugud-bird?'

She spread her wings, which are like the wings of a great eagle, and preened her head, which is the head of a lioness. Her eyes sparkled as though they were encrusted with jewels. I knew her for what she was.

I said, 'I am in terror of death, Imdugud. I am looking for a place where death cannot find me.'

She laughed. Her laughter is like the laughter of a lioness, soft and frightful. 'Death found Enkidu. Death found Dumuzi. Death found the hero Lugalbanda. Why do you think death will not find Gilgamesh?'

'Two-thirds of me is god, one-third is human.'

She laughed again, more harshly, a cackling laugh. 'Then two-thirds of you will live, and one-third will die!'

'You mock me, Imdugud. Why be so cruel?' I held out my hands to her. 'What harm have I done to you, that you should mock me? Is it because I drove you from the huluppu-tree? That tree was Inanna's. It was my duty then to serve Inanna. I asked you gently; I asked you well. Help me, Imdugud.'

My words seemed to reach her soul. Quietly she said, 'How can I help you, son of Lugalbanda?'

'Tell me where I can go that death will not find me.'

'Death comes to all mortals, son of Lugalbanda.'

'To all, without exception?'

'Without exception,' she said. Then she was silent a time; and then she said, 'Indeed there has been one exception. It is one of which you are aware.'

My heart began to race. Urgently I said, 'One who is exempt from dying? I cannot think. Tell me. Tell me!'

'In your madness and your despair you have forgotten the hero of the Flood.'

221

'Ziusudra! Yes!'

'He dwells eternally in the land of Dilmun. Have you forgotten that, Gilgamesh?'

I quivered with excitement. It was like a sudden fever. I saw there might be a hope.

Eagerly I cried, 'And if I go to him, Imdugud? What then? Will he share the secret of life with me, if I ask him?'

I heard the mocking cackle again. 'If you ask him? If you ask him? If you ask him?' Her voice was less like a lioness' now, and more like that of some huge strange crow. She fluttered her great wings. 'Ask! Ask! Ask!'

'Tell me the way, Imdugud!'

'Ask! Only ask!'

Now it was becoming harder for me to see her: the air grew thick and the dark needles of the tree seemed to be closing about her. Nor could I hear her easily any longer: her words were losing themselves in the sound of the beating of her wings and the snorting of her laughter.

'Imdugud?' I cried.

'Ask! Ask! Ask!'

There was a sharp cracking sound. The branch fell suddenly from the tree, as branches will do when the season has been very dry. It landed almost at my feet; I leaped back barely in time. When I looked up again I saw no sign of the Imdugud-bird against the pale blue-white sky.

29

Ziusudra. Yes, I knew the tale. Who has not heard it?

This is how the harper Ur-kununna sang it to me, when I was a child in the palace of Lugalbanda:

A time came long ago when the gods grew weary of mankind. The uproar, the clamor, that rose to heaven out of the Land was annoying to them. It was Enlil who was the angriest, exclaiming, 'How can I sleep, when they make so much noise?' And he sent a famine to destroy us. For six years there was no rain. Grains of salt rose from the earth and covered the fields, and the crops perished. People ate their own daughters; one house devoured another. But the wise and compassionate Enki took pity on us, and caused the drought to end.

A second time the anger of Enlil grew hot against mankind, and he hurled plagues upon us; and a second time the mercy of Enki brought us relief. Those who had fallen ill recovered, and new children were born to those who had lost theirs. Once more the world teemed with people, and our noise went up to heaven like the bellowing of a wild bull. Yet again did the rage of Enlil arise. 'This clamor is intolerable to me,' said Enlil to the gods meeting in council; and before them all he vowed to destroy the world in a vast flood.

But the lord of floods is Enki the wise, who dwells in the great abyss. The making of the deluge therefore was given into Enki's hands; and because Enki loves mankind, he saw to it that the destruction would not be total. There was at that time in the ancient city of Shuruppak a king named Ziusudra, a man of great virtue and piousness. By night Enki came to this king in a dream, and whispered to him, 'Leave your house! Build a ship! Abandon your kingdom and save your life!' He told Ziusudra to make his ship as wide as it was long, and to make a roof over it that was as sturdy as the vault that covers the abyss of the ocean; and he was to take the seed of all living things on board the ship when the great flood came.

Ziusudra said to the god, 'I will do your bidding, my lord. But what am I to tell the people and the elders of the city when they see me making ready to depart?'

To which Enki made this sly response: 'Go to them and say to them that you have learned that Enlil has come to hate you, and you cannot live in Shuruppak any longer, or set your foot in any territory where Enlil rules. Therefore you are taking refuge in the great deep, to dwell with your lord Enki. But when you are gone, tell them, Enlil will shower down abundance on the people of Shuruppak: the choicest of birds, the finest fishes, a rain of wheat. Tell them that, Ziusudra.'

So at the coming of dawn the king gathered his household about himself and gave the order for the building of the ship. All of them took part in the toil, even the small children, who carried baskets of pitch. On the fifth day Ziusudra laid the keel and the ribs. The walls were a hundred twenty cubits in height, and the sides of the deck were a hundred twenty cubits in length, and the floor was the size of a field. He built six decks, and divided the interior into nine sections with sturdy bulkheads between. He drove in the water-plugs where they belonged, he had a supply of punting-poles laid aside. The caulking alone required a whole measure of oil. Every day he slaughtered bullocks and sheep for the workmen, and gave them wine both red and white as though it were river water, so that they might feast as they did on the day of the new year. On the seventh day the ship was finished.

The launching was a difficult one: they had to shift the ballast about until the ship sat deep in the water. Then the king loaded all his gold and all his silver into her and put on board all the people of his household and all his craftsmen, and also animals of every kind, bringing them two by two, both the tame beasts of the pastures and the wild creatures of the field. The hour of the downpour would soon be at hand, he knew.

The sky darkened and the wind began to blow. Ziusudra went on board the ship himself and battened down her hatches. At dawn a black cloud appeared on the horizon; there was thunder, and a terrible wind. The gods rose up against the world, and lightning flashed: the torches of the gods, setting the world ablaze with their flashing. Tempests roared, and the rains came sweeping down. And the Land was shattered like a pot that has been tossed against a wall.

All day long the storm-winds blew out of the south, growing more terrible the longer they raged. The flood-waters gathered their force and fell on the Land like a conquering army. There was no daylight; no one could see anything; the crests of the mountains were submerged. The gods themselves became fearful of the deluge and shrank back, ascending into the loftiest heaven, the heaven of the Sky-father. There they cowered like dogs, crouching against the outer bulwark. Inanna the Queen of Heaven wept and cried out like a woman in childbirth to see her people tumbling into the sea. The gods wept with her. Humbled and frightened by the forces they had let loose, they sat bowed and trembling, and they wept.

Six days and six nights the wind blew and the tempest and the rain swept the land. On the seventh day the storm abated: the flood-waters no longer rose, the turbulent sea became still. Ziusudra opened the hatch of his ship and came out on deck. What he beheld struck him to his knees with terror. All was still. But he could see no land, only water stretching in every direction to the horizon. In awe and fear he covered his head and wept, for he knew that all mankind had returned to clay except those he had saved aboard his ship, and he saw that the world and everything that was in it had perished.

He sailed on and on in that great expanse of sea, seeking a coast; and in time he saw the dark massive slopes of Mount Nisir standing above the water. He went toward it; and there the ship came to rest. She held fast and could not budge. Three days, four days, five days, six, the ship rested against the side of the mountain. On the seventh, Ziusudra set free a dove; but she found no resting place, and returned. He loosed a swallow; but the swallow had nowhere to alight, and she too came back. Then Ziusudra let a raven loose. The bird flew high and far, and saw that the waters had begun to retreat: he flew about in a wide circle, he found something to eat, he cawed, flew off, and did not return to the ship. Then Ziusudra opened all the hatches to the four winds and the sunlight. He went out onto a mountain, and poured a libation, and set out seven holy vessels and seven more, and he burned cane and cedarwood and myrtle to the gods who had spared him. The gods smelled the savor of the sacrifice, and they came to enjoy it. Inanna was one of those who came, clad in all the jewels of heaven. And she cried, 'Yes, come, O ye gods! Let all of you come. But let Enlil not come, for he is the one who brought this deluge on my people!'

Nevertheless Enlil came. He looked about in fury and demanded to know how it had come to pass that some human souls had escaped destruction. 'You should ask that of Enki,' said Ninurta, the warrior, the god of wells and canals. And Enki stepped forward, and said boldly to Enlil, 'It was a senseless thing to bring on this deluge. In your wrath you destroyed the sinner and the innocent alike. It was too much. It was far too much. If you had sent a wolf to punish the evil ones, or a lion, or even another famine, or a pestilence—yes, that might have been sufficient. But not this terrible flood! Now mankind is gone, Enlil, and all the world is drowned. Only this ship and its people survived. And that has happened only because Ziusudra the wise king saw the plans of the gods in a dream, and took action to save himself and his people. Go to him, Enlil. Speak with him. Forgive him. Show him your love.'

Enlil's heart was moved by compassion. He had seen the devastation worked by the flood, and sorrow overwhelmed him. So he went on board the ship of Ziusudra. He took the king by one hand and the king's wife by the other, and drew them to his side, and touched their foreheads to bless them. And Enlil said, 'You have been mortal, but you are mortal no longer. Henceforth you shall be like gods, and live far away from mankind, at the mouth of the rivers, in the golden land of Dilmun.'

Thus were Ziusudra and his wife rewarded. There in the land of Dilmun they live to this day, eternal, undying, those two by whose faith and perseverance the world was reborn in the days when Enlil sent the Flood to scour mankind to destruction.

Such was the tale I heard from the harper Ur-kununna, when I was a child in the palace of Lugalbanda.

30

I wandered on, in misery and madness; but now my wandering had a purpose, mad and miserable though it might be. I could not tell you how many months it was I marched, nor across what steppes and valleys and plains. Sometimes the sun hung before me like a vast angry eye of white fire, sending up shimmering heat-waves that dizzied me as I plodded toward it; and sometimes the sun was pale and low on the horizon behind me, or to my left. I could not tell you which directions those were. I found rivers and swam them; I doubt that they were either of the Two Rivers of the Land. I crossed swamps and places where the moist sand was like muck beneath me. I crossed dunes and dry wastes. I made my way through thickets of thorny canes that slashed me like vengeful enemies. I fed on the flesh of hares and boars and beavers and gazelles, and where there were none of those I ate the meat of lions and jackals and wolves, and when I found no animals of any kind I ate roots and nuts and berries; and where there was nothing at all to eat, I ate nothing at all, and it did not matter to me. Divine strength was in me. Divine purpose was upon me.

I came in time to a mountain that I knew must be the one called Mashu, which every day keeps watch over the rising and the setting of the sun. I knew it to be Mashu because its twin summits reached to the vault of heaven and its breasts reached down to the gates of the nether world. There is only one mountain like that on the earth. They say that scorpion-men guard its gate, creatures that are half man and half monster, with arching tails of many joints that hold a fatal sting. So fearsome are these scorpion-men, so it is said, that the radiance of their eyes is terrifying; a splendor comes from them that gleams like fire in the cliffs; their glance alone strikes death. Perhaps it is so. I saw no scorpion-men when I made my ascent of Mashu. Or rather, I encountered some poor sad things that were monstrous enough, though far from terrifying, and it may be that others, hearing of them at second or third report, have construed them into frightful monsters. It is often that way with travelers' tales, I suspect.

But I will not deny that I felt a tremor of fear when I met the first of these creatures as I came up the middle of Mashu to the flattened place that lies between the two peaks. It must have been watching me some time before I spied it, standing on high ground well above me, its arms folded calmly.

By Enlil, it was strange to behold! I suppose it was more a man than anything else, but its skin was dark and hard and horny where I could see it, much like the crust of some scuttling sea-creature, or, yes, like the hard covering of a scorpion. I came at once to a halt when I saw it, remembering what I had heard of the guardians of this mountain and their lethal gaze. I flung my arm quickly

227

across my eyes and looked down. My heart leaped in dismay.

In a language much like that of the desert folk, the scorpion-creature said, 'You have nothing to fear from me, stranger. We get few enough visitors here: it would be a pity to murder them.'

Those words steadied me. I grew calm, and I lowered my arm and stared at the creature unafraid. 'Is this the mountain called Mashu?' I asked.

'It is.'

'Then I am very far from home indeed.'

'Where is your home, and why have you left it?'

'I am of Uruk the city,' I replied, 'and Gilgamesh is my name. And I have left my home because I seek something that cannot be found there.'

'Gilgamesh? Is that not the king's name, in Uruk?'

'How do you know that, in these far-off mountains?'

'Ah, my friend, everyone knows Gilgamesh the king, who is two parts a god and one part a mortal! Is there a happier man on earth than he?'

'I think there must be,' I said. Slowly I walked up the rock-strewn path until I stood level with the scorpion-creature. I said in a quiet way, 'You should know that I am Gilgamesh the king. Or was, for I have left my kingship a long way behind me.' We studied each other, face to face, neither of us, I suppose, quite knowing what to make of each other. My terror of the creature was altogether gone, though the strangeness of its skin awakened shivers in me. Whether the scorpion-being was part demon, or merely some pitiful thing deformed at birth, I could not tell you: but its eyes, staring out from that horror of a face, were sad gentle eyes, and I have never seen any demon whose eyes were sad and gentle.

After a time the creature turned, beckoning me to follow, and in a slow clumsy hobbling way it went around the curve of the hill to a little hut made of flat rocks and twisted boughs. There was a second scorpion-being there, a woman even more hideous than the other, with thick yellowish skin that rose in jagged crests and ridges like a heavy armor. Had the scorpion-man somehow managed to find a mate who shared his affliction? Or was this woman his sister, who had had the deformity from the same blood?

I never learned which. Perhaps she was mate and sister both: the gods grant that those two do not engender a race of their sort upon our world! Hideous though she was, she was kindly, and fell to work at once brewing a sort of tea of tree-nettles and ground nuts to offer me. The hour was late, the air was thin, the day was growing cold. Stars could be seen against the dismal gray of the afternoon sky.

The man-creature said, 'This wanderer is Gilgamesh king of Uruk, whose body is of the flesh of the gods.'

'Ah,' she said, as unsurprised as if he had told her, 'This is the goatherd Kish-adul,' or 'This is the fisherman Ur-shuhadak.' She poured the tea into a crude clay beaker and handed it to me. 'Even if he is a god, he will want something warm to drink,' she said.

'I am not a god,' I told her. 'I have a god's blood in me, but I am mortal.'

'Ah,' she said.

The other said, 'He has come here seeking something, but he has not told me what it is.'

The woman shrugged. 'He will not find it here, whatever it may be.' And to me she said, 'There is nothing here at all. This is a bleak and empty place.'

'What I seek lies beyond this place.'

Again she shrugged, and sipped her tea in silence. It seemed that she did not care why I was here, or what I sought. Well, why should she care? What was Gilgamesh and his pain to her? Here she lived in this terrible place, in this loathsome body, and if a wandering sorrowful king came along one cold gray afternoon in search of mysteries and fantasies, what was that to her? I studied her closely for a time. Her face was all folds and crevices, monstrous and repellent. But I saw that her eyes were soft and warm within that hideous shell, tender eyes, a woman's eyes. It was as though she had been attacked and devoured whole by something ghastly and strange, and now peered out from within its husk.

But the other had more curiosity. 'What is it you search for, Gilgamesh?' he asked.

'In Uruk,' I said, 'a stranger came to me—Enkidu was his name— and we fell into a friendship that held us with a bond stronger than any bond I know, stronger even than the bond

229

between lover and beloved. He was my friend. He and I endured all manner of hardships together, and we loved each other dearly.'

'And then he died?'

'You know that too?' I said, startled.

'I know nothing. But I see your grief like a black cloud about you.'

'I wept for him day and night. I would not even give him up for burial, until I saw that it had to be done. Perhaps I thought that if I wept enough, my friend would come back to life. But he did not. And since he died my own life has been empty. Since he died I have wandered in the wilderness like a hunter. No: like a madman. I see nothing awaiting me but death, and my knowledge of that death drains my life of all life. Death is my enemy.' I looked the scorpion-man close in the eyes. 'I mean to vanquish death!' I cried.

'We all must die,' said the woman in a dull downcast way. 'It comes none too soon.'

Fiercely I said, 'For you, maybe!'

'It comes, whether we want it to or not. I say, better to accept it than to do battle against it. It is a battle no one can win.'

I shook my head. 'You are wrong. How long ago was the Flood? Ziusudra still lives!'

'By special favor of the gods,' she said. 'He is the only one. That will not happen again.'

Her words were cold water in my face. 'Are you sure? How can you know that?'

The scorpion-man put out his hand to me. It felt rough as wood against my skin. 'Gently, gently, friend. You grow too excited; you will give yourself a fever. If the gods chose once upon a time to spare Ziusudra, what is that to you?'

'More than a trifle,' I said. 'Tell me this: How far is it from here to the land of Dilmun?'

'A very great distance, I think. You must go over the crest of the mountain, and down the difficult far side to the sea, and then—'

'Can you show me the way?'

'I can tell you what I know. But what I know is that no one has ever reached Dilmun from here, and no one ever will. The far side of the mountain is the darkest wilderness. You will die of the heat and thirst. You will tumble into ravines. Or you will be eaten by beasts. Or you will be lost in the darkness, and starve.'

'Only point out the way to me, and I will find Dilmun.'

'And what then, Gilgamesh?' the scorpion-man asked calmly.

I said, 'I mean to seek out Ziusudra. I have questions to ask him, about death, about life. He has lived hundreds of years, or perhaps it is thousands: he must know the secrets of all things. He will tell me how death may be vanquished.'

Both the creatures looked at me, and their eyes were pitying, as though I were the monstrosity and not they. But they said nothing. The woman offered me more tea. The man arose and hobbled to the back of his hut and brought me a kind of bread made from some wild seed of the mountain. It tasted like baked sand, but I ate the whole piece.

After a long while he said, 'No man of woman born has crossed the wilderness that lies ahead of you, so far as I have ever heard, and I have lived here a long while. But I wish you well, Gilgamesh. In the morning I will take you to the crest and show you the way; and may the gods guide you in safety toward the sea.'

He sounded as though he were talking to a child who against all reason must have his way. There was sadness in his voice, and some anger also, and resignation. It was clear that he felt I would only come to grief. Well, that was a reasonable thing to believe; and he had seen what lay beyond the mountain pass and I had not. It did not matter. I had no dread of coming to grief, for I had come to grief already, and it was my purpose now to move onward into the land that lies beyond grief. For that I must reach Dilmun, and speak with ancient Ziusudra, and if I must make that journey in sorrow and pain, in peril, in cold or in heat, sighing or weeping, so be it. I slept that night on the floor of the scorpion-creatures' hut, listening to the rasping dry scratchy sounds of their breathing. When dawn came they fed me, tea again and cakes of sandy meal, and as the sun burst upon us between the peaks of Mashu the scorpion-man said, 'Come. I will show you the way.' Together we clambered to the crest of the pass. I looked down into a bowl of tumbled jagged rocks the color of baked bricks, stretching downward as far as I could see. To the right and to the left lay wilderness: small twisted snag-armed trees in the higher reaches, a dense black forest farther down. It looked like a place from which all presence of the gods had been withdrawn.

'Are there wild beasts?' I asked.

'Lizards. Goats with long horns. Some lions, not many.'

'And are there demons?'

'It would not surprise me.'

'I have encountered their kind before,' I said. 'Perhaps they will prefer not to trouble me, since they know I will trouble them if they do.'

'Perhaps,' said the scorpion-man.

'Are there streams? Springs?'

'Very few, until you reach the lower forest. I think there must be water there, since the trees grow so thick.'

'You have not been that far down?'

'No,' he said. 'Never. No one has been.'

'That will not be true much longer,' I said, and took my leave of him with warm thanks for his kindness. He nodded but did not offer me an embrace. He was still standing at the crest of the pass long after I began my descent; it must have been hours later when I looked up, and saw his misshapen monstrous form outlined against the sky. Nor did he cease watching me after that. I caught sight of him twice more as I made my winding way downward, and then the crest was lost to my view.

31

It was a journey that held few delights and many challenges. I do not remember it fondly. For days I was descending the southern face of the mountain, and the heat was intense: the sun, as it climbed, beat against me like a gong that would not be silent. I thought the force of it would blind and deafen me both. The nights were bitter cold, with howling knife-keen winds. The rocks were sharp-edged and loose, and when I stepped on them the wrong way they slid, sending clouds of dry red dust up into my nostrils. Twice I injured my legs in the scramble; more than twice I cut myself by falling; I was constantly plagued by thirst; and furious clouds of stinging insects hovered about my face all the way down the slope, seeking my eyes. For food I had none but the lizards that I caught as they lay sleeping in the sun and the long-legged hopping insects that abounded everywhere. For water I chewed the twigs of the sad gnarled little plants, though their sap burned my mouth. At least I saw no demons. I saw some lions, as dusty and woebegone as I was myself; but they kept far away. I wondered often if I would live to see the end of the descent, and more than once I was certain I would not.

Yet it often happens that that which is held forth to one as utterly impossible turns out to be no more than extremely difficult, or even merely inconvenient, in the actuality. That was the case here. I will not pretend it was an easy descent: it may be that no man other than I could have accomplished it, excepting only Enkidu. But it proved to be altogether possible to achieve. I will say this much, that I would not care to attempt it again.

Then the fearful passage was behind me. When I was done with my descent of Mashu I found myself entering a dry high tableland where only small thorny plants grew: not a pretty place, but one, at any rate, that did not tax my strength to travel through it. I was many days in crossing it. I walked in the patient plodding way of a mule, or an ox in the yoke.

But as I made my way onward, the quality of the land began slowly to change. The light became less harsh; the soil, which had been red and barren, grew darker and seemed more fertile. A warm tender wind that carried moisture came to me out of the south. I passed through a vale so narrow that I could almost touch both its sides with my shoulders, and when I came out of it I emerged into a misty country of soft air and gentle sunlight, where a sweet shining dew fell into the valleys from the hills ahead.

How good that felt, when the dew wrapped itself around me and bathed my parched dusty skin! It might almost have been the garden of the gods, that place. Flowers bloomed everywhere, with a fragrance like none I had known before. There was pale green

233

grass, kind against my legs. The air shimmered as though it were silver. I saw the land unfolding before me like a great golden fan, wide and flat with green hills at the rim and a glittering sea somewhere farther onward. I could not say how long it would take me to reach that sea, but I knew that I would get there, and that I would find the blessed land of Dilmun upon its farther shore.

Still bruised and stiff from my long descent, wild-eyed, clad only in a lion's tattered and cracking hide, I walked in wonder through this land of beauty. It seemed to me that the fruits that hung heavy on the vines were fruits of carnelian, and that the leaves of the plants were lapis lazuli, with sweet lush fruit nestling among them. Wherever I looked I thought I saw living jewels: agate and coral, onyx, topaz.

As I walked amidst this splendor I felt my injuries beginning to heal. I was covered all over by the festering bites of the stinging insects and the wounds I had received from the sliding tumbling rocks; my hair and beard were filthy tangles with sores beneath them; my tongue was swollen from thirst: but I began to heal. I found a cool lagoon of pure blue water, and drank and cleansed myself, and rested a long while, listening to the droning of bees that never thought to sting me. Their sound was like a loving music. White birds with legs like stilts paused in their foraging to look at me, and it seemed almost that they smiled.

I was at peace. It was a long time since I had known peace of any sort; and I do not think that I had ever known peace of the sort I felt just then. There was a joy and a silence about this land that brought me to rest, as I lay by the side of that cool lagoon. I felt no urgent need to move onward, nor any to go back to my city of Uruk: I was content where I was. I wonder now if I had ever before known a time when I was content to be where I was; but I did not ask the question then, feeling no need for answers. A man truly at peace does not ask himself questions of that kind. But peace and joy are not native to my spirit, I think; I am not accustomed to spending my time in their company. For as I lay there I thought of Enkidu, who knew nothing of this wondrous place. 'Do you see, brother?' I wanted to say to him. 'The vines bear jewels for fruit, and the birds walk on stilts, and the air is sweet as young wine! Have you ever seen a place so beautiful, brother? In all your wanderings in the forest, have you ever seen a place like this?'

I could say it, but he would not hear me, and a terrible sadness came upon me in the midst of all my joy and peace. I would have wept, but I was beyond all weeping; and so I could not rid myself of my sadness.

Despair returned to my heart. I could not find my way back to that moment of peace. This place was beautiful, yes, but I was alone and could never forget that; and every breath I drew brought me only that much closer to my end. So once more I was enveloped in grief and brooding, which had come to seem my natural state.

Then in my sorrow I looked up toward the sun and saw Utu the bright god looking down at me. I sent him half a prayer, just the smallest of a request for some solace. And I thought I heard him say, 'Do you think there is any hope of that? How far you have traveled, Gilgamesh! And for what? For what? You will never find the life for which you search.'

'I mean to find it, great one,' I told the god.

'Ah, Gilgamesh, Gilgamesh, how foolish you are!'

I tried to look straight into the heart of the god, but I could not. So I turned and looked at him shining on the breast of the lagoon, and to the god in the pool I said, 'Hear me, Utu! Have I marched and roved all through the wilderness for nothing? Am I simply to lie down now in the heart of the earth and sleep for all the years to come? Let it not be so! Spare me from that long darkness, Utu! Let my eyes continue to see the sun until I have had my fill of it!'

I think he must have heard my prayer. But I cannot tell you what reply he made to me, for I heard none; and after some little time a cloud passed across the face of the sun, and I no longer felt the presence of Utu close by me. I rose then and wrapped my tattered lion-skin about me, and readied myself to move on. For all the beauty of this place I could not regain that sense of joy that I had known for a while here. But the despair had passed from me also. I was calm. Perhaps I felt nothing at all. This is not peace; but it is better than despair.

I went onward, feeling nothing, thinking nothing; and in a few days more the air brought me a new taste, sharp and odd, like the taste of metal on my tongue. It was the tang of salt; it was the tang of the sea. My long pilgrimage thus was coming near its end. From the taste of salt in the air, I knew that I must be approaching the shore of the land that lies opposite the blessed isle of Dilmun, where ever-living Ziusudra dwells. Of that I had no doubt.

32

I came into the city that lies upon the coast opposite Dilmun looking like a wild man, like a second Enkidu. It is not truly a city, I suppose, it is not a tenth the size of Uruk, it is nowhere near as large even as Nippur or Shuruppak. It is only a small seaside town, a village, rather; a place where fishermen live, and those who repair the nets of fishermen. But to me it seemed like a city, for I had been in the wilderness so long.

In truth it was a pitiful place. Its streets were unpaved, its gardens were sparse and ill-tended, the salt of the air was devouring the brickwork of its buildings. I saw what may have been a temple; at any rate it was raised on a little platform. But it was a small and shabby structure and I could not tell you the name of the god to which it was devoted. I doubt that it was any god of ours. The people here were slim and dark-skinned, and they went practically naked except for a strip of white cloth around their waists. As well they might, for it was as hot here as it is in the Land in the depths of summer; but the season here was not summer yet. A tawdry town; still, to me it was a city. I trudged through it, looking for lodging and someone who could tell me where I might hire a ferryman to take me to Dilmun.

I think any stranger would have stirred excitement in that sleepy village. Few travelers are apt to seek it for its splendor. Visitors of any sort must be rarities. But certainly it was bound to cause some buzzing when a man of giant size came marching through the shabby streets, wild-eyed and gaunt, clad in the skin of a lion, leaning on a great pointed staff. Some little children saw me first—they ran off in fright—and then a few older boys, and then one by one the townsfolk came to stare and point. I heard them whispering. They spoke a version of that language which the desert tribes speak, and which is spoken in many places on the borders of the Land. The way they used it here was not much like the way it is spoken by the people of the desert race who have come to live in the cities of the Land; but I could understand it well enough. Some of them thought I was a demon, and some a shipwrecked pirate, and some a brigand. I said to them, 'Is there a place where I can buy food and drink here, and a bed for the night?' They broke into laughter at my words—a nervous laughter, perhaps, or perhaps it was only that my accent was so barbarous. But then one woman pointed down a crooked muddy street to a little white-walled building, prettier and less ramshackle than any other in the vicinity. The breeze brought me a whiff of ale from it: a sailors' tavern, I realized.

I went to it. As I neared its gate, a woman appeared and looked out at me. She was tall and comely, with shrewd straightforward eyes and a strong body: her shoulders were almost as broad as a man's. For a moment she stared at me as if I were a wolf come to her door; and then with great force she slammed the gate in my face. I heard a bolt being thrust home within.

'Wait, what is this?' I cried. 'All I seek is a night's lodging!'

'You may not have it here,' she called from the far side.

'Is that the hospitality of this place? What did you see that frightened you so? Come, woman, I will do you no harm!'

There was silence. Then she said, 'It is your face that is frightening. It is the face of a murderer, I think.'

'A murderer? No, woman, no murderer, only a tired wayfarer! Open up! Open!' And in my weariness a terrible anger came over me. I lifted my staff and said, 'Open, or I'll smash the door! I'll break down the gate!' I pounded once, and once again, and I heard the wood creak. It would not have been a heavy task for me to shatter it. I pounded a third time, and then I heard the bolt sliding.

The door opened and she stood before me, looking not at all terrified. Her jaw was set, her arms were folded over her breasts. There was anger in her eyes to equal my own. Sharply she said, 'Do you know what the price of a new door would be? By what right do you stand there hammering?'

'I seek lodging, and these people tell me this is a tavern.'

'So it is. But I am not required to take in every wandering rogue who comes along.'

'You do me an injustice. I am no rogue, woman.'

'Then why do you have the face of one?'

I told her that was an injustice too: I had come a long way, and the journey had left its mark on me, but I was no rogue. I took some pieces of silver from the pouch at my waist and showed them to her. 'If you will not let me sleep here this night, then will you at least sell me a mug of ale?' I asked.

'Come you in,' she said grudgingly.

I stepped inside. She closed the door behind me. The place was cool and dark; I was glad to be in it. I held one of my silver pieces out toward her, but she brushed it aside, saying as she drew me my ale, 'Later, later. I am not as greedy for your silver as you seem to think. Who are you, traveler? Where do you come from?'

I had thought I would invent a name for myself; but suddenly there seemed no reason to do that. 'I am Gilgamesh,' I said, and waited for her to laugh in my face, as one might do if I had said, 'I am Enlil,' or 'I am An the Sky-father.' But she did not laugh. She looked at me long and close, frowning. I felt the presence of her, strong and warm and good. I said after a moment, 'Do you know of me?'

'Everyone knows the name of Gilgamesh.'

'And is Gilgamesh a murderer?'

'He is king in Uruk. Kings have bloody hands.'

'I slew the demon in the forest, yes. I slew the Bull of Heaven, when the goddess set him loose to rage in my city. I have taken other lives when the need was there, but always only when it was needful. Yet you closed your door to me as if I were a common highwayman. I am not that.'

'Ah, but are you Gilgamesh? You ask me to believe a great deal, traveler!'

'Why do you doubt me?' I asked.

Slowly she said, 'If you are indeed Gilgamesh of Uruk—and by your size, by a certain majesty that I see about you, I suppose that it could be that you are—why is it that your cheeks are so wasted, that your face is so sunken, that your features are so worn by heat and cold and wind? Is that the style of a king? And your clothes are filthy rags. Do kings dress that way?'

'I have been a long while in the wilderness,' I replied. 'Into Elam, and north to the land called Uri, and to the deserts, and over the mountain known as Mashu, and many other places besides. If I look weatherbeaten and worn, there is reason for it. But I am Gilgamesh.'

She shook her head. 'Gilgamesh is a king. Kings own the world; they live in joy. You are a man with woe in your belly and grief in your heart. It is not difficult to see that.'

'I am Gilgamesh,' I said. And because there was warmth and strength in her, I told her why I had gone wandering. Over one mug of ale and another I spoke of Enkidu, my brother, my friend whom I had loved so dearly, he who had chased the wild ass of the hills, the panther of the steppe. I told her how we had lived side by side, how we had hunted together and wrestled together and feasted together, how we had had many grand exploits together; I told her how he had fallen ill, and how he had died; I told her how I had mourned him. 'His death lies heavy on me,' I said. 'It was the most aching of losses. How can I be at peace? My friend who I loved has turned to clay!'

'Your friend is dead. You have mourned him; now forget him. No one grieves as you have grieved.'

'You do not understand.'

'Then tell me,' she said, and gave me still another ale.

I drew a deep draught of the sweet foaming stuff before speaking. 'His death puts me into fear of my own dying. And so, fearing death, I roam from land to land.'

'We all must die, Gilgamesh.'

'So I hear, over and over: from the scorpion-woman in the mountain, from Utu on high, now from you. Is it so? That I must lay me down like Enkidu, never to rise forever and ever?'

'It is the way,' she said calmly.

I felt hot fury rising. How many times I had heard that! *It is the way, it is the way, it is the way*—the words were coming to sound like the bleating of sheep in my ears. Was I the only one who disdained the sovereignty of death?

'No!' I shouted. 'I will not accept that! I will go on and on through all the world, if I must, until I learn how I can escape death's hand.'

The tavern-woman came to me and stood looking down at me. She let her hand rest lightly on my arm. Once again I felt the strength of her, and the tenderness within that strength. There was goodness-presence about this woman; she had the mother-force within her. Softly she said, 'Gilgamesh, Gilgamesh, where are you running? You will never find this eternal life that you seek. Can you ever come to understand that? When the gods created mankind, they created death also. Death they allotted to us, and life they kept for themselves.'

'No,' I murmured. 'No. No.'

'It is the way. Forget your quest. Live well, instead, while you live. Let your belly be full. Be merry, day and night: dance and sing, feast and rejoice. Put aside these tatters and let your garments be clean and fresh. Wash your hair, bathe your body, be always fresh and clean and pure. Cherish the little one holding your hand, cherish the wife who delights in your embrace. This too is the way, Gilgamesh. And it is the only way: live joyously while you have life. Stop your brooding; stop your seeking.'

'I cannot rest,' I said.

'Tonight you will rest.' She drew me to my feet. She was so tall that she came almost to my breast. 'I am Siduri,' she said. 'I live quietly by the sea, and sometimes strangers come to my tavern, but not often. When they come I treat them with courtesy, for what is my task on earth, if it is not to look after the comfort of wayfarers? Come with me, Gilgamesh.' She bathed me then, and washed and trimmed my hair and beard; and she made for me a meal of barley and stewed meat, and instead of ale we drank a fine wine of a clear golden hue. Then she laid me down on her couch and rubbed me and stroked me until all the weariness had gone from my body; and I spent the night clasped in her arms. No one had held me that way since I was a baby. Her breath was warm and her breasts were full and her skin was smooth. I lost myself in her. It is good sometimes to lose one's self that way; but one can never remain lost for long, so it seems. Before dawn I was awake, and restless, even with Siduri beside me. I told her that I must go; and again she said, gently, half reprovingly, 'Gilgamesh, Gilgamesh, where are you running?'

'I mean to go to Dilmun, and speak with Ziusudra.'

'He cannot help you.'

'Nevertheless, I will go.'

'The crossing is toilsome,' she said.

'Undoubtedly it is. Tell me how I may get there.'

'Why do you think you will find Ziusudra, even if you reach Dilmun?'

I answered her, 'Because I am Gilgamesh the king. He will see me. And he will help me.'

'Ziusudra does not exist.' said Siduri.

With a harsh laugh I said, 'Am I to believe that? The gods themselves rewarded him with an unending life and sent him to dwell in Dilmun. This much I know. Why do you try to discourage me, Siduri?'

'How stubborn you are!' She made a purring sound, and moved closer to me. 'Stay here with me, Gilgamesh! Live by the sea, live quietly, grow old in peace!'

I smiled. I caressed her cheeks and the deep bowls of her breasts. But then I said, 'Tell me how to reach Dilmun.'

She sighed. After a moment she replied. 'There is a boatman, Sursunabu by name, who serves Ziusudra and the priests of Ziusudra. He comes each month to the mainland to purchase certain supplies. I think he will be here in a day or two. When he comes, I will ask him to take you back with him to Dilmun. Perhaps he will.'

I thanked her. I held her a long while in my arms.

For three days more I sojourned in the tavern of Siduri by the shore of the warm green sea. She fed me well and bathed me and slept with me. I found myself thinking at times that this life was in truth not so bad, that it might not be impossible for me simply to go on and on like this, giving no thought to tomorrow, living only for the easy pleasures of the moment. Why not? What did tomorrow offer, except death and darkness? But I did not really believe that I could live that way for long. And neither did Siduri. On the fourth day, as I lay sleeping after a long night of lovemaking, she came to me and shook me by the shoulder and whispered, 'Awaken, Gilgamesh! The boatman Sursunabu has come from Dilmun. Up, dress yourself, come with me to the harbor, if you would seek passage with him.'

33

Dilmun! Holy isle! Paradise of the gods!

They tell such fabulous tales of Dilmun, all those whose business it is to be tellers of tales—the harpers, the priests, the story-spinners in the marketplaces. It lies in the south, where the Two Rivers run into the Sea of the Rising Sun. They say that it is a place where there is neither sickness nor death, where all is pure and clean and bright, where the raven does not croak and the wolf snatches not the lamb. It has been a habitation for gods: Enki dwelled there; Ninhursag dwelled there; and together they gave birth to gods and goddesses. Utu smiles constantly on Dilmun; flowers bloom without end; its water is the sweetest in the world.

But I have been there. I will tell you of the true Dilmun.

It may be a paradise indeed. Yet it is an earthly paradise at best, a gentle place but not without flaws. It has its share of the common hardships of the world. There are days when the sun does not shine; there are days when stormy winds blow. One can grow ill in Dilmun, and one can die; one may find mice gnawing in one's barley-sacks, or the grubs of insects; there are beggars there, and people born without legs or eyes, and other unfortunates. Still, it is a gentle place: I have known worse. The air is hot and wet, which is strange to us, for in the Land the hot season is the dry season, and the air is not moist; but in Dilmun the air is moist all the time, though there is little rain. In the winters the breeze is from the north and the heat is more easily endured. It is a small island, but very fertile, well watered, with rich groves of date-trees. The houses are white, with flat roofs. There is great prosperity.

The good fortune of Dilmun is its location in the Sea of the Rising Sun. It lives by trade, and lives well. Its ships go out not only to the cities of the Land lying along the Two Rivers, but far off to Meluhha and Makan and other kingdoms even more remote, of which little is known in Uruk. Through the marketplace of Dilmun pass copper from the mines of Makan and gold from Meluhha, rare timber from the countries of the distant east, ivory and lapis lazuli and carnelian out of Elam and the nations beyond, and also all the manufactured goods of the Land, our textiles and our utensils of copper and bronze and our fine jewelry. I have seen in the shops of Dilmun the smooth green stone that comes from some land beyond the edge of the world; no one knows its name, but they know that the stone comes from there, dug from the earth by demons with yellow skins. Everything of this world and the worlds beyond passes through Dilmun on its way to be sold somewhere else, and whatever passes through Dilmun creates more wealth for the merchants of Dilmun as it passes. If wealth is a hallmark of paradise, then Dilmun is a paradise. I can understand why Enlil sent Ziusudra there for his everlasting reward. Its merchants are plump and sleek. They drive hard bargains and live in fine palaces. Someday, I think, a king who does not understand the value of having such a port as Dilmun for the sake of the world's commerce will descend on it like a lion, and slaughter those sleek merchants so he may loot the riches of their bulging warehouses. That will be too bad for Dilmun; but until that day comes it will be a place where life is kind and common folk can live like kings.

In truth I was not in Dilmun long. What I found is that Dilmun is not the home of Ziusudra, although Ziusudra does indeed exist, even if he is not precisely the Ziusudra that the fables had led me to expect. He dwells not on Dilmun but on a smaller island without a name that lies perhaps half a league off its western shore. I learned that from the boatman Sursunabu. It was the first of many things I would learn about Ziusudra before I left those blessed isles.

This boatman was a gaunt old fellow with gray hair tied in a knot behind his head. He wore only a strip of ragged brown cloth about his hips, and his skin was tanned dark as leather. I found him in the harbor of the fishing village, loading things into a long, narrow vessel built of reeds covered with a thick coating of pitch. When we approached, he greeted Siduri amiably but without warmth, and took almost no notice of me.

The tavern-woman said, 'I bring you a passenger, Sursunabu. This is Gilgamesh of Uruk, who would speak with Ziusudra.'

'Let him speak with Ziusudra, then. What is that to me?'

'He needs passage to the island.'

With a shrug Sursunabu said, 'Let him find passage to the island if that is what he wants. And then let him see if Ziusudra will admit him.'

'Show him your silver,' Siduri whispered.

I stepped forward and said, 'I can pay well for my passage.'

The boatman gave me a blank stare. 'What need do I have of your metal?'

A bold fellow! But there was no haughtiness about him. He was merely indifferent. I had not encountered that before and it was a mystery to me.

In rising anger I said, 'Will you refuse me? I am king in Uruk!'

'Be wary, Sursunabu,' Siduri said. 'He takes refusals badly. His temper is fierce, and his love for himself is immense.'

I turned and gaped at her. 'What did you say?'

She smiled. It seemed a tender smile, not at all mocking. She replied, 'You alone of all mankind fly into a rage when you consider your death. What is that, if not love of self, Gilgamesh! You mourn your own passing. You weep harder for yourself than ever you did for your friend who died.'

I was amazed—both by the brutal bluntness of her words, and by the thought that there might be truth in them. I blinked at her; I struggled to reply. But I could find no answer.

She went on, 'You said it yourself. You grieved mightily for your Enkidu, but it was the fear of death, your own death, that drove you from your city into the wilderness. Is that not so? And now you run to Ziusudra, thinking he will teach you how to escape from dying. Has any man ever loved himself more?' The tavern-keeper laughed and looked toward the boatman. 'Come, Sursunabu, put a better face on things! This man is king in Uruk, and he dreams of living forever. Take him to Ziusudra, I beg you. Let him learn what he must learn.'

The boatman spat and went on loading his boat.

It was too much, the boatman's disdain and the sharp edge of Siduri's words. My wrath overflowed. There was sudden fire in my spirit. I felt a drumming in my head and my hand shook. Angrily I strode toward Sursunabu. There was a row of small columns of polished stones resting on the ground between me and the boat; these I kicked furiously aside, knocking some into the water, smashing others, so that I could get to Sursunabu. I caught him by the shoulder. He looked up at me, entirely unafraid, though I was twice his size and could break him as easily as I had broken those things of stone. At that fearless look my rage subsided a little, and I let go of him, catching in my breath, trying to cool the white-hot blaze within my soul.

As humbly as I knew how I said, 'I pray you, boatman, take me to your master. I will pay the price, whatever it is.'

'I told you, I have no need of your metal.'

'Take me anyway. For the love of the gods, whose child I am.'

'Are you? Then what fear do you have of death?'

I felt my anger returning at these bland uncaring rejoinders of his, but I fought it down. 'Must I kneel? Must I beg? Is it so great a thing, to take me to that island of yours?'

He laughed a strange thin laugh. 'It is a great thing now, O foolish Gilgamesh. In your rage you have smashed the sacred stones that insure a safe passage: do you know that? They would have protected us. But you have broken them.'

I was greatly abashed. I have rarely felt so sheepish. My cheeks flamed; I dropped to my knees and searched for the little stone columns. But I had fallen upon them too vigorously; they lay scattered in many pieces, and I cannot say how many I had kicked into the sea, but it was more than a few. Numbly I gathered up those that remained. Sursunabu told me with a gesture that it was futile. 'We will manage without them,' he said. 'The risks will be greater. But if you are the child of the gods, perhaps you will ask them to look after us during our crossing.'

'So you will take me!'

'What is it to me?' he said, shrugging once more.

Siduri came to me. She caught my hands in hers, she pressed her soft breasts against my chest. Gently she said, 'I did not mean to speak scornfully of you, Gilgamesh. But I think there was some truth in my words, harsh though they were.'

'It may be so.'

'Despite the things I said, I do hope you find what you seek.'

'I thank you, Siduri. For that wish and for all the rest.'

'But if you should fail to find it, perhaps you will come back here. There will always be a place for you with me, Gilgamesh.'

'There are many worse places to be,' I told her. 'But I think that I will not be coming back.'

'Then fare you well, Gilgamesh.'

'Fare you well, Siduri.'

She held me, and she offered a prayer, speaking to some goddess that was not any goddess I knew. She prayed that I would find peace, that I would come soon to the end of my wanderings. The only peace I could see for myself just then was the peace of the grave, and I hoped Siduri did not mean that; but I chose to take her prayer at its best meaning, and thanked her for it. Then the boatman beckoned me in his brusque sour way. I climbed in and took a seat at the prow, against mats of straw. He pushed us off from shore, running a short way out into the water before he leaped in beside me.

Silently we set forth for Dilmun. The gods protected us, even though I had smashed the things of stone, and our crossing was an easy one under bright skies. For a time we bobbed in open water—no longer green here, but blue with the deep blue of the wide sea—and there was no land in view anywhere, neither behind us nor before us. That made me uneasy. I had never been out of sight of land before. I felt the presence of the great abyss all about me. I thought I could look down into the water and see the mighty lord of the depths, giant Enki, in his lair. I imagined I beheld the shadow of the horns of his crown. And in the heat of day I felt a chill, a chill that comes from going too close to great gods. But I prayed to him, saying, *I am Gilgamesh, Lugalbanda's son, the king in Uruk, and I seek what I must seek: spare me until I find it, great and wise Enki.* My prayer sank into the abyss and I suppose it must have been heeded, for late in the day I saw a dark line of palm-trees across the horizon, and the white limestone walls of a large city shimmering in the last of the sunlight, with many ships drawn up on the beach before it.

'Dilmun,' Sursunaba grunted. It was the only word he had spoken during the entire crossing.

34

I stayed there five days, or perhaps six, while I waited to be allowed into the presence of Ziusudra. It was a restless time. From Sursunabu I had learned that the patriarch did not live on Dilmun itself, but had his retreat on one of the adjacent smaller islands, surrounded by a company of holy men and women. Few were admitted as pilgrims to that island; whether I would be one of them he could not say. In his curt and surly way he promised only to carry my request. Then he departed, leaving me behind on Dilmun. I wondered if I would ever see him again.

I tell you, I was unaccustomed to begging favors of boatmen, or to ask humbly for permission to journey here and there. But it was an art I had to learn, for there was no other way. I told myself that the gods had decreed these things upon me as one more stage in my initiation into true wisdom.

At a hostelry near the waterfront I found a pleasant lodging: a large, airy room, open on its seaward side to sunlight and breezes. That is not the way we build in the Land, where it is folly to make openings in walls; but our winters are more harsh than those of Dilmun. It did not seem wise to advertise my true rank in this place, so I gave my name to the innkeeper as Lugal-amarku, which is the name of the little hunchbacked wizard whose services I had used from time to time. Now he served me without knowing it.

There was no way I could disguise my height or the breadth of my shoulders, but I tried at least to hold myself in an unkingly way, with my chest made hollow and my chin pulled back. I met no man's eye unless he met mine first, and I said little to anyone except when it was unavoidable. Whether anyone recognized me I cannot say; but no one, at any rate, hailed me to my face as the king of Uruk.

The city swarmed with merchants and seamen of every nation. Some spoke tongues familiar to me—I heard the language of the Land a good deal, and also the desert-dwellers' language, which is native to Dilmun and all the regions nearby—but others came forth with amazing incomprehensible babble, like the stuff one might hear people speaking in one's dreams. How they understood it themselves I cannot say: one of the languages was all clicks and sneezes and snorts, and another flowed like a swift river, one word joining into the next without break, and a third was more sung than spoken, in a high chanting way.

Not only their languages were strange, but their faces too. One vessel that arrived on the first day had a crew with skins black as the middle watch of a moonless night, and their hair like tight wool. Their noses were broad and flat, their lips were thick. Surely they must be demons or men of some other world, I thought. But they laughed and sported like ordinary seamen, and no one in the harbor seemed to make a great deal of them. Just then a merchant passed by whose hair was shaven after the manner of the Land, and I halted him: sure enough, he was from the city of Eridu. I nodded to the black ones and he said, 'They are men of the kingdom of Punt.' That is a place where the air is like fire, which blackens its people's skins. He could not tell me where Punt is; he pointed vaguely toward the horizon. Later in the day I saw other black-skinned men who looked altogether different, for these had thin noses and lips, and long straight hair so dark it was almost blue. From their language and manner of dress I thought they might be men of Meluhha, which is far away to the east beyond Elam; and that proved to be the case. I hoped also to see the yellow-skinned demons who mine the green stone, but there were none of those in Dilmun. Perhaps they do not even exist, though the green stone certainly does, and very beautiful it is, too.

I said little and listened much. And learned some news of the Land that troubled me deeply.

This I heard one night at my tavern as I sat by myself sipping ale. Two men came in who were speaking in the language of the Land. I feared at first they might be of Uruk; but they wore scarlet robes trimmed with yellow, a style that is common in the city of Ur. Nevertheless I hunched myself down to look as inconspicuous as is possible for me, and turned my back to them. From their accents I knew after a moment that they were indeed men of Ur: the younger one had newly arrived in Dilmun, and the other was asking him for news of home.

'Tell me again,' said the older man. 'Is it really so that Nippur is ours?'

'It is.'

I sat bolt upright at that, and caught my breath sharply. Nippur is a sacred city: it should not be ruled by Ur.

'How did it come to pass?' the older man asked.

The newcomer said, 'Good fortune, and good timing. It was the season when Mesannepadda the king goes to Nippur to worship at the Dur-anki shrine and perform the rite of the pickaxe. This year he had a thousand men with him; and while he was there the governor of the city fell ill. It looked as though he would die; and the priest of Enlil came to our king and said, 'Our governor is dying, will you name another for us?' Whereupon Mesannepadda prayed long at the temple and came out to say that Enlil had visited him and had commanded *him* to take upon himself the governorship of Nippur.'

'It was that simple?'

'That simple,' said the younger man, and they both laughed. 'The word of Enlil—who will go against it?'

'Especially if it is backed by a thousand men!'

'Especially so,' said the other.

I clenched my hand tight around my beaker of ale. This was grim news. I had not taken action when Mesannepadda had overthrown the sons of Agga and made himself king in Kish as well as in Ur; it had not seemed a threat to Uruk, and I had had other matters to occupy my mind, as I have related. But Nippur, which in the time of Enmebaraggesi and Agga had owed allegiance to Kish, had been independent since Agga's death. If Mesannepadda, having taken Kish, had seized possession of Nippur as well, we were on our way toward being encircled by an empire in the process of formation. Surely I could not allow that. I wondered if they knew of it in Uruk. Were the people of Uruk waiting for Gilgamesh their king to return and lead them in war against Ur? What limit would there be to Mesannepadda's ambitions, if Gilgamesh did not set one?

And Gilgamesh—where was he? Sitting in a tavern in Dilmun, waiting to be summoned to the isle of Ziusudra so that he might somehow wheedle eternal life for himself! Was that how a king was meant to conduct himself?

I did not know what to do. I sat like stone.

But the newcomer from Ur was not done with his news. Old Mesannepadda was dead; his son Meskiagnunna had come to the throne. And he was losing no time showing that he meant to continue his father's policies. Mesannepadda had begun the construction in Nippur of a temple to Enlil. The new king not only was overseeing the completion of that temple but, by way of further demonstrating his deep concern for the welfare of Nippur, had given orders for the immediate restoration of the great ceremonial center known as the Tummal that had fallen into ruin after Agga's time. Worse and worse! These kings of Ur were treating Nippur as though it were their colony! It must not be, I thought. Let them build temples in Ur if they wished to build temples! Let them look after their own city and keep their hands away from Nippur. It was all I could do to prevent myself from rising up and seizing those two men of Ur and slamming their heads together, and commanding them to go back to their city at once and tell their king that Gilgamesh of Uruk was their enemy and was coming to make war on him.

But I held my seat. I had business in these islands with Ziusudra; I had come a long way to do what I had to do here; I could not leave just yet, no matter what responsibilities called me to Uruk. Or so it seemed to me just then. Perhaps I was wrong about that; quite certainly I was wrong about that. But I think it is just as well that I did as I did. Had I chosen at that moment to return to my city I would never have gained the most important wisdom that I possess.

I slept not at all that night. Nor did I rest well in the days that followed. I thought of very little but the arrogance of Meskiagnunna, prancing about in Nippur's sacred precincts as though he were its king. But I stayed in Dilmun. And on the fifth day, or perhaps it was the sixth, the boatman Sursunabu reappeared and said to me in his usual cheerless manner, 'You are to come with me to the isle where Ziusudra dwells.'

35

The island was low and flat and sandy, and—unlike high-walled Dilmun—completely undefended. Anyone might have beached his boat there and walked straight into the house of Ziusudra. At least the island had no defenses of the conventional sort; but when Sursunabu pulled his little craft onto the shore I noticed that along the beach were three rows of small stone columns of the sort I had so wantonly smashed in my foolish anger. I asked him what those were and he said that they were Enlil's tokens to Ziusudra, given at the time of the Flood. They protected the island from enemies: no one would dare trespass where such tokens were erected. Whenever Sursunabu journeyed to Dilmun or the mainland he always took some of them with him and set them up beside his boat to guard him. I felt even more ashamed then at the way I had scattered and broken those things like a wild bull with wrath. But evidently I had been forgiven, since Ziusudra was willing to have me come.

I saw what seemed to be a temple near the center of the island, a long low building with white walls that were brilliant in the hot sunlight. The hairs rose upon the back of my neck as I looked toward it: it came to me that within that building, just a few hundred paces from me, must be the ancient Ziusudra, the survivor of the flood, he who had walked with Enki and Enlil so long ago. The air was still; a great silence prevailed here. There were twelve or fourteen lesser buildings about the main structure, and some little farm-plots. That was all. Sursunabu conducted me to one of the outbuildings, a small square house of a single room, entirely without furnishings, and left me there. 'They will come for you,' he said.

It is a time out of time, when one is on the island of Ziusudra. I cannot tell you how long I sat there alone, whether it was one day or three, or five.

At first I was fretful and even angry. I thought of walking to the central house and searching the patriarch out; but I knew that that was absurd and would be damaging to my purposes. I paced my empty room, walking from one corner to the other. I listened to the noise and buzzing of my own brain, that unceasing sputtering inner chatter. I peered at the sea, dazzling my eyes in the fiery track of sunlight that blazed across its breast. I thought of Meskiagnunna king of Ur and all that he was attempting to do. I thought of Inanna, who surely was scheming in Uruk against me. I thought of my son the babe Ur-lugal, and wondered if he would ever be king. I thought of this, I thought of that. The hours passed, and no one came to me. And gradually I felt the great silence of the place seeping into my soul: I was beginning to grow calm. It was a wonderful thing. The noise and buzzing within my mind subsided, though it did not entirely die away; and after a while I was as still within as everything was without. At that moment it did not matter to me what Meskiagnunna might be doing, or Inanna, or Ur-lugal. It did not matter if they left me sitting in this place twelve days, or twelve years, or twelve hundred. It was a time out of time. But then I passed beyond that wondrous calm, and grew angry again, and impatient. How long would I be left like this? Did they not know that I was Gilgamesh king of Uruk? Urgent business awaited me at home! Meskiagnunna, king of Ur—Inanna—the needs of my people—Meskiagnunna—the care of the canals—would I be home in time for the ceremony of the lighting of the pipe?—the pageant of the statue of An?—Meskiagnunna—Ziusudra—Inanna—ah, the babble, the chatter of the mind!

And then at last they came for me, when I had made myself as frantic as a baited hound.

There were two of them. First came a slender solemn girl with a dancer's supple body, who I think could not have been more than fifteen or sixteen years old: she would have been pretty, if she smiled. She wore a simple robe of white cotton, and no ornament, and carried a staff of black wood carved with inscriptions of a mysterious kind. For a long moment she stood at the threshold of my door, regarding me in an unhurried way. Then she said, 'If you are Gilgamesh of Uruk, come forth.'

'I am Gilgamesh,' I said.

Just outside, a tall fierce-eyed dark-skinned old man, all planes and angles, was waiting. He too wore a cotton robe and carried a black staff, and he looked as though the sun had baked all the flesh from his bones. I could not tell how old he was, but he seemed of great age, and a surge of wild excitement went through me. Trembling, I said, stammering, 'Can it be true? Do I behold Ziusudra?'

He laughed a little. 'Hardly. But you will meet the Ziusudra at the proper time, Gilgamesh. I am the priest Lu-Ninmarka; this is Dabbatum. Come with us.'

That was strange, what he had said: *the* Ziusudra. But I knew I ought not to ask him to explain. They would offer me such explanations as they cared to when they cared to do it, and otherwise would offer me none at all. Of that I was sure.

They led me to a house of fair size close by the main temple, where I was given a white robe like theirs, and a meal of lentils and figs. I scarcely touched it; I had not eaten in so long, I suppose, that my stomach had forgotten the meaning of hunger. While I was there others of that priesthood came and went in the house to take their midday meals, and they glanced at me only casually, without speaking. Many of them seemed very old, though all were sinewy, sturdy, full of vitality. After they ate they prayed at a low altar that bore no image, and went out to work in the fields. Which is what I did also when Lu-Ninmarka and Dabbatum were done with their meal; they beckoned to me and led me outside, and put me to toil.

How good that felt, working on my knees under the hot sun! Perhaps they thought they were testing me, seeing whether a king would do the labor of a slave; but if that was so they did not understand that some kings take pleasure in the work of the hands. It was the season of planting barley. They had ploughed the land already in strips eight furrows wide, and they had dropped their seed two fingers deep. Now I came along behind the plough, clearing the field of clods, leveling the soil with my hands so that the barley when it sprouted would not have to struggle against hills or valleys. You may say it was a task that called for no great skill, and you would be right; nevertheless I had pleasure from it.

Afterward I returned to the dining-house. Another old man— ancient, even, withered and parched—entered as I did, and once again my heart leaped at the sight of him: was *this* one at last the Ziusudra? But one of the others hailed him by the name of

Hasidanum; he was simply one of the priests. This old man made a libation of oil and lit three lamps, and knelt over them for a time murmuring prayers in a voice too faint and feathery for me to hear. Then he sprinkled some of his oil on me. 'It is to cleanse you,' the girl Dabbatum whispered at my side. 'You have the pollution of the world still upon you.'

For the evening meal it was lentils again and fruit and a porridge of onions and barley. We drank the milk of goats. They used no beer here, nor wine, and ate no meat. The work of the afternoon had awakened hunger in me, and also thirst, and I lamented the lack of meat and drink. But they did not use them; I did not taste them again until I had left the island.

So it went for some days. I cannot say how many. It is a time out of time, on the island of the Ziusudra. I worked in the sun, I ate my simple meals, I watched the priests and priestesses at their devotions, I waited to see what would happen next. I think I ceased to care about Meskiagnunna, about Inanna, about Ur, about Nippur, about Uruk itself. That great calmness of the island returned to me, and this time it remained.

Every second day they went to the main temple for their high rites and ceremonials. Since I was only a novice I could not take part in these, but they let me kneel beside them while they chanted their texts. The temple was a huge lofty-vaulted room devoid of all images, with a gleaming floor of black stone and a red ceiling of cedar timbers. When I first entered I expected the patriarch to be there, but he was not, which caused me sharp disappointment. But I taught myself to curb my impatience: I thought perhaps they would not admit me to the presence of the Ziusudra while I seemed too eager for his blessing.

I listened to their rituals without at first understanding much of what was being said, since the language they used was a strangely old-fashioned one. It was plainly the language of the Land, but I think they must have been speaking it the way people spoke before the Flood. But after a while I saw how the words were fitted together and how they differed from the words we used today, and the meaning, or some of it, came clear to me. In these rituals they were telling the tale of the Flood; but what they told was nothing at all like the story I had heard so many times from the old harper Ur-kununna.

It began with the anger of the gods, yes: displeasure over the noisy brawling slothful ways of mankind. And the gods sent rain, indeed, week upon week of it; the rivers rose, bursting their banks, spilling across the plain, ripping open the walls of the cities and falling like wolves upon the low-lying streets and houses. Throughout the Land the destruction was dreadful and the loss of life was great.

But then the story began to diverge from the one I knew, as an unknown path splits from a well-traveled highway; and it led me to an unfamiliar place. I heard the name of Ziusudra, and listened close. And what I heard was this: 'The wise and compassionate Enki came to Ziusudra king of Shuruppak, and said to him, "Stir yourself, O king, and put aside provisions and useful goods of all kinds, and take yourself and your people to the high ground; for the devastation will be great." Ziusudra did not falter, but hearkened at once: he put aside provisions, he put aside useful goods of all kinds, and he loaded them on the backs of his beasts of burden, and he and all his people went into the hills, and there they remained as the flood waters raged in the lowlands. And they did not come down again until the storm had ceased.'

What was this? Where was the great ship into which Ziusudra had loaded the people of his household, and the beasts of the field two by two? What about the voyage across the sea which had come to cover the face of the Land? And what of the dove he sent forth, and the swallow, and the raven? Fables and legends, and nothing more? Was such a thing possible? The tale they were telling here had none of those pretty things in it. It was a simple account: a bad rainy season, turbulent rivers, a shrewd king acting swiftly to mitigate the disaster for his city. The longer I listened, the more ordinary the story seemed. When he came down from the hills, Shuruppak and all the cities of the Land were in a bad way, choked with mud, stained by water. The farms had been swamped, crops and animals had been lost, the stores held in the granaries were ruined. There was famine in the land; but in Shuruppak it was not so bad as in other places because Ziusudra had taken care to escape the worst of the storm. That was not all. No Land-engulfing sea, no ship of six decks, no dove, no swallow, no raven. I could not believe it. Such a simple story? It is not the way of priests to make stories simpler by the retelling. But what these priests were saying was that there had never been an all-destroying Flood, but only some heavy rains and some difficult times.

And if that were so, what of the rest of the story, the coming of Enlil to speak with Ziusudra and his wife, the great god taking them by the hand and saying, '*You have been mortal, but you are mortal no longer. Henceforth you shall be like gods, and live far away from mankind, at the mouth of the rivers, in the golden land of Dilmun*'—was that too a fable? And had I come halfway across the world for the sake of a mere fable? *Ziusudra does not exist*, the tavern-keeper Siduri had said. Was it so? How big a fool had I made of myself, in undertaking this quest? *Gilgamesh, Gilgamesh, where are you running? You never will find this eternal life that you seek.*

Despair came over me. I was lost in confusion and shame.

It was then that the old priest Lu-Ninmarka rested his hand on my shoulder and said, 'Rise, Gilgamesh, bathe yourself, put on a fresh robe. The Ziusudra wishes to see you this day.'

When I had made my preparations he took me to the main temple. I found myself to be strangely calm; or perhaps it was not so strange. The spell of the island was upon me. We entered the great room of the cedar beams and black stone floor and went to its rear; Lu-Ninmarka touched his hand to a place in the wall and it swung back as though by sorcery, revealing a passage that curved away into darkness. 'Come,' he said. He had neither a lamp nor a torch. We went forward, and at once I felt a damp clinging mist rising out of the earth, carrying a faint scent of salt. It is the water of the great abyss, I thought, that must climb the roots of the island and discharge itself into this tunnel. Lu-Ninmarka moved confidently in the darkness and I was hard pressed to keep up with him. I did not allow myself the ease of feeling my way with my hands, but walked steadfastly although I could see nothing. How far we went, how deep beneath the skin of the island, I cannot say. Perhaps we were only moving in circles, round and round the great central room following the coils of a vast maze. But after some long time we came to a halt in the darkness. Ahead of me I saw the faintest of amber gleams, as gentle and dim as the brief flickers of light which come from the glow-fires that sparkle in the summer night. Dim as it was, it startled my eyes; but a moment later I was able to see, after a fashion. I stood at the threshold of a small round room with earthen walls, illuminated by a single oil lamp mounted in a high sconce. Incense sputtered in a porphyry dish on the floor; and at the center of the room, sitting upright and straight on a wooden stool, was the oldest man I had ever seen. I had thought the priest Hasidanum was ancient; this one could easily have been Hasidanum's father. I felt awe like a choking hand at my throat. I who had walked with gods and fought with demons was stunned at the sight of the Ziusudra.

His face was like a mask: his eyes were white and sightless, his mouth was a dark empty slit. He was altogether without hair, devoid even of eyebrows. His cheeks were soft, his face was round. The other old men of this island had a gaunt, lean, sun-dried look about them, sharp edges everywhere; but the Ziusudra had passed beyond that gauntness and was smooth and pink and full-fleshed like a baby. His blind eyes were trained upon me. He smiled and said, in a voice that was deep and resonant, but hollow somewhere at the core, 'At last you are here, Gilgamesh of Uruk. What a long time you were in coming!'

I could not say a word. How could I speak to this man whose forehead had been touched by the hand of Enlil?

'Sit. Kneel. You are too big; when you stand you rise like a wall before me.'

I did not understand how he could know my stature, when he was unable to see: maybe his priests had told him, or possibly he felt the minute fluctuations of the currents of air in the passageway. Or perhaps he had the sight beyond sight; I did not know. That last was most likely. I knelt before him. He nodded and smiled a faraway smile. He put forth his hand to bless me, and touched it to my cheek. His touch had a sting; his fingertips were very cold. I thought they must be leaving white imprints on my skin.

He said, 'You draw back. Why?'

I managed to reply, in a hoarse rusty whisper, 'No reason, father.'

'Do you fear me?'

'No—no!'

'But you have an aura of fear about you. They tell me you are the greatest of heroes, that your strength is without limit, that all men hail you as master. What is it that you fear, Gilgamesh?'

I stared at him in silence. My overwhelming awe was ebbing, but still it was hard for me to speak; so I stared. He was still as stone except for the expressions of his face. I thought for a moment that he might indeed be a statue, some ingenious construction worked by ropes by a priest hidden in the floor. After a time I said, 'I fear that which every man must fear.'

From very far away he asked, 'And what is that?'

'I had a friend, and he was my other self; he fell ill and died. The shadow of my death falls upon me now. It darkens my life. I see nothing but that lengthening shadow, father. And it frightens me.'

'Ah, then the hero is afraid of dying?'

I could not tell if he was mocking me.

'Not of dying,' I said. 'Dying is only pain, and I know pain and do not fear him much. Pain ends. What I am afraid of is death. I am afraid of being cast down into the House of Dust and Darkness, where I will have to dwell for all eternity.'

'And where you will no longer be a king, and drink rich wine from alabaster vessels? Where no one will sing of your glory, and you will lack for all comfort?'

That was unfair. 'No,' I said sharply. 'Do you think comfort is so important to me, I who left my city of my free will to roam in the wilderness? Do you think I am in such great need of wine, or fine robes, or harpers to sing of my deeds? I like those things: who would not? But losing them is not what I fear.'

'What do you fear, then?'

'To lose myself. To live in that shadow-life that comes after life, when we are nothing but sad dusty empty things shuffling our wings in the dust. To cease to perceive; to cease to explore; to cease to journey; to cease to hope. All those things are Gilgamesh. There will be no more Gilgamesh, when I go to that dismal place. I have been on a quest all my life, father: I cannot bear that that quest will end.'

'But all things end.'

'Do they?' I asked.

He looked close at me as though he must surely be seeing into my soul with his milky sightless eyes and said, 'When we build a house, do we expect it to stand forever? When we sign a contract, do we think it is binding for all time to come? When the river floods, do the waters not recede? Nothing is permanent. The dragonfly lives in a shell when it is young; then it comes forth, and it beholds the sun a little while; and then it is gone. So it is with mankind. The master and the servant both have their little moment, their glance at the sun. It is the way.'

Those words again! They made me despair.

'*It is the way!*' I cried. 'You tell me that too, father?'

'Can it be otherwise? The same destiny is decreed for us all.'

Before I knew what I was saying I replied, 'Even for you, father?'

It was a crass and foolish remark, and my cheeks blazed as I said it. But he was unperturbed. 'Let us talk of me some other time,' said the Ziusudra calmly. 'Today we talk of you. I think this of you, Gilgamesh of Uruk: that you are not frightened of death so much as you are angry at having to die.'

'It is the same thing,' I said. 'Call it fear, call it anger—I see no difference. What I see is that the world is full of joy and wonder, and I have no wish to leave it. But soon I must.'

'Not soon, Gilgamesh.'

'Why, do you know the number of my days?'

'I? No, not at all: I would not deceive you on that score. But you are still young. You are very strong. You have many years ahead of you.'

'However many they be, they are too few. For their number is set and limited, father.'

'Which angers you.'

'Which distresses me greatly,' I said.

'And in your distress you have come to me.'

'I have.'

'Do you come seeking life from me, or wisdom?'

'I can conceal nothing from you. I come seeking life, father. Wisdom is another matter. I hope time will bring it; but what I must have is time.'

'And you think that by coming here you may win more time for yourself?'

'So I hope, yes.'

'Then may the gods grant you all that you seek,' the Ziusudra said. There was a long silence. His head sank forward on his breast and he seemed lost in brooding: he frowned, he pursed his lips, he sighed. I felt I had wearied him; I dared not speak. The moment was endless. Come, I thought, reach out to me, give me your blessing, teach me the secret of your eternal life. But still he sighed, still he frowned.

Then he lifted his head and peered at me with such intensity that I could not believe he was blind. He smiled. Softly he said, 'We must speak of these things again, Gilgamesh. I will send for you another day.' And he made the smallest of gestures: it was a dismissal. I felt an invisible curtain descend between us. Although the Ziusudra still sat before me, unmoving, *he was not there.* Lu-Ninmarka, who had waited all this while by my side, came forward and touched me by the elbow. I rose; I offered a salute; I took my leave. I followed Lu-Ninmarka through the dark maze to the upper world like one who walks in his sleep.

36

I worked in the fields and I went to the temple to hear them telling and retelling their tale of the Flood, and I took my meals of lentils and goat milk, and one day flowed into the next. I wondered vaguely about events in the world beyond the shores of this island, but I gave no thought to departing. Occasionally I saw the streets of Uruk in my mind, or the face of my wife or my son, or some man of the court: but they seemed like scenes out of a dream. Once I imagined I saw Enkidu before me, and I smiled at him but I did not go toward him. Another time Inanna slipped into my dreams, radiant, magnificent, more beautiful than she had ever seemed: seeing her, I felt no hatred for her scheming, only some mild regret that such beauty had been in my arms once and no longer could be mine. So the days went by. Uruk and all its contents had drifted away from me. And in the ripeness of time I found myself in that winding passageway once again, descending to the lair of the Ziusudra.

He sat as he had sat before, staunchly erect on his little wickerwork stool as though it were a throne. I felt the power of him. It surrounded him like a wall. In his own way he was a king; he was almost a god. It seemed to me that he dwelled on some plane beyond my understanding; I wanted instinctively to kneel before him the moment I came into his presence. I think I have never known another man who aroused such awe in me.

As soon as I entered he began to speak; but I could not make sense of what he was saying. Words rose from him as a column of thick smoke rises from a fire of green wood; and the words were as impenetrable as the smoke, so that I was unable to see through the sound to the meaning. His voice circled round and round me. He spoke the language of the Land, or so I believed, and his words were calm and self assured, as though he were presenting some closely reasoned argument; but no word followed upon the last in any manner I could comprehend. I knelt and stared. Then out of the murky flow I began to perceive a glimmer of understanding, as one sees sparks flying upward within the smoke. He was speaking, so it seemed, of the time the gods had sent the Flood as a punishment upon mankind and he had led his people to the high ground to wait the waters out. But I was not sure. There were moments when I thought he might be talking about the proper design of chariots, or about the places one goes to find deposits of rock-salt in the desert, or other such things far removed from the table of the Flood. I was lost in the tangled skein of his discourse; I was altogether baffled.

Then he said suddenly with perfect clarity, 'There is no death, if only we do the tasks the gods appoint us. Do you understand me? There is no death.'

He turned towards me, and seemed to be waiting.

I said, 'And so it was your task to resettle the Land when the waters receded; and for that the gods spared you from death. Then what is my task, Ziusudra? You know that I also would be spared from death.'

'I know that.'

'But the Flood will not come again. What shall I do? I would build a ship like yours, if there were need. But there is no need for one.'

'Do you think there was a ship, Gilgamesh? Do you think there was a Flood?'

By the faint flickering light of his little lamp I tried and failed to read the mysteries of his face. His mind was too agile for me; he danced away from my comprehension. I was losing hope that he would help me find what I sought. 'I have heard what they say in the temple here,' I said. 'But what am I to make of it? They tell a different tale in the Land.'

'Trust it as we tell it. The rains came; in Shuruppak the king gathered his people, and they put provisions aside and carried them to the high ground, and remained there until the fury of the storm was spent. Then they returned to the Land and rebuilt all that had been destroyed. That is what happened, those many hundreds of years ago. All the rest is fable.'

'Including,' I said, 'the part where Enlil came to you and blessed you and sent you to Dilmun to live forever?'

He shook his head. 'The king of Shuruppak fled to Dilmun in despair. He went there when he saw that it was folly to have saved mankind, since all the old evils still thrived. He left the Land; he gave up his realm; he sought virtue and purity on this island. That is as it was, Gilgamesh. All the rest is fable.'

'The tale has it that the gods gave you eternal life. Was that only a fable too? There is eternal life here, so it would seem.'

'There is no death,' said the Ziusudra. 'Have I not told you that?'

'You have told me, yes. We must do the tasks the gods decree for us, and then there is no death. But I ask you again: What is my task, Ziusudra? How am I to know it? What secret must I learn?'

'Why do you think there is a secret?'

'There must be. You have lived so long. You saw the Flood: that was ten lifetimes ago, or twenty; and yet you still sit here. All about you are men and women who seem as ageless as you. How old is Lu-Ninmarka? How old is Hasidanum?' I looked at the Ziusudra long and earnestly. My hands were trembling, and I felt within myself the first beginnings of the god-aura, the buzzing, the

262

crackling and hissing, all those strange things that come upon me in the times when I am almost coiled upon myself with need. 'Tell me, father, how I too can defeat death! The gods in assembly conferred life on you: who will call them into assembly for me?'

'You are the only one who can do that,' said the Ziusudra.

I could barely draw breath. 'How? How?'

He replied in the most offhand manner, 'First show me that you can master sleep, and then we will see about a mastery of death. You can slay lions, O greatest of heroes; can you slay sleep? I invite you to a test, a trial. Sit here beside me for six days and seven nights without sleeping; and then perhaps you may find the life you seek.'

'Is that the path, then?'

'It is the path to the path.'

The buzzing in my soul subsided. A new calmness came over me. He meant to guide me after all.

'I will attempt it,' I said.

The test was severe indeed: six days, seven nights! How could any such thing be done by mortal man? But I was confident. I was more than mortal; so I had believed since my boyhood, with good reason. I had slain lions and even demons; I could slay sleep also. Had I not gone day after day with no more than an hour or two of sleep in the seasons of war? Had I not marched through the wilderness by night and by day as though sleep were no need of mine? I would do it. I was sure of that. I had the strength; I had the zeal. I crouched on my haunches next to him and fixed my eyes on his pink smooth serene face, and set myself to the task.

And to my shame sleep came upon me in a moment, like a whirlwind. But I did not know that I had slept.

My eyes were closed, my breath came thickly; as I say, it had happened in a moment. I thought I was awake and that I sat staring at the Ziusudra; but I slept, and I dreamed. In my dream I saw Ziusudra and his wife, who was as old as he; and he pointed to me and said to her, 'Behold this hero, the strong man who seeks eternal life! Sleep came upon him like a whirlwind.'

'Touch him,' she said. 'Wake him. Let him return in peace to his own land, through the gate by which he left.'

'No,' said Ziusudra in my dream. 'I will let him sleep. But while he sleeps, wife, bake a loaf of bread each day, and set it here by his head. And make a mark on the wall to keep count of the days he sleeps. For mankind is deceitful; and when he wakes he will try to deceive us.'

So she baked bread and marked markings on the wall each day, and I dreamed that I slept on, day after day, thinking I was awake. They watched over me and smiled at my folly; and then at last Ziusudra touched me and I awakened. But this too was still in my dream. 'Why do you touch me?' I asked, and he replied, 'To awaken you.' I looked at him in surprise and told him hotly that I had not slept, that only a moment had passed since I had crouched down beside him and my eyes had not closed for so much as a moment of that moment. He laughed, and gently he said that his wife had baked bread each day while I slept and had set the loaves before me. 'Go, Gilgamesh: count them, and see how many days you have slept!' I looked at the loaves. There were seven of them: the first was like a brick, the second was nearly as stale, the third was soggy. The fourth had gone white about the crust with mildew; the fifth was covered with mold. Only the sixth loaf was still fresh. I saw the seventh baking over the coals. He showed me the markings on the walls, and there were seven, one for each day. So I knew that I had fallen asleep despite myself; and I understood that I had failed in my undertaking. I was unworthy. I would never be able to find my way along the path to eternal life. Despair engulfed me. I felt death coming upon me like a thief in the night, entering my bedchamber, seizing my limbs in his cold grasp. And I gave a great groan and awakened; for all this was still in my dream.

I looked to the Ziusudra and I put my hand to my head as if to free it from a shroud. I was lost in my confusions. To sleep, believing I was awake, and to dream, and to wake within my dream, and then to awaken in truth—and still not to know whether I dreamed or waked, even now—ah, I was lost, I was lost!

I pressed the tips of my fingers uncertainly to my eyes. 'Am I awake?' I asked.

'I think you are.'

'But I slept?'

'You slept, yes.'

'Did I sleep long?'

He shrugged. 'Perhaps an hour. Perhaps a day.' He made it seem as if to him the one was the same as the other.

'I dreamed I slept six days and seven nights, and you and your wife watched over me, and each day she baked bread; and then you awakened me and I denied that I had slept, but I saw the seven loaves before me. And when I saw them I felt death take hold of me, and I cried out.'

'I heard you cry,' said the Ziusudra. 'It was a moment ago, just before you awakened.'

'So I am awake now,' I said, still unsure.

'You are awake, Gilgamesh. But first you slept. You were not aware of it: but sleep came upon you in the first moment of your test.'

'Then I have failed,' I said in a hollow voice. 'I am doomed to die. There is no hope for me. Wherever I set my foot, there I find death—even here!'

He smiled a tender loving smile, as one might give a babe. 'Did you think our mysteries could save you from death? They cannot even save me. Do you see that? These rites we observe: *they cannot even save me.*'

'It is the tale they tell, that you are exempt from dying.'

'It is the tale, yes. But it is not the tale we tell here. When did I say that I was exempt from dying? Tell me when I spoke those words, Gilgamesh.'

I looked at him, bewildered. 'There is no death, you said. Only do your task, and then there is no death. You said that.'

'So I did. But you failed to take my meaning.'

'I took the meaning that I thought was there.'

'So you did. It was the easy meaning; it was the meaning you hoped to find; but it was not the true meaning.' Again the tender smile, so sad, so loving. Gently, he said, 'We have made our pact with death here. We know his ways, and he knows our ways; and we have our mysteries, and our mysteries defend us for a time from death. But only for a time. Poor Gilgamesh, you have come so far for so little!'

Understanding flooded me. I felt my skin prickling; I shivered with the chill of perception as the truth made itself manifest. I caught my breath sharply. There was a question I must ask now; but I did not know if I dared to ask it, and I did not think I would have an answer from him. Nevertheless after a moment I said, 'Tell me this. You are the Ziusudra: but are you Ziusudra of Shuruppak?'

He answered without hesitation. And what he told me was that which I had already come to comprehend.

'Ziusudra of Shuruppak is long since dead,' he said.

'The one that led his people to the high ground when the rains came?'

'Dead, long ago.'

'And the Ziusudra who came after him?'

'Dead also. I will not tell you how many of that name have sat in this chamber; but I am not the third, nor the fourth, nor even the fifth. We die, and another comes to take our place and the title; and so we continue in the observance of our mysteries. I am very old, but I will not sit here forever. Perhaps Lu-Ninmarka will be the Ziusudra after me, or perhaps someone else. Perhaps even you, Gilgamesh.'

'No,' I said. 'It will not be me, I think.'

'What will you do now?'

'Return to Uruk. Resume my throne. Live out my days to their allotted number.'

'You know that you may remain with us if you wish, and take part in our rites, and receive training in our skills.'

'And learn from you how to keep death at bay—though not to defeat him altogether. For that is impossible.'

'Yes.'

'But if I give myself to you, I can never again leave this island. Is that so?'

'You will not want to, if you become one of us.'

'In what way would that be different from death?' I asked. 'I would lose all the world, and have only a small sandy island in exchange for it. To dwell in a small room, and work in these fields, and say prayers at night, and eat only certain foods—to live like a prisoner on an isle so little I can walk from shore to shore in an hour or two—'

'You would not be a prisoner. If you remained, you would remain of your free choice.'

'It is not the life I would choose, father.'

'No,' he said. 'I did not think you would.'

'I am grateful for the offer.'

'Which will not be withdrawn. You may come to us any time, Gilgamesh, if so you choose. But I do not think that is what you will choose.' He smiled yet again and held forth his hand; and as he had done the first time he touched his fingertips to my face for a blessing. His hand was very cold. His touch had a sting. When Lu-Ninmarka led me back to the surface, I still felt the places where he had touched me, like white imprints against my skin.

37

I made ready to leave the little island. By orders of the Ziusudra I was given a fine new cloak, and a band to place around my head, and I bathed until I was clean as fresh snow. The boatman Sur-sunabu would take me across to Dilmun; there I would arrange for my journey home. My mood was somber, dark and subdued, and why should it not have been? The Ziusudra had said it all: I had come so far for so little. Yet I was not distraught. I had gambled and I had lost, but the odds had been great. Only a fool will weep when he asks the impossible of his dice and they do not provide it for him.

The time was nearly at hand for my departure when the old priest Lu-Ninmarka came to me and made a little speech, saying, 'The Ziusudra feels deep sorrow that you have undergone such long hardship and have wearied yourself so greatly without attaining any reward. By way of comforting you he has decided to disclose a hidden thing to you, a secret of the gods. He offers it as a gift, to carry back to your own country.'

'And what is that?' I asked.

'Come with me.'

In truth I felt so bleak that I had little yearning for any gift of the

267

Ziusudra's; I wanted only to get myself away from that place and take myself swiftly back to Uruk. But I knew it would be mannerless and uncivil to refuse. So I accompanied the priest to a far part of the isle where the land stretched into the sea in a long narrow point with the shape of a knife-blade. On the edge of that point I saw a great mound of thousands of gray seashells of a strange shape, all gnarled and rough on one side, smooth and gleaming on the other. Near them lay the sort of stones that divers use as weights when they go down into the sea, and some ropes to attach them to their legs.

'Do you wonder why they have come here?' Lu-Ninmarka said. He grinned. I think he meant it to be pleasant, but to me it was like the grinning of a skull, so lean and fleshless was his sharp-featured face. He picked up one of the gray shells, rested it a moment on the palm of his hand with its smooth side downward, and tossed it to the ground. Then he pointed out to sea. 'This is the place where the plant known as Grow-Young-Again is found: there, at the bottom of the sea.'

Frowning, I said, 'Grow-Young-Again? What plant is that?'

He looked at me in surprise. 'Don't you know it? It is the wonder of wonders, that plant. From it we make a medicine to cure the most implacable of illnesses: I mean the ravages of age. It is a medicine that restores a man to his former strength, that takes the lines from his face, that makes his hair grow dark once more. And the plant from which it comes lies in these waters. Do you see the shells here? They are its leaves. We dive for the plant, we bring it up, we extract its power, and we discard the rest. From its fruit we make the potion that preserves us from age. This is the Ziusudra's parting gift to you: I am to let you have the fruit of Grow-Young-Again to take with you on your journey.'

'Is it so?' I said, astounded.

'We would not jest with you, Gilgamesh.'

Awe and amazement silenced me a moment. When I could speak again I said in a hushed way, 'How am I to obtain this miraculous stuff?'

Lu-Ninmarka waved his hand towards the divers' stones, the ropes, the sea. He indicated that I should put off my clothing and go down into the water. I hesitated only a moment. The sea is

268

Enli's domain, and I had never felt much at ease with that god. It would be a new thing for me to enter the sea. Well, I thought, in my passage to Dilmun Enki had done me no harm; and as a boy I had dived into the river often enough. What was there to fear? The plant Grow-Young-Again waited for me in the water. I cast my cloak aside; I tied the heavy stones to my feet; I went stumbling forward to the edge of the sea.

How clear the water was, how warm, how gentle! It lapped at the pink sand of the shore and took on a pink flush itself. I looked toward Lu-Ninmarka, who urged me onward. It was slow going, with those stones. The water was shallow; I waded knee-deep for an endless time. But then at last I came to a place where the sunken shelf of the land dropped away and what seemed to be the maw of the great abyss loomed before me. Again I looked back; again Lu-Ninmarka signaled me onward. I filled my chest with air and cast myself forward, and the stones drew me down.

Ah, what joy it was to tumble into those depths! It was like flying, effortless and serene, but a flying downward, a pure sweet descent. I was altogether without fear. The color of the sea deepened about me: it was a rich sapphire now, shot through with strands of sparkling light from above. As I descended, the fishes came to me and studied me with great goggling eyes. They were of every hue, yellow banded with black, scarlet, azure, topaz, emerald, turquoise; they were of colors I had never seen before, and mixtures of colors that I would not have believed possible. I could have touched them, they were so close. They danced beside me with unimaginable grace.

Down, down, down. I held my arms high above my head and gave myself freely to the pull of the abyss. My hair streamed far out about me; a bubbling flow came from my lips; there was a thunderous pounding in my breast. My heart was joyous: through my entire body there flowed the keenest of delights. I could not say how long it had been since I had known such joy. Not since Enkidu had gone from me, surely. Ah, Enkidu, Enkidu, if you could have been there beside me as I made my way into the abyss!

The water was much cooler here. The shimmering light, far above, was pale, blue, remote, like moonlight made scant by heavy clouds. I felt firmness suddenly beneath my feet: I had reached the

269

floor of this sunken realm. Soft sand below, dark jagged rocks before me. Where was the plant? Where was Grow-Young-Again? Ah, here, here! I saw a multitude of it: stony gray leaves clinging to the rocks. I touched several of them lightly, in wonder, thinking, Is this the one that will do the magic? Is this the one that will turn back the years? I pulled one plant loose. That cost me no little pain. The outer surface of it was sharp and thorny, as though covered with tiny blades, and it pricked my hands like a rose. I saw a crimson cloud of my blood rise along my arms. But I had the plant of life and breath; I clutched it tight; I raised it jubilantly, and I would have cried out in triumph, if such a thing could have been done in that silent world. Grow-Young-Again! Yes! Perhaps eternal life could not be mine, but I would at least have some way of shielding myself against the bite of time's tooth.

Rise, now, Gilgamesh! Get you to the sea's surface! My errand was achieved; and I realized now for the first time that my breath was all but exhausted.

I cut myself free of the stones that were tied to my feet and rose like an arrow through the water, scattering the startled fishes. Brightness enfolded me. I burst through into the air and felt the blessed warmth of the sun. Laughing, splashing, lurching about, I flung myself onto the bosom of the sea and it sped me toward the shore. In moments I reached a place where the water was shallow enough for me to stand; and I went running onward until I was on dry land once again.

I held out my hand toward Lu-Ninmarka, showing him the gray uncouth thing I held. Blood still ran from the cuts it had made in my flesh and I felt the salt of the sea stinging in them; but that did not matter. 'Is this it?' I cried. 'Is this the right one?'

'Let me see,' he murmured. 'Give me your knife.'

He took it from me and deftly slipped the blade of the knife between the two stony leaves. With a strength I did not think he had the old priest split the leaves apart and turned them back. Within I beheld something strange, a pulsing pink furrowed thing as soft and intricate and mysterious as a woman's most secret inner place. But that was of no concern to Lu-Ninmarka; he prowled with his fingers in its folds and crevices and after a moment cried out and pulled forth something round and smooth and gleaming,

270

the pearl that is the fruit of the plant Grow-Young-Again.

'This is what we seek,' he said. Carelessly he tossed aside the stony leaves and the pinkness they contained; a bird swooped down at once to feed on that tender meat. But he held the pearl cradled in the palm of his hand, beaming at it as though it were the dearest child of his bosom. In the warm sunlight it seemed to glow with an inner radiance; and its color was rich and fine, with a blush of blue mingled with the creamy pink. He touched it lightly with the tip of his finger, rolling it about, taking the greatest of delight in it. Then after a few moments he placed it in my hand and folded my bloodied fingers about it. 'Put it in your pouch,' he said, 'and keep it as you would the greatest of your treasures. Carry it with you to Uruk of the high ramparts, and store it in your strongbox. And when you feel your years weighing heavy upon you, Gilgamesh, take it out, grind it to fine powder, mix it with good strong wine, drink it down in a single draught. That is all. Your eyes will grow clear again, your breath will come in deep gusts, your strength will be the strength of the slayer of lions you once had been. That is our gift to you, Gilgamesh of Uruk.'

I stared at the pearl with wide open eyes. 'I could have asked for nothing finer.'

'Come, now. The boatman awaits you.'

38

Sour and sullen and silent as always, Sursunabu the boatman took me across in the afternoon to the greater island nearby. Once more I found lodgings in the main city of Dilmun for a few days, until I could buy passage aboard a ship bound for the Land. Idly I wandered about the steep streets, past the open-fronted shops of brick and timber where the craftsmen in gold and copper and precious stones plied their skills, and looked down toward the beach and its ships, and past it to the broad blue sheet of the sea and the little sandy island. I thought of the Ziusudra who was not Ziusudra, and of the priests and priestesses who served him in the mysteries of their cult, and of the true tale they had told of the coming of the Flood, so different from what is told in the Land; and I thought also of the stony fruit of the plant Grow-Young-Again which swung in a little pouch about my neck and blazed against my breastbone like a sphere of flame. So at last my quest was ending. I was going home; and if I had not found what I had come seeking, I had at least attained some part of it, some means of fending off the fate I abhorred.

So be it. Now to Uruk!

There was a trading-ship of Meluhha in the port, nearly done with its business. It would go northward now as far as Eridu and Ur to sell its goods for the merchandise of the Land; and then when it was laden it would make its way back down into the Sea of the Rising Sun and sail off to the distant and mysterious place in the east from which it had come. This I learned from a merchant of Lagash who stayed at my hostelry.

I went down into the port and found the master of the Meluhhan ship. He was a small and delicate-looking man with skin dark as ebony and fine proud sharp features; he understood my language well enough, and said he would carry me as a passenger. I told him to name his price, and he named it: I judge it was half what his whole ship was worth. He stared up at me with eyes like polished onyx and smiled. Was he expecting me to bargain with him? How could I do that? I am king of Uruk; I cannot bargain. Perhaps he knew that and took advantage of me. Or perhaps he thought I was just a great hulking fool, with more silver than wit about me. Well, it was a steep price; he took from me nearly all my remaining silver. But it was no great matter. I had been away from the Land far too long; I would pay that much and more with a glad heart, if only he would carry me toward my home.

We made our departure, then. On a day when the sky was as flat and hot as an anvil the little dark-skinned men of Meluhha hoisted their sail and leaped to their oars and we headed northward into the sea.

The cargo was timber of several kinds from their own land, which they stored in bundles on the deck, and chests that held gold

272

ingots, ivory combs and figurines, carnelian and lapis lazuli. The captain said he had made his voyage fifty times and meant to make it fifty more before he died. I asked him to tell me about the countries that lie between Meluhha and the Land. I wanted to know the shape of the coasts, the color of the air, the scent of the blossoms, and a thousand other things; but he only shrugged and said, 'Why is that of interest? The world is much the same everywhere.' I had great pity for him, hearing that.

Among these Meluhhans I felt like a colossus. I have long been accustomed to the way I tower over the men of the Land, head and shoulders and breast; but on this voyage my shipmates came scarcely more than belly-high to me, and scampered about almost as if they were little apes. By Enlil, I must have seemed a monstrous thing to them! Yet they showed no fear of me nor any awe; to them I was merely a barbaric curiosity, I suppose, something that they would weave into their mariners' tales when they reached their homeland. 'Believe it if you will, we had a passenger between Dilmun and Eridu, and his stature was like that of an elephant! As stupid as an elephant, too, and as heavy-footed—we took good care to keep out of his way, or he might have trampled us flat without so much as noticing we were there!' In truth, they made me feel like an oaf, so little and agile were they; but in my defense I will say that the ship was crafted to fit men of a smaller size than mine. It was hardly my fault I had to go about in a crouch with my arms at my side, barely able to move without knocking into something.

The sun was white-hot and the cloudless sky was merciless. There was little wind; but so cunning were these seamen that they kept their vessel moving forward under the merest of breezes. I watched them in admiration. They worked as if they had a single mind; each carried out his role in the enterprise without need of command, laboring quickly and silently in the sweltering heat. If they had asked me to do some task I would have done it, but they left me by myself. Did they know I was a king? Did they care? They are an incurious race, I think; but they work very hard.

At dusk, when they gathered for their meal, they shyly invited me to join them. What they ate each night was a stew of meat or fish so fiery in its flavor that I thought it would burn my lips, and a sort of porridge that tasted of sour milk. After eating they sang, a strange music indeed, the voices roaming and twining to fashion eerie twanging melodies that coiled like serpents. And so the voyage went. I was glad to be apart from them, alone inside myself, for I was weary and had much on my mind. Now and again I touched the pearl of Grow-Young-Again that hung about my throat; and I thought often of Uruk and what awaited me there.

At last I saw the welcome shores of the Land dark against the horizon. We entered the wide mouth of the joined rivers and went onward, on and on to the place where the rivers divide. Then there was the Idigna, making its course off to the right; and there was the Buranunu, our own great river, branching to the left. I gave thanks to Enlil. I was not yet home; but the wind that reached my nostrils was a wind that had blown yesterday through my native city, and that alone was enough greatly to gladden me.

Not long afterward we docked at the quay of holy Eridu. There I bade the Meluhhan captain farewell and went ashore by myself. It would not have been wise to go on further with that ship, for its next port of call would be Ur; and that was no place now for me to go in the guise of a solitary traveler. They would know me in Ur. If I set foot without any army at my back I knew I would never see Uruk again.

They knew me also in Eridu. I had not been off the ship three minutes before I saw eyes flickering and fingers pointing, and heard them whispering in awe and wonder, 'Gilgamesh! Gilgamesh!' It was to be expected. I had been to Eridu many times for the autumn rites that follow in the wake of the Sacred Marriage. But this was not autumn, and I had come without my retinue. Little wonder they pointed and whispered.

It is the oldest city in the world, Eridu. We say that it was the first of the five cities that existed before the Flood. Perhaps it was, though I no longer have as much faith in those old tales as I had before my visit to the Ziusudra. Enki is the prime god of the place, he who has power over the sweet waters that flow beneath the earth: his great temple is there, and his chief dwelling place lies beneath it, so they say. I believe it must be so: you can dig anywhere in the low-lying ground about Eridu and discover fresh water.

Eridu lies somewhere off the Buranunu but is connected to the river by lagoons and good waterways, and it is as much a port as the river cities themselves. Its site is difficult, though, for the desert comes right down to the edges of the city and I think some day the dunes may sweep right over it. They must think so too, for they have put not only the temple but the entire city atop a great raised platform. There is much stone around Eridu, and the city's builders have used it well. The retaining wall of the platform is a massive thing faced with sandstone, and the stairs of the temple are great marble slabs. It is a thing to be envied, to have stone close by your city, and not to be compelled as we are to build only of mud.

The merchants of Uruk have long maintained a commercial house in Eridu, close by Enki's temple: a place held in common, where they can extend credit to one another and put their books in balance and exchange rumors of the marketplace and do whatever else it is that merchants do. It was there I went from the quay, moving unconcerned through an ever larger crowd of whisperers and pointers: 'Gilgamesh! Gilgamesh!' all the way. When I entered the trading-hall I found three men of my city working at their scribe-work with stylus and tablet; they sprang to their feet at the first sight of me, gasping and turning pale as though Enlil himself had come striding into their midst. Then they fell to their knees and set up a frantic making of the royal signs; wiggling their arms and waving their heads about like frenzied madmen. It was a while before they were calm enough to make sense.

'You are not dead, majesty!' they blurted.

'Evidently not,' I said. 'Who was it that gave that story forth?'

They looked warily at one another. At length the oldest and shrewdest-looking of them replied, 'It was said at the temple, I think. That you had gone into the wilderness out of mourning for Enkidu your brother, and you had been devoured by lions—'

'No, that you had been carried off by demons—' put in another. 'By demons, yes, that came out of a whirlwind—'

'The Imdugud-bird was seen in the rooftops, crying evil omens, five nights running—' the third declared.

'A two-headed calf was found in the pastures—they sacrificed it at the Ubshukkinakku—'

'And at the Sanctuary of Destinies, they—'

'Yes, and there was green mist around the moon, which—'

I broke into all this babble with a loud cry: 'Wait! Tell me this: at which temple was it that I was given forth as dead?'

'Why, the temple of the goddess, majesty!'

I smiled. That was no great surprise.

Quietly I said, 'Ah. Ah, I see: of course. It was Inanna herself who uttered the doleful news, eh?'

They nodded. They looked more troubled with each passing moment.

I thought of Inanna and her hatred for me, and her hunger for power, and how she had coolly put the king Dumuzi aside long ago when he had ceased to serve her needs; and I knew that my leaving Uruk must have seemed to her like a gift from the gods; and I told myself that I had done the most foolish of foolish things, running off in my madness and pain in search of eternal life, when I had the duties of this life to carry out. How she must have laughed, when she was told I had gone from the city by stealth! How she must have relished it when the days went by and I did not return, and no one knew where I was!

I said, 'Was she greatly grieved? Did she lament and tear her robes?'

They nodded most solemnly. 'Her grief was great indeed, O Gilgamesh.'

'And did they beat the drums for me? The lilissu-drum, the little balag-drums?'

They did not answer.

'Did they? *Did they?*'

'Yes.' A hoarse whisper. 'They beat the drums for you, O Gilgamesh. They mourned most grievously for you.'

My head roared. I thought my fit was coming on. I felt the buzzing within, I felt the hissing. I came close to them, so that they trembled from being so near to me, and I was trembling myself as I asked the question I most feared to ask: 'And tell me this, have they chosen a king in my place yet?'

Again an exchange of worried glances. Those hapless merchants quivered like leaves in an autumn gale.

'Have they?' I demanded.

'Not—yet, O Gilgamesh,' said one finally.

'Ah, not yet? Not *yet?* The omens have been inauspicious, I imagine.'

'They say the goddess has called for a new king, but the assembly has thus far chosen to withhold its consent. There are those who think that you still live—'

'It is very likely that I do,' I said.

'—and they fear that the gods will be displeased, if a king should too hastily be put in your place—'

'The gods will very likely be displeased,' I said. 'And not only the gods.'

'—but there is need, everyone agrees, for a king in Uruk; for you know, majesty, that Meskiagnunna of Ur is swollen with pride, that he has put both Kish and Nippur into his hand, that he looks now toward our city—and in these troublesome months we have not had a king—we have not had a king, majesty—'

'You have a king,' I said. 'Make no mistake on that score: you have a king. Let's hope that you don't have two, by this time.'

There was a certain lightness to my tone of voice, I suppose, but none in my heart. I felt a great weight within, and much bewilderment. Was I still king? Did I even deserve to be? The gods had placed me in command over Uruk and I had deserted my post: that could not be denied. For that, anyone might say, I am to blame. But can any blame attach to us ever, when the gods call all the tunes? Had the gods not also sent me Enkidu, and then taken him away? And was it not so, therefore, that it was the gods who had aroused in me the pain, the fear of dying, that had driven me forth on my quest for life? Yes. Yes. Yes. I did not think that I was at fault. I had only been following the dictates of the gods in all things. But where was the will of proud Gilgamesh, then? Was I nothing but the plaything of the remote and uncaring great ones to whom this world belongs? The servant of the gods, yes: I will not deny that. We are all servants of the gods and it is folly to think otherwise. But their plaything? Their toy?

Well, I could not linger then over such questions. I brushed them aside. If I am no longer king in Uruk, I thought, let the goddess tell me so. Not her priestess, but the goddess herself. I will go to the city; I will seek out my answers there.

Then I felt the strong presence of my father the hero Lugalbanda within me. I had not felt him in a long while. The great king filled my spirit with his strength and gave me much comfort. I knew from that that I need feel no shame for anything I had done. The things I had done were what the gods had decreed for me, and they were right and proper things. My grief had been necessary. My quest had been necessary. The gods had resolved to bring me to wisdom: I had simply obeyed their design.

No longer did I doubt that I was still king. I sent the eldest of the merchants off at once to the palace of the governor of Eridu, to tell him that his overlord Gilgamesh of Uruk had arrived in his city and was awaiting an appropriate welcome. I instructed the youngest merchant to seek passage that day aboard the next ship sailing toward Uruk, so that he could bear word that the king was returning from his journeys. And I sent the third man out to fetch me wine and roasted meat, and a high-breasted wench of sixteen or seventeen years; for suddenly the juices of life were coursing in my body again. In all this dark period of wandering since the time of Enkidu's dying, I had become a stranger to myself. I felt as though I had split in two, and the part that was Gilgamesh had strayed off somewhere leaving only a husk behind, and I was that husk. But now the vigor and power and life that were Gilgamesh the king were coming back into me. I was myself again. I was Gilgamesh, whole and complete. For this I gave thanks to Enlil the master, and to An the great father, and to Enki the god of the place I was now in; but most warmly did I give thanks to the god Lugalbanda from whose seed I had sprung. The great gods are far away, and we are at best like specks of sand to them. Lugalbanda stood close beside me, then and ever.

39

The Governor then in Eridu was Shulutula the son of Akurgal. He was a small round dark-skinned man with a huge blunt nose. Eridu does not have kings; kingship went from that city a long time ago, before the Flood. But though his rank was only that of governor, Shulutula lived like a king, in a grand palace of two twin buildings surrounded by an immense double wall. He received me nervously, since I was in his city out of season and he was taken by surprise; but his nature was a tranquil one and as soon as he realized that I was not here to depose him or to make great demands upon his treasury he grew notably more easy. That night he ordered up a great feast for me, and showered me with gifts, fine spears and some concubines and a beautifully made alabaster statuette the length of my arm, with eyes encrusted with lapis lazuli and shell.

We talked far into the night. He knew I had been away from Uruk some time, but he dared not ask why, nor where I had gone. I tried to get from him an account of recent events in my city, but he could not or would not tell me much, only that he had heard the harvest had been poor and there had been some flooding along the canals during the season of high water. But the center of his concern, plainly, was not Uruk but Ur. That powerful city, after all, was only a few leagues from Eridu; and already Meskiagnunna had gobbled up Kish and Nippur. What would be next, if not Eridu? 'How can we doubt it?' Shulutula asked me. 'He is seeking kingship over all the Land.'

'The gods have not awarded the high kingship to Ur,' I said.

He peered somberly into his wine-cup. 'Can we be sure of that?'

'It is not possible.'

'Once the kingship was in Eridu, was it not?' Shulutula said. 'Long ago, before the Flood. Then it passed to Badtibira, to Larak, to—'

'Yes,' I cut in impatiently. 'Spare me. I know the ancient annals as well as you.'

Though my brusque tone obviously ruffled him, he would not be deterred. I liked him for that. 'I beg your indulgence,' is what he said, and then with surprising boldness went right on, '—to Sippar and to Shuruppak. Then came the Flood, and everything was destroyed. After the Flood, when the kingship of the Land again descended from heaven, the place where it came to reside was in Kish, is that not so?'

'Agreed,' I said.

'Meskiagnunna has made himself the master of Kish; can it not then be said that the kingship has gone from Kish to Ur?'

Now I saw what he was driving at.

I shook my head. 'Hardly,' I said. 'The kingship resided in Kish, yes. But you overlook something. In the first year of my reign Agga of Kish came to Uruk to make war, and he was beaten and taken captive. Clearly the kingship passed from Kish to Uruk at that moment. When the king of Ur seized Kish, he seized only a hollow thing. The kingship had gone from it; it had gone to Uruk. Where it now resides.'

'Then you maintain that the king of Uruk is king over the Land?'

'Most certainly,' I said.

'But there has been no king in Uruk these months past!'

'There will be a king in Uruk again very shortly, Shulutula,' I told him. I leaned forward until I could almost touch his enormous gourd of a nose with the tip of my own, and said in a way that admitted of no uncertainties, 'Meskiagnunna can have Kish if he wishes it. But I will not allow him to keep Nippur, for it is a holy city and must be free; and I tell you this, he will never have Eridu either. You have nothing to fear.' Then I rose; I yawned and stretched; and I emptied the last of my wine. 'This is enough feasting for tonight, I think. Sleep calls me. In the morning I will visit the temples, and then I'll begin my homeward journey. I will require of you a chariot and a team of asses, and a charioteer who knows his way north.'

He seemed puzzled. 'You mean to go by land, majesty?'

I nodded. 'It will give my people more time to prepare for my homecoming.'

'Then I will provide an escort of five hundred troops for you, and whatever else you may—'

'No,' I said. 'A single chariot, and beasts to draw it. A single charioteer. I need nothing more than that. The gods will protect me, Shulutula, as they always have. I will go alone.'

He had trouble understanding that. He could not see that I had no wish to come marching into Uruk at the head of an army of foreign soldiers: I meant to enter my city as I had left it, alone, unafraid. My people would accept me as their king because I was their king, not because I had reimposed myself by force. When men are subdued by strength of arms, they do not submit in their souls, but yield merely because they have no choice. But when men are subdued by the power of character they yield to the core of their hearts, and submit in full measure. Any wise king knows these things.

So I took from Shulutula of Eridu merely what I had asked of him: a chariot, a charioteer. He gave me also some provisions and a quiver of fine javelins, in case we encountered lions or wolves along the way; but although he hovered around me anxiously trying to persuade me to accept some more imposing escort from him, I would not do it.

I stayed in Eridu five more days. There were purifications that I had to perform at the shrines of Enki and An, and a private rite in honor of Lugalbanda. Those matters occupied three days; the fourth, according to Shulutula's conjurers, was an unlucky day, so I stayed on for the fifth. Then I set out at daybreak for Uruk. It was the twelfth day of the month Du'uzu, when summer's full heat was beginning to fall upon the Land. The charioteer he gave me was a sturdy fellow named Ninurta-mansum, who was perhaps thirty years old, with the first flecks of gray in his beard. He wore across his breast the scarlet riband that announced he had pledged his life to the service of Enki. In a curious way it called to my mind a fiery red scar that had marked the body of old Namhani, who had driven my team long ago when I was a young prince in the service of Agga of Kish. Which was oddly appropriate, for the only charioteer I had ever known who was the equal of Ninurta-mansum in skill was Namhani: they were two of a kind. When they held the reins, it was as though they held the souls of their beasts in their hands.

At the hour of my departure I embraced Shulutula and pledged him once more that I would shield his city against the ambitions of the king of Ur; he slew a goat and poured out a libation of blood and honey at the main gate to insure my safe passage home; and then I rode out into the morning. We left the city by the Gate of the Abyss and went past the high dunes and a great grove of thorny kiskanu-trees, almost a forest of them: when I looked back, I saw the towers of the palace and temples of Eridu rising like the castles of demon princes against the pale early-morning sky. Then we crossed a rough stony ridge and went down into the valley, and the city was lost behind us.

Ninurta-mansum knew very well who I was and what was likely to happen if I fell into the hands of some patrolling squadron of men from Ur. So he gave that city a wide berth and swung around instead into the forlorn and desolate land on the western side of Eridu. It was all wasteland here, and a bleak bitter wind blew: the sand swirled up and took the form of tenuous ghosts whose melancholy eyes did not leave me all the day long. But I was not afraid. They were nothing more than swirling sand.

The asses seemed tireless. They flew onward hour after hour and seemed to know neither hunger nor thirst nor weariness. They could have been enchanted, or perhaps demons placed under a spell, so tireless were they. When we halted at sundown, they looked scarcely winded. I wondered what the beasts would do for water in this wilderness; but Ninurta-mansum began at once to dig, and straightaway a cool sweet spring came bubbling up out of the sand. Beyond doubt the blessing of Enki was upon that man.

When we no longer ran much risk of meeting warriors of Ur, the charioteer began to guide us closer to the river. We were on the Buranunu's sunset side and had to cross it somehow to reach Uruk; but that was no great task for Ninurta-mansum. He knew a place where at this time of year the river was shallow and the bottom was firm, and took us across there. We had one bad moment when the leftmost ass lost his footing and went down, which I thought would pull the whole chariot over. But Ninurta-mansum gripped the traces and leaned all his strength into holding us upright. The other three asses stayed firm. The one that had stumbled came up out of the river snorting and spewing, and got himself in balance; and we came out safely on the river's sunrise bank. Perhaps not even Namhani could have managed that.

Now we were in lands tributary to Uruk. The city itself was still some leagues to the northeast. I did not know whose land we had entered, whether it was Inanna's or An's or some magnate's of the city—it might even have been mine, for I had vast holdings in this district—but whatever it was, temple land or private land, it was land of Uruk. After my long absence I felt such joy at seeing these rich fertile fields that I came close to leaping down from the chariot and embracing the earth. Instead I contented myself with a libation and the brief rites of homecoming. The charioteer knelt beside me, stranger though he was in Uruk. He was a holy man, that charioteer: holier than some priests and priestesses I have known.

We were encountering farming folk now, and of course they knew me for their king, if only from my height and bearing. They ran alongside the chariot shouting my name: I waved, I smiled, I made the signs of the gods to them. Ninurta-mansum reined the asses in and we moved at a slow trot, so the people might keep up with me. They gathered in number, coming in from this field and that as the word spread, until there were hundreds of them. That night when we halted they brought us the best that they had, strong black beer and the red beer they like so much, and the wine of dates, and the roasted meat of calves and sheep. And they came one by one for hours, weeping with gladness, to kneel before me and express their thanks that I still lived and ruled over them. I have had richer feasts, but none, I think, that has touched me so deeply.

Of course the news that I was approaching the city preceded me to Uruk. It was what I intended. I was sure that Inanna had used my absence to take great power into her grasp; I wanted that power to begin to slip from her, hour by hour, as the citizens whispered among themselves of the coming return of their king.

Then at last on a day when heat danced in the sky like the waves of the ocean I beheld the walls of Uruk rising in the distance, copper-bright, shining in the sun. Is there a finer sight in all the world than Uruk's walls? I think not. I think that I would have heard tell of it, if there were anything to compare. But there is not, for ours is the city of cities, the goddess among cities, the city that lies at the heart and center of the world.

When I drew nearer, though, I saw an unfamiliar thing. On the plain outside the city, in the stretch of bare sandy land that lies between the High Gate and the Nippur Gate, splashes of brilliant color sprouted like huge flowers below the walls: puffs of scarlet and black, yellow and bright blue. These were a mystery to me until I was closer still; then I realized that tents and pavilions had been erected there. In celebration of my return, so I thought. But I was mistaken.

Instead of my good lords Bir-hurturre and Zabardi-bunugga riding toward me to meet me with troops and escort me into the city, which I might have expected, three women of Inanna came from those pavilions on foot. So I understood at once that there would be trouble. I did not know them by name, but I had seen them in the rites: they were high priestesses. They wore rich scarlet robes and had the serpent-emblem in bronze coiled about their left arms. When I was in hailing distance the one in the center, who was tall and stately with tightly woven black hair, made signs of the goddess at me and called out, 'In Inanna's name we bid you go no further!'

This was too brazen even for Inanna. I went rigid and caught my breath as rage began to rise in me; but then I forced myself to ease. Calmly I said, 'Do you know me, priestess?'

She met my eyes coolly. I sensed great strength in her, and formidable power.

'You are Gilgamesh son of Lugalbanda,' she said.

'Indeed. I am Gilgamesh king of Uruk, back from my pilgrimage. Or will you dispute that?'

In the same measured way she said, as though conceding nothing, 'It is the truth. You are the king.'

'Then why do the women of the goddess bid me halt in this place outside the walls? I would enter my city. I have been gone a long while; I am eager to see it again.'

We were like two swordsmen, testing each other with wary thrusts. 'The goddess asks me to tell you of the joy she feels at your safe return,' she replied with no trace of joy in her tone, 'and requires of me that I convey you now to the place of purification which we have erected outside the walls.'

My eyes went wide. 'Purification? Have I become unclean, then?'

Blandly she said, 'In dreams the goddess has followed your wanderings, O king. She knows that dark spirits have impinged on your soul; and she would cleanse you of their malign force before you come into the city. It is her way to serve, and this is her service: surely you know that.'

'Her kindness is too great.'

'It is not a question of kindness, O king. It is a question of the

284

health of your soul, and of the safety of the city, and of the divine balance and order of the realm, which must be maintained. And so the goddess has decreed these rites, out of her great mercy and love.'

Ah, I thought. Her great mercy and love! I nearly burst out in laughter! But I did not: I held myself in check. Well, I told myself, I will play this game out to its end. In my most courteous and formal way I said, 'The mercy of the goddess is sublime. If my soul is at risk, it must be cleansed. Lead me to your place of purification.'

As I stepped down from the chariot Ninurta-mansum glanced toward me, and I saw him frown. It should have been no concern of his that I might be giving myself over to treachery: he was Shulutula's man, not mine. Yet he was trying to warn me. I realized that he was the one who would die for me, if needs be. Giving him a reassuring clasp on the shoulder, I told him to take the asses to graze but not to get too far away from me. Then, going on foot, I followed the three priestesses of Inanna toward the pavilions below the walls.

Plainly she had been a long time in planning this. What was virtually a holy precinct had been constructed out here. There were five tents, one large with the reed-bundles of Inanna mounted in the sand before it, and four lesser ones in which all manner of sacred implements seemed to have been stored—braziers, incense-burners, holy images and banners, and the like. As I came near, priestesses began to chant, musicians to pound on their drums and blow into their fifes, temple dancers circled round and round me with joined arms. I looked toward the main tent. Inanna herself must wait in there for me, I thought, and suddenly my throat was dry and fiery knots tightened in my guts. Was I frightened? No, it was not exactly fear; it was a sense of some great finality closing in upon me. How long was it since she and I had been face to face? What transformations had she accomplished behind my back in the city, since then? Surely she meant to work my undoing today; but how? How? And how might I defend myself? Ever since my childhood—when she had been little more than a child herself—my fate had been entwined with this dark-souled woman; and it seemed certain that I was approaching now, within this great tent of scarlet and black that rose before me on the plain of Uruk, the ultimate collision of our destinies.

But I was wrong once again. The three priestesses raised the curtain of the tent a little way and held it back, indicating to me that I should go inside. I entered, and found myself in a perfumed place of rich lustrous mats and sheer draperies; and awaiting me at the center of it, seated kneeling on a low couch, was a woman of voluptuous form whose body was bare except for a glowing pendant of gold that hung between her breasts and the thick-bodied olive-hued serpent of the goddess, which was wrapped like a rope about her waist, moving in slow sliding pulsations. But she was not Inanna. She was Abisimti the holy courtesan, she who had initiated me into the rites of manhood long ago, she who had done the same for Enkidu when he dwelled in wildness on the steppe. I had been set and braced for Inanna; the surprise and shock of finding someone else in Inanna's place so stunned and staggered me that I recoiled and found myself all but hurled into a fit. I felt myself going over the brink of an abyss. I swayed; I shook; I pulled myself back with the last of my strength.

Abisimti looked toward me. Her eyes were gleaming strangely; they burned in their sockets like spheres of glowing carnelian. In a voice that seemed to be making a journey to me from some world that was not this world she said, 'Hail, O king! Hail, Gilgamesh!' And she beckoned me to her side.

40

For an instant I was twelve years old again and I was going with my uncle to the temple cloister for my initiation; I saw myself in my kilt of soft white linen, with the narrow red stripe of surrendered innocence painted on my shoulder and a lock of my hair in my hand to give to the priestess. And I saw again this beautiful sixteen-year-old Abisimti of my boyhood, whose breasts were round as pomegranates, whose long dark hair tumbled loose past her gold-painted cheeks.

She was still beautiful now. Who could count the men she had embraced for the goddess' sake before I first had come to her, or the men she had embraced since? But the number of those who had possessed her might be as great as the number of the grains of sand in the desert, and still they could not take her beauty from her: they could only enhance it. She was not young; her breasts were no longer quite so round; and yet she was still beautiful. I wondered, though, why her eyes looked so strange, why her voice was so unfamiliar. She seemed almost dazed. They have given her some potion, I thought: that must be it. But why? Why?

I said, 'I expected to find Inanna in here.'

She spoke slowly, as if in a dream. 'Are you displeased? She cannot leave the temple. You will go to her afterward, Gilgamesh.'

I should have realized Inanna would not go outside the walls of the city. To Abisimti I said, 'I am just as content, finding you. I was surprised, that was all—'

'Come. Put off your robe. Kneel down before me.'

'But what rite is this that we will do?'

'You must not ask. Come, Gilgamesh! Disrobe. Kneel.'

I was wary but oddly calm. Perhaps this was a true rite after all; perhaps Inanna meant only to serve, indeed, and had devised all this to cleanse me of Enlil-knew-what impurity before I went inside the city. I could not believe that the gentle Abisimti would be part of any plot against me. So I put aside my sword and laid down my robe, and I knelt on the mat before her. We were both naked, though she wore a pendant and a living serpent about her middle, and I had the pearl of Grow-Young-Again hanging on a string on my chest. I saw her looking at it. She could not have any idea what it was; but her brows came together for a moment.

'Tell me what I must do,' I said.

'This is the first thing,' said Abisimti.

She reached to her side and lifted in both her hands an alabaster bowl of wondrous slimness and elegance, carved with the sacred signs of the goddess. She cupped it and held it forward between us. There was dark wine in it. So we would pour out a libation, I thought, and then perhaps we would make some sort of a sacrifice—sacrifice Inanna's serpent, could that be possible?—and after that I supposed we would speak a rite together; and at the last, she would draw me down onto the couch and take me into her body. In our coupling I would cast forth whatever it was that had to be purged from me before I could enter Uruk. So I imagined things would unfold.

But Abisimti held the bowl toward me and said in a slow dreamlike whisper, 'Take this, Gilgamesh. Drink it deep.'

She put the bowl into my hands. I held it a moment, looking down at the wine, before bringing it to my lips.

And I sensed a strangeness. Abisimti was shivering in the great heat of the day. She was trembling all over her body. Her shoulders were oddly hunched, her breasts swayed like trees in a tempest, the corners of her mouth drew in and out in an odd quirking way. I saw fear on her face, and something almost like shame. But her eyes gleamed ever more brightly; and it seemed to me that they were fixed on me in the way that a serpent's eyes were fixed as it stares at its helpless prey just before striking. I cannot tell you why I saw her that way, but I did. She was watching: she was waiting. For what?

I said, suddenly suspicious once again, 'If we are to take part in this rite together, we must share everything. You drink first; and then I will take mine.'

Her head went back with a jerk as though I had slapped her.

'That may not be!' she cried.

'Why is that?'

'The wine—it is for you, Gilgamesh—'

'I offer it freely to you. Share it with me, Abisimti.'

'I am not permitted!'

'I am your king. I command you.'

She wrapped her arms over her breasts and huddled into herself. She was quaking. Her eyes no longer met mine. She said, so softly I scarcely could hear her, 'No—please, no—'

'Take a sip, before I do.'

'No—I beg you—'

'Why are you so afraid, Abisimti? Is the wine such holy stuff that it will harm you?'

'I beg you—Gilgamesh—'

288

I held the bowl out to her, pushing it practically in her face. She turned away; she clamped her lips tight, perhaps fearing I would force it into her mouth. Then I was certain of the treachery. I put the wine-bowl down beside me, and leaned forward, taking her by the wrist. Quietly I said, 'I thought there was love between us, but I see I may have been mistaken. Tell me now, Abisimti, why you will not drink the wine with me, and tell me truthfully.'

She did not answer.

'Tell me!'

'My lord—'

'*Tell me!*'

She shook her head. Then, with a force that astonished me, she pulled her arm free of my grasp and whirled around so suddenly that her snake took alarm and uncoiled itself from her waist, gliding loose of her. An instant later I saw a copper dagger in her hand. She had pulled it from beneath a cushion behind her. I thought it was intended for me; but it was toward her own breast that she drove it. Seizing her wrist, I held the tip of the blade back from her flesh. That cost me some little effort, for she had a kind of fit upon her and her strength was almost beyond belief. Slowly I prevailed; I forced the dagger back; then I wrenched it from her hand and hurled it across the room. At once she fell upon me like a lioness. Our bodies came together, slippery with sweat, in a wild struggle. She clawed at me, she bit, she sobbed and shrieked; and as we fought her fingers became entangled in the cord that held the pearl of Grow-Young-Again. She pulled; I felt the cord burning like fire against my neck as it went taut; then the cord snapped, and the pearl, rolling down my body, went bouncing away.

When I realized what had happened I pushed Abisimti aside and scrambled desperately after that most precious of jewels. For a moment I could not see where it had landed. Then I caught the gleam of its lustre reflecting the faint light of the brazier. It lay a dozen paces from me, or so. But Inanna's accursed serpent had spied the pearl also, and—the gods alone know why—was slithering swiftly toward it.

'*No!*' I roared, and sprang forward. But I was too late. Before I was halfway across the room the serpent reached the pearl and took it lightly in its mouth, as a cat holds a kitten. It swung around, facing me, to display its prize. For an instant its yellow eyes glittered with the most bitter mockery I have ever had to behold. Then the snake raised high its head and opened its jaws, and the pearl went sliding down its maw. If I could have seized that serpent I would have wrung it until it disgorged the stone; but to my horror the foul creature slipped cunningly past my grasp and made its writhing way toward the flap of the tent. On hands and knees I crawled quickly after it, but I had no chance of catching it. It was the subtlest of beasts. Delicately it put its snout to the sand and wriggled down into the earth in a moment and vanished from sight. In its place remained only a few bits of its speckled skin that it had sloughed off as it escaped. Already it was shedding its old self, and coming into the renewal of the body that had been meant for me. All my labor thus was a waste: I had toiled in far lands merely to obtain the boon of new life for the serpent. For myself I had gained nothing.

I stood stunned a moment or two. Then I looked back toward Abisimti. While I sought to regain the pearl she had seized the bowl of wine and had gulped a deep draught of it: her cheeks were dripping with the stuff. She rose to her feet in a frightful wild jerking manner, staring at me with such sorrow and love as nearly broke my heart. Every muscle of her body was writhing at a different rhythm: she looked like a woman possessed by a thousand demons.

'You understand—I did not want to do it—' she said in a terrible thick-voiced grunting way.

Then the bowl fell from her lifeless hands and she toppled to the floor virtually at my feet.

I thought I might go mad at that moment, or at least be swept into the tremors of a fit. But a strange calmness was upon me, as though my soul, buffeted so hard, had shored itself up by closing in on itself to make me invulnerable. I had no fits. I did not even weep. I looked down and saw the dark stain of the spilled wine in the sand, and calmly I scuffed other sand over it with my foot until it was hidden. Then I knelt and closed Abisimti's eyes, she who had been sent here to slay me and who had given up her own life instead. I felt no anger toward her, only pity and regret: she was a priestess, she had been under oath to obey the goddess' behest.

Well, her oath to Inanna had brought her now to the House of Dust and Darkness, where I too might now be arriving, but for that look of fear and shame I had spied in Abisimti's face as she handed me the poisoned wine. Now she was gone. And the pearl of Grow-Young-Again gone too, between one moment and the next. Siduri the tavernkeeper had spoken truly: *You never will find this eternal life that you seek.* But it did not matter. I was weary of chasing after a dream. The serpent's mockery had given me my answer: it was not meant to be, I must find some other way.

I donned my robe and strapped my sword to my side and went from the tent. The dazzling sunlight struck my eyes like a fist as I emerged. But after a moment I could see. The three priestesses of Inanna stood before me, gaping in amazement: they had not thought they would see me come forth alive.

'We have done the rite.' I said quietly. 'I am cleansed now of all impure things. Go you and look after the priestess Abisimti: she will need the words spoken over her.'

The leader of the priestesses said, bewildered, 'You have had the sacred wine, then?'

'I have made a libation to the goddess with it,' I told her. 'And now I will enter the city, and pay my respects to the goddess in person.'

'But—you—'

'Step aside,' I said easily. I rested my hand on the hilt of my sword. 'Let me pass, or I'll split you like a broiled goose. Step aside, woman. Step aside!'

She gave ground as the darkness yields before the morning sun, shrinking back, all but vanishing. I went past her to the waiting chariot. Ninurta-mansum, coming to me, put his hand to my wrist and gripped it hard. The charioteer's eyes were shining with tears. I think he had not expected to see me alive again either.

I said to him, 'We are done with this business here. Let us go into Uruk now.'

Ninurta-mansum took the reins. We rode around the bright-hued pavilions and headed toward the High Gate. I saw people atop the parapets, peering down at me; and when the chariot reached the portal of the gate it swung wide and I was admitted without challenge. As well I should have been: for they all knew me to be Gilgamesh the king.

'Do you see, there?' I said to my charioteer. 'Where the White Platform rises, at the end of this great avenue? The temple of Inanna is there, the temple that I built with my own hands. Take me there.'

Thousands of the citizens of Uruk had come to witness my homecoming; but they seemed strangely cowed and awed, and scarce any of them called my name as I journeyed past. They stared; they turned to one another and whispered; they made holy signs, out of their great fear. Through a silent city we rode down the wide boulevard toward the temple precinct. At the edge of the White Platform Ninurta-mansum brought the chariot to a halt and I dismounted. Alone I went up the lofty steps to the portico of the immense temple that for love of the goddess I had built in place of the temple of my grandfather royal Enmerkar. Some priests came out and stood in my way as I approached the temple door.

One said boldly, 'What business do you have here, O Gilgamesh?'

'I mean to see Inanna.'

'The king may not enter Inanna's precinct unless he has been summoned. It is the custom. You are aware of that.'

'The custom now is altered,' I answered. 'Stand aside.'

'It is forbidden! It is improper!'

'Stand aside,' I said in a very low voice. It was sufficient. He stood aside.

The temple halls were dark and cool even in the heat of the day, so thick were their walls. Lamps were burning, casting a soft light on the colored ornaments of baked clay that I had had put by the thousands into those walls. I walked swiftly. This was my temple. I had designed it and I knew my way in it. I expected to find Inanna in the great chamber of the goddess, and so she was: standing at the center of the room, fully robed and in her finest breastplates and ornaments, as though she had prepared herself for some high ceremony. She wore one ornament I had never seen on her before—a mask of shimmering beaten gold that covered all her face but her lips and chin, with the merest of slits for her eyes.

'You should not be here, Gilgamesh,' she said coolly.

'No, I should not. I should be lying dead in a tent outside the walls just now. Is that not so?' I did not let anger enter my voice. 'They are saying the words over Abisimti now. She drank the wine for me. She did your bidding and offered the bowl to me, but I would not drink from it, and so she drank the wine herself, of her own free will.'

Inanna said nothing. The lips below the mask were clamped close together and set in a tight thin line.

'They told me while I was in Eridu,' I said, 'that in my absence you declared me dead, and called for the election of a new king. Was that so, Inanna?'

'The city must have a king,' she said.

'The city has one.'

'You had fled the city. You ran off into the wilderness like a madman. If you were not dead, you might as well have been.'

'I went in search of something. And now I have returned.'

'Did you find that for which you started?'

'Yes,' I said. 'And no. It does not matter. Why do you wear that mask, Inanna?'

'It does not matter.'

'I have never seen you masked before.'

'It is a new custom,' she said.

'Ah. There are many new customs, it seems.'

'Including the custom of the king's entering this temple unsummoned.'

'And,' I said, 'the custom of offering the king, upon his return to the city from a journey, a bowl of wine that kills.' I went a few steps closer to her. 'Take off the mask, Inanna. Let me see your face again.'

'I will not,' she said.

'Take off the mask. I ask you.'

'Let me be. I will not take off the mask.'

But I could not speak with this metal-faced stranger. It was the woman of flesh and blood I sought to look upon again, the treacherous and beautiful woman I had known so long, she whom I had loved, in my fashion, as I had loved no other woman. I meant to behold that woman one more time.

Gently I said, 'I would see the splendor of your face once more. I think there is no face more beautiful in all the world. Do you know that, Inanna? How beautiful you have seemed to me?' I laughed. 'Do you remember the nights we made the Sacred Marriage together? Of course. Of course. How could you forget? That year when I was the new king, and I lay all night in your arms, and in the morning the rain had come. I remember. I remember those times before you were Inanna, when you called me to the chambers deep below the old temple. I was just a frightened boy then, and I scarcely knew what games you were playing with me. Or that first time, when they were saying the coronation rite for Dumuzi, and I wandered off into the corridors of the temple and you found me. You were just a child yourself, though you already had your breasts. Do you remember? Do you remember? Ah, Inanna, in time I came to understand the games you were playing with me! But now I would see your face again. Put down the mask.'

'Gilgamesh—'

'Put down the mask,' I said. 'Put it down.' And I called her by her name: not her priestess-name but her other, older, name, her birth-name, which no one had spoken since she had become Inanna. By that name I conjured her. At the sound of it she gasped and held up her hands in a secret goddess-sign, shielding herself. I could not see her eyes behind the mask, but I imagined that they were fixed on me, unblinking, piercing, cold.

'You are mad to call me by that name!' she whispered.

'Am I? Then I am mad. I would see your face once more, one last time.'

Now there was a quiver in her voice. 'Let me be, Gilgamesh. I meant you no harm. What I did, I did for the sake of the city—the city must have a king, and you were gone—the goddess commanded me—'

'Yes. The goddess commanded you to remove Dumuzi, and you did. The goddess commanded you to remove Gilgamesh, and you would have done it. Ah, Inanna, Inanna—it was for the sake of the city, yes. And for the sake of the city I grant you my pardon. I forgive you all your schemes. I forgive you what you have done in the goddess' name to harm me and to undermine my power. I forgive you your hatred, your anger, your fury. I even forgive you your vengeance, for it was you that called the gods down upon Enkidu whom I loved, and I think but for you he might be alive this day. But I forgive you. I forgive you everything, Inanna. If we had not been king and priestess, I think I would have loved you even more than I loved him, more than I loved life itself. But I was king; you were priestess. Ah, Inanna, Inanna—'

I did not use the sword. I took the dagger from my hip and put it into her side between the breastplate and the beads of lapis around her waist, and twisted it upward until I reached her heart. She made a single small sound and fell. I think she must have died at once. I let my breath forth slowly. At last I was free of her; but it had been like cutting away a part of my soul.

Kneeling beside her, I unfastened the mask and lifted it from her face.

I wish that I had not done that one thing. What had become of her since last I had looked upon her was difficult for my mind to credit. Her eyes had lost none of her beauty, nor her lips; but all else was a ruin. Some spreading blemish had seized her face and ravaged it. She was pocked and cratered, red and raw here, gray-skinned and sagging there: a nightmare hag, a demon-faced thing. She looked a thousand years old. It would have been better that I left her covered. But I had laid her bare, and I must carry the burden of that. I bent forward; I put my lips to hers and kissed her for the last time; then I fastened the mask back into its place, and rose, and went outside to the temple porch to summon the people and tell them of the new order of things that I meant to proclaim as I resumed my kingship in Uruk.

41

These have been busy years, and fulfilling ones. The gods have been kind to Uruk and to Gilgamesh its king. The city thrives; the wall stands high; we have painted the White Platform with a fresh coat of gypsum, and it gleams in the sun. All is well. We have many tasks yet to carry out, but all is well. I sit now in my chamber in the palace, inscribing the last of my tablets, for I think the tale is told. I will not cease striving—I will never do that—but a certain peace has come over me that I never knew before, and that is new; I had no peace in the times of which I have been writing, but now I do. I tell you: all is well.

It was easy enough to bring the soaring ambitions of Meskiagnunna of Ur back down to earth: that was my first enterprise after my restoration. I sent him a message confirming him in his kingship of Ur, and granting him the administration of Kish as an additional fief. He knew what I was saying, when I condescended to let him hold the cities he already held. 'But Nippur and Eridu,' I told him, 'I reserve to myself, as the gods have decreed: for they are the holy cities, subject to the rule of the high king of the Land.'

By that message I sent forth my claim to the supremacy. And at the same time I dispatched my army, under command of the faithful Zabardi-bunugga, to enter Nippur and persuade the soldiers of Ur to depart. I did not leave Uruk myself, since I had so much to do there—the choosing of a new high priestess, for instance, and the proper training of her so that she would understand the role she must play in my government.

While I occupied myself with those matters, Zabardi-bunugga managed the liberation of Nippur effectively enough, though not without some small damage. The men of Ur took refuge in the Tummal, which is the house of Enlil there, and it was necessary to break down the walls of that temple in order to remove them. I have sent my son Ur-lugal to rebuild the Tummal, now that Nippur is ours.

These are full times for me. Indeed, there is never a moment to rest. I would not have it any other way. What else is there, but to plan, to work, to build, to do? It is the salvation of our souls. Listen to the music in the courtyard; the harper plays, and by making his melodies he pays his birth-price. Look at the goldsmith, bending over his table. The carpenter, the fisherman, the scribe, the priest, the king—in the performing of our tasks we all fulfill the commandments of the gods, which is the only purpose in this life for which we were made. We find ourselves thrown by the whim of the gods into a chancy world, where uncertainty reigns; within that whirlwind we must make a secure place for ourselves. That we do by work; and my work it is to be king.

So I toil and my people toil. The temples, the canals, the city walls, the pavements in the streets—how can we ever cease rebuilding and repairing and restoring them? It is the way. The rites and sacrifices by which we hold back the surging powers of chaos—how can we ever cease performing them? It is the way. We know our tasks, and we do them, and all is well. Listen to that music, in the courtyard! Listen! Listen!

Soon—let it not be very soon, but I will be ready whenever the hour arrives—I must begin the last of my journeys. I will go down into the dark world from which there is no return. My musicians will be beside me, and my concubines and stewards and valets, my charioteer, my jugglers, my minstrels; and together we will make our offerings to the gods of the world below, to Ereshkigal and Namtar, to Enki, to Enlil, to all those who govern our destinies. So be it. It does not trouble me now to think of that prospect. I have never considered returning to Dilmun to beg a second pearl of Grow-Young-Again: that is not the way. That old priest who calls himself the Ziusudra tried to tell me that, but I had to learn it in my own fashion. Well, I have learned it now.

The light is going. There is the rite to perform tonight on the temple roof, and I must hasten to it; I am the king, it is my task. We honor Ninsun my mother, whom I proclaimed a goddess this time last year when her days on earth were done. Already I hear the chanting in the distance, and the scent of burning meat is in the air. So, now, an end to all my stories. I have spoken much of death, my great enemy with whom I have grappled so fiercely, but I will speak of him no more. I have feared him greatly. I have walked with terrible fear of his shadow. But I have made my peace with death now. I have come to understand the truth, which is that the escape from death lies not in potions and magic, but in the performance of one's task. That way lies calmness and acceptance.

I have done my work, and I will do more. I have made a name for myself that will last down the ages. Gilgamesh will not be forgotten. He will not be left to trail his wings mournfully in the dust. They will remember me in joy and pride. What will they say of me? They will say that I lived, and I lived well; that I strived, and I strived well; that I died, and I died well. I feared death as no man ever did, and went to the ends of the world to escape him, in which I failed; but when I returned I feared him no longer. That is the truth. I know now that we need not fear death, if we have done our tasks. And when we cease to fear death, there is no death. That is the truest truth I know: There is no death.

Afterword

We have no reason to doubt that Gilgamesh of Uruk was an authentic historical figure. His name occurs frequently in the king-lists of the Mesopotamian land of Sumer—what is now the southern part of Iraq—and it is likely that he lived about 2500 B.C. Beyond much question he was a strong and successful king; until the end of independent Mesopotamian civilization, two thousand years later, he was regarded always as the prototype of the great leader, a warrior and statesman beyond compare. Myths of all sorts grew up about him; he became a legendary culture-hero, who combined in himself the best traits of Hercules, of Ulysses, of Prometheus.

It is primarily with the historical Gilgamesh that I have concerned myself in this book, but I have dealt also with that mythical one who is the hero of the oldest work of tragic literature which has survived into our time. I refer to the Epic of Gilgamesh, which is perhaps two thousand years old—more than a thousand years more ancient than the *Iliad* and the *Odyssey*—and which may be even older than that. Our text of it, which is incomplete but conveys the essential story, comes to us in various forms that have survived by mere luck out of the ruins of antiquity. The longest known version was found by archaeologists in the nineteenth century in the library of the Assyrian king Ashurbanipal—the Assyrians were the final inheritors of the ancient Mesopotamian culture, long after the

Sumerian founders had been absorbed by younger and more vigorous races—and was set down on clay tablets about 700 B.C. In addition we have a fragmentary version perhaps a thousand years older, written in the language of the Babylonians who dominated Mesopotamia between the time of the Sumerians and that of the Assyrians; and there is also a version in the language of the Hittites of Syria, indicating that the story was widespread throughout the Near East. All of these are probably based on some Sumerian original that is lost to us.

The Epic of Gilgamesh is a profoundly disturbing work: a meditative poem on the necessity of death. Gilgamesh is shown to be a superhuman figure, confident to the point of arrogance, bursting with vitality; and yet the fear of his own mortality reduces him to a kind of paralysis, out of which he emerges to undertake a desperate pilgrimage to the immortal survivor of the Flood, Ziusudra (Ut-napishtim in the later versions). It is worth noting in passing that the entire tale of Noah and the ark as told in the Bible is almost certainly based on the Flood narrative embodied in the Gilgamesh epic, which precedes it by at least a thousand years and perhaps much more.

In retelling the story of Gilgamesh I have drawn freely on the original epic, relying mainly on the two standard English translations, that of Alexander Heidel (1946) and E. A. Speiser (1955). I have also incorporated into it the far older Sumerian poems dealing with other aspects of the life of Gilgamesh, making use of the translations by Samuel Noah Kramer (1955). But at all times I have attempted to interpret the fanciful and fantastic events of these poems in a realistic way, that is, to tell the story of Gilgamesh as though he were writing his own memoirs, and to that end I have introduced many interpretations of my own devising which for better or for worse are in no way to be ascribed to the scholars I have named.

Perhaps it need not be explained—but I will—that the two rivers referred to in the novel by their Sumerian names as the Idigna and the Buranunu are those known to later civilizations as the Tigris and the Euphrates. The ruins of Gilgamesh's Uruk are to be found near the modern Iraqi town of Warka, which is twelve miles from the present course of the Euphrates; but the literary and archaeological evidence strongly indicates that the river flowed much closer to the city in the time of Gilgamesh.

Finally, I wish to express my gratitude to various friends who read the manuscript in its preliminary stages and offered useful criticism. I am indebted in particular to Merrilee Heifetz for her rigorous scrutiny of the book and for the depth of insight and technical expertise that she brought to her reading of it. She provided an extraordinary and invaluable service.

—Robert Silverberg
Oakland, California
February 1984

Robert Silverberg
Lord Valentine's Castle £2.50

'In an archaic, feudal empire . . . Valentine, an itinerant juggler,
discovers through dreams and portents that he is his namesake Lord
Valentine, his body and throne stolen by a usurper. He sets out to win
his throne back . . . Valentine and his companions trek across the
forests and plains of Zimroel . . . to Alhanroel with its Labyrinth and then
to the heights of power at Castle Mount. Silverberg's invention is
prodigious . . . an near-encyclopaedia of unnatural wonders and weird
ecosystems. Silverberg, like a competent juggler, maintains his rhythm
and his suspense to the end' TIMES LITERARY SUPPLEMENT

The Majipoor Chronicles £2.50

Lord Valentine's Castle, the best-selling fantasy masterpiece,
introduced countless readers to the giant world of Majipoor, teeming
with humans, aliens and exotics, filled with magic and strangeness and
adventure. The *Majipoor* Chronicles explores further this complex and
colourful world ranging across its long history and vast terrain.

Valentine Pontifex £2.50

The triumphant conclusion to the *Majipoor* trilogy. Now re-established
as Coronal of Majipoor, Valentine is about to undertake the grand
processional. Soon he faces a planet-wide crisis as the shape-shifting
Metamorphs sabotage the crops upon which Majipoor's billions
depend. Only after this challenge has been overcome can Valentine
fulfil his proper destiny and succeed to the title of Pontifex.

Science fiction

☐ **The Hitch-Hiker's Guide to the Galaxy**		£1.75p
☐ **The Restaurant at the End of the Universe**	Douglas Adams	£1.75p
☐ **Life, The Universe and Everything**		£1.95p
☐ **Nine Tomorrows**	ed. Isaac Asimov	£1.50p
☐ **Profiles of the Future**		£1.95p
☐ **Rendezvous with Rama**	Arthur C. Clarke	£1.95p
☐ **The View from Serendip**		£1.75p
☐ **The Green Hills of Earth**		£1.50p
☐ **Red Planet**	Robert Heinlein	£1.50p
☐ **Tunnel in the Sky**		£1.50p
☐ **That Hideous Strength**		£2.50p
☐ **Out of the Silent Planet**	C. S. Lewis	£1.95p
☐ **Perelandra**		£1.95p
☐ **The Many-Coloured Land**		£2.50p
☐ **The Golden Torc**	Julian May	£1.95p
☐ **The Non-born King**		£2.50p
☐ **The Adversary**		£1.95p

☐	**Other Days, Other Eyes**	Bob Shaw	75p
☐	**Lord Valentine's Castle**	Robert Silverberg	£1.95p
	Majipoor Chronicles		£1.95p
☐	**Swan Song**	Brian Stableford	60p
☐	**The Time Machine**	H. G. Wells	£1.95p
☐	**The War of the Worlds**		£1.75p

All these books are available at your local bookshop or newsagent, or can be ordered direct from the publisher. Indicate the number of copies required and fill in the form below

12

....

Name_____
(Block letters please)

Address_____

_____

Send to CS Department, Pan Books Ltd, PO Box 40, Basingstoke, Hants
Please enclose remittance to the value of the cover price plus:
35p for the first book plus 15p per copy for each additional book ordered
to a maximum charge of £1.25 to cover postage and packing
Applicable only in the UK

While every effort is made to keep prices low, it is sometimes
necessary to increase prices at short notice. Pan Books reserve
the right to show on covers and charge new retail prices which
may differ from those advertised in the text or elsewhere